KELLY DEVOS

DAY ONE

inkyard
PRESS

ISBN-13: 978-1-335-09136-9

Day One

Inkyard Press
22 Adelaide St. West, 40th Floor
Toronto, Ontario M5H 4E3, Canada
www.InkyardPress.com

Printed in U.S.A.

DAY

ONE

JINX

Tomorrow.

I will save my brother.

Of course, I've been telling myself that every night for the past month. I'm no closer to my goal than when Mom shot my father and then kidnapped my little brother, Charles, off the beach in Puerto Peñasco.

Lately, it's been getting cramped down here.

It feels like we've been in my father's underground doomsday bunker for an eternity. The bunk beds, the dried emergency food kits, the command center, the indoor garden, the paranoid alarm systems—these things have become our whole world. Like a prison we've sentenced ourselves to remain in.

We're starting to snap at each other, the way people do when they spend too much time in one cramped place sharing a tiny bathroom. Jay Novak, my stepfather, is running out of reading material. Gus Navarro, my kind-of-boyfriend and my father's protégé, and MacKenna, my stepsister, are running out of political arguments. Toby, my stepbrother, barely says anything at all.

Things have gotten worse since last week, when I cracked Dad's code storage system. Dad was nothing if not meticulous, and he chose to store his complicated algorithms on dozens and dozens of old floppy disks. Each one had its own puzzle that had to be solved, and each disk could be used only once. I used to love antique computers, but I find myself missing modern laptops. Missing e-tablets and lightning-fast networks.

I could barely work on the encryption key for a couple hours each day. It was exhausting, and the thought of making a mistake kept me awake most nights. It's the type of thing I would have asked my dad about.

Except Dad is gone.

Forever.

We buried him in Rocky Point.

Now that we have the key, now that we know we *can* leave, things are more tense. Somehow, everyone was happier when we believed we were trapped here forever.

The weather has been getting warmer. The ocean is still cold. Too cold for swimming, but the March temperatures are perfect for sitting on the beach. The breezy days are a reminder of when I thought I'd have another future. One where I might be in Mexico on vacation and not hiding to save my life.

Tonight, it's my turn to watch the command center. I switch on the camera feed and stare at the stacks of video monitors. It's the same as always. We're alone. The Xcalak beach in Quintana Roo is deserted. The waves come in and out, brushing the sand smooth, creating a hypnotic black-and-white motion across the screen.

Navarro is asleep, snoring in the bunk nearest the desk, his dark head of hair turned away from me. I close my eyes for a moment, try to avoid looking at him. He saved my life. And here I am, lying to him. Keeping things from him.

But I have to.

Trying not to make too much noise, I lightly press a few keys on the ancient beige box of a computer that Dad had left behind for me to use. I wait until I can see the sun poking above the horizon line on the video monitors before I type the last line of code.

```
AT
<OK
!Allow up to 10 seconds to get a response from radio
Timeout 5000
AT&F
<OK
AT+XMM
<OK
AT+CXATT=0
Wait 25000
!Wait 25 seconds to allow for recalibration lag
AT+CXDCONT=1,"IP",""
<OK
AT+CXYQRYQ=1,0,64,384,0,0,0,0,"0Y0","0Y0",3,0,0
<OK
AT+CXYQMIN=1,0,0,0,0,0,0,0,"0Y0","0Y0",0,0,1
<OK
AT*YIAAUW=1,1,"","",00001,0
<OK
```

My arms are heavy with resignation as I press the last key to bring the satellite online.

After a while, everyone wakes up and we go through our morning routine.

At breakfast, we take up our usual places. Almost in the

center of the bunker, there's an old kitchenette set that, at one time, was probably in some hamburger diner. The chipped, yellowing Formica tabletop has seen better days, and its aluminum legs are dented and dinged.

Jay gives me an encouraging smile before he sits in the faded turquoise chair at the head of the table, and I exhale. I'm grateful for my stepfather's kindness, especially considering my mother framed him for a crime he didn't commit and left him for dead. My stepsiblings, Toby and MacKenna, crowd on either side of their father. Navarro slides into his chair at the opposite side of the table, and I sit between him and MacKenna. That leaves an open chair across from me.

Where Charles should be.

It's green pepper omelet day, which is one of my least favorite meals. There's something about canned, reconstituted scrambled eggs that never turns out quite right. The peppers have an odd metallic aftertaste. But Navarro insists we keep the meals in rotation.

I look out into the space behind the table, at the bunk beds that line the walls, the racks of dried enchiladas and bottled water, the planter boxes flanked by pulsing, hydroponic lights.

Toby lets his spoon fall into his empty bowl, and a shadow falls across his face as he leans back in his chair. "We've been here long enough. It's time. We have the key."

"We don't know if it works," Navarro says.

I frown at him. My *dad* made the key. "It works."

On the mess of old floppy disks and ancient computers, my father left two things. The code that formed the encryption key we need to hack into the computers of First Federal Bank—

MacKenna glances up from the paperback book she's using as writing paper. "And we have the name."

—and a message.

Take the key to Esmerelda Ojos.

The name.

Jay rubs his eyes. "We don't even know who that is. If she's dead or alive. Or how difficult it will be to find her."

Navarro is silent for a few seconds before adding, "One of us should drive south. Into a town. Get a computer with network access. Do some research. Report back."

In some ways, Navarro was the best prepared for our new way of life. He'd done tons of disaster drilling with his own family and trained with my father. In other ways, though, he's had it rough. He hasn't been able to contact his family. And he's having a hard time adjusting to life without the drills. That's what he's doing how. Trying to write the next chapter in Dad's book, *Dr. Doomsday's Guide to Ultimate Survival.*

My pulse quickens as I spend a second too long staring at Navarro's handsome, chiseled face. He thinks we have no way to communicate with the outside world.

I know I should have told him. Told him that I found the satellite dish hidden in the shed above the bunker, behind a retractable panel. That I knew how to bring it online. That we could get the information we need without leaving the bunker.

Navarro would have tried to stop me from activating the dish.

But I also know that operating the dish would be risky. Best-case scenario, my old "friend" Terminus, who now works for The Opposition, would be monitoring network traffic and watching internet searches. Looking for patterns. Looking for us.

And the worst-case scenario? That was my mother.

"I don't want to stay here," Toby comments. "We can't stay here forever."

Jay doesn't say anything. Some days, I think he and Navarro would like nothing better than to stay here. To wait. To hide. To see if the coming war is a storm that will pass.

But he should know better than anyone.

Rule one: Always be prepared.

My father would never have left us without a plan.

MacKenna's ponytail bounces as she gives me a small nod of encouragement.

This is *our* plan after all. We're in uncharted territory. No more master plans from my father. No more chapters in Dad's book. MacKenna and I are calling the shots, and maybe we don't know what we're doing.

I suck in a deep breath. "We have a satellite dish."

For the first time in weeks, Toby sits up straight and his shoulders aren't slumped down. "Does it work? Do we have internet access?"

An expression of horrified betrayal settles onto Navarro's face. "How long have you known this?"

Jay gestures toward the corner where the computers and monitors are clustered together on a steel desk. "Jinx, what does that mean? We can contact people? Or *they* can find us?"

They. The Opposition. The government. The National Police.

I hold Navarro's tense gaze.

He chews on his lower lip. "Susan. Tell me you didn't bring a satellite online and connect a computer to it. Tell me you wouldn't do that without at least discussing it with me."

Jay shifts his weight in his chair and clears his throat. One of our ongoing problems is that Navarro keeps forgetting who ought to be in charge.

Behind us, from the corner of the bunker, the old NeXT workstation beeps, and the black radiation-shielded monitor flickers on.

"Susan..." Navarro says. "What did you do?"

But I'm not going to play by the old rules anymore.

The plan is in motion.

"What did you do?"

My teacher said journalists have to be fair, to be open-minded and to support the civil exchange of ideas. But what's happening isn't at all civil, and I can't tell this story in a way that goes down smooth with your oatmeal.

–MacKENNA NOVAK,
Letters from the Second Civil War

MacKENNA

The inverted pyramid.

That's how we write stories.

I've got a draft going of my first field report.

Okay, MacKenna. Let's go. Let's do this thing.

FIELD REPORT #1; QUINTANA ROO, MEXICO

Dr. Charles Maxwell Marshall II, more popularly known by his hacker alias, Dr. Doomsday, was killed last month at the beachfront home of a deceased operative for The Spark in Puerto Peñasco, Mexico. Dr. Marshall, author of the bestselling survivalist book, *Dr. Doomsday's Guide to Ultimate Survival*, was shot once in the abdomen by his ex-wife, Stephanie Maxwell Novak. Sources believe that Ms. Novak is a high-ranking undercover agent for The Opposition's secret paramilitary force who had been covertly assigned to frame her second husband, Jay Novak, for detonating a series of explosions at First Federal Banks. The attacks, which targeted locations responsible for storage of the banks' paper records, backfired and triggered widespread financial and political instability.

Mr. Novak had been serving as security director at the First Federal Bank in Rancho Mesa, Arizona, one of five buildings destroyed.

Okay. Okay.

Those were the major points.

The widest part of the pyramid.

LEAD: Dr. Doomsday killed by wife. Jay Novak framed for domestic terrorism.

But if Mr. Johnson were here, he'd already have kicked this back to me.

Fact check: Jay Novak hasn't been cleared of charges.

Bias check: Where's your evidence that Jay Novak was framed?

Fact check: Who are your sources?

Bias check: You can't use yourself as an anonymous source.

But Johnson wasn't here and, anyway, no more teachers, no more books.

One of the few fringe benefits of being on the run with your dad, your brother, your stepsister and some total weirdo you picked up along the way is that you never have to go back to high school. No more dress codes. No more book reports. No more grades.

No more rules.

But also, no more school dances.

No graduation day.

My life is basically over.

Like, how does this even happen? One day I'm at my desk imagining myself at the White House Press Dinner, and now…

What would all my friends at school think if they saw me

looking like this? These days, I choose the pants I wear based on how many pockets they have. Some family of moths is dying of starvation now that I've pulled this horrible cardigan out of the closet.

I scowl at the flap of *Comanche Moon.*

Dr. Doomsday built this bunker, and he thought of everything. Except office supplies. So…no e-tablets. No old-fashioned writing paper either. There are precisely two pens, one chewed-up pencil and a stack of dusty paperback books.

So… I'm stuck writing my reports in the margins of a dead man's books.

Dr. Marshall's death occurred during a confrontation between Ms. Novak and Marcus Tork, a consultant for the National Police, ostensibly assigned to track and capture Mr. Novak.

Fact check: What was Tork's actual job title?
Like, who the hell knows? How would I ever find out?
Does it even matter?

However, sources now believe that Ms. Novak and Mr. Tork were working together to…

Fact check: To what? Did I even really know?
Okay. Keep it together, MacKenna.

…to recover digital bank data encrypted by Dr. Marshall. As an accomplished systems engineer, Dr. Marshall successfully implemented a zero-day exploit designed to corrupt financial records stored on First Federal's mainframe computers. The hack was timed to coincide with Ammon Carver's presidential inauguration, which took place in January prior to the explosions.

Fact check: First Federal Bank hasn't identified the hacker.

Source check: Who is available to explain a zero-day exploit?

I glance at Jinx, who's staring out into space, poking at a bowl of scrambled eggs. Checking out Navarro when she thinks I'm not watching.

Navarro is pacing around, glaring at Jinx for hacking or fixing or whatever she did to the satellite. He's clearly pissed we didn't ask for his permission. But we all know he would never have agreed with a plan to leave the bunker. Neither would my dad for that matter.

First Federal Bank is the country's largest and oldest financial institution. Facing the loss of both its paper and digital records, First Federal has struggled to pay deposits and properly collect payments. Congress has frozen electronic payment processing networks and authorized banks to remain closed if necessary. The situation has triggered widespread panic, including a series of "run on the bank" type altercations that have become increasingly violent.

Source check: *The Dallas Herald.*

Aha! Take that, Mr. Johnson. I have a citation.

I pull out a piece of folded printer paper. It's a news report, complete with pictures that show a bloody scene in First Federal's Houston branch. National Police in body armor are beating back men in jeans and sweaty shirts and pushing against women in housedresses as a mob presses into the interior of the bank lobby. The place was designed to have a charming, country-western vibe to it.

The scene is surreal. A rustic, homey riot.

Yeah, and also this article is more than a month old. I

printed it out the last time we stopped at an internet café. My last bit of actual news.

I reread my field report and check out what I've got so far.

Seriously, MacKenna. Pull yourself together.

Maybe it was a mistake to use *The New York Times Manual of Style*. Like, referring to the murderous psychopath as *Mr.* Tork almost makes me choke on my own spit.

I guess now I should say something about The Spark and the New Depression and how the bad times at the bank had turned a terrible economy into a desperate situation. But there was something wrong with all of this.

Like, it was *a* story.

But not *my* story.

My back and shoulders ache. Every afternoon, Navarro puts us through the drills. We run on the beach and load guns and try to karate kick each other. Hey, now I can shoot someone.

But…could I really shoot someone?

I can't deal with that right now.

I grab the book again, scribble out the sentences with my pen and start a new entry on the back inside cover.

FIELD REPORT #1: WHAT REALLY HAPPENED
Quintana Roo, Mexico

It was the afternoon of January 20th and I was living my old boring life in one of the million identical suburbs of Phoenix, Arizona, and basically thinking how it brutally sucked that Ammon Carver was gonna be president and that the only upside was that us journalists would have plenty to write about. But really, I thought things would be okay. I mean, all the stuff they told us in school about the power of democracy and the checks and balances of the Federal system had to mean something, right? And my dad had a good job, and we had a nice house.

Maybe The Opposition would screw people over. But deep down inside, I thought I wouldn't be one of the people.

I know that's way wrong, and I was trying to do my part. I donated money, and I went to rallies and gave Mr. Johnson, my journalism teacher, all kinds of shit for constantly eighty-sixing my articles about The Spark and canceling my profiles of David Rosenthal.

So there I was, and my biggest problems were really that, since my mom died, my dad worked all the time and my brother, Toby, was away at college. I was stuck at home with Stephanie, a step-mom who looked like she'd been manufactured in some robot dream-wife factory. And Jinx. My stepsister, who couldn't pry her eyes from her laptop screen.

My new stepfamily was strange. They had been living as prep-pers in some bizarro basement somewhere. Plus, Jinx's dad was Maxwell Marshall. THE Maxwell Marshall. Dr. Dooms-day himself. The doofus hacker genius who'd used computer skills that almost no one could understand to rig the elec-tion for Ammon Carver. Dr. Doomsday was the reason that The Spark lost. The reason that evil Carver was president and not Rosenthal.

The daughter of the man who'd wrecked the whole world car-pooled to school with me.

The one good thing was my new little stepbrother, Charles, who was eight but somehow able to figure out how to grow perfect, puffy marigolds in a small greenhouse in his room because he heard me say that it was Mom's favorite flower.

Anyway, back to January 20th. I was driving home from school with Jinx and Charles. Jinx wanted to stop for potato chips. I mean, almost nobody eats potato chips anymore. They're ter-rible for you, heavily taxed and will probably be illegal soon. But we had to stop. At a store that happened to be next door to the First Federal Bank building. That happened to be one of the banks that blew up. Maybe someday I'll get some e-tablets or at least some notebook paper and I can tell the story of how we almost died. How we went on the run. How we were chased across the desert by The Opposition, the National Police and God knows who else.

But right now.

Right now, if you're reading this, here's what you need to know.

My father is Jesen Oscar Novak. He emigrated from Lanvin, Croatia, when he was four years old. He was awarded the Silver Star for heroism in Operation Cedar Hawk. He was proud of being a veteran. He watched more golf than politics on TV. Stephanie used his computer to log in to the mainframe and trigger the explosions that killed more than two thousand people.

My father is absolutely innocent.

I don't know what history will make of Maxwell Marshall. I guess a lot of that depends on what happens next and who gets to write the history books. However, his finest hour will probably always be unknown. He created a piece of malware designed to destroy bank data, not to help The Opposition with their revolution but to help his children escape to safety. The Opposition believes we have the code that will repair the mainframe computers, and this is the only reason we are still alive. Marshall's zero-day exploit was an act of love. Not an act of defiance.

Dr. Doomsday loved his family.

Stephanie Novak or Stephanie Marshall or whatever she goes on to call herself is not a history teacher and was never really my father's wife. I don't know who or what she is. She took Charles, and I don't think it's because she loves him. Sure, he's her son, but when it's all said and done, he's the same as the rest of us. A pawn in her chess game.

Stephanie Novak will probably never get what she deserves.

Gustavo Navarro is for The Opposition. There's no getting around it. He's brave and smart and he's so in love with Jinx that he'd probably jump in front of a train for her. Dr. Dooms-day trained him and sent him to help us escape. And he's good. Maybe even as good as Marshall. But he's a good guy with bad ideas. And you can't outrun what you are forever. I think Dr. Doomsday said that in his book.

Right now, we're relatively safe here in Mexico. Our own country is in chaos. The Opposition has basically instituted martial law. David Rosenthal, the man who really ought to be president, is missing. The Spark is afraid. Banks are closed and people are panicking and the stock market has crashed. Jinx thinks she's got Marshall's encryption key to work. I don't really know what that means. The "key" is a bunch of gobbledygook computer code that looks like you let a monkey pound on a keyboard for a while. But she says it works, and I trust her.

And we have a name of someone who can help us. We're going to leave the bunker with the key and find Esmerelda Ojos. We're calling this a plan, even though my dad and Toby have yet to agree to it. Plus, we still don't have an answer to the big questions.

How will we get Charles back?

What will happen to my dad?

What will happen to all of us?

Jinx wants to get her brother back.

Toby wants a revolution.

Navarro wants to hide in the bunker.

And I want...

I put the pen down for a second and, like, I can feel the corners of my mouth fall into a frown. Mr. Johnson would give me an F for this report for sure. It has slang and all kinds of bias and about five hundred uncorroborated facts.

And, seriously, MacKenna, this isn't a story in the inverted pyramid format.

Who cares about the *New York Times* or style sheets? Who knows if I'll ever get this stuff published? Or if anyone will ever even read it. Screw Mr. Johnson.

This is my story.

I cross out the words *Field Report #1.*

I replace them with:

And I want...

I want to go back. That's what I want to write. Like, back to my life before any of this happened. Not only is that impossible, it's not right anyhow. The election of Ammon Carver exposed terrible problems that were hidden or ignored or covered up. These problems have to be solved. It's a real mess.

We have to clean it up.

I want...
I want a world where none of these things could ever have happened.
And I want to find out the truth about why they did.

I drop the paperback book in time to see Navarro, all red in the face, get up from the kitchen table.

"We have a name," I tell him as he passes me. "Esmerelda Ojos. Now that the satellite is up, we can use the internet to find her and—"

He turns around. "You don't know what you have. Or what you're doing."

He goes to the stairs and leaves the bunker. After his footsteps trail away, it's silent apart from a few clicks and beeps coming from the old computers in the corner.

Some part of me knows that this is the beginning of something.

The start.

Today is Day One.

Maybe you have heard it said that a nation will more willingly believe one big lie over many small ones. But the truth is far older. Caesar spoke correctly when he said that men will willingly believe whatever they wish.

—Comment by PRESIDENT AMMON C. CARVER to his daughter, ANNIKA CARVER, after issuing Executive Order 17881, Suspending Congressional Activities during the Ongoing Economic Emergency

JINX

For an hour or so, Navarro sits alone on the beach.

I watch him on the security monitor. He's got his back to the camera and faces the waves. He doesn't move as they roll in and out.

Toby's at the opposite end of the bunker, messing with a pile of books.

MacKenna stands next to him as if to supervise whatever he's doing, but she says nothing as he makes a series of stacks on his bed.

While Navarro's outside, I explain the situation to Jay.

I'm behind the desk of the comm center, listening to the whir of the machines. "Okay, so as you know, Dad encrypted all the bank's data. It can't be accessed or restored without a key, a piece of complicated code that he hid on disks in the bunker. We can't use the code here. These computers are way too slow, and the satellite dish Dad left is super old. But we can access the internet and use it to plan our next steps," I tell him. "Figure out where to go next."

I cough into my shoulder. When the computers run for too long, there's a faint whiff of burning plastic in the air.

Jay, who has remained in the kitchenette, drums his fingers on the table. He opens his mouth. And then closes it, as if he's thinking carefully about how to phrase something. After a pause, he clears his throat. "The boy is right though. You should have discussed the satellite with me before you activated it."

That's not really what Navarro said. But I appreciate Jay's efforts to keep some form of order. At least it feels normal.

Toby drops a stack of books with a loud thud. "I'm glad you did it, Jinx. We've been sitting around here discussing things. Drilling. Talking. Arguing. For a month. It's time to do something."

Jay again hesitates, thinking. "Perhaps, son. Perhaps. But—"

The return of Navarro interrupts Jay's train of thought. Jay takes a deep breath and remains silent, surveying the bunker.

I swivel the comm center chair around to face Navarro as he flops onto his own bunk. "But," he says, picking up the conversation, "we could have at least come to a decision as a group." Navarro folds his arms across his chest. "It also, apparently, didn't occur to you that Jay could have remained here in relative safety regardless of what we decided to do."

MacKenna and I exchange a look.

Actually, this very thing *had* occurred to us. But—

"I'm sure Stephanie knows where this place is. It's only a matter of time before she sends someone to look for us," MacKenna says.

—there is that.

"You don't know that," Navarro says. But I can tell he's thinking. About the rules.

Rule fourteen: Don't put your fate in the hands of your enemy.

"MacKenna is right," Toby says, staring down at a paperback. "Stephanie might not be looking for my father right now. But the instant that locating him becomes a political necessity, we'll be hearing from her again. I told you before. We should move him to a safer location."

Yeah, my mom might know about the bunker. But the bigger issue is—

Jay stands up, puts his hands on the back of his chair. "Excuse me, son, but you are all out of your minds if you think I'd remain underground, hiding like a groundhog afraid of his shadow, while my children run around fomenting a revolution."

That. MacKenna said there was no was Jay would let us leave the bunker without him.

Navarro stares at something in his lap.

Jay takes a few steps so that he's standing in the center of the bunker, midway between where I am at the desk and everyone else at their bunks. "I'm not a piece of old furniture that you need to find a home for." He clears his throat. "I've been trying to give each of you a little space to deal with the…"

He falters, and I wonder how he would describe what's happened to us. Or to him.

I wonder how he deals with all the betrayal.

I swallow a dry lump in my throat.

But as usual, Jay doesn't give much away. "To deal with the reality of our situation." He glances at me. "To each grieve in our own way." He continues to move toward Navarro so that he towers over the bunk. "But make no mistake. *It is essential to establish a chain of command. And I am in charge here.*"

Rule number eight.

It hadn't occurred to me that Jay might have read Dad's

book. Or maybe that bit of wisdom is something that my father and my stepfather have in common from their army days.

Jay stands up very straight. His dark hair has gotten a bit grayer at the temples since we arrived in Mexico. But the remnants of his military training emerge. "Here is the new drill. Jinx and MacKenna, I want a list of possible destinations. Places we could go after leaving here. Toby, Gus, you're with me. We'll handle supplies."

Given that this is the first time that Jay's given us any orders, there's a pause. But MacKenna comes to sit at the kitchen table, and that settles it.

The chain of command is established.

I turn my attention back to the computer.

I quickly write a program that does a public records search. It's based it on the theory that Esmerelda would be living in Mexico within a hundred-mile radius of the bunker. But the system Dad cobbled together is old and slow, and it takes a while for the program to run.

After the NeXT beeps again, I print out the results on paper I recycled from a weird survivalist cookbook which, thankfully, has recipes on only one side of the page.

I join MacKenna at the table, and we look through the papers. We make a list of all the people we find named Esmerelda Ojos along with notes about their location, how far away it is, how we'd get there.

"Here's one," I say. It's a newspaper article about a woman who opened a cantina in San Pedro, about an hour south of us. "This would make sense."

Pulling her cardigan tight around her chest, MacKenna shakes her head. "Look at the date of the article. If she's still alive, she'd be like a hundred and fifty years old."

Navarro and Jay are at the weapons cabinet in the corner

opposite the comm center loading supplies into bins. They appear to be taking inventory. Navarro mutters to himself and once in a while, I recognize a word or term here or there. *Glock* or *Colt* or *rounds*.

MacKenna swipes up the papers and neatens them. "So how many is that?"

I check the list I made on the back of a recipe for rattlesnake chili. "Fourteen Esmereldas," I tell her as I make my way back to the computers. "If we operate under the assumption that the person would be relatively close to my dad's age and then sort the list based on proximity to our current location, we could—"

Navarro groans and drops the bin he was holding onto the carpet.

MacKenna and I watch as he goes to one of the bookshelves and comes to the table with a weathered atlas. He opens it and places a yellowing paper map on top of my printouts. "Esmerelda Ojos isn't a person." He shoots me a glare. "It's a place."

He smooths out one of the wide maps and taps his finger at a spot a bit removed from the coast. "At least, that's how American tourists refer to the Ojos de Esmerelda Cenote. It's basically a network of flooded caves. It's pretty remote. My uncle used to take us scuba diving there when I was a kid. We had to stop the trips because the roads in that area haven't been well maintained since the New Depression. Not easy to get in." Navarro sighs. "Or out."

I decoded the message from Dad last week.

MacKenna's mouth falls open. "You've known that this whole time? When were you planning to tell us?"

He had been keeping his own secrets. I was trying to get us out of the bunker, while Navarro was trying to keep us in. "Maybe the same day *you* were planning to tell *me* about the satellite dish?"

Toby joins us and leans over the atlas. "This is what? Fifty miles or so from here?"

Navarro nods. "Fifty miles north." He adds, "When it would be safer to go south," in a low, ominous tone.

Jay presses the top on the plastic bin he'd been loading and then takes a seat at the head of the kitchen table. "I want you all to listen to me. No more secrets. Do you understand? Do *all* of you understand?" He looks pointedly at me.

It's Mac who answers. "Yeah, Dad. We get it."

"So we think what? That Marshall hid something in these caves?" Jay asks.

I shrug. "Maybe? I assume he stored equipment there. Or information. Something to help us deploy the code he wrote."

Navarro begins pacing in the small area around the table. "Those are dangerous assumptions. We don't know when Dr. Marshall loaded up those floppy disks, but presumably he hatched this plan while your parents were still married. We don't know what he may have told your mother. What she knows."

I catch his gaze, forcing him to look at me for the first time in a while. His posture softens a bit. And, anyway, he's wrong. My parents didn't talk. They hid everything from each other. "My mom was a spy for The Opposition while my dad was secretly sabotaging their leader. I'm pretty sure they didn't discuss these things." I try to give him a small smile. "Dad wouldn't have left us the instructions if he didn't want us to use them."

Navarro's shoulders stiffen. "He *didn't* leave anything for us, Susan. He didn't give us those disks or tell us where to find them. Dr. Marshall intended for us to come here and that's it. The fact that you know enough about his coding habits to figure out how he stored the key is dumb luck, not evidence of some master plan."

He glances at Toby, who is still staring at the atlas. "I mean, you really haven't thought this through, have you? We have no idea who Dr. Marshall left those instructions for. We're playing this game and don't even know all the players. We don't know what...or...or who we'll find in those caves."

Jay draws in a deep breath, and when he speaks again, it's with a fatalism that makes my blood run cold. "It doesn't matter. Either Stephanie knows about this place or she doesn't. Either there's something in the caves that can help us or there isn't. But either way, The Opposition is waiting for us to make a move."

MacKenna chews her lip.

Navarro runs his hand through his hair. "They're waiting for us to come up with Dr. Marshall's code. Waiting for us to leave here with the key in our pocket. This is exactly what Marshall *didn't* want. His instructions were to stay here."

I try to swallow the lump in my throat. "Gus. When my dad...died, he didn't know what we know. About Charles. I have to save my brother. And I can't think of a better idea."

Navarro sighs in defeat. "Well, we still could have discussed it first."

MacKenna pulls the atlas closer to her, slouches in her chair and traces a thin blue line with her finger. "So. How are we gonna get there?"

"Probably walk," he responds flatly. "There are a few dirt roads that will put us in the general area. But it's...well..." He glances at me, and his face turns red. "I don't know what the technical term is, but it's essentially like a rainforest or something."

I pull at a thread on my own sweater. Everything makes me think of my brother. Charles is the expert in all things botanical.

Toby is lost in his own thoughts. "So, it's a jungle out there?" he mutters.

"Glad to see you've still got your sense of humor," Navarro says. "You're gonna need it."

Jay crosses to the far side of the bunker, and I can barely hear him when he says, "I see no choice but to press on with this plan and see what develops."

He opens another plastic bin. "Everyone get ready. We leave tomorrow at dawn."

MacKenna pokes Navarro in the arm. "So, Ojos de Esmerelda? That means eyes of green, right? Why do they call it that?"

"Oh, you'll see," he tells her before joining Jay at the supply cabinet.

From the comm center, the NeXT beeps. A message appears on the screen.

SUSAN. THIS IS YOUR MOTHER.

All the dystopian books we've read. Everything we've been told about brave new worlds and doublethink. Sure, these stories are cautionary tales. But they aren't about some big systems collapse or a warning against evil dictators. Not really, anyway. They're about what happens when it's no longer important to regular people to do the right thing. What's happening isn't a crisis of government. It's a crisis of conscience.

—MacKENNA NOVAK,
Letters from the Second Civil War

MacKENNA

Well.

We've got enough guns to start our own militia.

They're stored in four black plastic tubs that fill up half of the camper of the cruddy truck Navarro picked up back in Guadalajara. He's got the tubs labeled with our names. It kinda disturbs me to see MACKENNA written in thick block letters on the side of a tub of Smith & Wesson M&P Shields and Glock 43s.

It also kinda disturbs me that I now know the difference between a Shield and a Glock. How to load and fire them.

Jinx gets way cooler guns. The kind that look like they belong to cops in old-timey TV shows. But Navarro says I have too much trouble with the grip safety. So, no Colt Governments for me.

I shudder. The old me wouldn't have considered any gun cool.

Oh, for the love of Pete. Calm down, MacKenna. Focus.

The old me wrote a paper called "Your Thumbprint Is Your

Weapon: How DNA-A Technology Killed Gun Culture." It was all about how old guns should be destroyed. How The Spark basically stopped school shootings and mass murders with the National Gun Control Act. All new guns had to be connected to the internet, and the user had to login to shoot.

Jinx could probably explain all the techie stuff.

The old guns though… The Spark wasn't able to get rid of them all.

And…here I am. Like a hypocrite. Carting around an arsenal of Dr. Doomsday's twentieth-century weapons.

I try to tell myself that our lives depend on it.

But where is the old me? Am I in here somewhere?

I have to be, right?

I'm sitting in the passenger seat of the truck, listening to Jinx and Navarro go through another one of their survivalist routines. It's kinda like a mating ritual for doomsday survivors. Watching them in the rearview mirror, I can tell Navarro is still mad. He's making that squinty-eyed face and keeps crossing his arms.

And hey…it's looking like it was a big mistake not to tell him about the satellite dish. After we got that cryptic message, Jinx pretty much threw that old computer off the desk and, like, destroyed anything that could even possibly communicate with anything else.

LEAD: Stephanie Marshall knows where we are and is coming for us.

"How many self-heating meals did you pack?" Navarro asks.

I have to hand it to them. They're running their drills.

"One hundred and fifty," Jinx says.

"That's only enough for ten days, Susan."

Jinx pushes her reddish-brown bangs out of her face. Sometimes she looks like Stephanie. She makes these faces, with her lips kinda scrunched up. Or sometimes, she'll reach for her neck, like she's playing with an invisible necklace.

Stephanie used to do that too.

The resemblance scares the hell out of me.

"This isn't a magic camper," Jinx says with an eye roll. "We don't have unlimited space back here. And if we haven't found something in ten days, we'll need to come up with…with…"

Navarro snorts. "With what? A plan better than this one?" The muscles in his arms kinda flex, stretching the fabric of his camo T-shirt.

I have to give it to Jinx. The guy is hot.

She picks up a bin of food and shoves it into Navarro's arms. "With another idea."

I lean so that I can see myself in the mirror.

Ugh. What I wouldn't do for a facial. Or some kinda moisturizer that doesn't smell like a banana snow cone.

I wonder if anyone ever thinks I look like my mother.

Toby and I both look like Dad. Even Mom used to say so all the time. These days, I try to think about Mom. Try to picture the exact color of her hair.

I can't.

That scares the hell out of me too.

Jinx and Navarro grow larger in the mirror as they come closer to me. The space that's right over the top of the truck's cab is a bed. They fill it with the bins, clearing enough room for us to be able to move around in the camper.

Dad gets into the driver's seat and pokes me lightly on the arm. "You're in the back."

When I stay in my seat a little too long, he adds, "We need Gus up here to navigate."

I get out and pass Navarro on my way to the small camper door. So it's me and Toby and Jinx in the back.

"We need to get going. Now," Jinx says. She can't stop pulling on strands of her hair. Or stop sounding and looking and seeming nervous as hell.

And…something's way wrong with Toby. Not, like, in the sense that something's wrong with me or Jinx. We're scared and freaked out all the time, and probably all messed up by what we've seen, and we miss home, we're worried about Charles, and we want our old lives back.

Toby is…different.

Like there's an icy storm raging inside of him.

Always.

We're totally smooshed in the back of this crappy camper, which, by the way, smells like an old man's dirty socks. Almost every surface is covered in wood paneling that's all scraped up. Like someone with freaky long fingernails used to be trapped in here.

Because the space is so narrow, I have to kinda turn sideways when I walk. Jinx and I move to the center and take a seat at a little table with a weirdly bright green top. Like a plastic lime.

It hurts my eyes to look at it.

Toby's on the floor of the camper with his back to the bed where we stashed the weapons. He's got his feet pushed against the tiny camper stove. He's staring, the way that a normal person might look out the window.

Except there's no window down where he's siting.

And he's not himself.

We play crazy eights for a while but, after about an hour, the ride gets so bumpy that the cards won't stay in place long enough for us to keep the game going.

"D-d-d-d-draw two." Jinx bounces up and down in her seat.

The truck hits a major bump, and the card pile spills all over the table.

"What's the point?" I push the pile into a neat stack.

It hits me that it's, like, way darker inside the camper than it was before.

I stand up. Or. I try to stand up. We take another mini hill, and I'm thrown back into my seat.

Okay. Here I go again. Up. Up. To the window.

Bracing myself using the sink, I make my way to the camper's wide window. We've completely left the coast. Tall, tropical trees surround the truck, blocking out the sun. It is like a jungle or a rainforest, and I wish I'd paid more attention in school when they explained the difference.

We haven't passed a house or a car or evidence of human civilization since leaving the beach. We could be the only five people on the whole friggin' planet.

A couple palm trees whiz by. There's something I recognize, at least.

Navarro didn't want to come here.

I'm getting this sinking feeling he's right. And I hate it.

I turn toward the cab. Toby's still sitting there, bouncing and bobbing along like he doesn't have any bones in his damn body. Like he's a flipping blob of Jell-O. Through the small window, I see Dad hunched over the steering wheel while Navarro has his face pushed into the atlas. In front of us...

Well.

It's like we're deliberately trying to drive into a tree.

The road, or the dirt path—or the, like, whatever, that Dad's trying to use as a road—is vanishing into a small point ahead of us. Navarro starts gesturing and pointing and yelling something.

Dad sideswipes a tree. He's driving way too fast. I fall over again, and I'm pretty sure that we've lost the driver's side mirror. I'm back in my seat.

Jinx gets up, but she moves with more purpose, heading to the supply bins.

My stomach bounces and lurches and drops.

And my brother is still…um…whatever.

Jinx is close to him, reaching above his head, into the bins. He takes to staring at her knees like he'll need to describe them to a police sketch artist later on.

"Toby! What the hell!" I yell at him.

He jumps to attention. "What? What's going on?"

"What's going *on*?" I shout even louder. "What's going on is that Dad is driving about a hundred miles an hour into the forbidden forest!"

He has the nerve to shrug. "What do you want me to do?"

"Act like you give a damn!"

Jinx is murmuring something to herself. She glances at the road ahead of us. "When we stop, we need to get ready to move!"

"Why are we going so fast?" I say.

She shrugs, too, but at least she has the decency to give me an actual answer. "I don't know. Maybe they see something." Jinx checks out the window again. "Maybe—"

Her "maybe" is cut off by a *boom*.

And then another.

A sound I've become too used to hearing.

Two shots. From a big gun. Like a rifle.

LEAD: The Opposition pursues family of fugitives through Yucatán.

Fact check: I can't verify who was chasing us. Everyone wants us dead.

Jinx clicks into mission mode, and before I can blink a few times, she's sliding into a holster with her Colt attached.

Boom again.

Dad hits the brakes.

Hard.

I pretty much face plant into the table.

That green tabletop realllllly sucks, and if I had any wind inside of me, it's totally knocked out.

Seriously, MacKenna. Get a hold of yourself.

"They're...they're...shooting. At us." I cough a bunch of times. That disgusting kinda cough that suggests I might have tuberculosis or something way truly gross.

Jinx is saying something in that high-pitched, semi-hysterical way she talks when she's saying things like, *We're all gonna die* or *Run!*

I catch only a few words here and there.

"Someone...shooting...tire...gunfire...blowout."

I hear the clacking of plastic as the bins up on the bunk collide with each other. The truck turns and rocks and spins and skids before hitting something.

If I had breath, I'd scream.

By the time I'm able to push my face off the table, Jinx is wearing her utility jacket and passing M16s to Dad and Navarro through the small window that divides the cab from the camper. She wraps another holster around her waist and grabs her backpack.

I'm hyperventilating as she makes her way up the narrow aisle in my direction. She drops my pack at my feet and presses a loaded Glock 43 into the palm of my hand.

I hate the feel of it.

"Stay behind me." She clutches her own M16.

Yep. That's Jinx.

"I think someone's out there," she says in a whisper.

Toby finally gets to his feet and manages to put a look on his face that isn't brooding lovesick vampire. Or bored. He watches Jinx as she passes. "She's always so eager to risk her life. Even when she has no idea what she's risking it for," he mutters.

Oh hell's bells.

That.

That right there was the problem. "We're risking our lives for Charles. And Dad. And anyone else about to be exterminated by The Opposition."

He loads his own gun. "Right. And truth, justice and the American way."

"Toby! You need to—"

"Shh!" Jinx tells me, waving her hand at me to pipe down.

I know she's right. Now's not the time for this. But fighting with my brother is the only thing that keeps my pulse going. That keeps the cold fear from overtaking me.

Because.

I think someone's out there.

The camper door has a small window. Jinx takes one finger and slowly pulls at the edge of the white curtain that hangs over it.

I can hear my heartbeat.

"You see anything?" Toby asks.

"No," Jinx whispers.

The door creaks as she pushes it open.

Slowly.

Slowly.

Rocks crunch under her boot as she lowers herself onto the ground.

She carefully closes the door behind her with a soft click that only a supervillain would be able to hear.

Toby follows her. He's got a bit of a jaunt to his walk, like he doesn't give a damn who or what might be out there.

He lets the door slam behind him.

I grab my own backpack, but I'm not ready to roll around the jungle with a loaded gun, so I gingerly place it on the counter.

Then.

I dig my fingers into my palms and focus on that pain… and force myself to go outside.

And outside.

Outside, there's…

Nothing.

And I do mean nothing.

We're in a narrow clearing between clusters of huge trees that tower high above the truck. The area is gloomy and shaded. I can barely see the sky, and the sky might be made of tree branches. It's like the land that time forgot. The sounds are things that creep me out. Rustling leaves. Screeching. Like maybe a monkey or something.

As far as the eye can see…trees. More trees. Tall trees. Everywhere. Deep greens. Green in every shade of green. And ground covered in tall grass that looks like it will be a major pain to walk in.

I come around to the side of the camper, where everyone else is already huddled in a small circle. Seeing them like that, it strikes me how much we've all changed. We're dressed in fatigues and camo Ts and windbreakers. Dad has grown a salt-and-pepper beard, and his hair has gotten longer and grayer.

We're, like, our own little army.

"You heard the shots," Dad is saying.

"It could be nothing," Navarro says, his voice filled with a tension that means it's not nothing. "There's lots of hunting out here. It's illegal. But with everything going on, it's probably not a priority for the Mexican police to be this far out."

Jinx nods. "Most of the Federales are deployed at the border." Somehow, she's managing to sound calm. But her knuckles are white from gripping her gun.

"But…" She takes a deep breath. "Somebody is out there."

I glance around in every direction. It seems like you could go a long time out here without seeing *somebody*. The trees are so thick. The forest so dense.

How would you find *somebody*?

Even if you were looking.

"We've got two blown out tires," Navarro comments, squinting at the truck. "From now on, I guess we're on foot."

"Someone should stay here," Toby says.

"Absolutely not," Dad answers. "We stay together."

Navarro open his mouth to speak.

There's a pause.

Like he's thinking what to say.

He starts again. "Jay. I think he might be right. We didn't make it as far into the forest as we wanted. We don't know how far we are from the caves. We don't know if whoever was shooting at us is nearby. If we end up wanting to come back here, it'll help to have someone stay here to guard the supplies. Make sure we're not surprised when we return."

Dad appears to be considering this.

"We have the radios," Navarro adds. "We can stay in contact."

"And enough guns to arm the whole National Police force," Toby says in a low tone.

He leans against the truck.

Casual.

Off.

Wrong.

We're silent again, the wind filling the space between us. I wish Dad would notice that something is really, really, *really* weird about Toby. But he's busy being Captain Commander of our expedition.

Mom would have noticed.

"I assume you're volunteering to stay?" Dad asks my brother.

Toby swats at a mosquito. "Oh, I long to be covered in insect bites and get malaria as much as the next man. But now that you mention it, I would prefer to stay here."

"We have bug spray," Navarro says through his teeth.

Jinx frowns at the trees. "I wish Charles were here."

I know what she's thinking.

Being city folk, it's always handy to have someone around who can keep you from walking right into poison ivy. And she misses him.

We all miss him.

Dad has made a decision. "Okay. You stay here. Keep the radio with you at all times. If the caves are close, we'll come back for you. If you see anything, alert me immediately."

Oh. Hell. No.

With Toby acting so nuts, there's no way I'm leaving him out here in the middle of nowhere all by himself.

"I'm staying too," I say.

Toby frowns. "Like hell you are."

Suddenly he's more lively than he's been in a month.

I know I've made the right decision. His left eye kinda twitches and he's chewing the inside of his cheek. He's trying hard to come up with a reason that I shouldn't stay. Like

when we were kids, and he'd try to get out of letting me walk
to the store with him.

He'd make up reasons. Like it was going to rain. Or the
walk was too long.

Mom never let him get away with that stuff—because he
acts like this only when he's up to something.

I give him a curt nod.

Because I know.

I see you, bro.

"It doesn't take two people to man the lighthouse here,"
Toby says.

"I'm staying."

"She's right," Dad says. "It'll be better for you not to stay
alone."

Navarro nods. "We need to move out."

A second later he steps into the trees and disappears.

Dad opens his backpack and hands Toby the radio. "Stay
alert."

Jinx slings her backpack over her shoulders and moves toward where I last saw Navarro. "Call if you need anything.
We're on channel two." She turns back. "Be careful."

"You too," I say.

And she's gone.

Dad gives me a hug.

Then it's Toby and me.

And the creepy swaying trees.

And the mosquitos sucking away all my blood.

And…

It's so quiet.

Something hoots.

Toby stands there for a few minutes, a scowl on his face.
Watching the space between the trees where Dad disappeared.

"Woo-hoo! Earth to Toby," I say, in as normal of a way as I can.

He ignores me, walking past me into the camper.

"Uh. Hello," I say. To myself. Or maybe the monkey in the tree.

I go back into the camper too.

Toby's packing another backpack. Filled with food and several more guns. Not the kind of behavior you'd expect from a guy who'd resolved to stay put.

"Hey! What are you doing?"

He ignores me.

"Toby!"

He lifts up the large, heavy pack and comes toward me.

I spread my arms out and block the door. "What do you think you're doing?"

He tries to give me the radio. "I'm leaving."

LEAD: Toby Novak leaves sister and deserts doomed mission.

Over my dead body.

"Oh *hell* no."

I keep my arms spread out to stop him from passing, and then we're in a bizarro pushing and shoving match. Like we're five-year-olds or something. It would have ended with both of us in time-out back when we were little.

It hits me that we're doing the exact opposite of what Dad wanted.

Stay alert.

It also hits me that I'm out of breath. Again.

"Wait. Wait. Wait." I put my hands up in surrender. "This is stupid. Exactly where do you think you're gonna go?"

He runs his hand through his dark hair. "Away from here!"

"Toby—"

"Mac," he cuts through me. "What are we doing? Dad won't even consider a plan that ensures his own safety. You and Jinx are living in some fantasy land that involves some-how getting back into America to—" he makes air quotes "—rescue Charles."

"You don't want to rescue Charles?" I demand.

"Of course I do!" Toby's face is totally red. "But in case you've forgotten, he's in the custody of a mass murderer. A superspy with the resources of the government at her disposal. You really think we're gonna beat Stephanie Marshall at her own game? I want to go back. Go back and do everything over...because I miss..."

I put my hands on my hips. "You miss what?"

My brother's anger threatens to simmer over, but at least he's showing emotion. Plus. The expression on his face. It's familiar. From those days when we were tiny, and Mom worked long hours in her restaurant.

"Is that what this is about? Mom? You miss Mom?"

I miss Mom.

"I miss everything!" he hisses through his teeth. "I miss our old house. My old life. My friends. I miss when my shift in the library ended at noon and my next class started at 12:05. My biggest problem was how to grab a sandwich and make it across Cady Mall before Professor Lidell took attendance."

I'm losing my brother.

And. Oh crap.

"Toby. Don't tell me."

This is about *her.*

"Don't tell me you're still pining away for that bleach-blonde bobblehead. You only knew her for, like, three days. And she's Ammon Carver's daughter."

"It's not about her."

Part of me thinks that it is. That, totally stupid as it seems, Toby thinks he's in love with Annika Carver and wishes he'd run away with her when she offered to take him.

"You know Dr. Doomsday thought she was totally cut-throat."

"He didn't know everything," Toby answers quickly. His expression softens. "Mac. You remember our old house? The birch tree?"

Don't cry.

"Uh...yeah. Mom planted all those flowers underneath it. That spot was always cool in the shade. Even in the summer."

Toby pats my arm. "I think there must still be a place in the world like that. Where nobody's heard of The Opposition. Or The Spark. I'm going south until I find it."

MacKenna. Don't. You. Cry.

Get angry again. Boil inside. Erupt like a volcano.

"So you won't help us? You were gonna sneak off and leave me here? Without even saying goodbye?"

He shakes his head. "*Help* you? Help you what? Commit suicide? The border is guarded by the entire Mexican Army and half the National Police. You won't get back across, and if you try, you'll be killed." He lets his hands fall to his sides. "If I thought you'd come with me, I would have asked. But..."

"What? But what?" I demand.

Something in the window has caught his attention. "Shh! I think I saw something."

All the muscles in my legs tighten.

He firmly pushes me aside and opens the camper door

slowly. "Stay here and be quiet." He's getting his gun ready as he steps outside.

It's like my feet are made of lead. So heavy. Immobile. I almost have to pick them up. But somehow. I make them go.

Step. Step. Step.

Over to the window. Where Toby was only a minute before. I can't see my brother out the small window. In fact, I can't see anything at all, other than the tall trees. The lower branches sway gently. Back and forth. Almost teasing me. Like they conceal all the secrets and will never reveal anything.

Even the monkey is quiet and gone.

Something silver streaks through the trees. Kinda like tinsel. I blink a few times.

The silver spot has vanished.

LEAD: Toby Novak vanishes in Macbeth's creepy, haunted forest of death.

That was terrible. On top of everything else, I'm losing my skills as a journalist.

Well. I've basically got three options. Stay where I am and do nothing. Call Dad on the radio. Or go outside and look around.

If I call Dad on the radio and it ends up being a piece of aluminum foil stuck in a tree or something, I'm gonna be super embarrassed.

What would Jinx do? She'd grab about ten thousand guns and go stomping around out there in her big boots, that's what. Plus, what if Toby was totally scamming me? Scaring the crap out of me while he ran off into the jungle on foot? The way he's been acting lately, I would absolutely not put it past him.

That's it.

I'm going out there.

"Toby," I whisper as I push the camper door open. "Toby," I say a tiny bit louder. "I think I saw something too."

It seems weird to add the word…*sparkly*. And yet. That's what I saw.

Oh. Crap.

No answer. And no sign of my brother either.

Perfect.

My brother took off and left me here.

I'm going to have to use the radio.

I'm going to have to call Dad.

My finger hovers over the talk button.

But before I can push it—

—a thick hand wraps around my throat.

There is an indelible link between love and loss. We will rightfully always fear losing what we love. But, of course, if you love nothing, you have nothing to fear.

—PRESIDENT-ELECT DAVID ROSENTHAL,
pirated national address

JINX

We've been walking less than fifteen minutes, and already my thighs ache and burn.

Sinking into the wet mud with each step, I follow Navarro, and the tall grass whacks my calves as he moves forward. He holds a compass up to his face and keeps us moving westward. Jay is a few paces behind me. Each time I glance back, he's scanning the jungle, no doubt looking for the source of the shots we heard.

My sweaty hands tremble.

I want to ask how long we'll be walking like this, but I know that would annoy Navarro.

Instead, I say, "What time is it?"

"A little after eleven," Navarro says.

I don't know how he manages to stay so cool and crisp and not be dripping with humid sweat…and… *Focus!*

Another cluster of long, yellow-green grass hits my shins. I remember Charles telling me that grass grows on every continent, even in the polar regions. There's something called hair grass that grows in Antarctica. I hope my brother is okay. That Mom is checking his blood sugar and making sure he takes his meds.

My arms and legs are suddenly so heavy.

The instant that I finished using the satellite dish to hunt for information about Esmerelda Ojos, I ran a search for my brother, and it found...nothing.

No news headlines. No references on any social media. I even hacked into his old elementary school. His file was archived and marked TRANSFER.

My eyelids flutter, gummy from tears that won't fall.

I'm lost in these thoughts when a spider the size of my palm emerges from the parted grass and comes to rest on the toe of my boot.

Oh God. Oh. My. God.

The thing is an off-brown color with long, spindly legs shooting out in every direction and a hairy hourglass-shaped body. It looks like a thinner version of a tarantula. I kick at it and find myself doing a weird little dance, hopping on one foot and making a series of disgusted gurgling noises. The little monster scurries off my shoe and toward a pile of fallen leaves.

I freeze, unable to take another step.

I've been chased all over the place by the National Police and The Opposition and whoever else. I shot a mercenary soldier in the face, helped deploy a drone loaded up with explosives and got pushed out of a moving truck.

This was just a spider.

In an instant, I'm flanked by both Jay and Navarro, who have their guns ready.

"What? What do you see?" Jay demands, scanning the trees.

My insides heat up with embarrassment and I feel my face getting red. "I saw… I saw…" I falter. But I know that making something up will endanger our lives. So I finish, "A spider," in a low, lame, defeated voice.

Navarro glances around for the spider that I've already kicked into the landscape. "A spider? Really, Susan?" His mouth twitches, like he finds this funny. "I thought maybe you stepped on a bear trap or something."

I scowl at him and try to save my dignity. "I doubt there are any bears in this swamp."

Jay puts a light hand on my upper arm. "Let's try and keep our composure here, okay? A lot of people don't like spiders, but we need to stay focused."

"You know, we have spiders back at home," Navarro says with a teasing smile.

My face gets even warmer.

He's right. There's an entire exhibit at the zoo called Arizona's Arachnids, and it's in a huge building. My mom used to take us there on Saturdays in the winter. We'd have cocoa and walk along, taking pictures of giraffes and zebras.

Those days are gone.

I go for a casual shrug. "When you're out in the desert, in the wide-open spaces, you can usually see them before they see you."

Navarro puts his hands on his hips and smiles. "Maybe. Unless they crawl into your shoes or find their way into your bag. You know, once when I was camping with my dad, a brown recluse spider got tangled up in his undershirt and—"

I sigh and give him a warning look. I do *not* want to know

where this story is going. Navarro smiles, but he takes pity on me and doesn't finish.

"We need to keep moving," Jay says brusquely, pushing past Navarro and taking the lead.

The smile falls from Navarro's face as he watches Jay move ahead of us. "He's different."

Yes. Yes, he is.

Desperate to change the subject, I say, "I wish I'd been able to find some information about your parents before we left the bunker." It was strange. I ran a search for information on Navarro's family and I found...nothing. Maybe my program had a bug.

He resumes walking, so I'm looking at the back of his head when he says, "I wish *you* would have told me in advance that you had decided to activate that satellite dish."

We're back to that again.

I take a few quick steps to catch up to him. "Look. I already told you—"

Navarro turns and waits for me to catch up. He reaches out and pulls a small leaf from my hair. His touch sends a strangely electric pulse through me. It's always like this. Like I could so easily forget we're out here running for our lives.

"I know. I know. I accepted your apology," he says.

I feel my lips pucker up in a skeptical expression. It doesn't sound like he has.

"It's true," he says, his cheeks going a little pink. "I do. I mean, I did. I...well...talking about my family makes me feel... I just... I want to tell you—"

Jay raises a hand to stop us from talking. He's about fifteen feet away from us and up to his knees in brush that seems impossibly long. "Hey! You hear that?"

We quicken our pace to catch up to him.

Navarro freezes but then relaxes a bit. "Sounds like running water."

I swallow as I arrive where the two of them stopped near a wide tree trunk. "Is that good?" I ask.

Jay nods and addresses his comment to Navarro. "I assume the water is runoff from the caves. Let's hustle." He takes off, walking twice as fast as before. We're moving deeper into the forest. Birds coo and chirp. The tall trees totally surround us.

"Should we call MacKenna?" I ask.

Navarro watches Jay for a second. "I don't know. I mean, we're headed in the right direction. But we don't know much more than we did before. We should press on and figure out if the caves are close." Then he, too, is gone.

Catching only occasional glimpses of the cloudy sky through gaps in the tree cover, I force my tired legs to push on through the grass. After about ten minutes, we find ourselves at a wide stream running between clusters of trees. It's filled with gorgeous aquamarine water.

It almost looks fake, like a jungle river ride at a theme park.

"Excellent," Jay says. "We'll make much better time walking alongside the creek."

Navarro frowns. "Maybe," he says. "But if we run into any hostiles, we'll be awfully exposed out here. The trees provide great cover."

Jay checks his watch. "We've been out here almost thirty minutes and haven't seen or heard anything. We need to get to the caves as quickly as possible. That water is nice and shallow. We'll make much better time walking through it than through that switchgrass."

"Yeah, but—"

Jay cuts through Navarro's objection with a curt, "Let's move out."

His brusque, military-like demeanor somehow alarms me. Mac and I formulated this plan without knowing what all the possible consequences might be. How it might change us.

I shudder.

Jay splashes into the water. Navarro and I follow behind.

I have to say, I'm enjoying Jay's plan much more than staying in the grass. The water is cool and clean and comes up to midcalf. Tree branches extend over our heads, forming an arch over the creek. From time to time, Jay steers us around a patch of mossy rocks or brush jutting out of the creek.

Little waves lap against the grass. A frog ribbits. Birds coo and hoot.

It's…beautiful.

I find myself bringing up the rear with about ten feet in between each of us. My body aches. I'm already exhausted. The M16 weighs over seven pounds, which doesn't sound like a lot but does get heavy after a while. I wonder how long I should wait before proposing that we stop for water and protein bars.

"This is wrong," Navarro says, slowing down and waiting for me to catch up.

My gaze darts all over. Through the deep green trees. Up at the darts of blue sky that occasionally appear through tiny breaks in the tree canopy. "I don't see anything."

He frowns. "The water. It's flowing in the wrong direction. It's moving toward the caves. It can't possibly be runoff. Plus, look at how fast it's moving."

My legs get heavier and heavier as I lift them in and out of the water to keep going. "Maybe we're walking in the wrong direction? And what difference does it make how the water moves? I don't get it."

Navarro pulls the compass from his pocket. "No, we're going the right way."

Jay is getting farther and farther ahead of us.

Navarro begins to walk again. "There were a couple of rivers marked on the map." He continues to stare at the compass. "Rivers run because water is moving from a higher elevation to a lower one. Like snow melting on a mountain and then flowing down, which means…"

He quickens his pace and mutters to himself.

There's a light breeze, and a lone green leaf sails from a high tree branch, coming briefly to float on the surface of the water near Navarro's boot. It disappears into the rushing water as he takes his next step.

But he freezes midstride, his boot hovering over the water.

And a second later I understand why.

Whispering.

From the trees.

Navarro turns back to me, his eyes wide with horror.

"Run!" he screams.

I barely manage to avoid falling into the water as I take off at a sprint. Navarro waits until I pass him before also getting into action. Jay's neck swivels around. Failing to find any targets, he fires his M16 three times into the air. It's probably designed to be intimidating. He takes off ahead of me.

Behind us, shots ring out, and feet splash into the water.

Someone is chasing us.

The boom of a rifle.

And shooting at us.

Ahead, the stream curves to the right, and Jay disappears

from view as he follows it around a thick tree. Navarro has managed to get a few paces in front of me. As he rounds the tree, he skids to a stop.

It's not hard to see why.

Jay is about twenty feet ahead of us, stopped where the stream ends.

At a cliff.

Navarro was right. The small river was flowing over a formation of jagged black rocks and into a valley. We're staring at a gulf between two plateaus. Directly across from us is another wall of massive trees that creates a dark, mysterious void.

We can't cross. We can't go back.

We are going to die.

I fight off the urge to scream. When has screaming ever helped me?

I can't help but slip and slide into Navarro, and we both come crashing down into the water with a splash that would be comical were it not for the fact that someone with a gun is chasing us through the jungle. I spin around a couple of times, catching a dizzy glimpse of three men in green fatigues making their way around the corner, coming toward us.

Fast.

It's The Opposition. It has to be.

"We have to jump!" Jay yells.

Down below, a wide river runs around clusters of dark rocks. There's no telling how deep the water might be or how sharp the rocks are. "Jump? Are you crazy? We'll be killed!"

Navarro's face is turning as green as the trees.

My heart drops into my stomach.

I think he's afraid of heights.

More shots. One ricochets off a tree trunk about six inches from Navarro and barely misses my left cheek.

Jay groans and tugs me up by my arms, yanking me the way a careless child would treat the doll they received last Christmas.

I'm not sure what I think he'll do.

But I'm definitely not prepared when he draws me in front of him and gives me a dramatic shove, sending me off the edge of the rocks.

Down. Down. Down.

My stomach lurches and heaves and turns.

Blurry black rocks.

And then.

Splash.

For a second, I'm relieved that the water is deep enough that I don't break my legs. But that feeling fades as I try to fight my way to the surface. Glimmers of green and blue sparkle above me.

I have to make it.

For Charles.

Frantically pumping my arms, I gasp for a deep breath as I reach the surface. I get one gulp of air before I'm drawn down again by someone else, probably Jay, landing in the water. Making it up again, I drag myself to the bank of the river.

It takes me a minute or so to figure out what in the hell is going on. The three men are on top of the cliff, yelling. If I had to guess, I'd say they're looking for solid footing.

So they can shoot us.

I shut my eyes for a moment.

I consider using the radio to contact MacKenna. Luckily

it's waterproof and should work, but it took two hours for us to walk here. What would she even be able to do?

In the water, Jay paddles in my direction.

Which leaves Navarro. My heart sinks when I can't see him, then jumps as he bobs to the surface a second later... but he's not exactly conscious. He's got a large, bloody gash on the side of his head, and he's not swimming.

I jump into the water again. Jay sees Navarro, too, and both of us push ourselves in his direction. I try to wrap Gus's arm around my shoulder, the way we used to practice in water drills, but I find myself getting sucked down below the surface again.

Jay is way more successful in helping Navarro out of the water.

Gus is semiconscious when the soldiers resume shooting at us.

"We have to move," Jay croaks.

We each flop one of Navarro's arms around our shoulder and drag him into the trees that flank the water. He moans and is able to take a few steps. The three of us quicken our pace, making our way as best we can through the wet, grassy jungle.

After a bit, Jay braces Navarro on a tree trunk and releases him.

Panting and gasping for breath, I try to get a look at the cut on Navarro's head. It seems kind of bad. Like he must have really taken a hit from one of those sharp rocks.

He swats me away. "Ow! Susan! No!"

"Stop it!" I tell him.

I dab at the blood with my finger. I'd be willing to bet he has a concussion, but he's standing up and talking now, which is a big improvement.

I leave him alone and poke my head out of the row of trees.

And I see it.

Two deep green eyes staring back at me.

Ojos de Esmerelda.

Two cave entrances sit side by side, each with green light streaming out of them.

I tap Jay on the arm. "We made it."

In the distance, water splashes.

My pulse picks up again.

The soldiers have decided to pursue us off the cliff.

The three of us break out of the trees and enter the cave on the left for no other reason than the entrance is the closest. We duck into the mouth and squeeze in between a rock formation jutting up from the ground. The run took the last bit of energy Navarro had. He leans over, slouching against the cave wall, with his eyes closed.

Voices echo in from outside the cave.

Jay and I both lost our M16s in the fall. He gives me an encouraging nod. We have to take these guys out. I withdraw the Colt from my side holster.

And. Hold. My. Breath.

Get ready.

We wait. In the cool greenish light of the cave. For the sound of approaching footsteps. Calm settles over me. I've dealt with this before. I can do this.

But.

A second later, the cold barrel of a gun presses against my temple.

In my peripheral vision, I spot a tall, broad-shouldered soldier in the same fatigues as the guys from the cliff. But he's dry. The hostiles, as Navarro had called them, had at least two teams and a much better plan.

We were herded into this cave.

"You just made a big mistake," the soldier says in a cold, hard tone.

"Wait. Wait. Wait," another male voice calls out.

The voice comes from a figure silhouetted at the cave's mouth. "It's her. That's Jinx Marshall."

I'm clutching my Colt so hard that I can't feel my fingers.

It's a voice I recognize.

And.

I'm not sure if things have gotten better.

Or worse.

Harold Partridge is one of these hackers who likes to pretend that technology just happens. That it's neutral or benign. Like if you only build the robot that builds the bomb, you can claim to be surprised by the explosion.

–MacKENNA NOVAK,
Letters from the Second Civil War

MacKENNA

Okay.

Like, once, in second grade, I wrote this book about what it would feel like to be an armchair. I drew all the pictures myself of this green recliner being carted from house to house and having a rad adventure. It was pretty cool, actually, and, of course, the teacher hung it on the wall.

But if I survive all of this—if live to see a world that isn't one big ole hellfire—well. I'm rewriting the book.

Because now I really know what it feels like to be lugged around like a piece of furniture.

Let me say. It's not a rad adventure.

I come out of the camper, into the clearing, or whatever you'd call the small space where Dad managed to squeeze the truck. I instantly get nabbed by some tall, beefcake guy who could be twinning with Jinx and Navarro. He's dressed in green fatigues. I would not be surprised to find out that he's wearing camo underwear. And, just like Jinx, he seems to be carrying about fifty guns.

LEAD: Quarreling brother and sister captured by The Opposition.

The supersoldier slaps a piece of duct tape across my mouth before I can even scream. He quickly tapes my arms behind my back, binds my feet and carries me away from the camper. Exactly like my imaginary armchair. The guy puts one hand under each of my armpits, lifts me up and holds me an arm's length away from his body. When we're in a narrow gap between a couple of trees, he drops me and props me up against a tree trunk.

We wait.

For a sec, I don't know what the hell is going on.

Some part of me registers that this ought to be terrifying. Like I should be having some kind of reaction. But I'm not. My palms aren't sweating. My insides don't jiggle like Jell-O.

I'm probably gonna die as soon as this rainforest rando sorts himself out.

All I can think about is how pissed Jinx is gonna be. If I live, my big reward will be another lecture on drilling. I can almost picture Navarro pacing, nodding and being all broody and disagreeable, while Jinx makes her smug pronouncements.

Leaving the camper without first radioing for help?

Jinx: Mistake.

Leaving the camper without a weapon ready?

Jinx: Mistake.

Going outside, one by one, without any kind of plan?

Jinx: Mistake.

I hate drilling, and I'm not good at it. At all.

Mistake. Mistake. Mistake. Mistake.

Oh yeah. But, really, this is all Toby's fault. Right. I'll tell Jinx that Toby ran off and...

Toby.

Yeah. My brother. I spot his bag near the door of the camper, where he must have dropped it. Crap. Now I really am scared. My palms sweat. My heart is beating so hard it feels like it wants to break out of my body.

Okay. Okay. Okay.

What if these creepazoids hurt my brother?

I shouldn't have let him go outside alone. I should have paid more attention. He took all that stuff with Annika way harder than I thought. Which is dumb. Annika Carver is nothing but an ornate urn, filled with the ashes of death.

But still. I should have noticed Toby was having trouble.

Okay, MacKenna. Take a breath and…

What would Jinx do?

First, she'd try to get her hands free.

This would be a really awesome time to realize that I'm double-jointed or have superstrength and can rip through the duct tape like the Hulk.

But no.

I'm only me, and being good at collecting pull quotes isn't a skill that comes in particularly handy right now.

I'm doing a lame job picking at the edges of the tape when some guy yells out, "All clear," from what sounds like the opposite side of the camper.

The guy comes into the clearing where we've parked the camper. Another soldier, like the one who's holding me. Except the new guy is driving some kinda small vehicle. It's camo green, and so quiet that it must be electric. It looks like a ruggedized golf cart that was designed by army rangers. The back, where the caddy might sit with the clubs, is loaded with fuel containers and food and…

My brother.

Plopped on the top shelf of the cart.

His hands and feet are taped, too, and he's been tossed on his stomach on top of a stack of cases of bottled water. Toby squirms around but stops when my gaze catches his. He flops over in defeat.

The first soldier picks me up and carries me to the cart. He dumps me on my butt on a rusted red fifty-gallon steel drum. It reeks of gas.

Both soldiers are white with cropped brownish hair. The one who nabbed Toby is a tad shorter and stockier. My guy is thin and wiry with a wide nose and chapped lips.

"We're taking them back to base?" Soldier One asks.

"Those are the orders," Soldier Two says.

Soldier One squints at our camper. "And the truck?"

My guy shrugs. "Leave it for now. We'll make some decisions as soon as we figure out who these kids are and what they're doing."

Soldier One drives the jolly green golf cart while Soldier Two walks in front, selecting a route. We follow the road we came in on for a while before cutting into the trees and the tall grass.

We jiggle and bob, and even my internal organs knock into each other. The scenery is one big blur that I can't focus on because my eyeballs are basically bouncing around like those craft googly eyes. I try to brace myself with my hands, which are still tied behind my back. This is a dumb process that accomplishes nothing and makes my thumbs sore.

Toby goes *oof* every once in a while. Usually when the guy driving steers us over tree roots or through particularly tight clumps of long grass.

Dents in the lid of the steel drum poke and scratch my butt.

"This is a lot of trouble for a bunch of stupid kids," Soldier Two calls out.

From the driver's seat, Soldier One snorts. "You didn't go in that camper. These stupid *kids* have buckets and buckets full of guns. I stopped counting at seventy-five."

I'm surprised that you can drive anything through this forest or rainforest or jungle or whatever. But the ATV seems to have been made for this terrain with its big high wheels that turn with ease.

Things are going about as well as they can be when you want to throw up but can't because your mouth is taped shut. Then. The ATV stops at the sound of three high-pitched pops.

"Shots fired," Soldier One says in a low voice. He doesn't bother looking around or checking things out. Which makes me think that the fire isn't coming from nearby.

Oh. God.

Jinx.

And Navarro.

And Dad.

It has to be.

Oh crap. Crap. Total crap.

I sniff in a few deep breaths through my nose, my nostrils burning from the stench of the gasoline. I have to stay calm. Jinx has been in tough spots before. It's usually the other guy who ends up getting hurt. I have to believe that they'll be fine.

Soldier Two reaches for a radio in the inside pocket of his lightweight green jacket. Soldier One taps the vehicle's horn lightly.

"We have our orders. HQ says radio silence," Soldier One says.

Soldier Two rolls his eyes.

More shots ring out.

Soldier Two climbs into the ATV. "Let's get a move on."
More gunfire.
And shouting.
Soldier One drives faster.
We come to the edge of a cliff. Looks kinda like Team Supersoldier took a wrong turn. I want to scream as Soldier One drives the vehicle…
Right.
Off.
The.
Cliff.
And…whoa.
Onto a path?
A weird lightness comes over me. A strange relief.

LEAD: Student journalist and her brother survive driving off cliff.

Fact check: It was too soon to conclude we'd survive.
It's kinda clever, actually.
There's an angled, paved road about five feet in width. It's been painted the same color black as the rocks of the cliff and decorated with plants here and there. It blends in remarkably well. You'd never find the thing if you didn't already know it's here.

LEAD: The Opposition runs a secret operation in the Yucatán wilderness.

For a couple of seconds, I'm happy to still be alive. But cold adrenaline returns and kills that feeling almost immediately. We're in the middle of nowhere, and these guys have a team and a base and an impressive infrastructure. They aren't poachers or hunters or mercenaries. They're The Opposition. Who else has these kinds of resources?

I consider throwing myself off the cart.

But what good would that do? I'm all tied up, and the supersoldiers would still have my brother, and I have to help Dad if I can.

So I sit here. Like a piece of furniture.

We descend into a valley between two cliffs made of black rocks that create a break in the thick overgrown forest. Below us, I can hear a river, the sound of water flowing like the soundtrack they play at the spa when I get my nails done.

Um. Back when I used to get my nails done.

The path zigzags down, down, down and appears to come to a dead stop at an enormous rock wall. We're coming along at a fast clip. Like we're gonna run right into it.

There's some yelling.

I can't tell who it is.

Any second now, Soldier Two is gonna ram us into a jutting, jagged rock.

Instead, he again reaches in his pocket, this time for a little key chain. He presses a button, and a low *thud* sounds out. A wide hydraulic door, perfectly concealed by rock cover, rises up. Once it's high above our heads, Soldier Two enters a code on a keypad.

A second door opens, and Soldier One drives our cart through the opening.

OTHER IMPORTANT FACTS:

-The Opposition (or whoever) has built a base out here

-They've created, like, a lab...in a cave

Goose bumps break out on the back of my neck. It's beautiful.

Sharp, yellowish-green stalactites drop from the ceiling and cast long shadows on the cave floor. Worktables covered with modern-looking computers sit between stalagmites shooting up from the cave floor. The area is really well lit by stand lights placed every few feet. On one side, a small pool of green water shimmers. Next to it, there's a long table with stacks of e-tablets, a row of printers and even a 3D fabricator.

How is this possible?

On the other side from the printers, several soldiers sit at a long table. It almost looks like a techie reenactment of *The Last Supper* painting by Leonardo da Vinci. They're all leaning in toward an older figure, sitting in the center.

It's a cave with power and computers.

Jinx would be in heaven here.

Crap. Jinx might be in actual heaven if The Opposition has already killed her.

"Where's the Professor?" Soldier One asks them.

Without looking up from his screen, the older guy says, "He's in C. We caught three more of them."

Caught.

Not killed.

Dad and Jinx and Navarro are still alive, for now. Relief fills me.

Soldier Two goes to a stainless-steel refrigerator, pulls out two cans of soda and tosses one to Soldier One. It whooshes over my head before I hear the sound of it smacking into a palm. Soldier One resumes driving the cart.

"You can't take the Bullfrog," Soldier Two says. "I need that stuff. I gotta get everything restocked."

Soldier One grunts. "So, what? I carry these two lumps over to C?"

When Soldier Two says nothing, Soldier One adds, "I'll bring it right back."

"Fine. But, Phil, if dinner is late, it's your ass."

We move past Soldier Two, sliding smoothly on another paved path that passes through a network of connected caves. The place looks like a more sophisticated version of Dr. Doomsday's bunkers. I catch a glimpse of a kitchen and a room full of bunk beds. Everywhere we go there are TV screens tuned to some kinda procession in the capital. Long lines of cars drive slowly past all the familiar monuments.

Continuing on, there are doors marked with large letters. A, B and…

C.

The door to C is another massive hydraulic door that requires a code to get through. This door leads to a more conventional-looking cave that's mostly filled with water. Light pours in through a wide mouth at the front.

Dad and Jinx are up there, next to several soldiers who have their weapons drawn. Tension radiates off their tight, military-like postures, and they're all sopping wet. Navarro leans up against the wall and he doesn't look so good.

They're in trouble.

Toby groans.

We're in trouble.

A thin figure stands up ahead. He's got his hands on his hips.

There's something familiar about him.

He turns at the sound of the squeaky wheels of the cart.

It's…it's…

It's Harold Partridge. Or Terminus, or whatever stupid name he's given himself. Jinx's weirdo hacker…um…friend? I mean, if you can call someone a friend after you try to strangle them with a phone cord. Jinx and Terminus knew each other from computer camp. Last time we saw him was at Goldwater Airfield when he was working for The Opposition and going on and on about how Dr. Doomsday practically walked on water.

And Jinx was trying to murder him.

Sure, he did help us escape from The Opposition. But he also helped The Opposition frame my dad in the first place. How much could we really trust the guy?

He's changed a little since the last time we've seen him. Terminus cut his purple hair into a cropped style that matches the rest of his crew. Like everyone else we've seen, he's wearing green fatigues and a camo windbreaker. There's something about him though. Something…well…he's not like other guys.

Soldier One…or uh…Phil…hoists Toby up and puts him in a seated position next to me. My brother's face is horribly red from pretty much being face down on the cart all this time. Toby gives me a nod that I think is meant to be reassuring.

Jinx stands about five feet away from Terminus, and her gaze is darting all over. I know what she's thinking. She wants to go for a weapon.

So no, I guess they're not friends.

Terminus comes my way and peels the duct tape off my mouth.

"What is this place?" I ask through the sting, the instant I can talk.

No one answers me. Jinx continues to scowl.

Okay, try again, Mac.

"I guess you're the Professor?" I say.

Terminus shrugs. His face turns red. "Ah. Yeah. That's what they call me."

I speak louder. With more authority. Fake it 'til you make it. "Okay...so...if you're the acting commander, who is the real commander? Like, who's in charge here?"

He smiles. An odd, off smile. He chuckles like a villain in a sci-fi movie. "Who's in charge here? Who. Is. In. Charge?"

Harold Terminus Partridge is SO weird.

There's an odd pause. He jerks his chin in Jinx's direction. "Technically? She is."

Terminus glances at the soldiers who brought us in. "Welcome to Fort Marshall."

The bravest of us are always the first to fall.

By the time we recognize our heroes, they are already gone.

—Statement by PRESIDENT AMMON C. CARVER,
on the death of DR. MAXWELL MARSHALL

JINX

I will not kill Harold Partridge.

I will not kill Harold Partridge.

I repeat this silently to myself.

First, there are the practical issues.

There are five soldiers in this cave and at least another three outside. They brought Mac and Toby in from another room. It's reasonable to think there are more people in there. I've only got seven rounds in my .45. I couldn't shoot them all even if I wanted to, and I certainly don't want to.

Second, we don't know who *they* are. Who they report to. Or what they know. If this really is Fort Marshall, then these guys aren't with The Opposition. But who are they with? We need to get that intel.

Third, MacKenna is giving me a look that says, *Be nice.*

Sigh.

She's right. I try to remember the days when Terminus and I were friends. The old summers at computer camp. Our late nights playing *Republicae.* Those days when my biggest problem was balancing video games and my homework. When I felt like I could count on him.

Terminus gets the soldiers to untie everyone and gives us water. They make sure to check us all for weapons and take all our remaining guns. Toby and Mac seem okay. Shaken but okay.

We're in a modern computer lab built in a network of scuba diving caves. "You're saying my dad built this place?" I ask.

Terminus pulls a candy bar from his pocket and bites into it. "Yep."

It's almost like a city in a cave.

It *is* impressive.

Even for Dad.

One of the guys, Phil, is also a medic. He eases Navarro into a folding chair and goes for a first aid kit. I dab at the gash on Navarro's forehead with a gauze pad.

"I'm fine," Navarro says, but he doesn't stop me from cleaning the cut.

"What happened to him?" MacKenna asks.

"He got hit on the head with a rock," I say.

She grimaces. "It looks kind of bad."

Navarro scowls. "I. Am. Fine."

"Lucky the rock didn't hit his pretty face though," Mac says with a teasing smile.

In spite of everything, I laugh. I think I've gotten a bit slap-happy, because I laugh too hard and for too long.

"I'm happy you two are happy," Navarro says, but he's more relaxed than before.

Phil covers the cut with liquid bandage and gives Navarro a pain reliever. "We need to watch for signs of a concussion. Keep me posted if your headache gets worse." The soldier returns to his cart and goes to leave.

Navarro gets up from the chair. "I am—"

"Fine," Terminus finishes. "Okay, tough guy. We get it."

I've never seen Terminus wear anything other than video game T-shirts and khaki shirts. I don't think he's brushed his hair...ever. "So, what are you doing here?" I ask.

"I might ask you the same thing," he says, continuing to eat his chocolate.

There's a pause.

A sort of stalemate that exists because neither of us wants to be the first to give anything away. MacKenna makes a small nod of encouragement. There wasn't much point in keeping things from Terminus. He is in control of Dad's lab.

We need his help.

"I was able to assemble the key to unlock the data Dad encrypted on the First Federal computers. The code block contained a note to come here. I assume that's because my dad left computers capable of interfacing with the bank's mainframe," I say.

"Yeah. He did." Terminus hesitates and his shoulders slump. "You want the tour?"

I nod and follow him, skirting a gorgeous pool of green water to a door on the wall opposite the cave's mouth. "Dad told you about this place?"

Terminus shoves his candy bar wrapper into his pocket, enters a code on a keypad and then presses his thumb onto a small screen. Dad replicated the same security system as in the bunker. "He had to. Marshall was secretive and one hell of a guy. But he couldn't lay miles of concrete or assemble all the furniture or install the networks by himself."

It's still so hard to think of my father in the past tense.

"Where does the power come from?" Jay asks as we pass a row of stand lights.

"Marshall came up with a network of solar generators. We have some gas ones for backup," Terminus says. He turns toward me, and his face goes pink. "That's what I worked on. I wrote the code that distributes power between the transformers, storage batteries and gas generators. It was the last thing he asked me to do, actually."

Terminus is silent for a minute.

The way he looks at me. Somehow he must already know that Dad is dead.

My eyes water a little, and I hope no one sees.

We enter a narrow hallway that's ordinary and gray. Stuff you'd expect to find in an office building and not a remote series of caves. We stop at a door labeled A. The room is a much larger version of the sleeping area in the bunker, with rows and rows of bunk beds that must sleep dozens of people. Here and there someone has tried to tape photos to the rocky wall. This doesn't appear to be working very well, as the pictures hang askew and a few have fallen to the floor.

"These are the barracks," Terminus says.

Toby enters the room, going farther inside than the rest of us. "How many people can this base accommodate?"

"Fifty, comfortably," Terminus answers. As if anticipating the next logical question, he adds, "We've got about thirty soldiers here now."

Through the door marked B, we find a large kitchen that opens into a wider mess area filled with steel picnic tables.

Toby's lips form a thin line. "So, you've got thirty people from The Opposition here?"

Terminus runs a hand through his now short hair and his face turns red. "From The Opposition? No. This place has nothing to do with The Opposition."

Confusion spreads across Toby's face. "But you... Then why..."

Terminus sighs. "Look, if you're going to ask me what Marshall was thinking when he designed this place, the short answer is, I have no idea. But he kept it off The Opposition's radar. We're absolutely sure of that."

"How do you know?" MacKenna asks, smoothing her ponytail.

There's another odd pause. "Because everybody in here is wanted by The Opposition. And they haven't found us yet."

Terminus walks past a door marked DATA CENTER, and my heart soars. I'm desperate to go in there. Dad clearly spent a ton of money and resources on this place, and I'm dying to know what type of hardware he chose for a bunker of this scale.

But MacKenna wants answers to questions that are probably more important than which servers my dad chose for his secret base.

"Wait. *You're* wanted by The Opposition? But you were helping them," she says.

She glances at Jay. We're the only two people who know that Terminus is the one who wrote the code that framed Jay for mass murder. That his work helped kill thousands of innocent people. I'm not sure why we didn't say anything. Actually, I *do* know. I was ashamed of being betrayed by a friend. I was supposed to know better.

A range of expressions run across MacKenna's face. She's trying to decide whether or not to say anything. She must decide against it, because she becomes very interested in fixing the zipper of her jacket.

Harold's face goes red and runs the color of one of my old ugly Christmas sweaters. "Well. I wasn't helping them good enough. First, I couldn't crack the encryption. Then, I helped all of you escape. I had to leave Goldwater right after you did. I vaguely remembered this place, so I came here." He bites his lower lip. "So, you cracked it, huh?"

I nod, also flushing with embarrassment. "But Dad left me decent instructions."

Navarro snorts. "Don't be so modest. He left us next to nothing. You figured things out on your own."

Terminus shrinks down even farther. "Marshall was right. I'm a crap coder."

Sigh.

Terminus did a lot of terrible things. He should feel bad. But.

I've done terrible things too.

"Dad never said that, Harold. I did," I tell him. "He thought you were brilliant."

Terminus manages a weak smile and leads us out of the bunker. Up ahead is the MAIN LAB door. He pauses for a second. "Thanks. But, Jinx. Do me a favor. Please don't call me Harold. Especially around the general."

"The general?" Jay repeats as we resume walking.

"Yeah," Terminus says. "When I arrived, there were a bunch of people already here. Mostly ex-army. Recruited by Marshall at one point or another. The general is the highest ranking. General Harlan Copeland."

"Copeland?" Jay's eyes widen. "He's *here*?"

"You know him?" Toby asks with interest.

Jay nods. "He was the commanding officer of Operation Cedar Hawk. A five-star general. If there's a medal, he's won it."

Terminus frowns. "Oh sure. He was an all-American hero. Until he told Carver he wouldn't round up supporters of The

Spark and put them in death camps or shoot citizens trying to cross the border. Then he became the same as the rest of us. Wanted for treason."

Jay continues to squint in confusion. "But...if the general is here, why did you say that Jinx is in charge?"

Terminus points to another keypad. "Care to do the honors?" he asks me.

I've been wondering the same thing. Whether my codes that open the other bunkers will work here too. I enter my code and press my thumb to the pad. The door clicks open.

The smile slides off Harold's face. "Well, when we first got here, there were a bunch of instructions from Marshall, addressed to Jinx. He clearly intended to leave her in charge. Although good luck dealing with the general."

I give Navarro a sharp look. My father *was* leading me here.

"I'd like to see General Copeland," Jay comments.

"We're getting there," Terminus says.

I walk into the main lab, and the first thing I see is a group of soldiers clad in camo standing around a large television mounted on a steel stand. On the screen, a funeral procession of black limousines with their headlights on crosses the screen.

And the headline.

Dr. Maxwell Marshall lies in state in the Capitol rotunda.

Our little group crowds in behind the soldiers, most of whom turn to stare at me.

Terminus sucks in a deep breath. "Sorry about your dad, Jinx."

More headlines scroll by.

President Carver: The nation has lost an innovator, a thinker, a warrior.

"We...we...buried him," I say, as the screen changes to a coffin draped in a flag. It's flanked by two marines in full dress uniform. Crowds, all in black, walk around, kept back by black rope and stanchions. "We buried him in Mexico."

President Carver: I have lost a great friend.

Phil, the medic, joins us at the screen. "We think The Opposition sent a team to Puerto Peñasco to retrieve the..."

The body.

President Carver: As Maxwell Marshall lived for his country, he died for freedom.

Mom clearly came up with some kind of a story to explain Dad's death.

"He was a hero," Navarro says.

The image changes again, this time to old footage of Dad shaking hands with Carver during the war. Dad's wearing a uniform I've never seen, with a bunch of stars and stripes that I don't recognize. Another reminder that he had this whole life I knew nothing about.

And now, I'll probably never know.

"Yeah," Toby mutters. "A hero. For The Opposition."

His tone turns my skin cold.

"What are they saying happened to Dr. Doomsday?" MacKenna asked.

I'm sure The Opposition isn't going around admitting that Mom killed him.

Phil catches my gaze. "Assassinated. By The Spark."

Right.

Terminus grabs my shoulder and draws me away from Dad's state funeral. I notice we're in a giant part of the cave, easily as large as all the other rooms combined. They've shoved desks in between rock formations. All the computers are...well... I don't know what they are. They're modern.

They're a bunch of custom processors and motherboards that look like they were manufactured in some future facility. They're housed in glass cases with colored lights pulsing and blinking.

They're something new.

"So," Terminus says, with an air of forced casualness. "Am I to understand that you're just strolling around with the access mechanism to the computers of the world's largest bank in your pocket?"

I actually wrapped the mini disk carefully in waterproof, signal-proof foil and put it in a side pouch, but that's probably splitting hairs. "Um. Yeah. I guess." It occurs to me that this makes me sound really idiotic, so I add, "It's protected by an OTP that overloads the power supply on the drive and melts the disk if you enter the wrong password."

"I'd expect nothing less," Terminus says.

From the look he's giving me, it's as if he might expect *more*. Terminus might be questioning our decision to travel around with the only copy of the key. But making duplicates was a risk. Every copy we made would have increased The Opposition's chances of recovering one. This key is my only hope of getting my brother back. Ultimately, I didn't want to do anything that might lessen my bargaining power.

It's cool in the cave, and I'm grateful that my clothes have mostly dried. But I still have water in my boots, and they squeak on the concrete floor.

We're nearing a long table with one old man sitting behind a laptop. The closer we get, the harder it is to tell *how* old the man might be. He's got short, silver hair and weathered tan skin, but has toned, muscular arms that boys my age spend all day in the gym trying to get.

"General Copeland?" Jay asks, extending his hand.

The general rises, revealing that he's a couple inches taller than Jay. A grin spreads over Copeland's face. "Major Novak?

Well, well. Some days I can't believe that it's been twenty years since Operation Cedar Hawk. That so much time has gotten away from me. How the hell are you doing, soldier?"

Jay also smiles. "About as well as you'd expect, sir."

Copeland laughs. "About as good as the rest of us, then, eh?" His smile fades. "Ah, but, as we always used to say in the great Third Army, *You ain't beat 'til you admit defeat.*"

"Yes, sir." Jay nods.

"No need to stand on ceremony here, friend." The general sits down and shoves out the chair next to him with his foot. He motions at Jay to take a seat, then turns to me. "Well, well. This is Jinx Marshall. *The* Jinx Marshall, eh?" he says. His bushy gray eyebrows travel up his lined forehead. "You look awfully animated for a girl who's supposed to be dead."

The rest of us shuffle awkwardly in front of the table while Jay takes the chair next to the general.

I'm...dead?

"She doesn't know," Terminus tells him.

Sometimes I feel dead.

"What are you talking about?" Navarro asks. I wish he wouldn't scrunch up his forehead. Blood oozes out from under the liquid bandage when he does.

"Well," Terminus begins. "You know...uh... Dr. Marshall was...um..."

General Copeland clears his throat. "Marshall is dead. A fact that Carver evidently decided he could exploit politically back home." His eyes narrow. "We believe The Opposition also wanted to pave the way for your mother to take a more... active role in their plans."

"Your mom is a total badass," Terminus says with an odd enthusiasm. He sits on top of the table but gets up immediately when Copeland shoots him a disapproving look. "They made her the head of the National Police yesterday and showed her on TV—"

My blood heats up and my heartbeat races.

My mom. I usually don't let myself think about her.

"The point is," Copeland interrupts, "they needed to dispense with you and your brother for their plan to work as intended. The Opposition spread the rumor that both of you were killed during the confrontation with The Spark that also killed Marshall."

"But…but…my brother…"

Oh. God. What if something's happened to Charles?

The flame of my anger snuffs out.

But…this can't be right. "If we were dead, I'd have found some mention of it in the news when I ran a search yesterday. There was nothing about my brother. Or Mom and the National Police. Or Dad for that matter."

Which is also…wrong. My father is being given a state funeral. The Opposition must have spent weeks planning it. I should have found some mention of the arrangements.

Instead, I found nothing.

"We believe your brother is fine, young lady," the general says.

I'm flooded with both relief and confusion. "But then…"

"The Steel Curtain closed three weeks ago," Terminus says.

"The *Steel Curtain*? That can't be right." Jay stares at General Copeland. "That's supposed to be a rumor."

"It's no rumor," Copeland says with a growl.

Suddenly, I'm even colder.

Mac elbows me. "Care to share your info with the rest of the class?"

I wrap my arms around myself. "The Steel Curtain is supposed to be a communication suppression system that can prevent people in America from sending or receiving data from outside the country. But it's not supposed to work."

What if it does? That would explain why I couldn't find out anything about Charles.

Or Navarro's parents?

"They were trying to develop it during Operation Cedar Hawk," Jay comments, stroking his stubbly beard. "Command said it was for scenarios where the enemy was exploiting cyber vulnerabilities or hacking critical information systems."

Toby frowns. "But it's a violation of international law. Even I know that. It's been more than twenty years since they dismantled the Great Firewall of China and all countries in the United Nations signed the Treaty of Katowice."

I nod. I had to stay focused. "And the treaty created an internet protocol and broadcast systems that supposedly makes something like the Curtain nearly impossible to implement."

Terminus digs into his pocket for another chocolate bar. "Yeah, well, nobody told that to Marshall. He went and made the damn thing."

Dad. Perfect.

That's why they were having the big funeral. It was a show. A pageant designed to make people feel patriotic about my father's terrifying work.

General Copeland stares at the TV screen on the wall.

I turn to face it and see that the news headline has changed. *Mexico orders the immediate deportation of all American citizens.*

"If all broadcasts are blocked, what are we watching?" MacKenna asked.

Terminus shrugs. "I managed to cobble together a way to get a pirated signal. I don't know how long it's gonna last though."

Toby continues to scowl. "So Carver is going to break international law again?"

"You can suspend Katowice in times of war," Jay says in a tone barely above a whisper.

"War?" Navarro repeats.

MacKenna plays with the end of her dark ponytail. "We're not *at war*."

"We will be," Copeland says.

The screen flickers and changes again. This time to a shot of the Golden Gate Bridge.

California announces secession from Union. Delivers notice to White House.

The old general continues to watch a group of people standing in front of a wooden podium. A man reads off note cards in his hand.

"We will be," the general repeats almost absently.

I don't know what any of this means to us or what our lives mean in the scale of a conflict that's been decades in the making.

I can think of only one thing.

"Where's my brother?"

Dr. Marshall. Dr. Doomsday. We wanted to believe he was for us. The Opposition told the world he was with them. Was he a man who fought for his family? Or a family man who worked for Carver? These are the two sides of the same coin. Whoever wins this war gets to flip it. Sometimes I think that's why Jinx fights so hard. Why she's so fierce. If we win, we get to answer once and for all. Who was Maxwell Marshall?

–MacKENNA NOVAK,
Letters from the Second Civil War

MacKenna

I don't know what to pay attention to.

Where I should put my focus.

A couple of hours ago Toby was fixing to take off. But he's still here.

Jinx still seems like she kinda wants to kill Terminus.

Navarro probably does have a concussion. He keeps blinking, like he can't focus his eyes.

But oh!

Terminus hooked me up with an e-tablet. A good one. With a decent screen and an e-pencil. No more writing in Doomsday's crappy paperback book. I make a couple of taps and start a document tab.

Sources.

Okay, MacKenna, start covering this story for real now.
Take that, Mr. Johnson.

I write *General Harlan Copeland* and watch as my script transforms into neat, typed letters. I make a few more notes.

Five-star general. Operation Cedar Hawk. Wanted for treason.

The general ignores Jinx's question and turns his attention to my father. "We have a lot to discuss. Why don't you get your kids settled and we'll talk more over dinner?"

Dad opens his mouth to speak, but Jinx talks first.

"Excuse me. This is my father's bunker," Jinx tells him. "I'm in charge now."

Oh yes! This is Jinx 2.0. The Jinx that talks back to adults and hacks bank computers and runs around in the jungle all loaded up with guns.

She's just like her father.

Or like her mother.

Oh. No. Nope. Nope. MacKenna, don't go thinking things like that.

"Think so, do you?" the general snaps at her. He waves his hand at the gorgeous cave. "What do you imagine building something like this costs? You think your father paid for it with the money he made teaching computer science three days a week at Arizona State? You think he built this place by himself?"

Jinx's face glows red.

"Sherman said, 'War is hell.' Well, I'm the guy you bring in when you need someone to stoke the fire. *Wars.* I make them. I run them. I win them. You think it's some kind of happy accident that I'm here, of all places?"

Copeland pulls his windbreaker down tight and squints. Like he's thinking of what to say next. "Marshall was a genius, but, young lady, he wasn't a one-man band. He wasn't even playing second fiddle."

Sometimes I think Jinx really needs to work on her poker face. Sometimes. It's like she's a cartoon, and a lightbulb is going off over her head. "It was you. At Goldwater Airfield. You helped us escape."

Well. Okay. That *is* kinda interesting. Back at the airfield, Marshall seemed to have his own little private army. They had guns and tanks and helped us get away from The Opposition. Now we know who those people were and what they thought they were doing.

LEAD: General Copeland helped my dad escape from Goldwater Airfield.

Copeland nods. "That was my team." He points to one of the soldiers watching TV. "Chuck over there took a shot in the gut that missed his kidney by two millimeters. Marshall convinced the people at the top that you're important to the war effort. I hope, Miss Marshall, for your sake, that he was right."

Navarro makes a series of odd faces. "Yeah...but...what? I thought that...weird kid is in charge? You know, the Professor?"

The old man actually laughs, and this time it's Terminus who turns red. "You musta hit your head pretty hard, son. The *Professor* is in charge of talking to the computers and making sure the lights stay on."

Jinx clenches her teeth. "Where is my brother?"

Copeland hesitates again. "We believe he's being held at AIRSTA North Bend."

Dad folds his arms across his chest. "The old coast guard base in Oregon? I thought that whole place was underwater."

That's right. "It is. Anything west of Eugene is flooded. Uninhabitable."

Navarro…man…it's like he's coming out of a haze. His eyes sharpen. "Maybe it's not."

No. *It is.* I did a whole report on it in junior high. The temperature increases, wildfires and melting glaciers had all increased sea level by more than five feet. "What are you talking about? They had to rebuild Interstate 5 because of water damage. I did a whole report on the little town called Cannon Beach. It used to be this quaint little place where—"

"They used to make taffy and build sanctuaries for puffins until a tsunami swallowed the town. Yes. Yes, I read the *New York Times* too," Copeland says in an exasperated voice. Here is a guy not used to explaining himself. "A few years ago, however, the government, under the direction of key members of The Opposition, invested in a reclamation system for the area."

"Reclamation?" Jinx repeats.

Copeland waves his hand in a flourish. "Dams, drainage systems, pumping stations. The point was to take back some land from the sea and have an area that the public perceived as off-limits. A perfect place for secret operations."

Secret. Operations. I scribble furiously.

LEAD: The Opposition operates a secret base under The Spark's nose in Oregon.

Navarro keeps on making a bunch of weird facial expressions. Each one is…

Guilty.

He knows something.

A good journalist always recognizes a source.

Jinx should be paying attention to this. But she's scowling at Copeland. "Like what?"

Copeland chews his lower lip.

"Why would they take my brother there?" Jinx asks, when Copeland doesn't answer her first question.

Dad is lost in his own thoughts, as if all of this information has already occurred to him. "Even if they got that base up and running again, there can't be more than a few ships and maybe a hundred people stationed there," he says.

"How many troops do you need to guard a five-year-old?" Copeland asks.

"He's eight!" Jinx tells him with a deeper frown. "And there's no way you're getting the key to the bank unless I get my brother."

I shift my weight from foot to foot. Jinx is kinda going rogue here, because this wasn't our plan. We were supposed to use the computers in this place to try the key ourselves. Not hand it over to some warmongering ex-military man.

Everyone's for Rosenthal.

That was supposed to be our plan.

But after what I've been through with Toby, I understand where her head is at.

Copeland scowls right back at her. "I'm in charge here, and if you do what I tell you, maybe I'll get you to your brother."

My dad clears his throat and runs a hand through his graying hair. "Who are the people at the top? Sir."

Maybe it's the *sir* that does it, or maybe the general has had his fill of obnoxious kids and, like, wants to talk to an adult. But his expression softens.

"As I said, we have a lot to discuss." General Copeland gets up from the table. "Partridge," he barks. "Take your friends to the barracks and find them bunks. Maybe share a few of those candy bars you're so fond of. We'll meet in the mess at 17:00."

"Yes, sir," Terminus answers in a sullen tone.

Dad stands up too.

Copeland jerks his head toward a small door behind the table. "There's something you need to see. Follow me."

Before Jinx or I can say anything, they're gone.

For some reason, they take Toby with them. Like, okay, he's nineteen and technically an adult. But an hour ago he was gonna walk off on foot and leave the rest of us for dead. He hasn't acted like an adult since we left for Mexico.

But he gets to go off with the grown-ups?

Because. I guess. There's something *he* needs to see.

This sucks.

"All right, let's go," Terminus says.

I assume that we're going back to A to share a room with the thirty other people, but it turns out that there are actually a few other rooms we haven't seen. One is labeled OVER-FLOW BARRACKS. In there, we find a few bunk beds, a more comfortable, dorm-style desk and a private bathroom. The mattresses are even a little thicker.

"This isn't too bad," I say, looking around.

Navarro sits on one of the beds and yawns. "I need a nap."

"You can't go to sleep," Jinx tells him in a high-pitched, alarmed voice. "You have a concussion."

Soldier Two from earlier ducks his head in the door.

"This is Galloway," Terminus says, pointing to Soldier Two. "He served under Marshall at Fort Dix."

Using my e-tablet, I make an addition to my Sources page.

Galloway. Tall. Around six feet. About 180 pounds. Black hair. Thirties. Wide nose. Not perfectly straight. Probably been broken.

"What's your first name?" I ask.

"Why?" Galloway moves closer and glances over my shoulder. "Sources? Sources of what?" He frowns. "I weigh two hundred. And, hey! I'm only twenty-nine."

"Sources of information," Terminus explains. "She's a journalist."

Galloway's face turns red. "Does the general know that?" And then. "Write down that I'm two hundred. And…and… I'm one of the only guys who can manually operate one of those damn hydraulic doors. Because I'm up every morning at six and at the weight bench." He thinks for a second. "Wait. No. You shouldn't be making reports at all. Unless the general authorizes it."

Okay. Don't roll your eyes.

Nope. They're rolling. Despite my best efforts. I. Am. Making. A. Face.

"I'm not making a report. I'm keeping information for later."

Galloway continues to eye me with skepticism.

Navarro yawns again. He's got the air of someone who thinks he's dodged a bullet. "We have no phone. No way to communicate with the outside world."

Galloway actually snorts. He points at Jinx. "That's Max Marshall's daughter. She could probably climb up on the cliff with a wad of aluminum foil and a hairpin and make some kind of radio transmitter."

Navarro is alert again. And more grumpy. He sits up straight with a scowl on his face, like he's now gonna be on the lookout to make sure Jinx isn't running off to build her own cell phone tower out of bits of trash.

Jinx turns red.

Oh geez. I have to laugh. Galloway's got her totally nailed.

Navarro scoots back on his bunk.

But, anyway, Mr. Johnson always said, *Sources can require persuasion.*

"Listen to me," I tell Galloway. "One of two things will happen. Either we're gonna die, or we're gonna be heroes. If we survive all this, people will want to know about us. You know. What we're like. Why we did what we did. If we survive, I'm gonna tell our stories."

This mollifies Galloway somewhat.

"Joe," he says. "Joseph Barker Galloway. Barker was my grandfather's name."

Joseph Barker Galloway? Rank?

He notices my scribbling. "Corporal. USMC."

He was a marine.

"You knew my dad?" Jinx asks. It's a good softball question. Terminus told us that most of the people here had served with Dr. Doomsday.

The way Galloway regards her, the way all the soldiers look at her, is weird. Really super weird. Like she's the Lady of the Lake or something. A ghost or an omen they were waiting for, maybe praying for. But one that seems unreal.

"That's right," Galloway says. "They had some of us enlisted guys providing air support for the colonel...for Marshall's unit."

"What was his unit doing?" I ask.

Galloway shrugs. "Dunno. *I* was pumping gas into helicopters. People didn't exactly stop to debrief me, you know?"

I fiddle with my new e-pencil. "Well. How did you end up here?"

Terminus gives the soldier an encouraging nod. "The general already told them about AIRSTA."

Galloway relaxes. "Yeah. Well. I was working transportation for the colonel on and off for a couple of years. During one of my leaves, he had me out here pouring concrete. Anyway, about six months ago I was running officers in and out of AIRSTA, high-level people, like the general…" He glances at Jinx. "And your father. Anyway, one day, Colonel Marshall comes out of the compound…and the way he looked…the way he was? It was just wrong. He told me if anything ever went wrong to come here." The man's shoulders slump. "So here I am."

"What went wrong?" Jinx asks.

I'm about to elbow her in the gut. I mean, seriously, Jinx? What went wrong is that a corrupt maniac rigged the presidential election and was now in control of our country.

But.

A hard expression works to conceal the sadness in Galloway's eyes.

"My mother," he says, flatly. "She was for The Spark. She got taken to the work camp outside Austin. She didn't make it."

Oh.

Oh. God.

Jinx saw something in Galloway that I couldn't see.

I think about Toby right then. And Charles. The cost of all this.

It's personal.

Mom once said that feeding an army was a job but feeding a person was an act of love. She resisted looking at the big picture. I'm not sure if she even knew the big picture existed. She fed anyone who came to the restaurant, whether or not they could pay.

It's always personal.

Galloway clears his throat and refocuses on Jinx. "Did Marshall say anything to you? Tell you what they were doing?"

I force myself to stand up straighter and write *AIRSTA* and *North Bend, Oregon* on my e-tablet. "We already know what they were doing. They were hatching a secret plot to blow up a bunch of banks, kill thousands of people and frame my father for it."

Terminus stares down at his shoes. "I... I don't think so," he says very slowly. "I think the violence at First Federal... I think that's what The Opposition was doing to detract attention from what they're really planning."

I almost can't take another breath. "What are they planning?"

"Something worse," Galloway says, gloom settling into his features.

Terminus moves toward the desk. "Did Marshall ever mention Project Cold Front?"

"No," Jinx says. Except something in her face says that maybe he did.

Navarro keeps his face in the shadows created by the bunk overhead.

Terminus moves to plop down into the tan leather chair at the desk.

This snaps Galloway to attention. "Nope. No time for lounging around. The general wants us to go for their truck. He thinks it's unwise to leave it out there in the open."

The *they* is us. We are them. They're going for our camper.

"Let's go," Galloway says.

Navarro pushes himself off his bunk. "I'm going too."

"What?" Jinx says, taking a few steps toward him. "You have a concussion. I'm supposed to monitor your headache and—"

His face turns red. "Susan, I'm fine. I'm supposed to stay awake. Which is going to be a lot easier if I have something to do."

"I don't know..." Galloway hedges.

"It's my truck," Navarro tells him indignantly. He's already straightening his jacket. "I've been floating in a river. My socks are still wet. I'd like some clean clothes. And if we're staying here, it would be great to have a toothbrush." He pats his jacket where his side holster is. "Where's my gun?"

"We can set you up with basic supplies." Galloway's face falls into a frown. "But I'm not giving you a gun."

"I'm going," Navarro says. He stalks out of the room.

I can't help but feel that he wants to get away from us.

"Then I'm coming too," Jinx says, following him into the hall.

Terminus and Galloway leave as well, and I hear fragments of a mumbled argument. "The general" and "unnecessary risk" and "follow orders."

Jinx returns after a few minutes.

Alone.

LEAD: Student journalist and daughter of legendary hacker stuck in scuba cave.

Not much of a story, Mac.

Jinx throws herself on the bed. "The general ordered us to remain in the barracks until 17:00," she says, doing a pretty good impression of Galloway's brusque drawl.

I write *Project Cold Front* on my e-tablet.

"So Dr. Doomsday never mentioned the Cold Front thing?"

Her forehead scrunches up in confusion, and she does that thing again where she reaches for a necklace that she's not wearing. "No…and yet…it sounds so familiar…"

I want to mention Navarro and his weird behavior, but I don't know how.

Her gaze darts all around, like she's hatching an escape plan. "What do you want to do?"

I don't get to answer.

My brother's face pops into the doorway.

"Good news," Toby says with a grin. "The general is gonna help us. We're going to California."

We've been told that our diversity will make us strong, and yet when a wise man builds a house, he does not choose the materials at random. He does not meander in his garden haphazardly picking up stones for his walls. His house is built of bricks, and each is the same as the next. And the house will stand.

—AMMON C. CARVER, Chairman, General Advisory Committee
Memo for the Record
re: Project Cold Front
Top Secret; Initialed as received by CMM

JINX

My stomach flops uncomfortably. "California?"

Mac says what I'm thinking. "If Charles is in Oregon, why would we go to California?"

And how would we get there?

Didn't we just find out that California has seceded from the Union?

Toby is grinning like a Cheshire cat. "The general has a plan. He'll explain it better than I can. But basically, he thinks that once we get to San Francisco, he can arrange ground transportation to North Bend."

"You seem awfully thrilled," MacKenna says in a sour voice.

I have a feeling his attitude change has something to do with what I saw on the TV in the main lab.

But I hope not.

Toby's head disappears from the doorway.

"Hey! Where are you going?" MacKenna asks, following him out the door. But Toby must have already disappeared into one of the other areas, because after only a few seconds, she comes back into our room and grunts in frustration.

"What's up with him?" I ask.

"What's up with *Navarro*?" she shoots back.

The motions of my stomach shift to a warm flutter. Navarro…he was…was acting odd. But then, we'd been shot at and jumped off a cliff, and he'd bashed his head on a rock.

MacKenna rolls her eyes. "Ugh. Stop thinking about how he looks in a wet shirt for a second. You don't think it's a little odd that he insisted on going back into the ultra-mega-creepy forest with Terminus and the merry major?"

I try to be casual. "Your dad practically tossed us off that cliff. Gus has a concussion and…you know him. Doing recon is part of the drill." I can't keep the bitterness out of my voice when I add, "It's what I should be doing."

My dad's work, computers he built, code he wrote, it's all over the place around here. I should be checking out the machines, testing the encryption key, researching my brother's location…and instead I'm stuck…in here.

"Let's look around," I suggest.

"Can't," MacKenna says flatly. "The general posted a guard at the end of the hall. That's why I had to come back. We're confined to this area. We can access the barracks and the kitchen only." Her face settles into a grumpy frown. "Why does everybody get to do what they want except us?"

She's pale with worry. Something is bugging her.

"We said no secrets," I remind her.

She takes a minute to adjust her ponytail, moving to the desk. "Before those soldiers grabbed us and brought us here, I caught Toby trying to leave." Mac takes the chair where Terminus was a couple of minutes before.

"Leave? What do you mean?" I ask. Toby was unhappy. And different than he was before. But we were all unhappy. And different.

MacKenna goes on with her back to me. "I mean, he got Dad to let him stay behind in the camper because he wanted to take off."

"On foot?" A jittery electric shock runs through my veins.

Her ponytail bobs up and down. "He had some vague and stupid plan to go south." She whirls around in the chair, staring at me with her big brown eyes. "One minute he's telling me that he thinks we're on a suicide mission, and then the next minute he's in here acting like he did that Christmas he found a brand-new bike under the tree."

My breath catches. *Oh, it can't be.*

"What?" she asks sharply.

When I don't immediately answer, she says with more force. "No more secrets."

I find myself fluffing the pillow on the bunk. Which is a stupid waste of time because it's filled with a cheap material and will never be more than a fabric blob.

Finally, I say, "I saw something. When I followed Navarro back to the main lab. You know who else is going to Oregon?"

"Who?" Mac growls.

I can tell from the expression on her face that she already knows.

"Annika Carver," I say.

MacKenna shakes her head slowly.

"They were showing it on the news. She's basically on a publicity tour. Going to military bases. Meeting with state lawmakers. Trying to build good will for Carver," I say.

"Oh Lord, was the political princess all dressed up in her

Sunday best and giving her royal wave?" MacKenna mumbles, "Elbow, elbow, wrist, wrist," as she does a pitch-perfect impression of Annika's gestures.

I nod. "Yep."

MacKenna drops her hands into her lap. "Perfect." But she perks up. "Let's see if we can get more info from Terminus when he gets back."

This, too, had been bothering me. "So, you're friends with Terminus now?"

The Terminus who helped frame her father for murder? The Terminus who was part of the reason we were on the run? The Terminus who was working with…my mom.

Her face goes red and she turns around again. "And what? You're *not* friends with him? You're the one who spent all your summers at computer camp with the guy."

"That stopped after I realized he wrote the code that framed *your dad* for murder."

"Maybe he didn't have a choice," she says.

I groan. "*You* said there's always a choice! You said we're here because of a series of choices. That our choices define us."

MacKenna returns to writing on her e-tablet. "I know! I mean, I think I do. And I still believe that. But. I don't know how to make sense of what's happening. I just… I just…"

Oh no.

I get up off the bunk and go across the room. I lean against the desk so I can see her face. "You like him. Like *like* him!"

"I do not," she says, too fast and with too much force.

I sigh. "He was working for The Opposition."

"So was your father," she says. "And unlike Dr. Doomsday, Terminus didn't get Ammon Carver elected or invent the Steel Curtain." Her words come out in a rush. "And, in case you haven't noticed, Navarro is *for* The Opposition."

"Gus isn't for The Opposition," I say, even as cold doubt creeps over me.

MacKenna pushes her chair away from the desk. "I keep trying to remember the old me. The one who spent all my nights writing profiles of David Rosenthal. The one who spent my allowance on markers and poster boards to make signs for our yard. The one who used a whole can of blue glitter on letters that spelled THE SPARK. Sometimes, I feel that me fading away."

"The Opposition wants a world where might makes right," I say.

She nods. "But look at where we are." She waves her hands around, pointing at the cave walls. "Your dad built this place. We don't know how or why or when. We're here with a bunch of outlaws, and what binds us together isn't an ideology, it's... it's..."

I know what it is.

"It's love," I say in a whisper. Or at least feelings. My dad led me here because he loved me. Jay is here because he loves his children. The soldiers are here because of the way Carver's regime has affected the people they cared about. Navarro is here because he...

I fight against a blush.

My thoughts are interrupted by MacKenna, who's still talking.

"Yeah exactly. I told myself, Everyone's for Rosenthal. Because I thought that this is a world where we all want the same things. I thought we all wanted cake on our birthdays, and hugs, and to be treated fairly, and to find someone to share our lives with. Instead we have this world. Not only do we not agree on what's right, this world is full of good people doing bad things and bad people doing good things for the wrong reasons," she says.

There it is. This is the world we'd inherited. It's complicated.

And messy.

But Terminus? He told us what he's about.

He's for bitcoin. His services are for sale to the highest bidder.

"We can't trust him, though," I tell her.

Like she always does when she can't make sense of things, MacKenna gets up and paces around, kicking over a metal trash can on the floor by the headboard of the bunk bed. She speaks into it as she leans down to pick it up. "Who can we trust? This morning, my brother, who I would have bet my life on, was gonna leave me for dead in the middle of nowhere. Terminus saved our lives. Which one of them is now more trustworthy?"

"Your brother," I say automatically, even though I understand what she's getting at. These situations…they are forcing us to reveal what we're really made of…testing us. What if we fail the tests? But still… Toby has to be the right answer. "Toby has principles. Terminus has an offshore, untraceable e-currency account."

MacKenna flops down on a bunk, her arms limp with defeat. "Toby has *love*…for…for that…that… Annika Carver. If it's like you say, if it's love that motivates people, then we're in trouble."

It's almost funny the way she says Annika's name. Like it's a curse word. "He doesn't even know her. And, anyway, we have each other," I say.

"Yeah. Yeah." She doesn't sound convinced.

I can't think of what else to say, so I blurt out, "Yeah, but you still like Terminus."

She sits up with her fists in tight balls. For a second, I think Mac might punch me, and I find myself flinching.

She breaks into a laugh. The sound eases the tension in my gut. We laugh and laugh and laugh.

"It's not like… I have a massive dating pool…to choose from," she says in between hoots of laughter. Then more seriously, "What should we do now?"

The smile slides off my face. "What *can* we do?"

We both know.

Nothing.

So we wait.

Copeland operates with military precision. At about five 'til five, Terminus returns to the barracks and takes us into the mess hall. It's crowded with men and women, all in fatigues, sitting on picnic tables with cafeteria trays in front of them. On the side of the room near the door, a crew works a buffet line, doling out chicken sandwiches, bags of potato chips and cartons of milk. It's a lot like our high school cafeteria.

If the cafeteria were in a cave.

And like the old lunchroom, this place seems to have cliques.

Toby sits at a packed table to the right of Copeland. Jay is on the general's other side. The old military man is in the middle of a story, soldiers leaning in, laughing and shaking their heads. They pay us no attention as we stand in the doorway.

Mac spends several seconds glaring at her brother.

The wide, round cave is lit by more lights on steel stands. No one has been particularly careful about where the lamps are pointed, so the lighting has a haphazard quality to it. The tables and chairs and rock formations cast shadows in all directions.

Eventually, I feel a light hand on my back.

I whirl around and find myself two inches from Navarro's nose.

My pulse almost comes to a stop.

He's drenched in sweat. His hair has long since outgrown the neat cut he used to wear, and wet, wavy tendrils curl up around his ears. More blood has run out from underneath the liquid bandage on his forehead, but at least it's dried.

Still, he manages to smell good. Look good.

And I look and smell like a swamp creature.

I lean in his direction until I see MacKenna smirk at me. "You…uh…got the truck?" I ask.

Navarro stares at Toby and the general. "We got stuck in the mud twice. I still can't get these idiots to give me back my weapon. But, yeah, the truck and the supplies are in a mechanical bay in another cave."

He's taken off his jacket, and his wet shirt clings to his chest.

I focus on how my socks squish between my toes. "Will they let us have our clothes?"

He nods. "Yes. I packed some supplies. That guy Phil said he'd take them to our barracks."

MacKenna fidgets with the tail of her T-shirt. "Where's Terminus?"

I knew it. She *likes* him.

Navarro doesn't get it. He steps between us and leans in close, his breath on my cheek. He gives us the type of status report that you'd compile about an enemy agent. "He's still over there. With two guards. There's an enormous area on the other side of the cliff. Storage and some other stuff. I can see why they need this Terminus guy, or whatever his name is. Dr. Marshall practically built his own power plant over there, and I've never seen computers like what they've got.

There's something big going on here, and I think your old friend knows more about it than he's letting on."

MacKenna flushes a deep shade of pink.

"You eating?" someone calls from the buffet line.

General Copeland gives me a searing look.

It lasts only a second.

It takes me a moment to realize that one of the soldiers, the one passing out bread rolls, is calling out to us. He motions for us to join the food line. In a few minutes, we've all got stainless-steel trays loaded with sandwiches, chips and grossly gelatinous chocolate pudding.

We go to the side of the mess hall farthest away from the door and from General Copeland's table. MacKenna takes a bite of her tofu chicken and chews robotically. Both she and Navarro continue to stare at Toby with matching suspicious expressions. He's acting almost like he used to. Lighthearted. Optimistic. His handsome features are relaxed. Playful. We're sitting alone but, once in a while, a soldier at a neighboring table steals a glance at us. At the table to my left, there's a black-haired girl who looks like she's barely older than we are. I give her a small smile, but her face maintains its professional mask.

"Your brother is suddenly in a real good mood," Navarro says in a surly tone, as another round of boisterous laughter erupts from Toby's table.

"Yeah," MacKenna agrees while chewing a chip. "Real good."

None of us notice Terminus until he drops his own steel tray at MacKenna's elbow. She startles and puts a hand to her chest. He gives Navarro a wary sigh. "No. I don't have your gun."

Like Navarro, Terminus is also sweaty.

"Where have you been?" MacKenna asks.

On the wall near the buffet line, two large flat-screen TVs are positioned on stainless-steel stands. Both are tuned to coverage of the mounting economic crisis back home. When Dad essentially put the First Federal records in lockdown, he cut off access to the banking records for millions of people. The monitors show people waiting in long lines outside bank branches with whatever paperwork they happened to save or print out. They have to try to prove how much money they kept in the bank. To prove they made their last mortgage payment. The electronic payment processing systems are still down. Bank vaults are guarded by rows and rows of National Police. Scenes flash across the screens.

Two police officers drag a bloody woman into a car.

A mob runs through a Walmart.

Senators try to explain the plan to bring bank systems online.

Terminus opens up a bag of chips. "I was at my workstation, making sure that the electrical load is properly distributed between the main solar generators and the battery backups. Sooner or later, you all are going to want to take a shower. Do you want there to be hot water when you do?"

On TV, signs scroll by.

Foreclosed. Bankrupt. Closed until Further Notice.

The flash drive suddenly burns in my pocket.

We have the code that could fix everything.

Phil enters the mess hall. He confers briefly with a couple of soldiers at the general's table and then approaches us. He taps Terminus on the shoulder. "The general wants you to set up the briefing in G."

Terminus rolls his eyes. "I'm eating."

"Eat in G," Phil says in a way that suggests it's an order.

The marine heads off to sit at the table with the dark-haired soldier. She smiles when she sees him.

"I'll see you in a few," Terminus says, mostly to MacKenna. He takes his tray with him as he exists the mess hall.

Navarro watches Terminus go and chews his bread roll. "I don't trust him. Or like him."

Perfect. Exactly what we need. More things to argue about.

MacKenna matches his suspicious gaze. "But you trusted Dr. Doomsday? That's who you could trust?"

My face heats up again. I'd tried to ask Gus about my dad on a lot of occasions. Somehow, we always ended up...doing other things. And all he ever said was...

"Dr. Marshall was a great man."

"Dr. Doomsday is a ghost. And you're making him into whatever you need him to be," Mac snaps back.

Except Mac is wrong. My father was a real person.

One whom we didn't understand.

I swallow the lump in my throat.

The argument is interrupted by the sounds of clanking trays and soldiers leaving the mess hall. Dinner is clearly over. After a few minutes, it's us, plus Toby, Jay and Copeland at opposite ends of the mess hall. After a minute or so, Toby approaches our table, leaving Jay and the general alone, their heads tilted together in a deep discussion.

He stands at the head of our table. "It's time for the briefing."

Mac's glare could bore a hole into her brother's head, but he takes no notice. We copy the soldiers and place our steel trays in a bucket at the end of the buffet line and then form a procession behind Toby who, in turn, takes us to the table where Jay is taking his last bite of the disgusting pudding.

"Let's go," Copeland says.

We find ourselves back in the paved hall that networks the caves together. My shoes squeak on the concrete, and since Terminus said the word *shower*, all I can think about is when I will be able to get clean and dry. We walk for quite a while on a long, narrowing path that I'm guessing runs behind the storage area Navarro mentioned. There are fewer lights, and they're spaced much farther apart than elsewhere in the caves. Large stalagmites line the path, and they're greenish brown and oddly bloated, like bulbs of garlic stacked on top of each other. Ahead of us, the cave roof slopes downward, creating a rounded rock wall. Copeland opens a door to our right, ushering us into a classroom. Like if we went to high school in a cave.

On the far side, there's a huge white screen. Orange-topped tables that each seat two people fill most of the room. Terminus is already sitting at a small table in the back, typing on a laptop that's connected to a large projector. He nods as we file past him.

Toby and Jay sit in the front row, taking a table together. Mac and I take the table next to them, leaving Navarro alone at a desk behind us.

Copeland stands at the head of the room with his attention focused on Jay. But the general turns to Terminus and says, "Bring the video up."

Terminus makes a few clicks.

Footage of a press conference in California goes up on the screen. It appears to be the governor, an aging but still handsome actor who has the air of someone who never thought he'd be put in charge of anything more significant than christening yachts or welcoming celebrities to theme parks. In the video, the muscled man is surrounded by more serious lawmakers, with the text *California secedes from Union* under the image.

The old general paces around in front of the image, casting an odd shadow over the governor's face. "As you may have seen, California has announced its plan to secede from the Union in protest over President Carver's election and his subsequent draconian policies."

Copeland's remarks seem like a bit of an understatement. If what we've heard is true—that Carver is rounding up political dissidents and putting them in death camps—then a state like California, a stronghold for The Spark, has few options but to secede.

He continues. "They notified Congress this morning. Command believes this is exactly the opportunity we need."

"What's Command?" Navarro asks.

"Or who?" Mac adds.

The general ignores their questions. He's good at ignoring us.

"As part of the secession plan, the state will allow all California residents to return home during the next seven days. They've organized a series of transports. The first one will leave tomorrow afternoon from Puerto Vallarta. *You* will be on that boat."

Copeland stares directly at me. "When you arrive in San Francisco, Command will arrange for your transportation to AIRSTA. The rest is up to you."

My heartbeat picks up. *The rest*...seems like a lot of stuff.

"Sir, how will we get on board?" Toby asks. "Surely they'll recognize us."

Copeland gives him an approving nod. I can almost hear MacKenna's eyes roll around. And I have to say, she's kind of right; the *sir* thing is way over the top.

"We have informants in key positions on the boat. The *USS Cory Booker* is transporting a significant number of people. We believe that with some minimal modifications to your appearances and the right documentation, you'll go unnoticed."

Modifications? Great. They want us to wear disguises. Dad would never have been for that plan. He would have considered these kinds of tricks unnecessary. We were raised to blend into the wallpaper. No disguise needed.

Terminus changes the image behind the general. Copeland now paces in front of an image of a massive silver boat. It's more like a floating military base. On the screen, a helicopter and an airplane take off from opposite sides of the deck.

"Whoa," Toby says.

"That's a federal military ship," MacKenna says. "It doesn't belong to the state of California."

"It does now," Copeland tells her.

"But…but…but…" I sputter, not quite sure how to finish. But…there *is* something going on here. Something Copeland isn't telling us. Even Jay now looks sort of, well, guilty.

On-screen, the image of the *Booker* fades to black.

"That's not really much of a plan," MacKenna grouses.

"Would you care to submit a counterproposal?" Copeland asks her.

She stares at her fingers, pressed flat on the orange desk.

Jay clears his throat. "The general has kindly filled me in on some of the details of the situation. I feel confident that he's recommending the best course of action."

Copeland hesitates for a moment. "We've come to the difficult decision that Colonel Novak will remain here. His face has been broadcast on every screen in every country in all the world. He'd be spotted in an instant."

"*Colonel* Novak?" Mac repeats, scowling at her dad. "You're supposed to be retired."

"Well, I'm going," Toby says with a dark edge.

"Yes, of course. Of course," the general says absently with the air of someone indulging a favored child. I glance at Mac. Her eyes are wide with worry. What is going on with Toby? How did he ingratiate himself with Copeland in such a short period of time...and why?

"What's Project Cold Front?" I ask.

Copeland ignores my question. "And of course, you'll be expected to hand over Marshall's codes to Command when you arrive at the Control Center," the general continues.

Oh. Of course.

I was pretty sure we'd get around to the quid pro quo sooner or later.

"In San Francisco? Before I even know if I'll be able to see my brother?" I ask.

MacKenna is concerned with something different. "Who is in command? Who are you people?" She addresses this question mostly to her father.

Jay remains silent.

"Those are the terms," Copeland says. "Take it or leave it."

Gustavo Navarro's origin story is not quite what he led us to believe. What he obviously needed Jinx to believe. I've always thought that we're all responsible for our own choices. But now I wonder how much choice we really have. In the end, I wonder if he understood better than any of us. Our stories are our weapons.

-MacKENNA NOVAK,
Letters from the Second Civil War

MacKENNA

Take it or leave it?

Well.

It's not even really a choice because, seriously, that Copeland guy isn't gonna let us stroll out of here with the encryption key to the First Federal mainframe.

The choice is really cooperate or don't.

Like it or don't.

Of course, we take the deal.

LEAD: Student journalist, hacker, doomsday prepper and wannabe soldier prepare for clandestine trip to San Francisco.

You know who really seems to like it?

Toby.

Like, when you're living in a cave with forty other people, trying to speak to someone privately is way difficult. Bordering on impossible. After the briefing breaks—or more like after we're dismissed—Terminus starts an argument with Copeland. They close the door, and it's another one of those big metal doors. So no eavesdropping. No help there.

If Jinx is right, Terminus knows more than he's telling us.

I spend a minute imagining his face. There's something so unusual about it. He looks like a doll made up of the parts of other dolls. His nose is a hair too short and his eyes are a little too squinty and his mouth is at a kinda odd angle.

Oh relax, MacKenna. It doesn't matter anyway.

We're leaving for San Francisco in the morning.

No more Terminus.

Ugh. I tell my brain to stop having these futile thoughts.

We're trying to save the world. We're trying to get Charles back.

LEAD: Two teen girls rescue brother from the clutches of Fascism.

OTHER IMPORTANT FACTS:
-I guess I'll write some when I get them.

Dad stays with Copeland and Terminus. I guess he's part of this operation now.

But this isn't Fort Novak.

It's Fort Marshall.

We go back to the barracks, and Navarro and Jinx do what they always do, which is to exchange a bunch of significant looks and stare at each other all the time. It sucks that this is what passes for dating in our new life. In another version of reality, they'd probably be making out while pretending to watch a movie. Instead, it's more like a silly, repressed teen soap opera. All that's missing is an emo piano soundtrack.

I have to wait and wait and wait and *wait* to talk to Toby.

Like, I have to mill around in that drafty hallway where the wind whips through and kinda whistles as it blows across the rocks. And I have to wait out there holding a bar of soap and a towel so that, when the soldiers pass by, I can act like I'm on my way to the shower. Which is weird and suspicious because we have a private shower in our barracks. Which my brother could have used instead of going to the other one attached to A.

Finally, finally, *finally* Toby rounds the corner from the main showers to our barracks. He's actually whistling. If he were a cartoon, he'd probably be doing a little jig while he walks. It's, like, jaunty. Yeah, jaunty. I've always wanted to use that word in a sentence, and here it is.

My brother's walk is really damn jaunty.

When he comes within a couple feet, anger surges. "What the hell is wrong with you?" Toby is wearing green sweats and a camo-green T-shirt. Like the soldiers do. I think he's trimmed his hair. "And…uh…what the hell are you wearing?"

He's got a gray sweatshirt in one hand and a towel in the other. He makes a comic show of examining the items one by one. "The guys said it gets cold in here at night. I grabbed some sweats. Just in case."

Oh. For real?

I'm about to blow. "The guys? The *guys*? You don't have guys. You're not one of *the guys*. You're my brother, and we're supposed to be working together."

Toby smiles at me like I'm a small child. He actually pats me on the arm. "We *are* working together. We're going to get Charles back. Like you wanted. Tomorrow, we've got a big day ahead. You need your sleep."

A big day? It takes a lot of self-discipline not to deck my brother.

What I need is honesty. "Oh. Now you wanna come? This morning you said it was a suicide mission. This morning you said we'd be marching into certain death."

His smile fades. "That was before."

He tries to step around me and go to our room.

It's a weird repeat of what happened this morning. Like all he wants is to get away.

"Before what?" I ask. "Before you took off with that creepy general? Or before you realized that Annika Carver is on her way to Portland?"

He's cold when he speaks to me. "Before we had an actual plan. Before we had help. Before we had resources."

This is such a bunch of crap. Like, we already *had* resources. We had Jinx's programming abilities, which so far no one has been able to match. We had Navarro, who ran our crew like the marines. We had guns and money. We had each other.

"You're still in love with her? Are you a total fool?"

His anger flares. His lips form a sneer. "I suppose you and Jinx have been sneaking around again. And as usual, drawing all the wrong conclusions. The general predicted this."

I put my hands on my hips. "The general *predicted* this? You know, if it weren't for me and Jinx, you'd probably still be sitting in a security office at ASU while the government debated which branch of the military was gonna come and execute you."

Toby tries to pass me again. "I barely know her, Mac. I'm not planning on running off to elope." He stops for a second and looks me in the eyes. "But she's one of us, you know. All she wants is a real friend."

Annika Carver is the kind of girl who carves up her friends and eats them like banana slices on top of her morning cereal. I'm about to say as much, when he goes on.

"You remember when I went through that phase where I was super into pinball?" he asks.

Yeah, sure I do. It was back when Mom was still alive and we lived in Colorado. Toby was twelve and had his braces and was all kinds of annoying. He begged Dad to put some doofus machine called Cirqus Voltaire in our basement, and the thing practically drove me nuts. It had this freaky green head that would pop out and shout, "I'm the juggler," or something, and—

"I always wanted to find a way to beat my high score. To beat the machine. But now? We're like those shiny silver pinballs. You, me, Annika, Jinx. Even Navarro. We're bouncing around from obstacle to obstacle. We barely understand the rules of the machine. And even if we beat it, what do we win?"

Oh. Sure. That makes a ton of sense.

Toby tries to push me gently to one side of the hallway.

I grab his arm. Hard. He flinches.

"What else did *the general* tell you?" I demand.

There's a pause, and he answers slowly. "That we have an opportunity. Not to beat the game. But to destroy it."

My blood turns to ice. "What does he want you to do, Toby? What does Copeland want?" It sounds like, in a matter of hours, Copeland managed to indoctrinate my brother. But then, only this morning, Toby was trying to ditch us.

He expression is calm and nonchalant. "Exactly what he said. Get to California. Hand over the encryption key. We'll get Charles back and then decide what to do next. Together."

This sounds like another one of the lies we tell ourselves. "You can't save her, you know. You can't save Annika from herself, Toby."

My brother shrugs and smiles blandly. Which pisses me off even more.

I let go of his arm. "The only reason Copeland is even talking to you—the only reason he didn't kill you—is because they need Jinx. They need her to fix the bank computers."

"I'm not sure that they do," he says, for a second looking and seeming like his old self, not cocky or jaunty or jokey. "I think they need something else."

"What do they need?"

He hesitates again. "Maxwell Marshall. And she's the closest thing they've got."

This time, he firmly pushes me aside and enters our room, leaving me alone.

Again.

Which leaves me no choice but to follow.

Back in the room, any hope of a discussion is put on hold when Phil arrives on the utility cart with several plastic bins of supplies. One thing I'll say about Dr. Doomsday—he, like, *really* loved things organized neatly.

We unpack the bins.

There are several boxes of hair dye. A pair of sharp scissors. A fake cast. A selection of bright scarves. A few wigs. Birth certificates and social security cards in unfamiliar names. A stack of passports. I open one and find my own face staring back. Except I have a short red bob instead of my long dark hair.

I have a new name.

Hannah Ashley Brown.

Hannah Ashley looks like the kind of girl who spends Saturday afternoon at the gourmet cupcake store unable to choose the perfect frosting and loves taking those internet quizzes to figure out her personality type.

Two things are clear.

One: I do not want to be Hannah Ashley Brown.

Two: I look crappy with red hair.

MacKenna, this is a revolution! Who cares how you look!

I pick up the box of hair dye and the scissors.

"You want me to do it?" Jinx asks. She's looking at her own paperwork, which shows her with a blue pixie cut. It doesn't look half-bad, and she can probably cover it up with a hat.

I can feel the tears coming as I head to the bathroom. "No," I say. "No offense. But hair design isn't one of your strengths."

Navarro laughs, but the sound is cut short as I close the bathroom door.

It's a small and cramped bathroom that looks like a slightly enlarged version of an airplane lavatory with a shower. I spend a couple of minutes strategically arranging the bottles of hair dye and scissors on the too-narrow steel bathroom counter. And then it's me and a horrible box of hair dye and an uncertain future.

Step one: perform an allergy test.

Nope.

I crumple up the instruction sheet without reading the rest of it. I've been to enough slumber parties to understand the basics. I open up the bottle of color and squirt it on my head. Fast. So I can't change my mind.

Then.

More waiting.

After a while, I rinse out the color.

And then it's time.

Well.

The easiest thing to do is going to be to put my hair in a ponytail and cut it off. That'll be about the right length, and I can try to fix the cut here and there. If I can.

I hold the ponytail in one hand and the scissors in the other. *Okay. Okay. Okay. Okay.*

This is so stupid, but I want my mom. I want a hug. I want to be back in my room. I don't want to cut my hair. It occurs to me, in that moment, that my hair is one of the things I really like about myself. I like the color. Dark brown, like tree bark. I like the fact that it's thick and smooth and straight without much effort.

Tears. Tears. Tears.

Not like a few little droplets that I can wipe away with my sleeve. They run down my face. I turn on the water so no one can hear me heaving with sobs.

What the hell is wrong with me?

My dad is wanted for a crime he didn't commit, and we're on the run in Mexico. My stepbrother is being held by a bunch of neo-Nazi goons, and my brother spends all his free time dreaming about being Ammon Carver's son-in-law.

LEAD: MacKenna Novak is a loser who cries about her hair while people are fighting and dying.

I'm a crap person.

So. Here I go.

I snip the ponytail and am left holding it in my hand, and it's done. I wash my face and leave the bathroom.

"You look…nice," Jinx says. Carefully. Diplomatically.

Navarro nods. "Very punk rock."

Toby is reading a book. Not a novel or a biography. This one is black and old, with the title in large white, block letters on the front.

The Crowd: A Study of the Popular Mind.

"Where did you get that?" I snap.

Toby stops reading long enough to glare at me.

We both know.

It had to have come from Copeland.

Jinx actually answers me. And at least has the damn sense to be concerned. "My father used that book when he taught systems modeling," she tells me. "It's old. Even from before Freud. It essentially says that when a person joins a crowd, they leave their individual judgment and morals behind. Dad used some of those ideas in his theories, especially the notion that if you can get people to view themselves as part of a group, they are more persuadable."

Navarro holds a box of blue hair dye. He acts like he's really reading how to apply hair color from roots to ends. But he glances up. "And more violent," he adds.

Toby lets the book fall onto his chest and watches Navarro. There's something unspoken that passes between them. Like they understand each other in a way they didn't before.

"Why does Copeland want you to read that?" Jinx asks.

"Why did your father give it to you?" Toby shoots back.

This is the new Toby.

Evasive. Weird. Different.

The old Jinx would have probably turned some shade of red and fidgeted with her shirt.

Jinx 2.0, on the other hand, says, "He didn't give it to me. I read it on my own. My father used the material as a basis for his experiments in group manipulation, mainly to help get Ammon Carver elected. His conclusion was that, if you got people to self-sort into groups and then made them mad enough, you could get them to do almost anything. So, why did Copeland give that book to you?" There's an accusation loaded in that question.

Toby gives her a fake smile. "He didn't give it to me. I'm reading it on my own."

She's about to say something else when Navarro intervenes. "Susan, you should get started on your hair or we'll be up all night." He passes her the box of dye.

Jinx's shoulders slump. She takes the box and goes into the bathroom.

She's been in there for a couple of minutes when there's a soft knock on the door.

Terminus enters.

In spite of everything, my stomach kinda flutters.

LEAD: MacKenna Novak is a loser who should be focusing on saving Charles and not developing feelings for some creepazoid hacker.

Fact check: I am NOT developing feelings.

Toby keeps reading and doesn't look up from his book.

"The general wants to see you," Terminus says.

Even though I haven't yet figured who *you* is, Navarro immediately goes to the door like he was expecting this. Waiting for it to happen.

I scramble forward. "Wait. I'm coming too."

Terminus and Navarro are already out of the small room and into the hall. I hear Toby call after me, but honestly, screw him. I have a few things I'd like to say to *the general*.

Out in the hall, Terminus and Navarro are double-timing it in the direction of the main lab, the way we originally came in. "Copeland's at the comm center. We'll—"

Since it's possible they'll go through some door that requires a one-zillion digit code, I call out, "Hey! Hey! Wait for me."

They freeze midway between where I am and where a soldier stands guard, right before the doors that would take us to the labs, mess hall and storage areas.

I catch up with them and watch a red-faced Terminus glance from me to Navarro to the guard in a repeated, circular fashion. "The general only wants him. I like your hair though."

"Shut up. And I don't care what the general wants," I tell him.

Relax, MacKenna. Relax.

Terminus sighs. "Evans?" He calls out to the soldier. "Take him to Copeland, okay?"

"I'm supposed to man this post, sir," Evans calls back.

"Just take him back there and I'll keep watch here."

Navarro resumes walking down the hall. But even from where I am standing, I can see that this makes the guard uncomfortable. "The general doesn't think you can be trusted to watch the girl. My orders are to remain here."

The girl. It has to be Jinx. Something about her scares the shit out of everybody.

"For God's sake, Evans, it'll take two minutes to walk this guy over there."

Evans opens the door to the main lab for Navarro. "Okay. But if anything goes wrong, it's your ass."

"Fine," Terminus says as the door clicks shut.

His eyes are blue.

He stands really close.

Too close.

"Listen," he says, softly.

"You listen," I say, making myself say something. "Why are they guarding Jinx?"

He shoves his hands into the pockets of his camo cargo pants. "Why do you think?"

I drum my fingers on my own pant legs and wait for him to answer his own damn question.

He does. "Because Marshall loaded her fingerprints, retinal scans, common access codes, you name it, into the security program, and I can't figure out how to get in there and make changes. She could access everything. See everything. And Copeland doesn't want her to see everything."

"Well, this *is* Fort Marshall," I remind him.

"Yeah, yeah. Well, unfortunately Fort Marshall is under new management."

"What is it that Copeland doesn't want us to see? Why does the general want to talk to Navarro?" I ask.

He answers too quickly. "I don't know."

I hate to admit it, but Jinx is right. There's something about Harold Partridge that can't be trusted.

"Do you *want* to know?" I ask.

Before he can say anything, I grab his arm and drag him down the hall. I plop his hand onto the thumbprint scanner. It accepts the entry, and then a small screen blinks a message.

ENTER CODE.

I stare at Terminus. Give him my most intimidating glare.

He takes two breaths, his fingers hovering above the keypad.

He quickly presses several buttons.

"Don't let anyone see you!" he says with a resigned sigh.

Now that I have hair the color of a stop sign, not letting people see me seems more difficult than it used to be. But. Whatever. "Obviously," I tell him.

He takes my hand.

No one has held my hand in so, so, so long.

We're back in the main lab room, which is somehow even

prettier at night. Or at least more mysterious. There are fewer lights on. The pool of water in the center of the cave, which was green and glowing, is more of a dark, secret abyss that reflects the golden lamplight. Most of the tables are empty. Two soldiers sit at desks on the opposite side of the water. One is wearing a headset and talking into a microphone, focusing deeply. Evans is there, too, talking to the other one. A female soldier with her blond hair knotted up neatly in a French twist.

They don't see us.

We keep close to the wall and duck behind brownish rock formations. Staying in the shadows. Terminus shoots me angry stares when my boots scuff on the concrete path or when I breathe too loud or when he's plain ole terrified that we'll be caught.

We make it to a stack of plastic supply bins around five feet or so from the long table where Copeland was seated when we came in. He's there again now, with his laptop open in front of him. Navarro stands before the general with his arms crossed over his chest.

The two of them are already in deep conversation, like two people who know each other quite well.

Copeland is talking in his gravelly voice. "We can keep the girl away from the computers until tomorrow morning. In fact, that's what we'll do. On orders from Command. But sooner or later…" He trails off.

"That's my problem," Navarro says quietly.

Copeland lets his hand fall onto the table. "Son, you should think hard about what you're gonna do next. Maybe you're not an asset to this mission."

Navarro looks shaken. Probably for the first time ever. And

this is a guy who's been in fistfights, gunfights, every kind of fight. "I gave Marshall my word."

"Oh sure," Copeland says. He adds in a cynical grunt for good measure. "Sure, sure. Everyone's all in for the great Maxwell Marshall. We're all following his big master plan. Tell yourself that if you want. But you're in love with that girl, and love is for fools. You know what's coming. What do you think your little friends are gonna say when they find out what you know? Who you really are?"

It strikes me cold that this is pretty much what I'd said to my brother.

Love is for fools.

Oh yeah. And Navarro is keeping secrets. Just like my brother.

"I'm approved for this mission," Navarro says. But there's none of his usual defiance. It's almost a plea.

Copeland nods. "Command says it's a go. But you should think about it."

As Navarro turns to leave, Copeland calls out, "Think about what could happen."

His words echo faintly off the walls of the cave.

Before I can make sense of what's happening Terminus is pulling me. Fast. Back to the door. We barely make it back inside the hall before Navarro and Evans return.

"What are you two doing?" Navarro asks, with suspicion.

"Waiting for you," Terminus says. He tries to lean against the wall, real casual-like. A move that doesn't pay off when a pointed rock scratches his shoulder. "Oh! Ouch!" he yelps.

I fight off the urge to smile.

Navarro rolls his eyes. "Well, here I am."

I follow him back to the bunker.

As I walk, it occurs to me that, in less than twenty-four

hours, Copeland has managed to divide us. To break us down. To have us questioning our own sense of purpose.

He, like Dr. Doomsday, understands things—understands how people operate.

Okay.

In the morning, we're going to California.

I go to bed with the general's words ringing in my ears.

Think about what could happen.

War is hell. Unless your everyday existence is hell. In which case, war is just war.

—GEN. HARLAN S. COPELAND to COL. C. MAXWELL MARSHALL
Log of the Interim Committee
re: Project Cold Front
Top Secret

JINX

We're ready.

"We look ridiculous," MacKenna says.

"I think that's sort of the point," I say.

And it makes sense.

The team at Fort Marshall issues us sets of clothes that look like things typical teenagers would wear. Jeans and band T-shirts and chunky necklaces. Toby and Navarro have baseball hats. They make them memorize information about the teams. The trick is to have something about you that everyone can remember. Like Mac's red hair or my short blue cut.

Something that can be easily changed when you need to blend in somewhere new.

I'm wearing a pair of jeans with the knees almost worn through, a green T-shirt with a picture of a T. rex that says DINOSAUR PUNS ARE PTEROBLE and a cardigan sweater that has rainbow-striped sleeves.

"I like it," Navarro says. "The blue hair suits you."

They hooked Mac up with something she would never ever wear. A preppy, striped shirtdress and a bulky knit sweater.

"This thing is itchy," she says, adjusting the gray sweater.

We're back in the briefing room, but this time Terminus is up front showing a series of images that contains facts about current events.

California theme parks have all closed pending further information about secession.

Our story, only to be discussed if someone asks, is that we were a group of college students traveling together for spring break when news of the secession broke out.

"Jinx," Terminus calls out. "Where are you from?"

"Culver City," I say. We've been made to memorize our fake bios.

"No," Terminus says with a groan. "Do not answer to Jinx. You should have ignored that question." He frowns at me. "What's your name?"

"Carrie Martin," I say, matching his sour expression.

Terminus turns to Toby. "How about those Dodgers?"

Toby points to his hat. "Angels fan here. Sucks that they've put spring training on hold though. Do you think the regular season will start on time?"

"Perfect," Terminus says. "Focus the attention on your hat. Get the other person talking. Perfect." He changes the image on the screen.

California governor orders energy rationing.

Terminus points at MacKenna. "Hey, Nancy! What time is it?"

"My name is *Hannah*," she says. "And I, like, don't have a watch."

"Okay," Terminus says with a gentle smile. "Next time,

though, maybe don't act like you absolutely hate the name Hannah."

"I *do* hate the name Hannah."

"It's not your real name," Toby tells her.

"Mom chose the name MacKenna," she says. "Not Hannah."

Copeland enters the bunker. "Transport is ready. How about you?"

"Ready as we'll ever be," Terminus says.

When Copeland exits the room and we all get up from our seats, we've been in the briefing room since 06:00. I'm glad it's over.

Navarro wears a skeptical expression that exactly matches how I feel inside. I have the computer stuff under control. Navarro is tough as nails. MacKenna is smart, and Toby keeps our group under control. But will it be enough?

Before I can think too much about that, Copeland is back. "Time to ship out."

We're shuffled out the cave corridor and into the mechanical bay that Navarro mentioned earlier. It's an enormous space with a height that is easily double that of the other caves. The entire area has been covered with smooth tile flooring. We walk past all kinds of vehicles. Carts, trucks, a small helicopter and even a boat on a trailer. Our old camper is on the far side in front of two huge metal pull-down doors, squeezed in between two cargo trucks.

As we walk, Mac keeps trying to catch her father's gaze. Jay seems almost determined not to look at her.

We arrive at an old Land Rover with a young black-haired woman behind the wheel. The vehicle has a faded, light blue paint job with several sticker-covered surfboards tied to the top. My father would have loved it. It's practically an antique. No autodrive. No GPS. No computers. Completely untrackable and untraceable. A couple soldiers are applying bumper stickers to the back of the vehicle and arguing about their placement.

Galloway, one of the soldiers we met when we came in, holds the driver's side door open and starts to introduce us. "This is Captain—"

The woman climbs out from behind the wheel, revealing the sun-faded leather interior of the Rover, which has the occasional tear with cotton stuffing popping out. She has the air of someone who's neat as a pin and trying desperately hard to look casual. She's clipped up some green hair pieces with bright barrettes into her curly style, but they're a little too perfect. She's clad in a weathered hoodie and boardshorts, but the getup contrasts with her military posture.

"I'm Josephine Pletcher," she says, cutting through Galloway.

"Uh? Really?" MacKenna asks, squinting.

Terminus enters the bay and stands next to MacKenna. "Actually, yes."

The woman ignores them. "You can call me Jo. We met at the St. Regis in Punta Mita. Since we all need to get to Puerta Vallarta before the ship leaves—"

"Say *boat*, Captain," Galloway corrects. "Civilians always get it wrong."

One of the soldiers putting stickers on the car mutters, "Most civilians don't know the difference between a ship and a boat."

The other one snorts out a laugh. "Most civilians don't know the difference between their asses and their elbows."

Copeland casts a disapproving look in their direction, and they immediately quit talking.

The woman starts again, as if practicing a speech. "You can call me Jo. We met at the St. Regis in Punta Mita. We all need to get to Puerta Vallarta before the boat leaves. I had a car, you had gas money."

"Good," Copeland says.

Jo resists looking pleased.

"Why is she coming with us?" Navarro asks.

Copeland chews on his cheek. "You didn't really think that we'd send you out without any adult supervision, do you?"

I wait for MacKenna to say something. I realize, once again, that I'm dependent on her to say the right things, ask the right questions. She remains quiet.

"I'm Maxwell Marshall's daughter. I don't need your supervision," I say.

Copeland smiles, and even Navarro makes an odd expression with a little squint and a bit of a pucker of his lips. Like he thinks I'm being ridiculous.

I guess I need to work on my witty repartee.

Toby speaks. "The captain will help us find our transport when we arrive in San Francisco," he says.

And to make sure we give the flash drive to Command.

Whoever or whatever that is.

I hate this plan. It runs contrary to everything Dad taught me.

Trust no one.

Now we're putting our lives in the hands of people we barely know.

What's the alternative?

I have to find my brother.

"All right, then," Copeland says.

Something else hits me. We're leaving Jay behind.

MacKenna fights off tears. "So...so...you'll be here when I get back?"

"Of course," Jay says as he pulls his daughter into his arms. It doesn't sound like the truth. It sounds like what parents say when what's true is ugly. It's the voice of a father who doesn't want to tell his daughter that Santa Claus isn't real. "I'm proud of you. I'll always be proud of you."

"Dad... I..." MacKenna begins.

"I know. I know," he says, planting a kiss on her forehead.

Jay says goodbye to Toby before turning to me. He wraps me in a warm hug. "I want to say good luck. But I know you don't need it."

We don't have to do this. None of us do. We can stay together. We can come up with another plan. Over his shoulder, I watch Mac wipe her tears on the sleeve of her cardigan. My dad is gone. And now, she's losing hers too.

Everything is slipping away. Everything is being lost.

"This isn't fair," I whisper. "There has to be another way."

"We've all known for a while that this would have to happen sooner or later," he says with a small, sad smile.

I still feel responsible. "I'm sorry for everything."

He hugs me again. "I'm not. Everything included a lot of good times too." He adds, "Hug Charles for me when you find him."

Galloway hands us each a phone, a move that seems unusually risky. But he says, "We've modified these radios to look like phones. You can use them to contact each other within about a mile or so, which should be fine for the ship." I turn the small rectangle over in my hand. They've put my radio in a case covered with glittery pineapples. Is Carrie Martin the type of girl who likes pineapples?

Later on, I'll have to take this thing apart and find out what's really inside.

Terminus must read this thought on my face. "Of course they put trackers inside them. But it's in your best interest that they know how to find you. You might get separated."

Toby nods. "Or things could be chaotic when we get to the port in San Francisco."

Copeland motions for the rest of us to pile into the car. "When you get on the ship—"

Oh nope. I do not need this condescension.

I've been drilling with my dad since I was ten years old.

"Don't be memorable," I say, climbing through the passenger side door and into the back. The rear of the Rover contains four seats, two on each side of the vehicle. The seats face each other. The space between is filled with colorful duffel bags, the kind kids our age would carry. I slide down to make room for MacKenna, who enters next. Navarro takes the seat opposite me.

"Do enough recon to stay aware of any issues, but otherwise, remain out of sight," Navarro says, with an eye roll.

"Stick to your story but don't give unnecessary details," I say.

"Keep your radio with you at all times," Navarro says.

I'm about to add the cardinal rule. Rule number one.

Always be prepared.

But Copeland holds up his hand. "You will immediately follow any and all orders issued to you by Captain Pletcher."

"That's Jo, sir," the captain tells him.

"Yes, of course, soldier," Copeland says. He comes around to the passenger side and approaches my window. "I imagine that I don't need to ask if you have the disk drive, do I?"

"No," I answer flatly.

We're all surprised when Toby doesn't take the fourth seat in the back. Instead, he goes to the passenger side and sits next to Jo.

Soldiers are coming into the bay, lining up against the walls and filling up the spaces between the various vehicles. There's something odd about the way they regard us. It's like we're a battalion headed off to war. Jo turns the key, and the engine of the Rover roars loudly to life. The soldiers break out into a cheer.

My gaze focuses on Terminus.

My old friend.

One more person I'll probably never see again.

He gives me a small wave.

So much for Mac's dating options.

She leans over me, shoving her head toward the general. "Who's in Command?" she asks. She can't keep a certain amount of desperation out of her voice.

"You'll see." Copeland gives the door a couple taps, and Jo hits the gas.

The Rover emerges into a canyon composed of black rock. She steers us onto a narrow dirt path flanked by huge green trees. When we make it onto the actual highway, Navarro presses Jo for details, trying to find out who she is, how she got to Quintana Roo and why she's working for Copeland.

"It's a waste of time for me to tell you," Jo tells Navarro.

"We have time," he says. "Nothing but time, in fact, considering that we're going to be on the road for the next twenty-nine hours." He tries a softball. "Why do you get to use your real name?"

"I'm not a fugitive," she says.

"We're gonna be trapped in this car for twenty-nine hours?" MacKenna asks in a dead voice.

No one wants to answer.

Instead.

We drive.

We all have a bunch of stories. There are the stories we tell the world. Mostly about why we're doing the things we're doing. And then there are the stories we tell ourselves. If you get to the point where your enemy knows those stories, you're already dead.

–MacKENNA NOVAK,
Letters from the Second Civil War

MacKENNA

Call me MacKenna.

Some hours ago—never mind how long precisely—having no cell phone and no proof of my real identity, and nothing in particular to interest me in Acapulco, I thought I would sail about a little and…

Oh. Ugh.

My efforts to turn this trip into *Moby Dick* aren't doing anything to calm my nerves.

Maybe Ishmael could be stoic, but I'm scared out of my mind.

I press my sweaty palms onto the crappy cotton dress from Fort Marshall.

Okay, MacKenna. Try to look bored and not like this itchy dress is driving you nuts.

But honestly. Did they really have to dress me up like I was president of The Opposition Youth League?

LEAD: Four teen fugitives on a rescue mission stow away aboard a navy ship.

IMPORTANT FACTS:

-*Who:* The Mexican government ordered all American citizens to leave the country.

-*What:* The *USS Cory Booker* is a totally new naval acquisition that was stationed in San Diego before it was commandeered by the governor of California. It's like a floating city with a flight deck where planes can land and a deck below where little boats can come and go.

-*When:* Everyone has to be out by the end of the week.

-*Where:* Ship sails from Puerto Vallarta to San Francisco.

-*Why:* This transport is the last official way to get home. Anyone who misses it has to find their own way out or risk being arrested by the Federales.

We're pressed into a huge crowd which, as a huddle, is making its way down a long, wide, wooden pier. I imagine that there are normally a lot of ships here, but today the pier is empty except for the *Booker*. A few boats are already out to sea, and occasionally a horn toots.

As we get close to the massive gray-and-white steel structure, the ship fills my whole vision. It's all I can see on either side. The bottom of the ship is painted with a red stripe, but only a bit of red pokes out of the water. As we make our way down the pier, I have to watch my step to avoid tripping on rubber mats tossed all over the ground at odd angles. Twice Jinx trips on cables running from the ship. Navarro gives her a look of warning.

When I'm twenty feet or so from the entry ramp, the *Booker* blocks out the breeze and pretty much makes its own weather. My mouth falls open as two helicopters approach from opposite directions and make synchronized landings.

"VIPs," a man behind me mutters.

QUOTES AND BACKGROUND INFORMATION:

"It smells like crap."–Teenager in death metal concert tee.

"That's probably jet fuel."–Probably his mother.

"We better hope The Opposition lets us make it to California."
–Random man.

It's hard to get quotes when you have to hide and can't talk to anybody.

We've been in a long, winding line for almost an hour. In keeping with our cover story, Jo waved goodbye to us, the supposed strangers she'd picked up at a dive hotel, as soon as we parked on the pier. She fell in with a crowd of adults who were far more assertive in trying to get on the ship than we were. She's at least fifty people or so ahead of us in the line, with a completely neutral, passive expression, occasionally making casual conversation with the people around her. The ramp zigs and zags a few times and is guarded by both Federales and navy personnel. When Jo arrives at the entrance, she manages a bored yawn as the navy woman checks her paperwork. Then she disappears through the door.

And is gone.

I can't take it anymore.

I have to get out of this horrible cardigan. I shrug it off and tie it around my waist.

My passport falls out of the pocket. Jinx and I have to scramble to pick it up. A couple of people in line make annoyed, impatient noises. I can almost hear Jinx's thoughts.

Nice work, Mac. There's nothing at all memorable about your Charlie Chaplin impersonation. If only I had an organ-grinding monkey.

We pass several more soldiers in blue jumpsuits, all clutching large assault rifles. These guns are different than the old ones collected by Dr. Doomsday. They, like, have electronic displays on the front with messages like LOGIN, READY and AUTO HEAT SYNC on them. These kinds of weapons are illegal for civilians to own. Maybe that's why Marshall decided not to use them.

As we near the door where a trio of soldiers inspect documents, a woman three places ahead of me is suddenly jerked out of line and hauled off down the pier. She cries hysterically and kinda slumps over. Her polka-dotted sundress drags on the ground as they carry her away.

My pulse picks up.

More than anything, I want to run.

I want to go back to Dad.

Jinx checks her watch, a bright green thing with glow-in-the-dark happy faces on it. Normally, Jinx wouldn't be caught dead in something like that. "It's around three," she says. "I wonder if we'll be at sea when the sun sets."

It's exactly the right kinda thing to say…bland…forgettable.

"I bet a sunset on the water is beautiful." I fight to keep the edge of panic out of my voice.

We come to the metal podium, and Jinx steps back to allow me to go first. For a second, I kinda think, that's crappy. Like if there's a problem, I'm the one who's gonna be in trouble.

But then.

I realize this is the drill. She's got the disk drive. The only thing we have of any value. The only chip we have to bargain with. She has a plan to get away.

What is it that Dr. Doomsday said?

Always be prepared.

Jinx is prepared. To run.

My heart beats so slow as I take my place in front of the podium. A male soldier opens my passport and transport au-

thorization letter. He compares the picture to my face, checking and checking again. "Hannah Ashley Brown?"

"Yep," I try to lean on one leg. The way I used to when
I took selfies.

"What's your destination?" the man asks.

"Home," I say. This is what pops out of my mouth. Even
though I'll never go home again. I have no home. "Uh...
Santa Monica," I stammer when the soldier gives me a hard
look.

He runs a highlighter over my papers and hands them back
to me. "Remain in an orderly line and follow the yellow ar-
rows up to the hangar deck. You'll receive your tent and
mealtime assignments. For safety, stay in your tent whenever
possible." The man dismisses me with a nod. I go through the
door and, out of the corner of my eye, I see Jinx take my place
at the podium. Jinx emerges a second later looking relieved.

The two of us continue along slowly until Toby and
Navarro are also in.

The worst is over. We're on the ship.

You know what's not over?

The line.

Like the soldier told us, we follow the reflective yellow ar-
rows through a mazelike hallway. Inside, it's different than
I expected. There's stuff everywhere. Steel beams poke out
all over the place. There are stacks of wood and equipment.
There's an order to it though.

It's like an organized mess.

We pass through a door that looks like it belongs on a submarine, but someone put some thought into how to make
the place, like, cheerful. The floors are bright blue. The wall
has a wide yellow stripe on the bottom of it.

Then.

We. Wait.

And wait and wait and wait, until my feet ache and my back is stiff from carrying this dorky bag they gave me, and I can't stop yawning.

When we finally emerge on the hangar deck, I can barely hear myself think. A place where you'd normally park airplanes has instead been converted to a massive tent city. Everything is gray. The walls. The flooring. Everything. The dull roar of voices in a thousand conversations fills the wide space. On the side opposite us, a makeshift cafeteria has been set up.

Every few minutes a navy person inserts someone into the front of the line, causing groans and delays. The people are clearly VIPs. I think I recognize an actor from one of those superhero movies.

I try to make conversation with one of the navy women monitoring the line.

"So...uh, how many soldiers are on this boat?" I ask.

"We're sailors, ma'am," she answers brusquely. "When the ship sails, we'll have sixty-seven officers and 1,067 enlisted personnel on board."

Sailors not soldiers.

Ship not boat.

I make a mental note for when I write my article later.

We're finally given our tent assignment. Copeland's connections must be good, because he arranged for the four of us to be in the same tent, which simplifies matters a great deal. There are more naval personnel shouting directions and orders. We stay in a long queue and finally end up in a small tent along a wall. It's in a pretty good location. Not too close to the cafeteria, the elevators or the huge hole where the hangar opens to the sea.

After all that time in Doomsday's bunkers, I feel right at

home. Air mattresses covered with basic bedding have been tossed in the tent. There's a set of paperwork on one of the beds that contains our meal schedule and bathroom schedule.

I'm not sure what happens if you want to take a shower.

I dump my bag on one of the mattresses, open it and rifle through the contents. A toothbrush. Some lotion and...two other dresses that are exactly the same as the one I'm wearing. With different-colored ugly stripes.

Because this is my look now.

Yay.

My brother climbs onto the top bunk.

Jinx reads the paperwork. "According to this, our dinner time starts at 19:00. We have thirty minutes to get there and get our rations."

"Or?" I ask.

"No food," Navarro answers with a shrug.

I yawn for the millionth time. "What do we do now?"

Toby is already reading that stupid, stupid book Copeland gave him.

"Now? We wait," he says without even glancing up.

The next day passes uneventfully at sea.

We have breakfast.

And go back to our tent.

And lunch, and go back to our tent. And finally, dinner.

Despite the fact that everyone is supposed to remain in their tents, a lot of people seem to be treating this trip like a free cruise. As we come and go, I catch glimpses of people lounging around the hangar deck, especially at the large opening in the back where the ocean breeze wafts in, but also, on the small balconies that line the side of the ship. Well-dressed passengers lean on the industrial railing, taking pictures of themselves. Taking pictures of the planes that occasionally come and go. Sailors shoo people dressed like tourists away from equipment. I overhear a man asking some navy guy if they've got any deck chairs. The sailor spits out a curt, "No sir," before hustling away.

In between eating scrambled eggs and ham sandwiches, Navarro drills. He does laps around the deck and briefs us. Like it really helps to know that some general or other is on board, or the son of some actor is asking for organic baby food.

Navarro says one thing that seems to concern my brother.

After lunch he says, "I overheard a few of the navy people talking. There's concern about retaliation. Carver has a press conference scheduled for later today."

"Retaliation for...?" I repeat.

Toby understands more about this than I do. "It's unclear whether Governor Clooney had the legal authority to assume control of this vessel. General Copeland was concerned about this as well."

I see red spots. Here's another reminder that my brother was keeping things from me. Having conversations behind my back.

"So?" I say. "What difference does that make?"

Toby resumes his reading, leaving Navarro to answer. "Governor Clooney told the world that it was necessary to use this boat to allow California citizens stranded in Mexico to return home. But that was after the official secession. So, is this a proper use of his emergency powers, or an act of war against the federal government? And if Carver decides it's an act of war, what will he do to retaliate?"

That question hangs in the air.

About an hour before dinner, Navarro goes out on one of his drills. Since Copeland wouldn't let me take my e-tablet with us, Jinx is trying to help me find something to write on. She swiped a CPR pamphlet at lunch and is currently rifling through our bags in hopes of finding a stray pencil.

"Nope. Nope. Nope," she mumbles as she zips and unzips the duffels.

Toby puts down that damn book. "I'll be right back. My radio is on channel two."

"Where are you going?" I ask.

He's already got his hand on the door when he answers. "I'm going to speak to Jo."

"To Jo?" I'm off the air mattress and I can't get down fast enough to stop him. He's gone before I can ask what he needs to talk to *Jo* about, why I can't come, too, and how he even knows where she is.

"I'm sick of this," I say.

Jinx nods distractedly. "Me too," she says. "But it's almost over. We'll be in San Francisco by midnight." She drops Navarro's bag.

"That's not what I mean." I mean, I'm tired of this total bull with my brother. "Let's go."

She freezes and turns to me with her mouth in a tight O. "Go? Go where?"

I tap my fingers on the metal lockers. "It doesn't bother you that Toby and Navarro are off doing whatever they want while we're—"

"Navarro isn't doing whatever he wants," she points out. "He's following the drill. And he reports everything back to us."

This is true.

But.

"Yeah...well, my brother is doing whatever the hell he wants," I say.

"Okay…" Jinx looks worried.

I move toward the tent flap. "I'm gonna find out what he's doing."

A look of resignation crosses her face. "Okay. Okay. I'll go with you."

Then. We drill.

Jinx makes us spend five minutes on some zillion-point checklist. *You have your radio? Is it switched to channel two? Do you have your identification?*

She goes on and on and makes a point of putting on the weirdo fanny pack she carries the disk drive in.

"Why are you taking that?" I ask.

"I have to guard it at all times," she says. There's an eye roll contained in her tone. Like she's telling me something super obvious. Something that I ought to know.

When we leave, I'm Hannah Ashley Brown in the horrible cardigan with my passport in my pocket. We agree to keep our radios off unless there's an emergency.

The tent city is packed.

But Toby is long gone.

"Um…so…where do you think Jo's tent is?" I ask Jinx.

She's already taking the lead. Strolling past me. "They wouldn't go to her tent," she whispers. "There's probably three other people in there. And, anyway, it would be needlessly conspicuous. They would pretend to run into each other in a common area. The cafeteria. The back of the hangar. We should check those places. If anyone asks, we're headed to dinner."

Right.

We're on a drill.

And she turns out to be correct.

We walk around the deck, making occasional conversation

about the ocean breeze or things to do in San Francisco. And
we're walking for a long time. The *Booker* is longer than several football fields. Staying in the middle of the boat, we're
mostly able to avoid getting stuck in the clusters of people
who are moving from tent to tent. We're walking and walking and walking...

Then.

I spot Toby and Jo on the...I guess...starboard side? There,
on one of the open-air landings. They're doing a great job
pretending to be flirting college coeds, but I can tell their
conversation is serious. And there's something about the two
of them. They're staring out at the open, empty sea. Toby
seems scared.

Jo looks like she's waiting for something.

I quicken my pace, but my intention to confront my brother
is disrupted.

Jo pats him lightly on the arm. He nods and takes off.
Fast. Moving in the direction of our tent. I'm about to suggest that we do the same. Maybe Jinx is right. We'll be in
California in a few hours, and then I'll have plenty of time
to yell at my brother.

But.

Jo spots us.

She looks...angry.

She motions for us to join her on the landing. We walk in
that direction and as we go, she waves her hands dramatically
for us to hurry. So much for being incognito.

I try to be casual and lean against the metal railing.

"What the hell are you doing here?" she asks in a mixture
of shock and anger. "You have your orders. You're supposed
to be in your tent." Her composure is slipping away. "Shit.
What the...hell are we...gonna do?"

Jinx's face shifts into worry. "Do? Do about what?"

I grind my teeth. "Oh, so my brother can roam around up here but—"

She grabs my arm. Hard. "I sent your brother to the tent to get you and escort you to the…" She trails off. Her eyes widen. Jinx and I have our backs to the sea, so I have no idea what she's looking at.

I'm about to wave my hand in front of her face.

Ahead of us on the hangar deck, there's a beautiful woman in a bright green dress that flaps romantically in the breeze coming in through the doorway. She's twirling a pair of binoculars and in the middle of listing her favorite restaurants in the Filmore when she gasps. A melodramatic, over-the-top type of gasp. Like from a soap opera.

All that's missing is a record scratching sound effect.

I'm about to roll my eyes, except people everywhere in the hangar deck are pointing and waving and shouting.

"Oh no," Jo whispers.

I whirl around to face the ocean.

I can barely make sense of what I'm seeing.

Way off in the distance, on what can only be the coast of California, is the kind of thing I've only ever seen in old news footage. From the Manhattan Project. From tests of the atomic bomb. From Hiroshima.

A cloud. Cold. Black. Massive and mushroom in shape. Rising so high that it might extend into space. Every minute or so, bursts of lightning illuminate the dark billows of smoke.

I can't think. Or speak, or move.

Jinx grabs Jo's arm and shakes her. "What's that? What the *hell* is that?"

Jo doesn't answer. Maybe she can't. And, anyway, part of me knows.

It's Carver's retaliation.

There's more yelling, and then the low rumble of thunder. Like the sound associated with the cloud of death is finally reaching us on the ship. Next to me, a mother holds a small girl who clutches a tiny doll. It's got long black eyelashes that flutter.

Jo grabs one of my arms and one of Jinx's. "Come on!"

She starts pulling us toward the front of the ship.

All hell is breaking loose.

An alarm siren blares, and a series of announcements begin. Mostly instructions to us civilians about remaining calm and staying put. But there are also some to navy personnel as well. We do our best to move forward, and I catch snippets of conversation as we move.

I thought we dismantled all our nuclear weapons.

Did you see the size of that blast? That's no nuclear bomb.

What is it, then?

Something…else.

A woman screams, "Rogue wave!"

Sure enough, off the starboard side, a wall of water heads toward us. It's hard to tell exactly how big it is, or how fast it's moving. But it's huge. The size of a skyscraper, or bigger.

More screams.

The wind picks up.

Somewhere in the back of my brain, the journalist is talking.

BACKGROUND INFORMATION:

-A rogue wave is a freak phenomenon that occurs without warning in the open sea. This isn't a rogue wave. It's the result of that explosion. Of whatever is happening in California. It's The Opposition's revenge.

We can't go forward.

There's no going back.

Jinx shakes Jo again and yells, "What are we going to do?"

There's no answer.

If you desire an America where everyone looks like you, loves like you and worships like you, then you do not love your country. You love yourself.

–PRESIDENT-ELECT DAVID ROSENTHAL
Pirated national radio address
On the use of the Cold Fusion Bomb

JINX

MacKenna stands like a statue designed to show people how to play freeze tag.

We have to go.

Now.

Dad always said, *Things will break down faster than you think.*

I'm tugging on her arm now. Hard. So hard. But it's like her feet are bolted to the metal deck.

"Come on!" I shout right in her ear.

We are going to die.

I know I've thought that before, but this is different. The size of that blast. The massive wave that's about to hit the ship. People don't survive things like this. I'll probably never see Navarro again. Not even to say goodbye.

I'll never see my brother again either.

Mac waves her hand in the direction of the swelling ocean. "What…what…what…"

I squeeze her arm even harder. "We have to stay focused on what's in front of us." That's what my dad always used to say.

What's in front of us is Jo shouting into her radio.

I push my face into hers. "Where's Navarro?"

"And my brother," MacKenna adds, coming closer.

"Safe," Jo tells us through clenched teeth. "Which is more than I can say for us if we don't get a move on it." She ducks back into the hangar bay and weaves through the crowd, leaving us with no choice but to follow. Most of the people around us are either trying to get in or out of the stairwells or elevators. Jo drags us toward a small door that looks like a janitor's closet.

Once again, I find myself in the position of not knowing where I'm running to.

Jo has a small device in her left hand. As we get closer to the door, I realize it's an electronic key, a way to move around the ship. She opens the door and, instead of being full of mops, the place is a computer room. Inside, the electronics look remarkably similar to the ones back in the cave. The same kind of technology that my dad had used. You can't buy stuff like this at the mall on a Saturday afternoon. There are a few clear plastic screens, blinking blue displays, a large monitor that displays a grid and blinks with error and warning messages. On our left, I spot a desk with a couple of workstations.

Jo closes and locks the door.

It's cool and a bit quieter in here. Still, the screams from the deck filter in and make me jump.

"What is this place?" MacKenna asks.

I've been wondering that same thing. There's some cool tech in here but not enough to run a ship this size. "Um, maybe a backup control room? A redundancy in case there are issues with the equipment in the main control center." My guess is that you can run critical systems, like navigation, from this room.

There's another door opposite the way we came in. I continue going that way, but Jo stops to use her radio. "It's a weapons dispensary."

Static and chatter erupt from the device. "I've got them. We're in transit," she says into the radio. "Proceed to the *Perun*." She presses the off button.

Jo goes to the desk. The screen pulses every couple of seconds, but otherwise it appears to be working. She presses a few keys on the keyboard. First the screen reads LOGIN. And then WELCOME.

She releases a loud breath. A sigh of relief. "The password works."

I can't see how this is relevant or important. "So? We need to get to Toby and Navarro."

"We will. But first, *you* need to lock the door to the well deck," Jo says. "Do whatever you have to do to override the locking mechanisms so that they can't be unlocked by any passkey other than this one." She drops her electronic key onto the desk next to me.

"The well deck? What's the well deck?" I frown in confusion.

Her eyes squint in anger. "I'm giving you an order."

This *order* could have dangerous consequences for everyone. I'm not in the navy, but when your ship is about to be hit by a wave the size of the Empire State Building, the idea of messing with the door locks strikes me as...bad.

I stare at Jo and then MacKenna, whose expression alternates from confused to horrified. Mac turns her back to me and puts her head into a porthole.

Jo scowls. "The boats in the well deck are the only way off this ship. We were supposed to already be down there when all the commotion started. Now we need to stop everyone else from getting there before we do." She pushes the chair in my direction and steps away from the desk.

I take the chair and wheel myself toward the terminal. "Yeah…but…what? You want to make it *harder* for people to evacuate?"

Jo stands next to MacKenna by the porthole. "You two are the ones who went AWOL on deck. If you'd stayed where you were supposed to, this wouldn't be necessary," she says, jabbing her finger in Mac's direction.

My stomach drops. She's blaming us. Blaming us for whatever is about to happen.

When I remain frozen, Jo yells, "This is war!" She pushes me in front of the workstation. "I'm the officer in charge, and I order you to lock the well deck."

My face heats up. "But you realize that—"

My thought is cut off by a series of screams loud enough for us to hear. Meanwhile, the ship is actually rocking. This behemoth vessel that's bigger than the street we used to live on is being pushed from side to side.

My stomach turns over.

I guess it's seasickness.

Jo braces herself on the desk. "Rule four," she says. "Do what you have to do."

An order from Dad from beyond the grave.

I force myself to access the terminal. It's a UNIX workstation. With a few clicks, I'm able to find the well deck and lock it like Jo asks. I find a way to disable most of the lower-level passkeys.

But.

The door is only really going to be half the problem.

Guns are the other half.

The navy sailors have them.

We don't.

The door opposite the workstation clicks, indicating it's now unlocked. Jo nods in approval. "We need to go," she says, grabbing the passkey. The noise out on deck is growing louder.

I shake my head at her. The clear touchscreen at my elbow labelled WEAPONSYNC must be what controls the DNA-A guns. I've never hacked an AK relay system before, but Dad told me that the system basically works like a hub. The guns have to check in to receive a license to fire every sixty seconds. I think I can scramble the incoming genomes to make it look like the system is processing the same amount of data. But none of the sequences will match.

In theory.

I push the system access button on the screen and get started.

```
import time, re, gseqlib

# genode snippet hidden in program ROM
# find genone snippet
promoter = 'ttgaca.{15, 25}tataat'
chromosome = promoter[0:35]
promoter.write(0, reversed(chromosome))
# determine if write was successful
result = re.finditer(promoter, chromosome)
if result:

print("success")
```

"What the hell are you doing?" Jo yells from the open door.

"I'm jamming the guns!" I shoot back. "We'll survive a lot longer without everyone shooting at us."

She actually looks impressed. But she says, "If The Spark

loses the war, tech like this will be why. This is not how you should weaponize your military."

"Keeping people from running around shooting at each other with impunity is why the war is worth winning," MacKenna says.

I get up and go in her direction. MacKenna is midway between me and Jo, staring at what's going on in the porthole. As I pull her away, a massive wave emerges over the railing and sucks a thin man into the ocean. People run in every direction. Falling down. Getting trampled. A blonde woman holding a crying baby streaks by the window.

It's everything I can do not to scream.

A second later, we're racing through a labyrinth of hallways. Jo clearly trained for this eventuality, because she's leading us with a sense of purpose. Like someone who knows exactly where she's going.

We knock our way through screaming crowds.

And.

We're running downhill.

The decline becomes steeper, and a couple inches of water run underneath my feet. I slip and slide and almost smash into MacKenna. She's barely managing to stand up straight by keeping one hand on the hallway wall.

I realize.

The ship is sinking.

And then I realize.

Oh. My. God.

Jo pushes through the next door, bringing us face-to-face with three sailors. Two woman and a man, all three wearing matching stupefied facial expressions. They appear to be inspecting the next door in the hallway, like they're stunned that it's locked.

One of them has an electronic key like Jo's, and she's no doubt wondering why she can't use it to unlock the door.

I can't let myself think about what this means. Given the size of that wave outside, this ship was always going to sink. Most of the people on it were always going to die.

Don't think about that.

Rule four: Do what you have to do.

Jo told us that Toby and Navarro are somewhere safe, and I guess that's where we're running to. But we're on a sinking ship, and the place we were going was just destroyed by the biggest blast in human history.

"You can't be down here," the navy is man saying.

"I'm Captain Josephine Pletcher of the provisional militia of the New United States, and on behalf of the government of an Independent California, I order you to stand down," Jo says sternly.

This has the effect of making the three sailors even more confused.

There's the sickening sound of creaking metal and rushing water. And I can tell.

It's time.

My heartbeat surges.

Breathe.

Jo goes for the guy, landing a punch on his nose with a disgusting *crack*. He bounces off the wall of the narrow hallway like a pinball. She kicks him in the stomach as he lands on the floor. I step to the woman nearest me and yank the rifle free from her grip.

Strike to the face to disable.

Strike to the ribs to incapacitate.

Strike to the kneecap to immobilize.

The woman sort of gurgles and coughs up blood.

All those drills with Navarro have paid off.

This has gotten easy.

Too easy.

The last sailor gets ready with her gun. She taps the screen and attempts to fire.

I brace myself for a shot that never comes.

My gun script seems to have worked.

Terror takes over the soldier, and she takes off the way we came in, heading up to the hangar deck.

Jo uses her passkey, and we go through the door the navy people were guarding. It becomes clear why it is so important. Jo leads us into a massive area larger than a football field that's basically a staging bay for various kinds of smaller boats. Right in front of us, a wide mouth opens to the chaotic sea, which is churning dark waves. The plan must be to get to a lifeboat, but going out there in these conditions somehow feels worse than staying where we are.

The *Booker* tilts to the side. MacKenna grabs my arm, digging in her fingers. We're both fighting to stay standing.

Jo leads us through the deserted bay.

A lone figure mills around near a ramp that extends from a really weird-looking boat that's already partially submerged in the water.

It's...Terminus.

He's smoking a cigarette and pacing around. "Oh thank God," he yells.

A couple of things hit me.

First, it's really noisy in here. Many of the different boats must be turned on. Motors roar and percolate and gears grind. Water crashes against metal panels. The alarm siren continues to blare. The air is heavy with salt water and the smell of rust.

The plastic aroma of synthetic oil. We pass through a couple of clouds of exhaust from idling boat motors.

The thing behind Terminus can only be…a submarine.

A really large submarine.

MacKenna releases my arm and stumbles forward.

She almost collapses onto Terminus, who has to drop his cigarette to catch her. My mouth falls open in shock. Tears burst out of Mac's eyes. "I've… I've…done something terrible."

Terminus hugs her. Awkwardly. The way you would hug the weird kid who got all sentimental at the end of computer camp. I'm not even sure he can hear what she said. "It's okay," he tells her. "But we need to get on board."

Terminus is already tugging MacKenna down the ramp. The thing, the submarine, that they're headed to, is super odd looking. Something out of Jules Verne.

One side is made of a series of rounded glass pieces that look kind of like bubbles stacked on top of each other. But the clear material is thick enough that I can't quite make out what's going on inside. Blue light emanates from the glass, and everything's blurry.

The rest of the craft is constructed from the same sleek metal as the *Booker*. And like the rest of the ship, it's new, clean and modern.

I lean in close to Jo, who for some reason remains put.

"Uh…so I guess the *Perun* is a submarine?" I ask.

She nods and points to the ramp. "One that's gonna be submerged in about two minutes. So let's get a move on. Toby and Navarro are already on board." She stares at the doors where we came in, and I can see why.

Navy personnel stream into the hangar.

And also…General Copeland.

He's wearing a uniform I don't recognize, and, well...basically strolling toward the *Perun*. The navy people regard him with a weird awe, as if they're seeing a ghost. He takes long strides, like nothing can touch him.

He breezes past us.

Jo ushers me down the ramp and through a narrow door. We're barely inside when...

The submarine sinks beneath the surface of the water.

Floating down.

Down.

Down.

Into the abyss.

We're leaving.

Leaving them all.

Thousands of people.

To die.

It's narrow and cramped and dimly lit inside. We're in a passageway formed by the thick glass on one side and a metal wall on the other. Terminus is holding MacKenna up.

"You were supposed to stay in the tent," Navarro says. But he reaches out and pulls me into a warm hug, and my lungs release a massive breath as some of the tension drains from my body. I'm hugging him, and MacKenna is holding on to Terminus, and Copeland is trying to squeeze by to get around us.

"We should have done something to stop this," Mac whispers.

"Like what?" Terminus says. "Carver launched an attack against Americans in American waters. Because of him, the *Booker* was always going to sink. The navy barely had enough emergency transports to cover their own personnel and VIPs. There was nothing we could have done."

Toby gives him a hard look.

I reflexively pat the waist pack with the disk drive in it. It's still there.

Copeland is going toward what I suspect is the control center of the sub.

In a tiny voice, I say, "I guess we're not going to California."

Copeland turns around and hesitates for a second under the cool blue light and panels of bubbled glass.

Watching the chaos above.

"There is no more California."

You can never tell what some people are capable of.

That's rule number seven in Dr. Doomsday's book.

But my question is, how do I know what I am capable of?

Sometimes I lie awake at night and wonder if Dr. Doomsday is right.

Would I do anything I had to do in order to survive?

–MacKENNA NOVAK,
Letters from the Second Civil War

MacKENNA

There must have been something we could have done.

The look on Jo's face when she saw us on the deck—she knew.
She knew what was about to happen.

LEAD: The *USS Cory Booker* sinks in the Pacific Ocean.

I'm about to open my mouth and say as much, but something about Toby stops me cold. The way he's looking at me.
Like I'm a nuisance. A weakness. An obligation he'd rather
not be saddled with.

My insides are absolute ice. The only way I know I'm still
alive is that Terminus pats my back once in a while.

Jo remains there with us in the entryway of the *Perun*.

Jinx presses her face to the glass, probably trying to see the
mayhem above us. "Where are we going? How deep can this
thing go?" she asks, tapping the thick glass.

"As deep as it takes," Jo says. "Listen." For some reason she stares at Navarro when she says, "All of you. We're on our way to Command."

We are almost on our way to the floor when the *Perun* jerks to the left. Jinx is inches away from a face full of pretty blue glass. Navarro's thick arm steadies her.

"What the hell was that?" I ask. I'm in Terminus's arms again and rapidly heating. Thawing.

Jinx still has her chin pointed up. Her voice shakes. "Debris. From the *Booker*."

Sure enough, a piece of metal the size of a car zooms by us, missing the glass by about a foot. Yellow lights on the metal wall begin to flash.

It's like a stab to the heart.

Jo's shoulders tense. "Things could get rough for the next few minutes. Lieutenant Novak, you're in charge of these civilians. Make sure everyone gets strapped in."

Lieutenant Novak?

My mouth falls open. I know that's not me, so it's obviously...

Toby says, "Yes, ma'am." He motions for us to follow him.

Jo goes the same way as Copeland, leaving us to follow my brother, who is walking in the opposite direction and who has a lot of explaining to do.

OTHER IMPORTANT FACTS:

-The Spark said it had suspended government research when the New Depression hit. But clearly that wasn't true.

-This sub is super high-tech.

-Whoever designed it really, *really* liked blue lights. If you've ever wondered what it would be like to live in a sapphire ring, here you go.

My doofus brother takes us into this room that's basically like one of the break rooms on the *Booker*. White metal lockers line the wall to our left. There are ruggedized, white metal beams overhead that glow in various shades of aquamarine thanks to the lights. One of the walls has a mural of abstract ocean waves.

It's like someone took a submarine and tried to decorate it like a spa.

To our right, I see a couple rows of leather seats, like the kind they make for pilots. Each has a five-point safety harness.

"Okay, now if you'll take a seat…" Toby begins. He continues on with a ridiculously detailed description of, like, how to fasten the harness.

There are no windows in here and nothing really to look at. Like, couldn't The Spark have sprung for a few cat posters or something for the walls?

Okay, MacKenna. Get a grip.

Any place seems as good as the next. Toby's talking as we all take seats. Each row has five chairs, and we take four in the front row, leaving the seat in the middle for my brother.

The *Perun* jerks again, and my stomach lurches. I've got the impression that we're descending more quickly than before.

Whoa. Hold steady. How does that go again? Those who panic, don't survive.

Toby continues to stand, facing us and talking like he's giving a prepared speech. "And then click the final buckle—"

My right eye twitches. "We know how to use a damn seat belt, Toby!"

Oh yeah, everyone but Terminus already has their restraint on. He's fumbling with the last latch. Jinx and Navarro watch my brother with different expressions. She's confused.

But Navarro?

It's like he's seeing a rival.

My brother frowns at me and sits in the *second* row.

Away. Separate. Well, he can run but he can't hide.

"So, you joined the rebel army without discussing it with anyone?" I try to turn my head around to get a glimpse of him.

He hesitates before answering, and when he does speak, there's a formality to him. "I've joined the provisional militia of the New United States under the command of General Harlan Copeland. And I did discuss it with someone. Dad."

My stomach burns. "You're telling me Dad told you to do this?"

"Nobody *told* me to do it." Toby's tone is sharp. "I'll be twenty years old next month, and I don't need anyone's permission to enlist, and I—"

An announcement goes out over a speaker. *"All personnel at your stations. Brace yourself for evasive maneuvers."*

"I thought you were going to be a schoolteacher!"

He makes an impatient noise. "Where would I teach? At the Florence ADX Supermax Prison? Our old lives are gone. And honestly, so is that world."

I'm tempted to take off my seat belt and have it out with my brother.

No, Mac. This is not the time to smack your brother.

The *Perun* shivers. There's a loud *bong*, and then the sub lurches.

Oh crap. I take in deep breaths to fight nausea.

"What the hell was that?" Terminus asks.

Toby ignores Terminus and the mayhem around us. "Everything is so personal for you. For *all* of you. Jinx wants to find her brother. You both want...revenge. Partridge wants to erect a giant statue of the great Maxwell Marshall in the town square—"

Terminus turns, like, um, green. Like he might throw up. On me.

Oh. Ew.

He clutches his stomach. "Hey…why…are…you…bringing me…into—"

Terminus gives me his hand, and it's cold and sweaty.

"And Navarro…" Toby trails off. Like, yeah, we all know that Navarro is hopelessly in love with Jinx. Except, from the expression on my brother's face, maybe he means something different.

Anyway, I'm not buying any of this. "This is about her, isn't it? Like if you become some extra fancy war hero, you'll get the girl? You're gonna get killed. And for what? Annika Carver?"

Everyone in my row is still.

"Stop being a child," Toby says. "It is *not* about her. What did you think was going to happen? We'd find Charles and Jinx goes back to her video games and you return to making political slogan posters and everything is the way that it was? MacKenna, back home people are starving. The New Depression has become an emergency. There's food rationing and energy rationing and a black market for almost everything. Ammon Carver is putting people in death camps because of their political beliefs. Today, he murdered thirty million people whose only crime was that they had the guts to stand up to him! If I lose my life, it will be for my country. For my principles. For my honor."

This whole thing sounds awfully rehearsed. And then I remember.

Toby's meeting with Jo on the deck.

The way they both stared out at the sea.

Waiting.

Oh God. "You knew what was going to happen."

Toby says nothing.

"That psychopath Copeland *knew* that..." I don't even know how to finish my sentence.

There's another long pause. Which I guess is what will happen now every time my brother lies to me. "No one *knew*. Not for sure." More hesitation. "Well. I guess some people probably did."

I look up and down my row to see if anyone else is hearing this. For some reason, it's Navarro who's turning red.

Jinx sucks in a deep breath. "Could someone at least explain *what* is happening? Like where are we going? How does this get me to my brother?"

I kinda resent the fact that she thinks that the problems with *her* brother trump the problems I'm having with *my* brother. But. Toby is here and Charles is gone.

Except Toby is sort of gone too.

I'm not sure we can just go to Portland to get him back.

There's another sharp pull to the right, and Terminus moans.

I don't think any of us will be hungry for dinner.

Toby says nothing, and even weirder, it's Navarro who kicks things off.

"The Spark has to be managing its operations from somewhere," he comments.

Jinx frowns. "You're implying that The Spark has a hidden base? In the middle of the ocean?" She jerks her head all around. Like she's searching for a window to look out of.

"You're *also* implying that Copeland works with The Spark," I say.

If there ever was someone who seemed to have gone totally rogue, it was Copeland. My guess was that Copeland worked for Copeland.

"Terminus!" Jinx says, reaching across both me and the empty seat to swat at him. "You've been working with these people for months. Who are they? What did they tell you?"

Terminus does his best to straighten himself out. "What you have to understand is that...now...there's The Opposition...and...everyone who opposes them. All sorts of...um..."

Clang. Clang. Clang. More banging metal on metal.

He draws in a deep breath and continues. "So everyone else is loosely organized under The Spark because—"

Toby makes an impatient noise. "It's not The Spark. It's the—"

"Provisional government of the New United States," Navarro interrupts. "We know."

It's odd. Their sudden rivalry. They were never exactly friends, but now...

I roll my eyes. Of course, Toby's behind me, so he can't see it.

Toby speaks in the same rehearsed way as earlier. "It's important to note that David Rosenthal is the lawfully elected president of the United States, and he has assembled a coalition of people with diverse political perspectives—"

Navarro says what I'm thinking. "Oh, for God's sake."

Clank. Creak.

And then it's like we're on a crappy roller coaster. My butt leaves my seat, and the harness digs into my shoulders. Then back down again. Up and down.

"Oh no," Terminus says. He adds in a rush, "Basically, The Spark is in control of anything not held by The Opposition. Both groups are preparing for a war. Copeland is The Spark's warmonger-in-chief. That's all I know."

Those horrible navy scrambled eggs turn over in my stomach. I'm barely able to keep my food down, but Jinx is unbuckling her harness. This is Jinx 2.0. The badass who apparently doesn't care if she gets her head knocked off by the roof of a submarine.

But she has a plan. That works.

Sort of.

She grips her seat and stands.

Meanwhile, Toby is saying, "The general is not a warmonger—"

"*He* says he *is*," Navarro spits back.

Toby's voice rises in alarm. "You can't do that." The thing is, he's too alarmed. Jinx does bizarro dangerous stuff all the time, and he barely even notices. "Jinx! Sit down!"

The sub descends sharply again, and Jinx ends up in Navarro's lap.

"Susan—" Navarro's voice is full of queasiness.

He's about to wrap his arms around her when she stands and pushes up again. Her boots bang, very, very heavy on the metal floor. She makes it to the second row and falls into the seat next to my brother.

"What the hell is this thing? And where are we going?" she asks him.

"You have to put on your harness or—"

"I know you know!" she yells at him.

"Fine!" he says in defeat as we take a major hit and Jinx is thrown into the air. Toby has to pretty much catch her, and then she's in *his* lap. "But buckle your seat belt!"

Terminus leans over into the empty space on his right side and throws up.

The small space we're in fills up with the smell of stomach acid.

And...Navarro is out of his seat.

I'm retching and sure I'll be puking up bacon bits any second. I cover my mouth with my hand, and it strikes me how cold it is. My skin feels cold and clammy and plastic. My breath on my palm is cool too.

Behind me buckles *click* into place.

"Okay. I'm buckled," Jinx says.

A pile of partially digested corn runs onto my boot. Oh. So. Gross. I jerk my foot back as far as I can. Stomach acid rises up and burns my throat.

Navarro must be having the same problem because he says, "Ah! Disgusting."

"The *Perun* is an experimental submarine that was in development at a naval base in San Diego," Toby begins. "It's noteworthy because it can travel to extreme depths and also pressurize passengers as it descends."

Jinx flicks Terminus in the head. "How is that even possible? How would they be able to—"

Terminus pants. "If you're going to ask me ten thousand technical questions about…what computational power is needed to…or how they're pressurizing us without first taking our biometrics…"

Oh. Crap.

He pukes. Again. Or at least he tries. There must not be anything left in his stomach because all that comes out is some whitish drool that gets stuck on his face.

"Can you keep it together, Partridge?" Navarro says.

The nose of the submarine must be pointing down, because we are being tilted back, like patients in dental chairs.

"Oh, don't mind me," Terminus answers. "I'm only expunging my small intestines over here."

Jinx flicks him again. "Terminus—"

"I don't know, Jinx," he says in a weak voice. "I've never seen the damn thing before today."

The *Perun* levels out, and we go for a minute without any turbulence.

The alarm siren goes silent, and the blue lights stop flashing.

"So Gus is right," Jinx says. Yelling at first. Then in a normal voice. "The Spark built a control center at the bottom of the Pacific Ocean? Command is a deep-sea habitat?"

Toby resumes in a fatigued voice. "The Federal government actually built it, but The Spark was able to seize it, since we largely control California. Very few vehicles are capable of reaching this depth. DS-SEALAB XVI was thought to be the safest place to bring Command."

We're going to the bottom of the damn ocean.

Okay, MacKenna. Don't hurl.

Take deep breaths. Stay calm.

"What do they intend to do with Susan?" Navarro asks in a strange voice.

It's a strange question too.

"Help her find her brother," Toby says. In that voice he always used when Mom would catch him watching TV and not folding his laundry.

I'm tired of this conversation that I can only hear and not see. I'm gonna have to go back there.

I unbuckle, force myself to stand and face the three of them. I'm a little relieved that despite their conversation, they are totally a mess. Jinx's blue hair is sticking almost straight up, and Navarro is the color of an old asparagus.

Huffing and puffing, I ask, "*Who* is in command?"

"I don't know!" Toby says.

Navarro catches my gaze. "He's lying, you know. The Spark provoked that attack. I told you this from the very beginning. That everyone seeks power. That ideologies are really nothing more than control mechanisms. A way for the strong to dominate the weak."

"You're wrong," I tell him.

Everyone's for Rosenthal.

That one thing still has to be true.

"The Spark is fighting for a future that is fair for everyone," Toby says. I guess he's gonna take my side on this one issue.

"The only difference between The Spark and The Opposition is that the latter is honest about its intentions," Navarro tells him.

"What do you know about being honest about intentions?" Toby fires back. "You ought to be asking what they're gonna do to *you*."

"What are you talking about?" Jinx asks.

Toby ignores her. "And here we are. The same lazy stuff all the time. There are bad people on both sides. That's what you want to say, isn't it? Well, I hate that argument." He glances at me. "I've *always* hated it. It reeks of cynicism. And it totally lets people continue to do bad shit forever. Because whatever action that you want to take to stop bad shit from happening is always equated with the bad shit itself. It makes the morality the same for the victim and the perpetrator. Makes it wrong to kill a killer. Makes someone who recovers their stolen property the same as the thief."

A year ago, I would have made the same arguments. Before I saw my brother watching that explosion. If The Spark knew about that thing and didn't warn people...

"That blast," I ask Terminus. "What did it come from?"

He has his eyes closed. "Some kind of cold fusion bomb. We think."

I fall into my chair as I picture it again. The dark cloud that swallowed everything whole.

Cold fusion is supposed to be impossible.

Toby and Navarro continue to argue.

"You're the one who acts like a child. A child who is going to be very disappointed when you see what The Spark really intends to do," Navarro says.

"Hello!" Jinx waves a hand in front of his face. "What do they really intend to do?"

There's no time for an answer.

We experience another knock.

This time Toby explains, "We're docking with SEALAB. They have to align everything exactly to maintain proper pressurization."

Proper. Pressurization. I guess this is what will keep our brains from turning to mush.

Jo—*Captain Pletcher*—is back, in a uniform that matches the one Copeland was wearing. "It's time," she says, and I hear the nervousness in her voice.

I have to help Terminus out of his seat, and we hobble along behind her. Jinx is worried again. Which is pretty normal, but Navarro and Toby eye each other with a newfound animosity.

We're back in the glass partition.

Back in the low blue light.

Except there's no seascape. We must be right up against something because the view beyond the glass is complete blackness.

Copeland and a small group of soldiers, almost silhouettes, wait near the door we entered when we boarded. They steal glances at Jinx.

The door opens slowly into a cheerful, almost sunny environment.

Copeland and his soldiers, including Toby, stand at attention and salute.

There. Handsome. Dark hair trimmed and perfectly combed. Casual in a crisp white shirt and pair of khakis.

My hero.

LEAD: Command is David Rosenthal.

God gave us life. Then He gave us war.

–AMMON C. CARVER
to MAXWELL MARSHALL
Kennebunkport, Maine

JINX

I did not see this coming.

I have to say, never ever did I think that Toby would join The Spark's army.

And Rosenthal was dead.

I mean, he had to be, right?

Although I tried to pretend otherwise whenever MacKenna was around, I'd always assumed that The Opposition had Rosenthal killed. No one had seen or heard from him since the inauguration back in January. He was the intellectual and practical leader of The Spark. The Opposition couldn't let a guy like that stroll around.

But where could he hide?

I guess the bottom of the ocean was as good a place as any. Because here, up close and in person, is David Rosenthal.

He's taller than he looks on TV.

MacKenna's mouth hangs open.

We're in what basically looks like a glass box surrounded

by dark, black water on all sides. Tracks of lights hang from the ceiling, giving the room a warm, familiar feel.

David Rosenthal could film a campaign ad any minute. He's neat, clean, with perfectly pressed slacks and combed hair. Unlike us. We look like we've been crawling through a storm drain or something.

I'm meeting the well…sort of president…and I smell like BO and fish and vomit.

I press my arms into my sides, hoping he won't notice me.

Rosenthal stares at me for an instant before speaking to the general. "At ease, old friend."

Copeland's troops fall into a more relaxed stance.

Rosenthal steps forward to shake the general's hand. "Glad to have you on board."

Copeland smiles. "Wouldn't miss it."

"No, I suppose not." Rosenthal glances from face to face. "Well, I'll start the introductions. I'm David Rosenthal, of course," he says with a politician's careful smile.

The general introduces his team of soldiers next, including Jo and finishing with, "This is Toby Novak, Colonel Novak's son. He's a new recruit."

Toby shakes Rosenthal's hand. He and MacKenna wear matching facial expressions, both staring in awe at their hero. Terminus might throw up again.

Rosenthal turns to me. "You're obviously Miss Marshall. I only met your father on one occasion. But his reputation lives on. My condolences. And now the issue with your mother, well, it's one hell of a situation." He smiles while shaking my hand and patting me lightly on the upper arm.

Copeland points to MacKenna. "This is Novak's daughter. She's quite a fan."

MacKenna waves. "Everyone's for Rosenthal." Her face turns red.

"I appreciate the support," Rosenthal says. His gaze lands on Navarro, who's behind me, hovering in the submarine doorway.

But Copeland continues the introductions. "Harold Partridge," he says with a gesture.

Rosenthal actually laughs. "Right. Terminus, isn't it? I can't say I appreciated it when you hacked the State of New York's database and gave my personal cell phone number out as the hotline to report portable toilet outages. But bygones, I suppose."

Terminus stares at the shiny floor.

Rosenthal's smile fades. "And last but not least, Gustavo Navarro. Well, well. Misery acquaints a man with strange bedfellows, eh, Harlan."

"Something like that, sir," Copeland answers.

Rosenthal *knows* Navarro?

Navarro is wearing an expression that seems oddly frightened. I try to get his attention, but he stubbornly refuses to look at me.

Something's wrong. I resist the urge to wipe the little beads of sweat forming at my hairline. Whatever scares Navarro terrifies the absolute hell out of me.

"Okay, let's start the tour," Rosenthal says. He's pretty chipper considering The Opposition just killed millions of his supporters and destroyed his California stronghold. He gestures at the glass walls. "This is what's called the Moon Room. It's the main point of entry but can also be used as an observation area. When we turn on the exterior lights, you can actually get a very nice view of the sea life down here. But we're keeping the lights off in the interest of good security."

Rosenthal opens a door opposite the submarine, leading us into a huge, wood-paneled room. It's a break area. There are Ping-Pong tables, vending machines and comfy sofas placed strategically in a way that's designed to allow small groups of people to relax. "Welcome to DS-SEALAB XVI. It was designed to be a long-term research facility for the navy. It's a fairly unique station in that it can generate power and breathable air for a month without being resupplied."

In the center of the room, a few people in dark blue jumpsuits watch a television that's tuned to a presidential press conference. Ammon Carver's face fills the screen.

Carver begins to speak in his gravelly voice.

"Three hours ago, a federal airplane dropped one bomb on the city of Los Angeles, California. This bomb was one thousand times more powerful than the weapons phased out as part of our participation in the Nuclear Weapons Ban Treaty. It was ten thousand times more powerful than the bomb dropped on Hiroshima, which was the largest bomb used in the history of warfare."

MacKenna blurts out, "They killed everyone in California!"

Rosenthal's face shifts to a look of sympathy. "In Southern California, yes, I'm afraid so. The Opposition has certainly shown the world what they're capable of."

What they're capable of.

What about what *we're* capable of?

I know I should keep my mouth closed, but I can't. "Don't you think you should have tried to stop them?"

Rosenthal glances at Navarro. "We did, young lady. We recruited your father for that purpose, in fact. But his efforts weren't as successful as we might have hoped. So here we are."

That last bit comes across sort of…menacing.

MacKenna looks confused.

We continue our trek across the break room.

On TV, Carver drones on. He's wearing his blue suit and red tie. Same as always.

"With this, my fellow Americans, I regret to inform you that the Second Civil War has begun. The Spark began this war with an act of defiance designed to destroy and destabilize American unity and union. That rebellion has now been answered in full. The deployment of the world's first cold fusion bomb serves first to quash the treason in our midst and then as a warning to other nations who might be tempted to view current events as a sign of weakness. The United States is, was, and will remain the most powerful nation on this earth."

We follow Rosenthal and he goes left across the break room, opening a door and going into a white hallway. It's glossy and smooth and belongs in a space station. But here, too, everything has a comfortable yellow light. He continues his tour. "Carver wasn't briefed on SEALAB's existence until late in January, which gave us enough time to take control of it."

The door to the break room behind us has shut, but Carver's voice continues to play on the station's speaker system. "We're monitoring communications from the mainland," Rosenthal says, explaining the noise. "It's quiet in my office. We'll be able to talk there."

"Top scientists have long theorized that cold fusion was an untapped source of unspeakable power. But that power remained elusive. Meanwhile, The Opposition, who objected to the elimination of nuclear weapons, were convinced that the nation was unprepared for modern war. We spearheaded Project Cold Front, a secret effort to find weaponry to replace our nuclear arsenal."

An ache builds in the back of my throat. Dad had clearly found out about the cold fusion bomb and been scared into leaving The Opposition and helping The Spark.

We continue walking with Rosenthal pointing out various doors. Storage. Research library. Various laboratories. We come to a smooth white door with a man in a full suit pacing in front of it. "Harlan, you probably remember Brian, my chief of staff. He can help you get your people settled and then show you to your private quarters. We'll meet for a drink when you've had time to relax."

I wave shaky fingers at Toby. He doesn't even bother to say goodbye to us as he leaves with Copeland.

Terminus has to grab MacKenna's elbow to stop her from going after them.

We resume walking and come to a large glass window. It's a room filled with workstations and huge glass monitors. Several people are at work, tapping on keyboards and pressing animated touch screens. "This will interest you, Miss Marshall," Rosenthal says. "This is the main computer control station and it…" He drones on about the makes of the computers, their processing power and their ability to monitor our biometrics even as we move about the habitat. But something else catches my attention. One of the monitors is tuned to the press conference. For a minute, two video loops replace Carver's face.

One was that stock video of my dad shaking Carver's hand. And the other.

Is Gus. Or at least what Navarro will look like in twenty years. It's footage of a man who could be Navarro's father, leaning over a microscope in a white lab coat.

Navarro still won't look at me.

Carver's audio continues.

"A team of researchers led by Dr. Peter Navarro and our own hero, Dr. Maxwell Marshall, worked feverishly at military bases in Phoenix, Arizona, Santa Fe, New Mexico, and Portland, Oregon, developing

a new technique that fuses deuterium with palladium metal to produce the most powerful weapon the world has ever witnessed."

Peter Navarro.

I'm heavy and frozen in a stony state of shock.

"The cold fusion bomb has laid to waste anything within two hundred miles of the blast radius, including the cities of Los Angeles, San Diego, Riverside and Palm Springs, with the zone of destruction extending as far north as San Luis Obispo. As a preemptive measure, The Opposition successfully evacuated the small communities living in western Arizona and southwestern Nevada. While these areas may experience some adverse weather conditions in the coming weeks, we believe that they will largely be unaffected by the effects of the cold fusion process."

But.

Peter Navarro?

I grab Navarro's arm and force him to look at me. "You told me your father sold restaurant supply equipment!" I say in a whisper.

His brown eyes plead with me. "He did! When he first came to this country, he had a restaurant supply business while he went to school."

"The new technology created by Doctors Navarro and Marshall does not utilize radioactive material and, as such, rebuilding efforts in California can begin at the conclusion of this terrible conflict."

Rosenthal is still giving the tour, mostly to Terminus, who is the only one really listening. "And here are the researcher dormitories. You've all been assigned rooms for tonight..."

Navarro, MacKenna and I have fallen back a few feet.

"So what? He's actually some kind of scientist?" MacKenna whispers.

"An electrochemist," Navarro says in a defeated tone.

"In the coming months and years, there are, no doubt, those who

*will question my decision, my motives and even my patriotism. There
is no denying that the number of casualties in California is high. Our
own estimates put the death toll at nearly thirty-five million. Millions of lives lost in an unnecessary war brought forth on our own soil
by The Spark. While I am deeply saddened by this turn of events,
I can only say that I felt called by a higher power to act in defending
the world's oldest democracy by whatever means necessary."*

We arrive at a fork in the hallway. "The kitchen and dining areas are that way," Rosenthal says, pointing left.

The betrayal hits me like a slap. "You lied to me!" I whisper through clenched teeth.

Navarro was the one person who had never lied to me.

*"There are those who will say that I had other options. That many
of the people who forfeited their lives were innocent of any blame. I
pray for each soul, but I firmly believe that their sacrifice was made
in the interest of ensuring that our people, our freedom and our way
of life will endure."*

Rosenthal points to the right, "My office is this way."

Navarro shakes his head. "I did not lie."

"You said you came here for me," I tell him, a curious pang
twisting through my chest. *Only me.*

Navarro stops and puts one of his hands on each of my
shoulders. I'm almost lost in his brown eyes. "I did. I gave
up my future, risked my life. Risked everything. For you."

*"While we have now won the battles of science and technology,
the rebellion of The Spark and David Rosenthal continues. We have
learned that The Spark, working in conjunction with known terrorist
Jesen Oscar Novak, plans ongoing military operations in a number
of areas with their ultimate goal to topple the lawful government of
our United States and replace it with a non-Democratic one headed
by Mr. Rosenthal."*

"My father is not involved in this," MacKenna says, shaking her fist at the speaker mounted near the ceiling.

Terminus turns and gives her a look. A look that says maybe Jay *is* involved.

The numbness continues to spread over me.

"We demand the immediate surrender of the State of California and of all armed forces currently reporting to The Spark. Anyone who surrenders voluntarily will be shown some measure of mercy. We demand the full and unconditional surrender of David Rosenthal, General Harlan Copeland and terrorist-at-large Jesen Oscar Novak. Additionally, all party affiliates of The Spark will report to a processing station in their area."

Navarro moves his face very close to mine, forcing me to stare right into his deep brown eyes. "I thought you of all people would understand how it feels to be defined by the choices of other people." He rubs my cheek with the tip of his thumb, leaving a warm trail behind.

"If these demands are not met within twenty-four hours, the federal government will have no choice but to make additional use of the cold fusion bomb. San Francisco is our next identified target. To David Rosenthal, I say surrender or prepare for annihilation."

Rosenthal places his hand on a trackpad mounted to the wall of a door that blends in remarkably well with the hallway. It clicks open. "And here we go."

If Rosenthal has a reaction to the news that Carver plans to pulverize Northern California to match Southern California, he doesn't show it. He remains polished and pleasant. Carver's voice continues to echo in the hall.

"Our response to the Second Civil War must be swift. Action must be immediate. We can and will do whatever is necessary to ensure that government of the people, by the people, for the people will live on."

I fight off a shiver.

We enter into a room that is an almost perfect replica of a government office. There's a massive mahogany desk, a red leather chesterfield sofa, bookcases with law books and old war reference manuals lining the walls, and even an oriental rug on the floor.

How do you get this stuff to the bottom of the Pacific Ocean?

David Rosenthal closes the door behind us, and it is quiet in this room. He gestures for us to sit at a circular table. There are only four chairs. Navarro stands behind me with his hands on the back of my chair. I wish I could see his face. I wish I could know what he is feeling.

"No doubt, you're all eager for a bit of downtime to refresh. However, I think it's wise if we get some of the basics out of the way at this point." Rosenthal isn't going to leave us to wonder about the basics for long, because he adds, "General Copeland tells me that you're in possession of some data that would repair whatever is wrong with the computers at the First Federal Bank."

It seems strange to be talking to the man who was elected president like we're equals. To be sitting with him at a table.

Everyone's for Rosenthal?

"Well...um..." I begin. I can feel my face getting hot. Terminus sits to my right and nods in encouragement. "My father encrypted all of the data on the bank's mainframe. He made the data inaccessible, unless you have a code block, a kind of key, that decrypts the data. We were able to assemble the key and place it on a disk drive." I unzip the pack around my waste and remove the small black drive.

Rosenthal holds out his hand.

I hesitate and turn to MacKenna.

This is our leverage. Our last hope of getting Charles back.

"Give it to him," she says.

I drop the device into Rosenthal's palm.

"And using the code on this drive, you could fully restore the First Federal systems?"

"Yes," I say.

"All of them?" he clarifies.

"The data would be current as of when the computers crashed," I say.

"So all the data as of January? Did Marshall make any copies of this?" Rosenthal asks.

"Dr. Marshall didn't even make that one," Navarro says in a cold voice. "Susan did."

Rosenthal gives Navarro a bland smile. "And, *Susan*, did *you* make any copies?"

I shake my head. And I hope it was a gamble that will pay off. I've been hyperfixated on the notion that someone will steal the code and take away my leverage to get my brother back.

Even though Dad said, *Always have a backup.*

Panic is settling somewhere inside of me.

Rosenthal drops the drive on the red patterned rug.

He stares at it, as if he's wondering whether he ought to pick it up.

Instead, he stands and steps on the device with the heel of his black leather shoe.

Never meet your heroes lest they disappoint you. That's what people say. Of course, it's always possible that reality won't align with imagination. But when we make choices about who we love or who we follow, we expose our own character. What do you do when you look down and it's your own feet that are made of clay?

–MacKENNA NOVAK,
Letters from the Second Civil War

MacKENNA

"Jesus Christ! What the hell are you doing?" Navarro says.

Jinx is on the ground collecting the tiny pieces of the disk drive. Picking them out of the carpet. "Um…um…maybe we can fix it…somehow…"

Terminus is down there too. "With what? Magic glue?"

"How am I going to get my brother back now?" Jinx mumbles.

Navarro paces around. "I told you not to trust him!"

He addresses this comment to me, and I address myself to Rosenthal.

"Mr.…President… Rosenthal…why did you do that?" I stand up.

"Because it's my job," Rosenthal answers sharply. All his friendliness has vanished.

But. But. But.

Navarro is giving me an *I told you so* stare.

"How is that your job? You're supposed to help people!" I say.

Rosenthal ignores me.

Jinx stands. Her head swivels from the crushed plastic pieces in her hand to Rosenthal's face and back again. "What about my brother?"

"Do what you're told, and you'll get your brother back," Rosenthal tells her. He walks to his desk and presses the touch screen. He speaks into the air. "Brian, get these kids where they need to be."

Brian, the man in the suit who we saw in the hall, bursts through the door. "Okay, kids, I can show you to your quarters."

I blink over and over again. As if I can make myself see something different.

Brian is almost shoving Jinx, Terminus and Navarro out the door. "Are the three of you going to make me call the MPs?" He's been in the office with us for maybe two minutes, and his suit is all rumpled and wrinkled.

I walk by myself. Slowly. With the ocean floor falling from under my feet.

I hesitate at the door, turning back to Rosenthal. "I really believed in you."

All those hours at rallies. Making posters.

Can I get them back?

Rosenthal draws in a deep breath and shoves his hands into his pockets. "Miss Novak, suppose we fix the bank computers. What would happen?"

Um. Well. "Things would go back to the way they were before?"

He nods. He really is kinda handsome, for an old guy. "But do you think things were right the way that they were before? We live in a world where two percent of the population controls eighty percent of the resources. My job is to make sure that the future is better than the past. For as many people as possible. This financial crisis is an opportunity to fix some of that. In the short term, things have to get worse before they get better."

Okay. But. "That's easy for you to say while you're comfortable in here and people are going without food out there."

LEAD: David Rosenthal destroys bank data to overhaul economic system.

Jinx and Navarro continue to argue with Brian in the hall. Their voices are getting louder.

Rosenthal joins me at the door. "I'm giving a speech in an hour. Let's see if I can convince you." The instant I'm in the hall, he closes the door.

A speech? Where? And for who?

"I don't know!" Brian is saying, tugging down his suit jacket. He's a short, thin, balding man who was born to book appointments for more important people. "And you'll see the general after dinner. There's a full briefing scheduled."

He herds us the same way we came. To the door that Rosenthal identified as the dormitories. "Orders are for you to remain here until dinner. You'll be escorted to the dining hall at seven. Then you'll receive information about your mission. If you'd like to listen to the president's speech—"

"What mission?" Navarro asks, still trying to push his way past Brian.

Our shoes are squeaking on the tile floor.

"How is Rosenthal giving a speech from the bottom of the ocean?" Jinx yells.

I can't help myself. "Who is it for? All the puffer fish and krill down here?"

Brian sighs dramatically. "He's addressing the nation via a

pirated signal. Turn your monitor to input four if you'd like
to watch. It starts in an hour." He leans on the door, shut-
ting it with all his weight, before we can say anything else.

There's a panel of lights mounted to the wall near the doorknob. One turns red.

We're locked in.

I'm pretty sure my childhood hero just had me placed
under house arrest.

I try to shake off the feeling that Navarro is right. That all
politicians are the same. That all this was predictable.

I'll think about that later. Right now. Focus.

The dormitory area is actually really nice. Like, if we
weren't in constant mortal peril, and if my knight in shining
armor hadn't fallen off his horse, I might be enjoying myself.
We start off in a large common area full of the same type of
furniture as in the break room. Recliners. A bright blue sofa
with gem-colored pillows piled on it. It's the perfect environment to curl up with a cup of cocoa and a book.

But.

No cocoa.

No books.

And Jinx. Repeating, "He destroyed the drive," over and
over.

Then there's Navarro.

He's able to resist saying *I told you so.* But I wonder if that's
only because he's relieved to not have to answer any more
questions about his own father. I'd almost rather have him
argue with me. Because watching him pace around and open
every closet and drawer like an assassin's gonna pop out really gets on my nerves.

LEAD: Peter Navarro built that terrible thing we saw from the ship.

Fact check: Make that Dr. Navarro *and* Dr. Doomsday.

Bias check: I'd need a quote to establish that the cold fusion bomb was terrible.

Except that explosion was quite damn obviously terrible.

Terminus falls into one of the recliners and buries his head in his hands. "Oh, does anyone have any milk of magnesia?" We ignore him.

Four bedrooms and a bathroom connect to the common room. We each claim a room and then find a tiny door that looks like it ought to be for a closet but is, instead, for a little kitchen. There's a little coffee maker and a minifridge. Everything is empty.

I'll be leaving a note for housekeeping.

We take short showers and change into the clean jumpsuits left behind in the dorm closet.

With nothing else to do, I end up turning on the monitor. Terminus is nearly asleep in his chair but, otherwise, I'm alone in the common room. I think Jinx and Navarro are fighting or making out or something.

After a while, a bright blue graphic and a fancy seal that reads the Provisional Government of the New United States appears. It dissolves into Rosenthal standing at a podium. He's obviously somewhere here in SEALAB, but if you didn't know that, you wouldn't know that. The room he's in has been modelled after the press briefing room at the White House. Rosenthal's dressed in a well-fitted navy suit and pastel blue tie. His wife, Celia, is behind him in a tasteful sky blue dress. General Copeland flanks Rosenthal's other side.

Rosenthal gives the camera a piercing stare and begins speaking.

"My fellow citizens, it is with a heavy heart that I address you this evening, in the wake of the massive destruction and loss of human life that occurred in Southern California earlier today. I am David Rosenthal, the properly, democratically elected president of the United States, and I am deeply saddened by the unprecedented move by acting president Ammon Carver..."

"Turn that off!" Navarro shouts from the bedroom he chose. "I've had enough of Rosenthal for today."

I move the volume slider down. But I keep it on. This speech could be important.

Jinx comes out of her room a second later. "You're the one who's so worried about what they might be planning. We should go out there and figure it out."

"Since assuming office using dishonest and duplicitous methods, Mr. Carver has allowed a difficult economy to devolve into a crisis. He's suspended the routine operations of the government, disbanding Congress and..."

Navarro follows Jinx. "I wasn't suggesting that we go out there and—"

Terminus sits up, looking alive for the first time in a while. "Oh no. No. No. I'm not sneaking around the secret underwater military base where the president is being guarded by General Copeland. No. Just. No."

"How would we get out even if we wanted to?" I ask, turning away from the screen. "We couldn't get out of our room back at Fort Marshall."

"My dad built *that* security system," Jinx says. "This is crap." She holds up a black duffel bag. "Plus, they let Terminus bring a bag."

Jinx plops the bag on the table in front of me, and the monitor rocks from side to side. I watch Rosenthal's face bounce around as she unzips Terminus's bag. "I'm sure he must have something in here that—"

I try to pay attention to Rosenthal, but it's almost impossible with them fighting in the background.

"...*resulting in the deaths of millions of civilians. In the past twenty years, The Spark made great strides toward a more just, equitable and democratic civilization. We've stabilized wages, protected civil rights for all, introduced universal health care and passed landmark legislation to repair damage done to our environment. But The Opposition has been reluctant to relinquish their position of unearned social and economic privilege and unwilling to...*"

Terminus waddles out of his recliner. "Hey! Don't look through my stuff."

A pair of underwear flies over my head. "Okay. Here we go," Jinx says.

Navarro makes a disgusted noise. "You touched his underwear."

Jinx ignores him and holds up an e-tablet. "This has minimal functionality, but we should be able to get it to run a script that..."

Rosenthal keeps talking.

"*It is tempting to think that if we acquiesce to Carver's demands, things will go back to normal. But, friends, I ask you to stand with me and envision a world where systemic poverty is not normal, where injustice is not normal, where challenges to basic freedoms are not normal. To build that world we must...*"

Terminus tries to get the e-tablet from Jinx. "That's not yours. It's for..."

I look up in time to see Terminus stare at me and blush.

He brought the e-tablet for me. His face goes totally red and it's kinda cute.

Ugh. Seriously. Focus.

Jinx rolls her eyes and holds the e-tablet out in front of her where Terminus can't reach it. "It's for MacKenna. I know. She can have it as soon as I unlock the door. I'll even clean the screen so my fingerprints won't be on it. Get me the data cable for this thing."

"You know, when I said your father left you in charge, I didn't mean of me personally," Terminus tells her.

"To build that world we must work together now. Dare to do the difficult work that lies ahead. If there is to be war, then, however reluctantly, we must fight. If there is to be injustice, we must resist the temptation..."

Jinx is at the door, ripping the plastic cover off of the electronic door lock system.

"What did Rosenthal say to you anyway?" Navarro asks. "Back there in his office."

"He said he's doing his job," I say.

Navarro groans. "*Lying* is his job. He's a politician."

Am I still for Rosenthal? *Everyone's for Rosenthal.* Do I still believe it?

Terminus leans over Jinx's shoulder. "That's how you're going to do it? A recursive function? Why not just..."

"It should say something about the nature of our fight that men like General Copeland, men of unparalleled valor and unequaled leadership, are willing to..."

I know I probably look and sound like a big goon. "Maybe he's for real."

What if he could be?

"Tell yourself whatever you want," Navarro says.

"Got it," Jinx says. And sure enough, the door is open a crack.

Terminus stares at the door. "When they toss us out into

the freezing deep sea to be food for whatever weird, bio-luminescent, poisonous creatures are floating around out there, I want it on the record that I opposed this idea."

"Stay here, then," Navarro tells him flatly.

Rosenthal leans toward the camera, and it's like he's addressing me personally.

"I, myself, have lived a life of some privilege and comfort, and there are those who might rightfully say that it's easy for me to urge us all to hold out for a better tomorrow when there's a chicken in my pot today. But friends, I say to you…"

"Let's go," Jinx says.

I can't look away from Rosenthal.

"I say to you truly. I can see the Promised Land so truly and completely. Right in front of us. The time is now. We're ready. Are you with me?"

Am I?

Jinx hesitates by the door. "Okay…so you're staying here, then?"

I turn the monitor off. "No. I'm coming."

Jinx pokes her head into the hall. It's all clear.

"I guess we're assuming there's no video surveillance?" Navarro says.

"I'm sure there's CCTV," she says with a shrug. "But Rosenthal is probably still speaking, and everyone is either watching him or helping him. Copeland is in that briefing room too. That's what I'd be watching. Plus, this is obviously designed to be a research station. The security isn't that good."

Oh sure. *Obviously.*

Jinx takes a left out of the dorm, but Terminus tugs the sleeve of her jumpsuit.

"The computer lab is the other way," he says.

"So you want to go in there and ask to borrow a workstation? We need to find an empty office. I say we try Research," she says.

We follow her, trying to do our best to keep flush with the walls and watch for cameras. We come to the door labeled RECORDS.

"I bet nobody's in there," Terminus says.

Navarro is able to jimmy the records door open with a small knife he found in the kitchenette of the dorms. Terminus is right. It's empty of people, with a lone metal desk and a strange-looking rectangular computer on top of it. It's also tiny, and there's no way all four of us will fit. Navarro and I stand watch while Jinx and Terminus go in the room. Snippets of their hushed arguments waft into the hall.

Jinx: Check common username and password combos from Fort Marshall—

Terminus: Oh sure, let's just announce ourselves because—

Jinx: The alternative being what? A brute force attack? We don't have time—

My boots squeak awkwardly on the floor. Navarro and I look at each other and then look away. Finally, I blurt out, "So my dad is a fake terrorist and your dad is a real one?"

His face runs pale. "You're really good at making idle conversation, you know? You could have tried the weather, the decor in here or how marvelous we all look in these jumpsuits."

There's a pause.

"And my father had about as much choice over whether to get involved in Project Cold Front as yours did in the bombings of those buildings."

I'm sure he's right.

"I'm sorry. I..."

"Shh!" He waves a hand at me.

It's so like Gustavo Navarro to tell me to shut up when I'm trying to apologize. But then I hear it too.

Voices.

Getting louder.

"Susan! Time to go," Navarro whispers into the crack in the door.

"One minute," she tells him.

"We don't have a minute!"

He's right. Again. I really hated this trend of Navarro always being right.

Voices fill the hall, echoing off the white, shiny walls, getting louder. It's a couple people I can't identify and two voices that I can. Copeland and... Toby.

I've got this choking sensation. Like when I have a piece of popcorn stuck in my throat.

My situation barely improves when my brother rounds the corner alone.

"You aren't supposed to be here," he says. Tension lines his face. Copeland and the other soldiers must have stopped a few feet before they turned the corner. Toby looks around in every direction. He's thinking about turning us in. I can see it in his eyes.

My own brother is going to rat us out.

Navarro steps close to my brother. "They're going to kill her, you know. They might kill all of us, to be thorough. But it's Susan they really need."

"No, they're not." Toby shakes his head. Slowly. Uncertainly.

"There always has to be someone to blame," Navarro almost spits at him.

Jinx and Terminus emerge from the small room.

"We got it," she says.

The two of them eye Toby uncertainly.

LEAD: Teen hackers steal secret files from The Spark.

The journalist in me has a thousand questions about what they think they've got. But the me who's just a girl has only one.

What the hell has happened to my brother?

The general's voice is growing louder again.

"Go," Toby says in a low voice.

We take off at a run and don't stop until the dormitory door is safely shut behind us.

The time has come to move the resistance from the sofa to the street.

–PRESIDENT-ELECT DAVID ROSENTHAL

Pirated national radio address

JINX

I shut down the machine and head into the hall with Terminus.

I'm surprised to see Toby and even more surprised when he tells us to run away. But two things are now clear. Toby doesn't really have our back anymore, and Copeland is psychotic.

I'm sweating when we burst back into the dorm.

I stash the e-tablet under the coffee maker while Navarro fixes the electronic log-in panel. It's Terminus who manages to look the least suspicious of all of us. He's back in the easy chair holding his stomach.

There's no time to think about what we saw on the SEALAB computer. About what we know. I barely have time to catch my breath.

There's a knock on the door and then Toby pushes it open without waiting for a response from us. "It's dinnertime," he says. Behind him, several soldiers lean in, maybe to get a glimpse of us.

And then we're back in the white hallway, our jumpsuits

making us look like a crew of club kids trailing behind the real soldiers in their serious uniforms. This time, Toby seems determined to, well, supervise us a little bit better. He takes us to a table for six. Jo joins us a couple minutes later. She seems far more comfortable than when we were together on the *Booker*.

Maybe because Rosenthal is at SEALAB, the dinner is a fairly fancy affair. We have a waiter. It's prime rib, cute little potatoes and asparagus. The meat might even be real. But neither the president of The Spark or General Copeland eats with us. Our dining room is filled with the people we saw working in the computer lab and the soldiers who arrived on the sub with us.

We mostly chew in the silence of MacKenna glaring at Toby.

"So you're gonna sit there and cut your meat into tiny pieces?" she says.

"Would you prefer I try to chew large pieces?" Toby shoots back.

"I would prefer..." she begins hotly but peters out. Maybe she doesn't know what she'd prefer, or she would rather not say anything in front of Jo.

Or maybe she'd rather not say anything in front of Toby.

Cool air hits my neck, and I shiver. I wish they'd given us a sweater with our jumpsuits.

Terminus tries to make conversation with Jo. "So, what should we expect during the briefing?"

"Nothing," Jo says repressively. "They only want her." She jerks her chin at me.

Navarro drops his fork. "Over my dead body."

Jo finishes chewing a mouthful of potatoes. "I wouldn't

say things like that if I were you. There are plenty of people around here who'd love to see that happen."

"Go to hell," I tell her. Jo Pletcher didn't see what I saw on the Research computer. She doesn't know anything about Peter Navarro. Or what he really did.

She bites into a bread roll. "He's for The Opposition."

Navarro's face turns red. "I'm… I'm…"

Do any of us even know what we're for anymore?

"Sure. Just like you are *for* letting the *Booker* sink without warning anyone. There's a five-year-old and her doll at the bottom of the ocean right now, FYI," I say.

Jo grips her fork so tightly that her knuckles go pale.

"Okay, okay. Let's all relax," Toby says.

This is both reassuring and…odd. This is the old Toby. The one who wanted everyone to get along and be happy. But then, Jo Pletcher is his superior officer.

"Whatever," Jo says, checking her watch. "It's time anyway." She turns to Toby and is less certain. "The general asked you to attend the briefing?"

Great. Military politics.

Toby nods. Casually. "Probably so Jinx will feel comfortable."

Yeah right. Copeland cares so much about my comfort.

"And you're headed topside tonight anyway," Toby adds.

"Right," Jo says. Her shoulders relax. "In the *Perun*. Operation Turquoise Eagle is a go."

We leave our empty plates and the table and make our way back into the hall. The soldiers from earlier wait to escort everyone but me back to our room.

"I'm coming with you," Navarro says through clenched teeth.

"We're all coming," MacKenna says, mostly to Toby.

Jo stares at her, as if daring Mac to start a fight.

Terminus seems very interested in something on the wall.

"It's okay. I'll be fine," I say, putting my hand lightly on Navarro's arm. "I'll be right back."

Anyway.

I already know what they want.

Before anyone can object, I turn to go with Toby. Behind me, I hear them continue to argue, but the noise fades as we go our separate directions. It's been a long time since I was alone with Toby, and it's hard to remember the days back when I used to have a massive crush on him and my biggest wish was that he'd come home from college on the weekends and swim in the pool. But now?

"So. You joined the army?" I ask.

SEALAB must essentially be a circle or a ring, because we walk around a series of rounded corners and arrive at what feels like the side opposite from the dorms. Ahead, two soldiers guard what I assume is a door.

Toby stops for a second and turns to face me. He looks the same as always. Same dark hair. Dark eyes. Pale skin. His features organized in a way that would make him a perfect model for a toothpaste or hair gel ad. The dark blue uniform accentuates his handsome features. He leans in toward me in a way that would have made me swoon one year ago.

"Nothing has changed, you know," he says. "We're still a family. After everything that happened, I wanted to find a way to do something that would matter. To make what we've been through matter."

"I have to get Charles back," I say, my heartbeat slow and sluggish.

"We will," Toby says in a voice that sounds hollow in the empty hallway. "We'll bring him home to us."

Part of me thinks that maybe Toby's not part of *us* anymore.

We arrive at a long room with more soldiers on guard. It's a standard gray office, like a doctor's waiting room. There are some bland office chairs, an American flag in one corner, a large poster of a government seal on the opposite wall and little else by way of decoration. It's brightly lit. Almost too bright.

Toby salutes the soldiers as we pass. The room contains several doors, but the one opposite where we came in is attended by two more soldiers. Which can only mean that Rosenthal is in there. One of the soldiers holds the door open for us.

We enter a conference room decorated in the style of Rosenthal's office, with a long, luxurious wooden table surrounded by plush office chairs on wheels. Sleek round lights hang from the ceiling, making it look like the room is filled with tiny UFOs. Rosenthal sits at the head of the table with Copeland at his right.

Toby stands at attention and salutes.

How does he even know when to do this?

Copeland smiles. "At ease. And good news, soldier. The president has finished signing your promotion papers."

Jo's instincts were correct. Toby is being fast-tracked for success.

"Congratulations, Captain Novak," Rosenthal says.

"Thank you, sir."

Copeland motions for us to take seats in the center of the table.

As we move farther into the room, I notice two other people seated at the long table. One is Brian, Rosenthal's creepy enforcer, and the other is a thin Asian woman in a tailored beige jacket. She nods at me and looks me over.

"Of course, we'll have to do something about her hair," the woman says.

I reach up instinctively to touch the blue pixie cut that I sort of like.

"Whatever you think is best," Rosenthal says.

The woman takes notes on an e-tablet.

On the wall we're facing, there's a projection screen filled with the image of a military base. Thanks to the files Terminus and I stole, I recognize it as the Los Alamos National Laboratory. It's a secret facility in New Mexico where they test new weapons.

And where, right now, they've got one of the only three cold fusion bombs that Dr. Navarro managed to build before he was killed. Also thanks to that file, I know that Gus's father is dead.

I'm not sure who's supposed to talk first or what the protocols are when dealing with people like Rosenthal and Copeland, but I'm tired of wasting time. I address myself to Copeland. "I thought you said they're holding my brother in Oregon."

Copeland glances at Rosenthal. "That's what our intel suggests. But the deal is, you help us, we help you."

My face heats up and I glare at Rosenthal. "I already helped you. I gave you the encryption key to the First Federal computers, which you decided to destroy in the interest of making people pissed enough about the economy that they'll join your revolution."

Toby shifts in his seat, his face a mixture of awkwardness and fear.

"Our revolution." Rosenthal's handsome face falls into a passive, unexpressive mask that reveals nothing. "I'm sure Dr. Marshall must have filled you in on some background here, so why don't we stop playing games. Tell us what you know, and we can fill in any needed details."

Rosenthal clearly didn't have much of an understanding of Dr. Doomsday.

My father never filled anyone in. About anything.

Everything I know came from what I could skim in the five minutes before we were chased out of the records office.

I muster up all the false bravado I can. "I *know* that The Opposition only built three of those cold fusion bombs. I know that they've deployed one, so they have two left—at Los Alamos and AIRSTA in Oregon. But those don't work. For one thing, Peter Navarro wasn't able to stabilize the tech before you had him murdered. For another, he and my father sabotaged the other two. Probably intentionally. So Ammon Carver can get on TV and pound his fists all he wants, but he probably can't destroy the city of San Francisco tomorrow."

Brian leans forward. The floating light creates long shadows across his face. "We didn't have Dr. Navarro murdered, young lady."

"Well, my father said you did," I lie. "And he was usually right about such things."

Copeland mirrors Rosenthal's flat effect. "Peter Navarro was the only person alive who could get cold fusion to work. You saw what that bomb did with your own eyes. We had to take him out, and if that makes your boyfriend cry, too bad."

My pulse surges, and I cast a sideways glance at Toby, whose face has run quite ashen. "Dr. Navarro didn't *want* to work for The Opposition," I say. "He was *helping* you. There was no need to kill him."

Copeland can no longer hide his annoyance. "Peter Navarro thought The Opposition often had the right idea. Same as your father. Same as me. Like the rest of us, he had to rethink things when he saw what they were prepared to do. By then, it was too late."

He's raising all these questions to which there are no real answers. How much did my father or Dr. Navarro really ever repudiate the philosophy of The Opposition?

Rosenthal hesitates, choosing his words carefully. "Some people are too dangerous to live. Your father understood this idea. He frequently acted on it."

Copeland presses his lips into an impatient line. "There are a lot of things about this world you don't understand."

It takes everything I've got not to jump across the table at him. "I understand that The Opposition believes the wrong things. And now The Spark is *doing* the wrong things."

I eye Copeland. Could I take him? Sure, he's probably pushing sixty. But. A career marine. A veteran of every war I ever read about in my national history class.

He'd crush me like a potato chip.

The woman remains silent but makes more notes.

Rosenthal, the consummate politician, steers the conversation back where he wants it to be. "What *we're* doing is trying to ensure that those weapons are rendered inoperable. Permanently. What *you're* doing is trying to get your brother. Given that we believe Charles Marshall is being held at the research facility at AIRSTA, those strategic interests align."

I suck in a deep breath. "Isn't it a little too coincidental that they took my brother to the exact location where you need me to go?"

"Miss Marshall," Rosenthal says in a new tone of warning. "It is clearly *not* a coincidence. It's a trap. But it validates our theories about what's happening behind the scenes."

"You know what a black box system is?" Copeland asks.

"Of course," I answer automatically. "It's a computer system where only the inputs and outputs are known." Suddenly, the pieces click into place. The Spark knew that my father had taken the cold fusion missile systems off-line. But they didn't know how or how long it would last. Depending on how Dad had deployed the system, other users might not even be able to see how it worked or to make changes to the code. Or the systems might periodically troubleshoot and reset themselves. Meaning the bombs might be off-line forever...or repaired next week.

They don't know.

Rosenthal taps the table, and a new image appears on the screen in front of us. It's a technical diagram of what looks like a giant screwdriver. "In layman's terms, Dr. Navarro thought he could insert a piston made of palladium metal into deuterium to achieve a cold fusion reaction. Research went on and on. He worked with Marshall, who believed that you could get the whole thing to work if you got a computer system to control the various processes of nucleosynthesis."

"You'd need a PhD in physics to understand this stuff," Copeland mutters.

"Dr. Navarro *had* a PhD in electrochemistry," I say coldly.

Toby scratches his neck. He's having trouble maintaining his cool.

The image on-screen changes again. This time to a massive explosion in a wide-open desert area. Rosenthal keeps talking. "The point is, they tested the cold fusion system and it worked, and it scared the hell out of them—that's when Marshall reached out to us."

Copeland nods. "We dispensed with Navarro, and that gave Marshall an opening. The missile in Phoenix was already operational, so there was nothing that could be done there. But

Marshall was able to ensure that the bombs in Santa Fe and North Bend were never brought online."

The way Copeland talks about this stuff. Like assassinating a government researcher was no big deal. Like, *Oops, wrong button.*

Plus, the insinuation is clear.

My dad knew they intended to kill Peter Navarro and went along with it. And then Peter's son decided to risk his life saving me, over and over.

My heart does a series of somersaults.

"But we don't know how," Rosenthal adds.

Okay. Breathe.

"And you think if he recycled code bases from his other projects, then my details might be built into the system. My fingerprints, my retinal scans. I might be able to log in," I say.

Copeland nods. "That was our theory. But it was confirmed when The Opposition moved your brother to that facility. Believe me, there are a million better places to take a five-year-old than AIRSTA."

Sigh. "He's eight."

"The story with the brother is good," the woman murmurs. "We can use that. Especially as The Opposition has put forward the information that he's dead. The fact that the two of you are not dead will clearly undermine the legitimacy of their messaging."

My face heats up. "It's not a story! And who are you? You—"

Rosenthal holds up a hand to silence me. "We want you to—"

"—you want me to break in there. Into a highly guarded military base, where they are obviously expecting me," I say with a sigh. "And what? Delete the code? Destroy the machines that it's running on?"

It's Copeland who answers. "Yes. To all of the above. We'll get you in. You make sure Marshall's code gets permanently deleted. We'll get you out. You can take your brother with you when you go."

Oh sure. That sounds easy.

"What about the missile in Santa Fe?" I ask.

For some reason, Copeland looks at Toby when he answers. "We believe that the computer system in Oregon interfaces with both missiles. Once it's down, once we're sure the missile can't be fired, I have a crew in place ready to destroy the facility."

There's a slight pause and then Copeland adds, "Captain Novak will be leading your team. Who has a better incentive to get you in and out safely?"

My mouth falls open.

Toby *will be in charge of getting us into AIRSTA?*

For the past couple months, we haven't even been able to get Toby to do twenty minutes on the treadmill.

"I'll be training intensively over the next week," Toby says, defensively.

"We'll get you up to speed, Captain," the general agrees.

"This operation will set The Opposition back several years and, clearly, after we win the war, we won't be allowing any future research of this kind," Rosenthal says.

"Very nice," the woman says. "I'll need to get a version of that on video for inclusion in postwar news coverage sizzle reels."

This time, even Toby asks, "What?"

Copeland gives him a small smile. "Captain, we need a big win."

Rosenthal nods to his assistant, Brian.

"This is Amelia Aoki," Brian says, pointing to the woman. "She's handling our public relations efforts."

He uses a small remote to change the image. This one is of me. An illustration of me, labeled ARTIST'S RENDER-ING 5. I've still got my old hair, which in the sketch has been drawn in a sleek ponytail with a few loose tendrils curling around my face, and I'm wearing a uniform that looks like it could belong to a superhero flight attendant.

Never in my life has my hair been that neat, or have my cheeks been that rosy, or have I stood so perfectly straight.

People are dying.

And Rosenthal is…making propaganda?

The woman rises. "World War I had Uncle Sam. World War II had Rosie the Riveter. Operation Cedar Hawk had Commander Contreras…and we've got…you." Amelia gives me a disapproving look. "Boring…generic…you."

"Well, wait now," Toby says.

The plan is simple. Amelia clicks through her presentation. The Spark is going to "brand" me, building on the work that The Opposition was already doing with my father. While I'm in SEALAB, we'll tape a series of interviews that Amelia's team will release through "the right channels." Then they'll send a marketing team with us to AIRSTA.

They'll broadcast our operation.

Like a television show.

It's the stupidest thing I've ever heard.

"No," I tell them flatly. "I'm taking my team."

"Your team?" Copeland repeats, carefully accenting each word.

"Yeah," I say. I sit up straight, trying to remember every-thing I know about assertive body language. "MacKenna, Terminus and Gus." I look at Amelia. "Gus can operate the camera. MacKenna is a writer, and she's already working on reports. Your people can edit the stuff they create as it comes through."

Copeland actually looks a bit relieved. I seriously doubt that there are many marketing people eager to volunteer to go with teenagers into a war zone.

"You think we're letting you take Peter Navarro's son into AIRSTA?" Amelia asks. "Or that idiot, Harold Partridge?"

I shrug, as fakely casual as I can. "Terminus is actually an expert in machine language coding. He worked with my father for years. Since you don't know anything about how Dad wrote the missile system, including what languages he may have used, sending Terminus is smart. And I won't go without Gus."

I'm surprised when Copeland agrees. He's being a little too accommodating.

"Okay," he says slowly. "But I make no assurances about your friends' safety. Our deal covers you and your brother only."

Rosenthal casts a sideways glance at Copeland.

Suddenly, I'm very cold. They're putting it all on me.

The responsibility for everything that's about to happen.

I can't think of what to say, so I blurt out, "And I'm keeping my hair."

Amelia glares at me.

"This is going to be fun," she says.

We said we wouldn't split up. We said we'd stay together. But at some point we became Us and Them. For a while I secretly thought that Dr. Doomsday got it right all along, when he wrote, "Do what you have to do to survive." But then I realized that's not quite it. And *then* I realized…it should be:

Do what you have to do to be able to live with yourself.

—MacKENNA NOVAK,
Letters from the Second Civil War

MacKENNA

Jinx is gone for a long time, leaving me stuck in a tiny room with Navarro, who can't sit still, and Terminus, who can't stop complaining.

So my entire world is now:

Terminus: They put a lot of pepper on those potatoes.

And.

Navarro: Susan has been gone too long.

And.

Terminus: And like horseradish on the meat. It's messing with my stomach.

And.

Navarro: I told you we couldn't trust these people.

I don't know Terminus well enough to be able to say whether he's always this obsessed with his stomach. Like, the sub ride was tough on all of us, and naming every ingredient in our food probably won't accomplish anything. But I do know Navarro, and this behavior is pretty typical for him.

I try to use the monitor again, but I guess it's too much

to hope that we'll get movie channels down here at the bottom of the ocean. Cycling through the various inputs, I find only black screens.

Be patient, MacKenna.

Nothing to do but wait.

Except.

Thanks to Terminus, I've got an e-tablet again... I think. This seems like the perfect time to work on my reports.

I get the e-tablet back from where Jinx shoved it. Behind me, Terminus is muttering about how chives make him queasy, and the heavy steps of Navarro's boots fill the small space.

Taking the e-tablet back to the room I claimed as mine, I flop down on my stomach on the twin bed. I'm about to create a new set of files when I notice that my old notes are already there. Terminus made a point of saving my tablet from Fort Marshall and bringing it back to me.

I can't help but smile.

Jinx is wrong about him.

Harold Partridge is okay.

I also notice that Terminus and Jinx managed to download a folder from that computer they hacked. It's called Operation Turquoise Eagle. Oh. Background research.

Yes.

I tap it, and it expands into a crap ton of files that all have labels that would make a journalist drool. Background, Cold Fusion Theory, Crowd Psychology, Marketing... The list goes on and on.

One folder catches my eye.

Personnel.

As I open it, I tell myself I'm not looking for information about Terminus. Which is good. Because there isn't any in that file. Instead there's a folder called Jesen Oscar Novak.

The first part are his service records. Mostly, I know all this stuff. His Silver Star. His promotions. There's some pics of his assignments during Operation Cedar Hawk.

The next part makes my blood boil. It's a bunch of documents that are marked with red and blue official-looking and scary names like NSA Upstream Collection and Homeland Security Data Intercept. Some are translated reports from various foreign governments. The Spark was spying on The Opposition.

And they'd collected reports written by Stephanie Marshall. About Dad.

Why she targeted him.

Subject's repressed grief over death of his wife five years ago and ongoing anxiety concerning the upbringing of his children has left him with a deep desire for a family unit that exists in an idealized proto-American, heteronormative state. As such, he's highly vulnerable to women with conventional beauty and old-fashioned mores. He is unlikely to view his domestic partner as a strong, independent operator.

Great. I think Jinx's mom was basically saying that Dad was a fool for pretty women. She, like, monitored him like a lab rat during their marriage:

Subject continues to display little or no interest in current events and rarely discusses past military service. I met with [name redacted] today for several hours—my absence attracted no notice.

Yep. That's what she was doing when we all thought she was teaching homeroom or grading extra credit assignments. Meeting with people whose identities were a secret—even to other spies. And my dad was probably home grilling corn on the cob.

I wish Jinx were here, because there's a weird document that's like part of some kind of surveillance or something. Most of the names have been blacked out. In some sections, most of the words have even been blocked out.

WIRETAP NO: ███████ Approved by: Hon. ██████

███████████████

Sunday, ████████████████

████████████████ : *There's concern in high places that Max has gone rogue.*

    Agent S. Marshall: *My current assignment doesn't provide the time or adequate resources for me to effectively monitor him but—*

    Agent ██████ : *Has anyone ever been able to effectively monitor Colonel Marshall?*

    Agent ████████ : *You're just pissed because last week Marshall had you tailing an ice cream truck halfway to Baja.*

    ████████████ : *If he can't be controlled, he'll have to be eliminated.*

    Agent S. Marshall: *You know,* ████████ . *You never learn. My husband is the greatest weapon The Opposition has in its arsenal. There are better ways to handle him than with threats of violence.*

    Agent ██████ : *If you'd done a better job handling him, we wouldn't be here.*

    Agent ████████ : *Yeah, well, you volunteering to take him out,* ████ ?

    Agent S. Marshall: *It would be like trying to kill a ghost.*

I don't know what to make of any of that. I close those files and open one called Operation Overview.

Then. My heart stops.

My eyes travel over a set of new commission papers.

Oh God. Oh God. Oh God.

Like Toby, Dad has joined the Provisional Army of the New United States.

He has a mission.

Operation Turquoise Eagle.

Survival Probability: >10%

I want to punch something or kick something or *do* something.

Dad lied right to my face when he said he'd wait for us at Fort Marshall and, honestly, I was a total fool for believing his crap. I should have known that he'd never ever sit around playing cards while we ran around with The Spark's little army. He signed up to lead a small force into the cold fusion research lab at Los Alamos in New Mexico. They're going to destroy one of those damn missiles.

At least, they're going to try. According to the mission, they have to wait for another team to take out another missile in Oregon and then evade a massive military force to get to the Los Alamos facility.

Dad's team is going in.

They aren't expected to make it out.

I wonder if Dad discussed this with Toby. I don't know which would hurt more. If my brother knew...or if he didn't.

Plus, it gets worse.

In another folder, colored red and marked TOP SECRET, is a folder called Operation Objectives. The primary objective is listed as "Create fear, shock and outrage." Not only did The Spark leak their plans to The Opposition spies, Copeland doesn't expect the other team in Oregon to succeed. The real objective is to instigate battles that will scare the hell out of everybody. It's clear from the way this stuff is written that Rosenthal doesn't know.

One line stands out: Command not advised of sub-level operations.

Copeland wants a war.

He's hoping The Opposition will find a way to detonate another one of those damn cold fusion bombs. And he isn't going to wait around for one to happen on its own.

Dad is walking into a trap.

Seriously, MacKenna. You have to do something.

Maybe I can get to Rosenthal, but, like seriously. On what planet will he believe some kid over his top general?

No.

It's up to me.

I have to warn Dad.

And I remember my brother's words. *You're headed topside tonight anyway.* Jo Pletcher is leaving on the submarine in an hour.

I have to be on it too.

LEAD: Student journalist must stow away on experimental submarine.

Um...okay...but how?

I fluff up my pillows and shove them under the covers, making a human outline. The way I used to do when we lived in Boulder and I used to sneak out to sleep in Janie MacDonald's tree house. It's getting late, and if I play my cards right, Jinx and Navarro might assume I've gone to bed. I feel like I should pack something. But we've got absolutely no gear.

I turn off the light to my room. A small night-light pops on next to the door. It looks calm. Kinda serene. I grab the e-tablet.

When I go back into the common room, Navarro has finally gotten tired of wearing a hole in the rug and decided to take a shower. I can hear the water running in the small bathroom that's next to his bedroom.

Terminus leans over in the armchair, moaning and talking to himself. "How come no one else was bothered with how greasy that gravy was? I mean—"

I toss the e-tablet into his lap. "Shh!" I say. And then I add in a whisper, "I need you to do that thing with the door again."

He sits up. "*Thing* with the door?"

"Open. The. Door," I say, with a fierceness I hardly feel.

I go to his room, position his pillows in the center of his bed, grab his bag and turn off the room lights. In the common room, Terminus has opened the door like I've asked, but he's got an expression on his face that's equal parts terror, horror and shock.

I poke my head into the hallway. It's quiet and empty, and still cheerfully and brightly lit. The same as before. It's weird being down here, where there's no day and no night.

"Come on," I whisper, motioning for him to follow me. There's no way in hell I'm letting my father go into that research lab.

Not without me anyway.

I put the tablet in Terminus's duffel bag. "The *Perun* is headed to the surface," I tell him. "I'm going with them…

"…and you're gonna help me."

Geniuses like Maxwell Marshall might create civilization. But fanatics like Ammon Carver create history.

—AMELIA AOKI
Report: The Image of the Second Civil War
Stamped: Top Secret

JINX

By the time Toby and two other soldiers escort me back to the dorm, it's past nine. We exchange a series of tense glances as our boots click on the clean white tile floor. The old Toby might have come into our room to talk. To reassure us. The new Toby is off with Copeland's team to his own quarters near the Moon Room.

Sooner or later MacKenna will have to confront the new Toby.

We all will.

I step into the dorm, and Toby closes the door without saying goodbye.

I've got a package of paperwork now, and it's full of reading and instructions from Amelia. Mostly scripts to memorize. Ridiculous things they want me to say and the way they want me to sit or stand when I say them. There's a tab called BRAND GUIDELINES. Which is a lot of garbage about keeping my uniform neat, not ever being too sweaty and staying in my "reluctant hero character."

Oh blargh.

I'm dying to get back to all the *real* intel. That briefing was total crap. There was something that Copeland wasn't telling me. Probably a lot of somethings, actually. The files we stole off the research computer contained tons of stuff I didn't have time to check out. They probably explained the real nature of our mission.

I'd be willing to bet that MacKenna has been reading while I was gone. Which is good. She's way better at research than me, has read more than me and knows a lot more about Rosenthal than me. She'll know what's going on.

In the common room, Navarro is alone. All the lights are off except a single lamp on a squat end table next to his chair. He's taken a shower and is sitting in the chair where Terminus was sitting earlier.

"Um…hi," he says, his face turning pink.

"Hi," I say. It's supposed to sound casual. Instead, it's… guilty.

Even from my position behind the sofa, I can smell the sharp mint of the shampoo that must be in the SEALAB bathroom. Somehow Navarro manages not to look dorky in these stupid blue jumpsuits we're all wearing. His top button has escaped from a frayed loop, and I can see a hint of toned chest.

Focus.

I force myself to go to the kitchenette, flip on the small light and look for the e-tablet. "You'll never guess what Copeland and Rosenthal want to do." I try to talk the way we always talk. The way we focus on what's happening.

Never on what's happening between us.

"You mean that they want to make you some kind of war hero?" he says.

Well, apparently, he *can* guess.

I rummage around under the coffee maker and in the basket of coffee filters and tea bags sitting next to it. No e-tablet. I go toward the bedrooms. The door to Mac's room is shut, and I'm about to open it when Navarro says, "I think she's asleep. It's been…things have been…um…you know."

Do I know that it's 9 p.m. and we nearly died in a bomb blast, a sinking ship and the submarine ride from hell? Yeah, I do know. The exhaustion sinks in as I remember the day's events. I can see why Mac might have wanted to get some sleep. I'm cold and heavy with the weight of everything that's happened. All the loss. All the destruction. Today, we saw mankind at our worst and, even though we saw a lot of the destruction from afar, everything came at a huge personal cost for countless people.

Tonight, how many sisters are missing their brothers the way I miss Charles? How many people have no hope of ever seeing the face of someone they love again?

I hesitate with my hand on MacKenna's door and then slide it open a crack to reveal her dark room and the silhouette curled up on her bunk.

"Can we…talk for a minute?" Navarro asks.

My pulse flutters. What would we talk about? How we're united in the fact that our parents did terrible things for which we might never be able to atone?

I decide that the e-tablet can wait and close MacKenna's door, then go back to Navarro in the common room. I take a seat in the center of the sofa, leaving me a few feet away from the cascading shadows created by the flickering lamp. Placing the binder from Amelia on the coffee table in between us, I'm about to brief him on everything that Copeland said.

Instead.

"Susan," he begins in a quiet voice. "My father—"

My father's choices are probably the reason that Peter Navarro is dead.

"He's a hero." I scoot to the end of the sofa, closing the distance between us.

There's a long pause.

"I know," he says with a small sniffle. "But I'm probably the only one who ever will."

"Well, I know too." I reach for his hand. I wonder how much of Gus's opinions about The Opposition and The Spark were forged out of the ashes of what happened to his father.

In the end, maybe everything is far more personal than we want to admit.

His warm fingers wrap around mine. "I never wanted to lie to you. Or keep things from you. I thought it would be safer if you didn't..." He stares off into the darkness of the corner of the room.

I don't want to lie to him either. Or keep secrets. Or hide behind cryptic phrasings. He needs to know, and I need to tell him. "I think..." I trail off.

I think my dad sold your dad out to buy time to defect to The Spark.

What are the right words for that?

"I think my dad—"

"He told me," Navarro interrupts. He avoids my eyes.

Almost dizzy with shock, I bite my lower lip. "He told you? He told you what?"

Navarro sighs. "That he and Pops worked on Project Cold Front together. It wasn't exactly optional, you know. When it became clear that the tech was going to work, it scared the absolute shit out of them. They decided to make contact with The Spark in hopes of stopping the program. Dr. Marshall got to Rosenthal at some point, but it was too late. The

Spark already knew about the operation and had a plan in place to..." He sniffs again. "To kill Pops. Your dad had to decide between..."

Between sabotaging the missile computers or helping Dr. Navarro.

And I guess we know what he chose.

Do what you have to do in order to survive.

My pulse flutters. "You knew? All this time, you knew that? And you still helped me anyway? Why?"

His face puckers into a pained expression. "For you," he chokes out. "I told you—"

I came here for you.

That's what he said that very first night we were on the run.

I don't care how he intends to finish that sentence.

Copeland may be right. I may not understand anything about this world, and I may always be wrong about my place in it, but I do know one thing for certain.

Navarro is the one thing I really need to survive.

Pushing myself up from the sofa and leaning awkwardly forward over the table...

I press my lips to his.

Hard.

Maybe too hard.

He freezes.

Mac thinks we're off making out all the time, but the truth is, this is only our second real kiss, and the first one lasted only a few seconds because there's no real privacy in a Doomsday bunker with five people. So this is not typical behavior.

I'm about to pull back...and maybe run away and hide somewhere.

Then.

He leans forward, too, and rises so I'm not hunched over

in some weird position. The tip of his tongue glides along my upper lip. We're both standing up now, and his warm hands wrap around my back.

All the times I'd spent imagining.

Gustavo Navarro.

His lips on mine. His hands on me.

Here we are.

We almost knock over a cheesy wooden eagle on the coffee table as he backs me to the door of his room. Inside, it's dark and cool and quiet.

Unsure what comes next, in the tiny sliver of light created by the open bedroom door, I fumble the first several buttons of his jumpsuit. He sucks in a deep breath as I reach the one at his naval and run my fingers lightly over the muscles created by long days preparing for the end of the world.

And then.

He shrugs out of the jumpsuit and closes the door.

Just this once.

The end of the world can wait.

The world will survive for one night.

Tonight.

My brother resisted the argument that both sides were the same, even though both sides were prepared to use the same methods to advance their causes. I'm not sure he ever asked himself if you could do wrong while trying to do right.

–MacKENNA NOVAK,
Letters from the Second Civil War

MacKENNA

LEAD: Journalism student and morally flexible hacker stow away on futuristic clandestine submarine to intercept doomed military mission.

IMPORTANT FACTS:

-Jo is leading a team to Santa Fe, New Mexico.

-There she'll meet Jay Novak, who has recently enlisted in the Provisional Army of the New United States.

-Novak's unit will try to permanently disable a cold fusion missile.

-But the plans for the mission have already been leaked to The Opposition. Even though the operations take place in areas controlled by The Spark, The Opposition plans to have a huge force on hand.

I go through this in my head. If we were at home, Mr. Johnson would totally accuse me of burying the lede. The big story here is that the town of Santa Fe is about to be the site of the first major battle of the Second Civil War. Oh yeah, and The Opposition plans to kill whoever happens to be in a one-hundred-mile radius.

But all I can think about is Dad.

He's walking into a trap, and he has no idea.

We're all becoming footnotes in the big story.

QUOTES AND BACKGROUND INFORMATION:
God, it would take too long to summarize everything. Who could I quote? There are only a handful of people on earth who even have some clue as to what's gonna happen.

Hello! Earth to Mac! Argue with yourself later. Right now, we need to get on the submarine, which is probably leaving any second.
One of the files Terminus and Jinx managed to steal is a map of SEALAB. Terminus brings it up on the screen of the e-tablet, and we spend a few seconds trying to get oriented. The underwater station was designed for research, and Jinx was right. The security isn't great. Like, whoever built this place mainly expected nerdy scientists to be going from lab to lab. They hastily installed cameras in the parts of the station where Rosenthal is being kept, but otherwise there's not a whole lot to worry about.

Well. Except for all the soldiers milling around.

The first fifteen minutes of our adventure are spent in a supply closet, trying not to choke on the smell of pine cleaner and moldy mopheads.

"This plan is stupid," Terminus says.

"Why didn't you say that before?"

"I did say that before!" he whispers. Terminus taps an area on the map. It's a computer supply room. "I have an idea," he says.

We snake around the network of halls, listening hard for the echo of voices. Terminus motions for me to duck and crawl underneath the glass window that looks into the computer lab room. Next to a door with a large sign that says AUTHORIZED PERSONNEL ONLY is a smaller door called STORAGE. Terminus uses the program he created earlier to unlock it.

It's an odd room in the shape of a C. The center is filled with racks of high-tech computers, extra monitors, spare parts of things I mostly don't recognize. Small white night-lights create odd shadows and here and there, red and blue lights blink as part of devices I don't recognize. There's something that maybe looks like a speaker, and a few replacements for the alarm panels like the one on the wall of the dorm.

Terminus finds a stainless-steel utility cart behind the series of racks. It has two shelves. He tells me to climb onto the lower shelf, and then he builds a fort of equipment, placing steel and plastic computer parts all around me.

His duffel bag lands on the shelf above me with a *thonk* that makes my ears ring.

"Whatever happens...stay quiet," Terminus says.

He pushes the cart clumsily out of the storage room.

Apparently, Terminus's big master plan is to push the cart around and act like he knows what he's doing.

OTHER IMPORTANT FACTS:

-He does not know what he's doing.

-One wheel of this cart squeals so loud that people on the mainland can probably hear.

It's really uncomfortable down here. Like, everything Terminus stacked on this cart has sharp corners that keep pressing into my legs and arms. I'm sitting cross-legged and hunched up in a ball, and one of my feet is falling asleep, and I think I might have pulled a muscle in my neck and—

Oh crap. Several voices are coming closer and closer.

Footsteps grow louder.

We almost knock into three pairs of work boots.

Calm down, MacKenna.

"Partridge? Where do you think you're going?" a deep voice asks.

These soldiers must recognize Terminus from Fort Marshall.

"You know this guy?" a female voice asks.

"He's supposed to be keeping an eye on Marshall's kid," the man answers.

"I thought that's what *we're* doing," the woman says.

"*We're* escorting her to and from the briefings. *He's* supposed to be keeping an eye on things from the inside," the man says.

My blood boils hot, and it takes every ounce of self-control I've got not to bust out from behind the computers.

LEAD: Morally flexible hacker is a spy.

A third man's voice adds, "They say she's just like him. Like Dr. Marshall." The guy can't keep the awe out of his voice.

There's something off-putting about this. Navarro was right. They want Jinx for something. And also. It's starting to really suck how often Navarro is right.

The least Terminus can do is to make up a halfway believable lie.

Instead.

"The *Perun*," Terminus volunteers. He's trying to sound bored, but there's an edge to his voice. "Copeland wants this stuff loaded in the supply bay."

"He asked *you* to do it?" One of the smaller pairs of boots wiggles around. "Why?" the woman voice.

"The general doesn't ask. He orders," Terminus says. "But feel free to call him. Copeland's in a meeting with Rosenthal. I'm sure he'll be thrilled to be interrupted."

"Okay," the woman says uncertainly. "Maybe one of us should go with him."

"We've got our orders," the third man says.

"Get back to your barracks ASAP, huh, Partridge?" the first man says.

"Right," Terminus says, this time finally achieving the dull tone he's been going for. "Because I really want to hang around in the hallway all night."

The boots resume moving and grow fainter. Our busted, squeaky-wheel cart gets going again. When I can no longer hear people shuffling and chatting, I punch the steel shelf above me.

Ouch.

I make a loud *bong* sound and rub my hand, which kinda throbs.

Terminus leans down. "*Shh!* I can explain."

I'm strangely disappointed by the knowledge that Terminus is a double agent. Not only does it mean that Navarro was right. Again. But also… I thought…

I try to stay mad. "You better!"

QUOTES AND BACKGROUND INFORMATION:
"You like him!"–Jinx Marshall.

Ugh.

I wonder if Navarro and Jinx have noticed that we're gone. What will happen when they figure out we're gone? Is it too late to go back?

But then there's my father.

There is no going back.

I bounce and bop around on the bottom of the cart. All I can see is strips of white wall as it goes by, and it's hard to tell how fast we're going, or how long it's taking. Occasionally, we take a corner or stop at a door. When my scenery changes to the dark glass of the Moon Room, I can see that we're close.

My head hits the shelf as we take the entry ramp to the *Perun*.

"Shh!" Terminus says again.

I rub the top of my head.

Yeah. Sorry if my concussion is bugging you, bro.

We're back in the blue light of the submarine, and queasy jitters churn in my stomach. According to the file, the *Perun* is on its way back to Puerto Peñasco. Once there, the crew will meet my father, who'll take over command of the mission. Not only will we have to hide for more than forty-eight hours on the submarine, but I don't know what will happen when we get to land. Dad will be pissed, and he might not agree to call off this mission.

I feel like I've had ten cups of coffee.

I mostly catch smells. Sea water. Salt. The rubber of cables. Lemon cleaner.

Finally, Terminus stops the cart, moves several of the monitors, and offers me his hand.

I don't take it. Instead, I try to get off the cart on my own, rolling over clumsily onto the floor. We're in a supply room, or maybe a small janitor's closet, that contains stacks of paper towels, toilet paper, a few brooms and a couple of hoses. There's one blue lightbulb on the ceiling in the center of the room.

"You've been spying on us!" I tell him, the instant I can get up off the ground.

"*Shh!*" he says, shaking his head.

I'm so tired of him saying *SHH!* over and over.

I don't want to *SHH!*

I'm about to open my mouth to argue when Terminus grabs my arm. He's still shaking his head. And he whispers, "I was never gonna spy! But I had to say something, or Copeland wasn't gonna let me come." His eyes are unexpectedly earnest when they meet mine. "I had to come."

I'm not sure.

What if Dr. Doomsday was right?

Trust no one.

Except…even Dr. Doomsday didn't believe that.

Plus, it got him killed.

Oh. Also.

Seriously, whoever designed these jumpsuits should be sent to bed without their supper. They are scratchy and uncomfortable, and the whole time I've been wearing one, I've been either too hot or too cold.

"For God's sake," Terminus says, giving me a light shake. He goes on in a tense whisper. "Look at where we are! If I was trying to spy on Jinx, why would I be here? Do you know what's going to happen to me if we get caught?"

I try to wrap my arms around myself in a hug. The truth is, I have no idea what would happen to him or to me. I know only that I don't want to go along with Dr. Doomsday's cynical worldview. That worldview is tearing the world apart.

Doing my best to force myself to relax, I nod. "Okay. So now we wait?"

"No," he says. "We need to get to a computer."

This seems like Jinx's and Terminus's answer to everything, and this room seems as good a place as any to hide. "Why not stay here?"

Terminus slowly opens up the janitor's closet. "Did you ever study submarines and deep sea habitats?"

Nope. Nope. Nope.

I shake my head. I can't see how pointing out the gaps in my reading is going to help us.

He waves his hand and motions for me to follow him.

Voices echo from everywhere, filling the narrow hallways.

My heart thuds violently in my chest.

Terminus takes my hand and drags me after him. My feet flop along like they're hanging from my body. A loud tone sounds over the intercom. I clamp my hand over my own mouth to keep myself from screaming.

All around us, voices get louder.

We take a sharp turn down a narrow corridor that ends abruptly a few feet in front of us. Terminus pushes me as far back into the darkness as we can go. A group of soldiers carrying equipment and packs proceeds down the main hall, passing by without turning our way.

The instant that they're gone, Terminus tugs me back into the hall and pushes me through a door marked with a red square label. I find myself in a beautiful, spacious room, furnished like something out of *Architectural Digest*, Submarine Edition. Everything is still metal and kinda industrial, but the edges are smoothed out. Surfaces are curved and polished. Concern has been given to the comfort of the person who stays here.

The room has a small private shower.

Terminus approaches a wide steel-and-teak desk.

"Where are we?" I ask.

"VIP quarters, I think," he says as he takes a seat at the plush desk chair.

Seeing the expression on my face, he says, "I'm betting that the occupant will be on duty for a while."

"I still don't understand what we're doing here," I say. "We could have hidden with the mops and brooms and been quite comfortable."

He makes a few taps on a touch screen. "Without food, water or a bathroom?"

Ugh. Right.

Jinx, if I ever see you again, I'll apologize for mocking all your survival drills. If you were here, we'd have food, water and jackets. Probably weapons. And probably a plan that's better than sneaking around like overgrown rats and praying no one notices.

"Fine. So that wasn't an ideal hiding spot. I can't imagine that hanging out here and waiting for Copeland to get back is much better."

Terminus types on the keyboard. "We're not hiding here. I need to adjust the expected headcount of the life support systems. Hang on." There's a pause. And then, "Okay. I think that should do it. I hope."

That sounded...not great. "Umm..."

"So back in the old days when people went to deep sea habitats, they had to go through this process of compression and decompression. It meant a couple of days in a special chamber when you arrived down below and more time in another chamber when you returned to land. The *Perun* and SEALAB, they have a system that gradually changes pressure as needed. They're constantly measuring biometrics. Checking vital signs," he says.

Ah. I see.

"If the computer finds more people than it expects..." I take a guess.

"There's probably an alert," he agrees. He's still tapping.

"What are you doing now?"

"Um," he says, staring at the screen. "Looking for a good place to hide. You know. Vacant quarters. Storage rooms. Hmm. The sub is pretty full up."

After a minute, he gets up from the desk. "All right, I think I found the place."

The place is the kitchen food storage area. I nearly have a series of heart attacks while we try to get there, but we make it.

We're able to move a stainless-steel rack of food about eighteen inches from the wall, creating a space for us to hide. We crouch behind massive cans of stewed tomatoes and stacks of cereal boxes.

Then, we wait.

We're slumped behind the cans for several hours, until the kitchen staff comes in and out of the room. Despite the fact that it must be in the middle of the night, they appear to be serving lunch. They're making fruit salad with canned fruit and assembling sandwiches and loading bags of chips into metal containers.

While we wait, I try to do a bit more reading on the e-tablet. Terminus is right about the sub. It's an example of super advanced technology.

Experimental technology.

It's quiet after the meal, and it seems like a good time to get something to eat and drink ourselves. I don't know how long it's been since we had dinner. My throat feels as dry as the desert back in Phoenix.

Terminus suggests that we split up, or at least take turns sneaking around. Getting supplies. Using the bathroom. By *bathroom*, what he actually means is that we'll use the large kitchen sink.

"That's so gross," I tell him.

"Yeah. Well. The nearest bathroom is outside the main control room. We have no idea what the food prep schedule is. We shouldn't take any more risks than necessary," he says in a frustrated whisper.

I leave him cramped and awkward in our makeshift fort while I check things out. Glancing at the sink, I decide to try to hold it until later. I creep around the small kitchen. One of the racks has boxes of protein bars and another is full of bottled water. I'm stuffing the pockets of my dorky jumpsuit when something cold presses to the back of my head.

My blood turns to ice. I've done enough drilling with Jinx to know that it's the barrel of a gun.

Okay. Okay. Um. What was the drill?

I'm gonna get shot.

I'm pretty sure I'm supposed to turn and strike the person's nose with the palm of my hand. Or maybe gut punch or…

"Don't even think about it."

It's Jo. Who hates us, but probably won't kill us.

"Turn around," she says. "Slowly."

Jo steps back a few feet. She's positioned in front of the sink, leaving me in the center of the room. Terminus stays put behind the cereal.

The thing is, Captain Josephine Pletcher, the supreme supersoldier, is scared out of her damn mind. Like, if I had a mirror right now, we'd probably look the same.

Absolute terror fills Jo's eyes. "Don't even tell me that Jinx Marshall is on this sub?" She pokes her head around me, like she expects Jinx to pop out from every corner.

Out of all the things that should concern her, I'm not sure why this thought fills her with such fear.

"No. It's only me. Listen—" I have to figure out a way to get through to her.

She scowls at me. "Where is she?"

"Jinx? Back at SEALAB. But—"

Jo's shoulders relax, but her eyes retain their skeptical squint. "You expect me to believe that the daughter of Maxwell Marshall sent you off on the *Perun*? By yourself?"

My anger flares. "She's not the boss of me! And anyway—"

Jo moves around the kitchen, glancing here and there while also trying to guard me. She peeks behind the rack. "Partridge! Oh perfect."

Terminus climbs out from behind the rack with his hands in the air. "Come on, Jo. Put down the gun. There's nowhere to run and, seriously, are you gonna shoot us?"

Jo presses her lips together like she'd enjoy nothing more than taking us out. She sighs. "All right. Let's go." She waves the gun toward the mess hall.

"Where are we going?" I ask.

"To the general. Where do you think?" she shoots back. But something catches her eye. She ducks behind the rack and returns with our e-tablet.

This is getting better and better.

Terminus and I are in the center of the kitchen as Jo tries to herd us into the mess hall.

Planting my feet firmly on the ground, I stay right in front of her. "You have to listen to me." Even though Terminus gives me a look of warning, I go on, pointing at the e-tablet in her hand. "Back at SEALAB, Jinx got ahold of these files. At Los Alamos, The Opposition knows we're coming. Copeland is sending my father into certain death."

"And…you want me to do…what? Exactly?" she says. Slowly. Coldly.

I wonder what Jinx would have done if she were here.

"All we're trying to do is talk to my dad. Please." I try to catch her gaze. Josephine Pletcher has stubbornly refused to tell us anything about herself. But she must have a father. She must understand how I feel. "Just let us hide until we reach the port."

Terminus's face goes blank. I can't tell what he thinks of my plea.

A mixture of voices fills the mess area. I recognize the cooks from earlier.

But also.

Copeland.

In a second, people will be in here setting up for the next meal service or something, and it won't be possible to hide anymore.

"Please," I whisper.

Terminus shakes his head. A small, barely noticeable gesture.

The seconds tick by as Jo stares at me. "Sir, we have a problem in here," she calls out in a loud clear tone.

Copeland enters the small kitchen with two male soldiers in tow. With his rigid posture, the general seems oddly out of place. No doubt it's been a while since he was on KP. He's wearing an outfit that's similar to ours but way cooler. He's got blue pants and a jacket made out of the same material as our jumpsuits, but a cozy dark navy undershirt.

The two soldiers glance from Jo to us and then to the general.

"If I'm about to find out that Jinx Marshall is on this sub, it's gonna mean someone's ass," Copeland growls. But there's genuine worry behind the tough exterior.

Clearly Jo's concern wasn't misplaced. But why is everyone so freaked about Jinx's whereabouts?

"She's not with us," I tell him.

"Sir," Jo says, in her usual brusque professional manner. "I don't believe Miss Marshall is on board the *Perun*. But I'm about to order both thermal computer and manual sweeps."

"Good. Carry on," Copeland says.

The man at his right asks, "Sir, should I contact SEALAB to confirm Miss Marshall's location? Or alert them to the presence of our stowaways?"

Copeland's angry stare might bore a hole into my forehead. "No. Maintain radio silence. Give Captain Pletcher whatever support she requires."

Jo hands Copeland the e-tablet. "Sir, they had this with them. They say the device is full of files relating to the mission."

The general turns to the two men. "Go up to the control room and request the sweeps that the captain mentioned."

"Yes, sir," the tall man answers. The two of them take off up the corridor.

Copeland waits until the two soldiers are gone before turning to Terminus. "Partridge? You're really turning out to be a pain in my ass. Being in Max Marshall's good graces will only carry you so far, and I think you've reached the limits of the great man's largess." There's a sarcastic edge to these words.

"We know about Operation Turquoise Eagle!" I say with as much energy as I can muster. "My father is walking into a trap."

"Jay Novak understands a great deal more about what's really happening than you do, young lady," he tells me curtly.

His insinuation hits me right in the gut. Dad had been acting so strange. He probaby knew he was on a suicide mission, and he didn't care.

The general hesitates. "And anything else?" he asks.

I can feel the blank expression overtake my face. "You've got a plan to get millions of people killed. What else is there?"

"Nothing," he says, tucking the tablet under his arm.

All of a sudden, I know I have made a terrible mistake. I have really messed up. Something else is going on. I was so impulsive, so rash, that I've screwed up our chance to find out what it is. Worse, we've taken the e-tablet from Jinx, so she has no way of figuring out Copeland's real agenda either.

LEAD: Irresponsible journalist and the guy she sort of wishes was her boyfriend are about to get thrown out of high-tech sub into Pacific Ocean.

Ugh. No one will care. No one would read that story.

"Captain, escort our stowaways to quarters until I decide what action to take."

Copeland is already walking away when Jo answers, "Yes, sir."

She herds us down the hall the same way we came in, toward Copeland's quarters. Our boots land with squeaks and thuds on the metal grated floor.

"It says in that file that the other mission, the one in Portland, is doomed. They don't expect any survivors," I say, trying to match her cold voice.

She walks between Terminus and me and uses an electronic key to open the door on her right. Jo practically pushes us into a comfortable-looking room, similar to Copeland's, but not quite as nice. The kind of place an assistant would stay.

Her lips settle into a hard smile. "For your sake, I hope you're wrong. Jinx Marshall is going on that mission. And your brother? *Captain* Novak? He's leading it."

The last thing I see is her smug expression as the door slams closed. I have messed everything up so bad.

Well. I'm crying.

Again.

Terminus reaches out and pulls me into another hug. "I should have told you before," he says. "She was never gonna help us." The words rumble in his chest. "Her full name is Josephine Pletcher Copeland.

"She's the general's daughter."

The masses are moved by the marvelous. The unlikely. The un-provable. The conspiracy theory. A crowd might follow a hero. But a society needs an icon. And an icon needs magic.

–AMELIA AOKI
Report: *The Image of the Second Civil War*
Stamped: Top Secret

JINX

It's early in the morning when I wake up, crowded with Navarro on the small bunk. Curled up in the space between his chest and the wall.

My neck is cramped. Also, he snores. Still, it's the safest and most secure I've felt since, well, a long time.

I wonder if Charles is alone. If anyone is taking care of him. That thought jolts me awake.

Navarro is already awake too.

"I'll wake up MacKenna." I scoot to the foot of the bed and crawl out, falling onto the floor. "We should decide what to do."

Navarro nods but he reaches out and grabs my hand. "Susan, there's something else," he says in a hoarse whisper. "When we get to Oregon…if we have a chance to destroy that thing… I have to take it. My father died because…"

Because he didn't want that cold fusion bomb to fall into the wrong hands. I give his hand the most reassuring squeeze I can muster. He closes his eyes as I pull the ugly jumpsuit up around my shoulders. Then, I creep into MacKenna's room.

It's perfectly quiet.

The room is sparse and dark with a short, square night table that has an alarm clock with a blue display. According to the clock, it's 6:03 a.m.

But.

Something's wrong.

MacKenna doesn't move or snore or...

Breathe.

I hit the light switch. A cheerful, yellow glow spreads across the room.

The form in Mac's bed has a lumpy rectangular shape. I rip back the scratchy wool blanket to find her pillows arranged in a long mass. Someone put them there to make it look like MacKenna was asleep in her bed.

I race back into Navarro's room.

Poking him several times in the ribs, I say, "MacKenna's gone!"

He yawns and mutters, "What are you talking about?"

I shake him. Hard. "MacKenna's bed is empty."

In a panic, I make a run for the dormitory door. The access panel hangs off like it did when we used the e-tablet to hack the locking mechanism.

I'm ransacking the tiny kitchenette searching for the e-tablet when Navarro emerges, buttoning up his jumpsuit. "Terminus is gone too."

Perfect.

My hands shake. "Someone's taken them."

Navarro takes my hands in his. "No one's taken them. They left, Susan."

Hot anger floods my insides. "How can you say that? We agreed that..."

That we'd stay together.

Navarro takes my hand and guides me to the sofa in the common room. "We're in a secret underwater base at the bottom of the ocean. Where would *they* have taken Terminus and MacKenna? And why?"

Rosenthal and Copeland hadn't wanted Terminus or MacKenna to be a part of the next phase of our mission. But they didn't seem particularly bothered by the idea either. Still, they aren't being honest, and there is more happening here than we understand.

We have to find MacKenna.

Now.

I'm about to jump up from the sofa when Navarro grips both my hands in his.

"Think about it," he says. "Terminus has been with Copeland for months. Why kidnap him now? Why bother putting the pillows in the bed? That was clearly designed to fool us. Why am *I* still here? You heard what Jo said." His eyebrows arch with worry. "They'd like nothing better than to dispense with me. But here I am."

The angry energy drains out of me. Part of me can't believe that MacKenna would leave us here.

Leave me here.

I shake my head. "It could be a trick. Designed to get us to cooperate or..."

Navarro fiddles with the top button of the jumpsuit. "You really think Rosenthal needs to trick us into cooperating? What choice do we have *but* to cooperate?"

The idea of someone deliberately fiddling with the alarm

panel to mess with us did sound pretty stupid. My arms flop down in defeat.

"No offense, Susan, but I warned you about this," he continues. "That day at the gas station. MacKenna's impulsive. Reactionary. And we don't know anything about Harold Partridge's real agenda."

That day at the gas station seems like a lifetime ago. But MacKenna left us then too. For Jay.

I frown at Navarro as warm anger flares in the pit of my stomach. "So you're saying, I told you so? That's the best you've got?"

He ignores this. "I'm thinking the same thing. MacKenna found something on that device related to her father. Then didn't stick around long enough to share it with us." Navarro can't keep the frustration out of his voice.

How does he always seem to know what I'm thinking?

And.

What do we do now?

"We need to think," I say. I hate to admit it, but since we left the bunker, we've lost control of our own fate. We're at the mercy of Copeland or Rosenthal. People we don't know and can't trust. "We need a new plan." I don't wait for him to remind me that he thought our original plan was doomed to failure. "Let's assume we're right. MacKenna wanted to help Jay. That means she and Terminus snuck out of here and onto the *Perun*?"

The sub was, after all, the only place to go.

Navarro brushes a random clump of blue hair off my face, leaving a trail of warmth that lingers on my cheek. "I think that's the only explanation. The fact that no one has shown up looking for them probably means they're on their way topside."

We're quiet for a minute.

"What specifically did they tell you in the briefing?" Navarro asks.

I shrug. "They've brought in a marketing consultant to turn me into a war hero. Or the idea of a war hero. You're going to handle the camerawork. Rosenthal said we'd spend the next week or so in training."

"Okay. Okay," Navarro mutters.

Suddenly, what we need to do becomes clear. "All right. We need to go back to sleep." Or pretend to sleep anyway. "When they get here this morning, we've got to act surprised."

"Okay," Navarro says.

"Then we train. Go along with what they say. But we need to steal whatever equipment we can. Find out whatever we can. Then. When we get back on land, we make a break for it."

"Agreed." He leans over to kiss my forehead. "There's one thing though."

"What?"

He squints. "It has to be just us. We can't trust Toby. He's one of them."

Mom is off running the evil empire. Dad is dead. Jay and MacKenna are gone. Toby is the only family I have left.

"Gus... I'm not sure. For all we know, he's off with MacKenna right now." That thought stings in a way I wasn't prepared for.

"Maybe," Navarro says. "But we don't tell him anything until we're sure one way or the other. I need your word on that."

"Okay," I say with a nod.

Navarro goes over all the likely scenarios, but in broad

strokes we agree to wait until someone mentions MacKenna and then be shocked to find her missing. We fix the alarm panel, put the pillows back the way we found them and then sit there for a while in silence.

Eventually there's nothing left to do but go back to our own rooms and wait to be escorted to breakfast. There are a few pairs of sweats and blue T-shirts in the closet that look more comfortable than the jumpsuit. After I change, I toss and turn alone on my own bunk. I can't relax. My mind drifts. I try not to think too much about what just happened between me and Gus. I find myself thinking about the old nights in our house in Rancho Mesa. The summer storms of the monsoon would blow the branches of the mesquite tree against my window. Sounding like jagged pointy fingernails. Something terrible. Trying to get in.

My mom would wrap me in a blanket and plop me on the couch in between her and my dad. They'd be there, working on their laptops, and I'd fall asleep with the rain coming down, safe between the two of them. Knowing nothing was coming to get me. Mom would kiss me on the forehead.

Was any of it real?

Or was my mother always a sleeper?

Always pretending.

A little before seven, I hear the door to the dorm open and someone moving around in the common room. I open the door to my room a crack and peek out. It's Toby.

He's casually making a cup of coffee using the small pot in the kitchenette. Not the demeanor of someone whose sister is off on an experimental submarine.

I fluff up my hair, scrunch up one leg of my sweats and make a big show of stumbling out into the common room.

"Morning," Toby says. Bland. The way that you'd greet an old acquaintance.

Not a family member.

He takes his coffee and sits on the sofa. There's a large plastic binder and a stack of e-tablets on the table in front of him.

"Hi." I yawn out the greeting and sink into the armchair.

Navarro comes out a minute later carrying two cups of coffee. He hands me one of the cups. He's put cream in the coffee. The way I like it.

Toby picks up the binder. "We should get started. Breakfast service ends at 08:00. Where's Mac? And…uh…what's his name?"

"Terminus," Navarro says.

In some ways, I think Navarro's got it easier than me. He's always surly and brooding. It's up to me to carry shocked and surprised, despite the fact that my insides are jiggling like a bowl of potato salad.

I shrug and yawn again. "Asleep, I guess. She must have been tired, because she was already in bed when I came back from the briefing."

Toby rises and moves toward the closed bedroom door. "Mac? Mac?"

Either this is the acting performance of the decade, or Toby has no idea that his sister took off. Navarro gets up as well and heads to Terminus's room. To continue the theater of acting like we expect to find him.

Toby skids into the common room. "Okay. What the hell is going on? Where's Mac?"

"What do you mean?" I ask. I go into MacKenna's room, open the small closet, forage around in her bunk, checking under the pillows and blankets.

"She's not here!" Toby says with a mixture of panic and shock.

Navarro enters Mac's room as well. "Terminus is gone too."

Toby whirls around to face Navarro. "What the hell are you talking about?" Then he turns back to me. "You're telling me that my sister is gone? That she took off without saying anything to you?"

"Did *your sister* say anything to *you*?" I shoot back.

He looks like I've punched him. But. We're both thinking the same thing.

MacKenna didn't trust Toby enough to even say goodbye.

And then.

"What the hell am I going to tell the general?"

Those words are like a knife against my throat.

Toby runs his hand though his cropped hair. His eyes are lit up with horror. That's his concern. Nothing about his sister. Or about me.

"I thought Copeland left," I say.

"He'll obviously be back," Toby snaps.

Navarro was right.

Toby is one of them.

And we are on our own.

Jinx always hated Dr. Doomsday's drills.

But it's getting harder and harder to pretend that those plans weren't the only things keeping us alive.

–MacKENNA NOVAK,
Letters from the Second Civil War

MacKENNA

Terminus has now beaten me at sixty-seven consecutive games of checkers.

"It's one of the first programs I wrote," he explains. "I had to memorize common moves to create the program's AI."

Then we play poker. Then crazy eights. Then hearts.

LEAD: Being trapped on a submarine is really boring.

Scratch that. There's no story here.

I let the story get away from me. Literally. Jo carried the e-tablet off, and I watched it go.

They've kept us in this room on the *Perun* the whole time. A soldier always guards the door. Our meals are delivered. Sometimes by Jo, who always seems to enjoy ignoring my questions. Sometimes we hear Copeland's voice outside the door. His room is near ours. His tone is always brusque. Orderly.

I can't make out his words through the heavy steel door.

The only upside is that Jinx isn't here to make me feel like an idiot. Somewhere out there she's trapped in her usual shame spiral of blaming herself for everything. Somewhere out there, Navarro is pacing around and making that brooding vampire face and muttering to himself about what idiots we are.

At least I'm not there to listen to it.

QUOTES AND BACKGROUND INFORMATION:
"Do what you have to do in order to survive." –Dr. Doomsday.

"So, you didn't see anything in the files?" I ask Terminus. Again.

The first fifty times or so that I asked him, he was pretty chill.

But now.

Barely able to contain his annoyance, he drums his fingers on the small table where we've set up the sixty-eighth game of checkers. "No. Jinx was at the terminal in the records office, and we were barely in there two minutes." He pushes a black checker forward in an opening move he told me is called Old Faithful. "And no. For the last time, back at Fort Marshall, they didn't tell me anything about their plans."

I frown at him and move my own checker, which he immediately captures. "They must have said something."

He grunts. "They said a lot of somethings. Except it was all like, 'The lights are off in A.' Or, 'The backup generator is coming on too frequently.' Or, 'My workstation won't let me log in to the mainframe.' Or, 'We're not getting a signal for the—'"

"Got it!" I say as he takes another one of my checkers. "You think—"

"Yes. I think they're fine," he says.

"You had access to the computers. Back at Fort Marshall," I say. It sounds like an accusation.

His eyes meet mine. They're a deep shade of blue. His shoulders tense. "All the interesting stuff was in an encrypted partition. I didn't have the tech I needed to hack it. Jinx might have been able to log in. It seemed like Marshall left her all the systems permissions. But Copeland was hell-bent on keeping her away from a terminal."

I try to sound casual. Not like the acid of worry is chewing away at my insides. "Navarro said he thinks Copeland is gonna kill Jinx."

Terminus relaxes and smiles. He's got a cute little dimple on his left cheek. "Navarro seems like the type of guy who can't be happy unless he thinks a hundred people are out to kill him before breakfast."

"They don't know what we know," I say, finally voicing what's been eating me up. "About the mission." About the futility of it.

"It doesn't matter to them," Terminus says, focusing on the board. "They're not sending Jinx to Los Alamos. She'll be fine."

"Where are they sending her?"

Terminus doesn't answer, and the tension of the question remains in the air.

A chill comes over me. I go over to the bed and return with the wool blanket as Terminus captures yet another of my pieces. "I think we're emerging," he says.

To me, the motion of the sub is almost undetectable.

"The temperature," he says. "You ever notice how quickly we get warm or cold? The computer is constantly making adjustments to pressure and oxygen levels. But it's not perfect. When there's a change in depth, there can be a bit of a lag in the system."

I nod. Sometimes it's hard not to feel like Terminus might know more than he's letting on. Sometimes I worry that Jinx is right. That Terminus can't be trusted.

MacKenna, you can't think about that. Seriously.

Terminus risked everything to come with me. Now he's the only friend I have.

There's a knock at the door.

It's Jo. She's back in her uniform with her hair twisted into a neat knot. "You're relieved," she says to the man standing at our door.

"Yes, ma'am," he says, leaving in the direction of the control room.

It's busy in the passageway. People are coming in and out of the general's room. Terminus must be right. We're almost at the port. I hold the door open so that Jo can come in. But she remains in the cramped narrow passageway. A soldier carrying an armful of gear has to squeeze around her.

"We'll be topside in thirty minutes," she says. "I'm on guard duty until then."

She reaches to close the door.

I put my foot out so she can't. "You tell that undertaker of a father of yours to get down here and tell us what the hell is going on."

At the mention of the fact that Copeland is her father, the smirk slides off Jo's face. "Take that up with your own dad. You'll be seeing the colonel in about an hour."

The colonel. At least walking into certain death earns you a promotion.

She pulls more firmly on the door, giving me a split second to yank my foot out of the way before it slams shut.

My heart drops.

Because I realize.

I have to face Dad.

We leave the *Perun* via a hatch in the center of the submarine that leads to a flat-top deck wide enough for us all to stand on. We're a short distance away from a small wooden pier in front of a beach house. The scene is eerily similar to the location where Stephanie shot Dr. Doomsday.

It might even be the same beach.

But today there is no man flying a kite. No kids with a ball.

The beach is empty.

I grip the railing to avoid being blown into the water by the heavy winds. Salt water sprays me in the face. The sub people have waterproof boots and jackets. Terminus and I are getting soaked.

Maybe I'll get swept into the sea before Dad can, like, yell at me.

If we survive this whole ordeal, I'm gonna go live in a cornfield in Nebraska or someplace where I never have to look at the ocean again.

We have to take turns being ferried to the shore by a motorboat that comfortably holds only about fifteen people. From the boat, I can already see my father's tall form standing on the dock. His posture is stiff. His anger easy to see even from a hundred feet away.

Terminus helps me off the boat and onto the pier.

I'm dripping wet and my teeth are chattering.

The boat motor continues to roar for a minute and then

cuts out, leaving the air quiet except for the chatter of a few soldiers and more distant shouts coming from the *Perun*.

My father meets me at the end of the pier. He's dressed in green camo fatigues with a NOVAK name patch on the left side and some kind of insignia on his arm. He's also got a gun in a shoulder holster.

No hug. No greeting.

"What the hell do you think you're doing?" he says.

"D-D-D-ad... I..." My shivers render me incoherent.

Dad's shoulders slump, and he finally hugs me. "I told you to stay with Jinx."

I fight back tears. "You...told...me...you were staying... at Fort...Marshall."

Except...he never really did say that, did he.

"Come on," Dad says. He takes my hand and draws me onto the beach. To Terminus, Dad says, "There's food and supplies in the main house. We'll meet you there shortly."

Dad points to a large stately mansion about a quarter mile away from the pier. It's white, at least two stories and flanked by dozens of tall palm trees that sway in the breeze. The place is perfect for the billionaire owner of a tequila factory.

The house is surrounded by an ornate iron fence.

"There's a gate on the far side," Dad says. He has to talk loud over the wind. "Hopefully they'll recognize you."

We walk in that direction together. Soldiers from the sub pass us, moving with a greater sense of purpose. We arrive at a small pastel-blue tent. Dad motions for Terminus to keep going while he holds the tent flap open for me.

He doesn't wait for me to explain. "You have to go back to Fort Marshall."

LEAD: Retired ex-army major wants to sacrifice self for his children.

No. No. That wasn't the story.

LEAD: Father wants to atone for the past.

For Mom's death. For marrying Stephanie. For everything. *But, Dad. You can't fix this.*

"Copeland is sending you into a trap," I say as calmly as I can. "The Opposition knows you're coming."

His eyes are unexpectedly cold. "You disobeyed me, smuggled yourself on board Copeland's submarine and ran over here to tell me that? Los Alamos is a top-secret research facility. *Of course* it will be well guarded."

My anger flares. "I mean, Jinx stole a bunch of files off some computer at SEALAB. They were full of all kinds of information about your mission. They *know* you have almost zero chance of survival. The real point of your mission is to start a big war. Copeland thinks that The Opposition will be able to get those cold fusion bombs to work before you get there. He lied to you."

Dad's face becomes hard. "Really? Because I don't recall seeing you there when he briefed me."

The fire of my anger is extinguished like a candle whose flame has been blown out. All the oxygen has been sucked out of the tent. My pulse flutters.

He knew he was gonna die.

"Wait. Wait…" I stutter. "You…you…"

"Actually, MacKenna," Dad says, not waiting for me to finish, "it's *you* who lied. You promised me that you'd stay with your brother. That you'd keep yourself safe."

"Toby's now a walking G.I. Joe doll," I say. *Who is off on his own mission to find Annika Carver.*

From the pier, the boat motor cranks on, creating new noise in the tent.

Dad raises his voice. "You're going back to Fort Marshall. Wait there until—"

"Until what? You're dead?"

"Until this is all over."

This will never be over.

I make one last attempt to reason with him. "There's something wrong with all of this. Something wrong with the other mission too."

This gets his attention. "What do you mean? What did you see?"

For the thousandth time, I want to kick myself for not hiding that e-tablet. "I didn't *see* anything. But I know that..."

Honestly, what do I really know?

IMPORTANT FACTS:
-The e-tablet contained all the important facts.

"I know there's something wrong with that mission," I finish lamely.

Dad makes the same face as he used to when I'd try to convince him that my doll had a cold. "It's dangerous. But I have to do whatever I can to make sure it's successful. Because Toby's on that mission. And so is Jinx."

A wave of horror washes over me as the story races through my mind.

IMPORTANT FACTS:
-Toby, Jinx and Navarro are on a super dangerous mission.

-Jay Novak agreed to go to Los Alamos because he thought the rest of his family was going to AIRSTA.

-The rest of his family included me.

OTHER IMPORTANT FACTS:
-MacKenna Novak is the worst.

-The. Actual. Worst.

Dad and Jinx and Navarro and even Toby are fighting to save the world and fighting for each other and I...am gonna be sitting on my ass in a cave while everyone else risks their lives.

As if sensing my thoughts, Dad puts a gentle hand on my arm. "You always try to do right. You came here to help me. You have such a passion for helping others and a fierce self-lessness. Don't change that. But for now, you have to promise me that you'll go back to Fort Marshall."

He stares at me. I open my mouth, but nothing comes out. "Promise me," he presses.

"I promise."

As I say the words, I know they're a lie.

The main house is strange. Like, it was obviously built to be some rich person's vacation retreat but has been completely overtaken by a military operation. Folding tables are crammed into every room, their metal legs scraping against the ivory travertine tile. Plush, oversize sofas and chairs are pushed against the walls and into the corners of each room.

I'm on the second floor, in the master bathroom, where first aid kits and boxes of generic supplies like razors and shaving cream and tampons are stacked on opulent marble countertops. There's a walk-in closet where five-thousand-dollar suits and resort wear dresses probably used to hang that's being used as a uniform dispensary.

I've got five minutes to change into dry clothes. I have to choose from the spare stuff in the supply cabinet. It's a bunch of random things that people have left behind. Nothing really fits, and I end up with jeans that have to be rolled up at the ankles and cinched with a belt, a University of Indiana T-shirt that's a size too small and a purple jacket with a large hole in one sleeve. It's got a name written on it in marker.

MARSHALL.

I doubt this used to belong to Dr. Doomsday. But after everything we've been through, this small thing feels like an act of defiance.

Or a lucky talisman.

Terminus is pacing around at the base of the dramatic circular staircase. He has changed, too, although he managed to find better stuff. He's got a basic gray sweatshirt and a pair of cargo shorts. He leans on the railing and opens his mouth like something romantic should come out. Except we're not in *that* movie.

As I arrive at the bottom of the stairs, a door opens and Dad emerges from a room that was maybe the family game room or something. I think I see a pinball machine back there. He clamps a hand on Terminus's shoulder.

"It's time," Dad says.

He ushers us through a large kitchen with posh steel appliances and out a side door.

A man in khakis is about ten feet away from us with his back to the house, smoking a cigarette. The wind puffs his hair into a pompadour as he turns.

Galloway.

He salutes Dad.

"At ease," Dad tells him.

It's weird how quickly my father has fallen back into his military routines.

Together, the five of us walk to the end of the driveway. The Land Rover we took to meet the *Booker* sits there with the bright-colored surfboards still mounted to the roof. Someone must have returned to the pier and driven the car back here.

Dad nods at Galloway. "Escort my daughter to the safe house and wait there for further instructions."

Galloway glares at me but says, "Yes, sir."

We approach the car and Dad hugs me again, the same way he did when we left for the *Booker*. But it means something different now.

Maybe Dad has decided to sacrifice himself for me and for Toby and for Jinx and the mission. But he can stuff it if he thinks I'll go along with his plan. I'm gonna do whatever I have to do to figure out what Copeland is really up to. Whatever I can to make sure we survive.

All of us.

LEAD: Student journalist decides to write her own story.

Terminus eyes me suspiciously as I get into the front passenger seat. Normal MacKenna would have taken the backseat and spent the drive scribbling on a scrap of paper. But I have to do what Jinx would do.

We have to get rid of Galloway.

He steers the car out of the drive and onto a cul-de-sac. The road has been freshly paved, and two other enormous houses are on the street. I have the sudden idea that, all over the world, these kinds of places are exactly the same. I catch a glimpse of a soldier in fatigues crouched down on the coral roof of the house across the street.

The Spark has commandeered this neighborhood.

Galloway turns onto a wider street and speeds up past a large market.

Behind us, the ocean scenery begins to fade in the rearview mirror. It's gradually replaced by thicker vegetation and deep green trees. It's late in the afternoon when we hit the highway back to Quintana Roo. I recognize a few landmarks on the road. A fruit stand that advertises beef jerky. A billboard for a beach resort.

Wait for it. Wait for it. Wait for it.

Eventually we hit the Sonoran highway toward Santa Ana.

Terminus tries to make conversation. "How are things back at the base?"

"Boring," Galloway says after a long pause.

You'd think the guy would be thanking us for saving him from certain death. "You seem awfully pissed for someone who's gonna be sleeping in a comfy bunk tomorrow instead of being shot at by The Opposition."

He glares at me again. "I volunteered because I want to do something important. Not babysit the colonel's disobedient children."

Ugh.

Cars on the highway become fewer and less frequent. The farther we go into Mexico, the longer it's gonna take us to get back to the border.

It has to be now.

Too bad. I always liked Galloway.

Right now.

Galloway is bigger. Stronger. Better prepared.

Jinx once told me that all you really need is nerve.

Nerve.

MacKenna, you must become nerve.

I turn to the side and catch Terminus's eye. He shakes his head. It's subtle. Like he knows what I want to do and is warning against it.

Galloway stares straight ahead. Watching the road.

I. Am. Nerve.

Drawing in a deep breath, I use the palm of my hand to hit Galloway in the face, thrusting up from under his nose.

The Land Rover veers toward the shoulder. I grab the steering wheel while Galloway mumbles something.

"What the fuck is wrong with you?"

That's what he says.

I'm asking myself that question too. My heart thuds in my chest. You can probably hear it beating from the moon.

Terminus leans forward. He's got his sweatshirt off and uses the sleeve to put Galloway in a choke hold. I'm surprised he's going along with this. In for a dime, in for a dollar, I guess.

The car is slowing down, and we're swerving from side to side as Galloway pulls at the sleeve around his throat and Terminus breathes heavily and I. Can't. Breathe.

We've got maybe a minute before Galloway is back in control.

Leaning over him, I reach for the lock of the driver's side door. Galloway keeps struggling with Terminus but frees one of his hands to grab my hair. Among my other problems, I'm probably gonna be bald.

Now's not the time for that, Mac.

I ignore the sharp jabs of pain as my hair is ripped from my scalp. I'm able to get the driver's door unlocked and open. The door bounces open and shut a couple of times before I shove it with enough force that it remains open.

Terminus thrusts his upper body into the center of the front seat. He presses Galloway in the direction of the open door. The soldier waves his arms wildly and tries to gag out a few words.

Are we really gonna toss Galloway into the street like a stack of old newspapers?

Do what you have to do in order to survive.

Am I following Dr. Doomsday's rules now?

I kick Galloway in the side. Hard. With all the energy I can muster. At the same time, Terminus gives Galloway a solid push, and the two of us are able to get the soldier out of the car. He skids along the gravel for a few feet as the car rolls slowly down the almost deserted road.

Terminus scrambles over the seat, slides behind the wheel, shuts the door.

He hits the gas hard.

The old engine roars.

In the rearview mirror, I can see Galloway get up. He chases the car for a few paces in a useless gesture. He's mad as hell. But he'll live.

"Well…that…was…something," I pant.

I rub my scalp to confirm I still have hair. My gut aches and my head aches and everything aches.

LEAD: Journalist and hacker steal car and go it alone.
IMPORTANT FACTS:
-None.

Terminus grips the steering wheel hard. It takes him a minute to regain his breath. "We have to get off the main road. We need to ditch this car. They're gonna come looking for us."

"Who?" I ask.

"Everyone."

Le Bon said that political influence is a matter of prestige. Crowds follow famous faces. When he said this, it might have been true. Between then and now, information began to flow at a pace the likes of which the Frenchman could never have imagined. The happy hometown mayor can be evil in the next news cycle. A powerful person is a few downvotes from being completely forgotten. Today, building the model of a hero on a foundation of prestige is akin to placing a statue on a pillar of sand.

Jinx Marshall, the reluctant hero, the girl with no real purpose other than the almost laughably simple notion of getting her brother "back," wields the inherited authority of the patriarchy. The king of doomsday has died and passed the scepter her way.

The beauty of Dr. Maxwell's reputation is that no one agrees on what he did, who he worked for or what he believed. He's gone. He's everywhere.

His prestige can't be taken away.

Because it doesn't really exist.

—AMELIA AOKI
Report: *The Image of the Second Civil War*
Stamped: Top Secret

JINX

I'm getting a logo.

MacKenna is gone and I'm in an advertising meeting.

It's early in the morning, we're going over the "branding" of our mission. I get to choose from three final logo designs *workshopped by the team*. Amelia displays them on the screen in a room that was intended for research but has been hastily converted to a conference room. We're crammed together at a high blue table, similar to what we had in our biology class, while pieces of scientific equipment have been stacked in the corner next to the screen.

"We need to make sure that you're not perceived as being associated with any state sanctioned authorities," Amelia tells us. This is why we don't get to wear the uniform of the New United States Provisional Army or talk about The Spark in any of our official videos.

Which is fine because I have no idea what I'd say about The Spark and MacKenna isn't around to explain everything.

With every passing moment, I'm reminded of how much I depended on her.

The first logo appears in front of us. It's a stupid-looking tilted *J*, beveled in bronze. The second one is a cartoony bomb in orange, similar to the cover of Dad's book.

Amelia makes a face at the sight of it. "Obviously the team came up with that one before the events in California. It's probably not a great fit now."

Yeah. Probably not.

It's the four of us in the briefing room. Me, Navarro, Toby and Amelia. Seeing Amelia outside of Rosenthal's war room, it's clear that she's much younger than I originally thought. She's probably around Toby's age. Like yesterday, she's wearing her own clothes, but today she's far more casual. She's got her black hair up in a neat topknot.

I want to ask why she gets to wear jeans and a cashmere T-shirt while the rest of us are stuck in these scratchy, ugly jumpsuits.

Amelia presses a button on the remote on the table in front of her.

The third logo fades onto the screen.

This one is the best. It's a silver bird. They've created a little animation loop of light flashing across the metallic surface.

"What is it?" I ask.

"A Cooper's hawk," Amelia says, reading off an e-tablet. "According to our brief, you're from Arizona, right? I guess they have those in the desert?"

Navarro rests his elbow on the table and leans forward. "We do," he says, placing his hand on his chin. "They hunt by concealing themselves in the brush and then catching their prey by total surprise."

Amelia looks at the screen. "Well, I think the pattern on their feathers is so attractive."

"We'd find them sometimes. When we hunted," Navarro says. I can tell that the *we* means him and his father. "They'd have broken chest bones or fractured wings from diving through the bushes."

Amelia makes a few more taps on her device. "I don't think the team went that deep with their research." She replaces the image of the logo on the screen with video of several hawks in flight. They have gorgeous brown-and-white-striped feathers and long tails that sweep the blue sky as the birds glide along gracefully.

I stare at the screen. "They're…beautiful."

"They're reckless," Navarro says flatly.

I flush at the sound of his voice. We exchange a quick glance.

"That sounds about right," Toby adds with a glare.

I don't know what passed between Toby and his commanders after we discovered that MacKenna was gone. But whatever it was, he blames us for it.

Navarro glares back. "If you get too close to their nests, they dive-bomb with enough power to knock a grown man to the ground."

"That sounds about right," I say, trying to lighten the mood.

It doesn't work.

Sigh.

"Well, if we really need a logo. Then…it has to be the hawk," I say.

"Perfect," Amelia says. She makes a couple of taps on her e-tablet.

The image on the screen changes to the ridiculous drawing of me that I'd seen during the meeting with Rosenthal. Words, glowing in blue, surround the picture of my face.

POWER. POISE. POSTURE. PRESTIGE. POLITICS.

She shines a laser pointer over POLITICS. "I put *Politics* on there as a decoy." Amelia stares right at me when she speaks. "Your mission can't be perceived as political. You need to stay on message. Make sure people think you're trying to get your brother back."

My face heats up. "I *am* trying to get my brother back."

"Good. Yes. Exactly," she says with an enthusiastic nod. "Stay with that. Our research indicates that crowds respond positively to the brother story. The dead dad angle is fine too. The main thing is to avoid seeming like you're trying to assist The Spark."

My hands ball into fists.

Navarro shakes his head in confusion. "But we *are* assisting The Spark."

"Yes." Amelia brushes a stray lock of hair off her neck. "But our focus groups were found to be more persuadable by heroes whose actions align with the principles of The Spark but who resist entrenched political affiliations. We think this explains the ongoing popularity of Dr. Marshall. According to our polling, even among people who generally dislike him, Maxwell Marshall has been able to retain his image as honest and credible."

"According to your polling?" I repeat. "The Opposition has been building a cold fusion bomb and The Spark has been *polling*?"

Amelia gets up from the table and hands out the e-tablets. As she passes Toby, she gives him an *I told you so* look.

So there it is. Us and them.

"Okay. Now, let's talk about our mission," she says, coming to stand next to the screen.

The slide changes to the word POWER in neon lettering. It pulses and flickers.

Navarro and I exchange a look.

We have our own mission.

And it begins now.

The next day, Toby and Navarro argue over who's in charge while I do POISE! Apparently, I slouch, mumble, say "um" way too much, use too many "filler words," make unattractive resting faces and have no inflection when I talk.

Amelia films me and has me monitor my own image on a large screen. At least my dad never made me stare at my own giant head. "I need a more active face," she says. "You need to look engaged, even when you're not speaking. A sentence should flow like a roller coaster. Level inflection in the beginning, upward inflection in the middle and then end on a down note to show that you're confident in your message."

So…basically I'm becoming a walking state fair attraction.

I finally get a computer. It's been so long since I had a machine that wasn't one of the awful beige boxes, my pulse flutters in excitement. It's a sleek, thin laptop made from a white titanium. The metal is cool under my fingertips.

"I hope you know I went out on a limb to get this for you," Amelia tells me as she hands it over. She's dressed in yet another casual, comfortable outfit. "A lot of people think that letting you have access to a computer without a high level of supervision is a really bad idea."

At these words, Toby makes a sanctimonious little nod.

Clearly, he's one of the people.

Amelia smiles. "But I think it's essential for the success of our mission for you to be able to practice ahead of time." She hangs on to the computer a couple of seconds longer than necessary. "Don't make me regret it."

My heart drops a little.

She almost certainly will regret it.

Sort of.

I mean, it's nice to finally have a machine in my possession, but there's nothing much I can really do with it. Someone has tried to mimic Dad's security programs and his file architecture. But whoever they got to do it didn't understand my father's work. I seriously doubt he'd set up the systems at AIRSTA or Los Alamos this way. And it's not like I need to practice using their file upload system. My dad had us work on more complicated utilities at computer camp in the third grade.

After a dinner of macaroni and cheese, I set up the laptop on the coffee table in the common room. I managed to swipe a network cable from the break room, and I find a data port behind the sofa. I'm able to access the drives I saw on the research office computer. A handful of folders appear on the screen, but they're empty.

Someone deleted all the files.

Navarro leans in toward me. He makes the generic soap we're both using smell incredible.

"I'm guessing there used to be data in those files?" he asks, checking out my screen.

I nod and make a few more clicks. "Whoever deleted them knew what they are doing. They did a secure erase and re-populated the server with garbage data. There's almost no way to recover anything."

"MacKenna got caught," Navarro says.

He has to be right. It's the logical conclusion. Copeland,

or someone working for him, must have confiscated the e-tablet. That's how they knew to delete the data.

"Or betrayed," I say. We can't trust Terminus. "This is my fault. Maybe if we hadn't been…" My face flushes at the memory of the night MacKenna disappeared.

"It's not our fault. She could have told us what she planned to do. She didn't have to take Terminus. It was her choice," he says.

We're always making choices.

That's what MacKenna told me back in the desert.

I don't know what to say to Navarro. He looks so young and sweet and perfect. I transfer the papers to the table, cover him with one of the scratchy wool blankets and turn off the lamp.

Navarro and I are awoken early by a loud knock from two soldiers who haul us off to the break room before we can shower or even brush our teeth. We eat breakfast in silence.

Rosenthal's creepy assistant, Brian, approaches the table in the mess hall where Navarro and I sit alone. I'm chewing a mouthful of oatmeal and can't really do much of anything besides grunt a greeting.

It's left to Navarro to say, "Morning," as I nod along.

"Finish up," Brian says curtly. "We're convening the official mission briefing."

I gobble up the last of my breakfast and join a crowd that includes Navarro, Toby, Amelia and several soldiers. We walk down the white hall to the area that contains Rosenthal's quarters. The president is seated at the same table as when I last saw him. He's dressed the same. Neat slacks. A polo shirt in another pastel color. This time, mint green.

A male soldier stands near the door and another sits at the

table two seats from the president. E-tablets have been placed at every seat at the glossy table. Rosenthal motions for us to sit down.

"Time to save the world," he says.

I take the same seat I had five days ago. Across from Rosenthal.

Brian remains standing. "We're sending you in with our top guys," he says cheerfully. "Our very best!"

Navarro freezes for a second before sliding into the chair next to me.

"They're not all guys," Rosenthal clarifies.

"Correct, sir," Brian says. He moves to the front of the room and begins his presentation. My hawk logo appears on the projection screen.

We go over the schematics of AIRSTA. Which parts are believed to be abandoned. Which are occupied. Based on satellite imaging, Rosenthal's people have a good idea which buildings have power and water and security. Which access roads are usable. Which routes are heavily monitored. But Carver took the satellite grid off-line when he implemented the Steel Curtain, so their intel is a month old and they don't know how many troops may have been deployed there since the war officially began.

We work until lunch. Brian ends the briefing with and enthusiastic, "Tomorrow, you'll hit the ground running!" like we're about to get on a tour bus and participate in a track meet.

Navarro and I are given box meals and sent back to the dorm. The instant we're back in the room, I hit the bathroom. I take a quick shower and change into my sweats. When I come back out, Navarro is sitting on the sofa, opening a bag of chips and studying the diagrams of AIRSTA.

He glances up, and I almost melt under the intensity of his gaze.

I shiver.

"Okay," he says, pushing my box dinner across the table in my direction. "Let's assume that Rosenthal is lying about everything. What do we actually know?"

I've been thinking about this as well. I flop down on the sofa next to him. "Nothing. We don't even know that my brother is actually at AIRSTA. In fact, based on the schematics, it seems like an odd place to hold him."

Navarro stares out in space for a second. "Agreed," he says with a sigh. "And Rosenthal...his plan...they're setting us up to fail." He drums his fingers on the table.

Opening my box, I pick through a cheesesteak sandwich, bag of veggie chips, apple and a carton of juice. "You mean because The Opposition is expecting us?" I ask.

He rubs his chin, thinking hard. "Well, they clearly placed Charles on that base so we'd come there. But remember when Jay said there were about 160 troops stationed at AIRSTA?"

"Yeah." We haven't seen Jay in almost a week.

He puts his sandwich on the low table and tries to cut through it with a plastic knife. "Let's assume that's a pretty good baseline estimate of what we'll encounter when we get there. And Copeland is sending us in with a platoon, four squads of eight people."

I can't stop staring at him. Why does he look so much better in his jumpsuit than I ever do?

Focus.

Rosenthal is giving us enough people to attract notice... but not enough to win.

"The Opposition will be expecting us. We'll make a lot of noise," I agree. I fight off the uneasy feeling in my chest.

"Right." Navarro drops his sandwich and takes my hand. "What would Dr. Marshall do?"

It's a rhetorical question. Almost an admission that we're already overpowered.

But.

"Don't put your fate in the hands of your enemy."

"Rule fourteen," Navarro agrees. "Right, Dr. Marshall would get away. Risky though."

A cold resignation settles over me. "The briefing doesn't really change anything. The Spark only wants us to die at the right time. We have to stick with our plan to get away."

"We'll be going it alone. No backup," he says.

That was something else that had been bothering me.

"Back there. In Quintana Roo. It was Fort Marshall. Not Fort Copeland or Fort Rosenthal. That's why they need us. There are people out there still loyal to my father."

Navarro nods slowly.

"What we really need to do is get away from...everyone," I say.

Navarro draws in a deep breath before dropping my hand and returning to his cheesesteak. "It's gonna be rough. And we'll have to..."

Go without Toby.

"I know."

"Tomorrow, then," he says.

Tomorrow we get away.

I didn't know what to make of our meetings with Rosenthal. Or of The Spark's continued association with the warmonger Harlan Copeland. There was this question that I couldn't bear to ask myself.

What if, in the end, political parties are incapable of putting a stop to the injustices they themselves are busy creating?

–MacKENNA NOVAK,
Letters from the Second Civil War

MacKENNA

We drive in silence for about ten minutes.

"I thought you said we needed to get off the main road," I say.

Terminus rolls his eyes. "Sure. Any idea where we should turn? Or where we're going?"

Okay. Um. No.

"So how exactly can I get on the planning committee for our little adventures? Is there an application process? Do I need references?" He tries to keep it light, but it doesn't work. There's an edge to his words.

"Sorry," I mumble. "I thought it was obvious that we needed to get away."

He's not wearing his sweatshirt, and I notice that his white T-shirt has THANK YOU written on it in red bubble script. Kinda like what they put on bags for take-out food.

Terminus glances at me for a second. "Well, it *wasn't* obvious. And even if it was, it would have been smarter to *get away* from Fort Marshall, where we might have been able to steal supplies and maybe even a computer."

My anger flares. "Right. Because it would have been easier for us to fight, like, fifty people than one distracted guy."

"Right." Terminus mirrors my tone. "Did you notice that Galloway had a phone in his jacket pocket?"

I had *not* noticed.

I keep screwing up.

MacKenna Novak is the worst.

"Probably an untraceable burner. We could have at least taken it before you broke his nose. Then we'd have GPS. And a map." Terminus sighs. "Okay. So Galloway did pack some stuff. We have gas. Probably enough to go a couple hundred miles. We've got some food. Maybe a day's worth. But what then?"

We have no information. No money. No plan.

"Both The Opposition and The Spark will be looking for us," Terminus says. "We've got no way to get across the border. No phones. No way to contact Jinx. No way to contact anyone."

We continue to drive on the two-lane Sonoran highway. It's been a while since we've seen another car.

He taps the steering wheel. "We've got no friends."

Of course, it will be almost impossible to get in contact with Jinx.

We pass a large billboard for a place called DOLLA-PALOOZA. A dozen cheerful doll faces mock me from the signpost. A smiling stork has a speech bubble coming out of its cartoon bill. The same phrase is printed in Spanish and English.

Your new best friend is waiting for you…

Tu nuevo mejor amigo te está esperando…

DOLLAPALOOZA in 5 km.

Oh perfect.

Part of me wants to get back to the time when I still believed babies came from the cabbage patch and my only real problem was stopping Toby from eating all Mom's cookies.

But. Also.

"We do know people," I say.

At least, Dr. Doomsday did.

I'm about to tell Terminus about Dr. Doomsday's friends at the border. Mr. Antone helped us before. Yeah, and there was that guy. Fernando. Would they help us?

Before I can put that question to Terminus, a plain black car kicks up a cloud of dust, driving onto the highway from the dirt lot in front of a minimart. It pulls up close to our rear bumper. Terminus sucks in a gasp.

Cool adrenaline courses through me. "It's The Opposition!"

Terminus hits the gas. His voice is high-pitched and freaked out. "It's probably our people," he says. "Otherwise they'd be shooting at us."

A low, loud *boom* follows his words. A blast from a gun.

A big one.

"Okay. Yes! That's The Opposition!" he screams.

A bullet whizzes over my shoulder. There's a *crack*, and a hole bursts open in the windshield. A long series of lines break across the surface of the glass, making it impossible to see out the front of the car.

I scream.

"Oh shit!" Terminus says.

There's more shooting and yelling and another *boom*.

I turn around in my seat. Behind us there are now several vehicles locked in a firefight. Terminus must be right. We've got both The Opposition and The Spark chasing us. A dark SUV rams the sedan that's on our tail. The crash is enough to let us break free of the melee. We continue to speed ahead.

But Terminus can't control the Land Rover, and we break into a skid. I should have put my seat belt on after we tossed Galloway from the car. But I didn't, and I'm thrown against the car door as we veer off the road and kick up a cloud of dust.

Keep calm, Mac. Keep it together.

Even though I brace myself, I'm all over the front seat. The car runs over low bushes and the pockmarked desert earth. We're jostled up and down, and I hit my head on the roof. Finally, we rock side to side and come to a stop in front of a series of small roadside restaurants.

"What do we do? What do we do?" Terminus asks over and over.

I'm not used to this.

I'm used to traveling with Jinx and Navarro, who have a backup plan for how to eat a bowl of cereal.

"Um. Um. Um."

Geez, MacKenna. Stop stammering and figure it out.

More shots. The rear passenger window explodes.

"We have to get out of here!" I yell.

Without waiting for a response, I force myself to open the Land Rover door. I'm hit with the smell of delicious grilled chicken and a mouthful of dust. We're right in front of an orange-colored shack with a large sign.

POLLO ASADOS SINALOA EL VICKI

I got a C in Spanish, but I think that means there's someone inside named Vicki cooking up some chicken. As I'm making sense of this, men stream out of a taco shop next door to Vicki's. People run in every direction, and there's shouting in a mixture of Spanish and English.

Terminus sits like a statue behind the wheel of the car.

Crap.

For a split second, I feel some sympathy for Jinx and Navarro. Is this what it's like to deal with me? Is this what Jinx felt like when she had to drag me through that pharmacy on the day this all began?

Okay.

I have to stay low, and we have to get out of here.

I dodge a screaming kid riding by on a rickety bicycle and run around to the driver's side, then yank open the heavy door and tug Terminus into the chaos.

It's like lugging a potato sack. I drop him onto the dirt.

"Oh God. Oh God," he repeats. He sinks down and rests his head on the Land Rover's tire. "Oh ouch." He immediately puts his face up again.

Jinx wouldn't leave without the supplies, so I open the back door next and hustle in. I find a khaki military-style pack in the cargo area and grab it.

When I get out of the car, Terminus is actually standing up. Which is an improvement.

Taking his hand, I lead us around the corner of the chicken place. We duck behind the building. We're actually in a small town with a few houses and shops. I scan the area. There are a couple of cars, but it's too risky to try to steal a vehicle. We have no choice but to take off on foot. The mayhem seems like it will buy us time.

"Let's go." I'm thankful for all the jogging I used to do.

Slinging the pack over my shoulder, I take off at a run.

Galloway's backpack contains three steel bottles full of cold water, two extra T-shirts, a compass, a paper map of Mexico, four protein bars, an extra pack of cigarettes, a book of matches, a first aid kit, a Swiss Army knife and a wristwatch.

Which is how I know that we've been walking for almost exactly two hours.

Two looonnnggg hours.

I forced Terminus to jog for a mile or so before we took a break. That's when we dug around in the pack and scanned the area to see if anyone was following us.

Oh yeah. We've got binoculars.

"I don't think anyone's following us." I check out the desert landscape.

I feel strangely comfortable here. It's the same kind of desert as back in Phoenix, and a familiar orange light is falling over all the brown and yellow plant life.

The sun is going down.

Soon it will be dark.

Galloway didn't pack a flashlight.

Terminus coughs again. The dust is getting to him. "Why should they bother following us? All that's gonna happen is that we're gonna die out here."

If Charles were here, he'd know what all these plants are. Even this brush that's never noticed by anybody. Even these cacti that seem to exist for no reason other than to have defensive needles and spikes jutting out from them.

It all has names.

Like us.

"We're not gonna die," I snap. "Puerto Peñasco is maybe like twenty miles from here. We have food and water, and that's not too far to walk."

"Oh sure," he says, in between another round of coughs. "We'll just stroll around Rocky Point even though the Mexican government has ordered all Americans out of their country."

I miss Charles. And Jinx. And Toby. Even Navarro. I can't think about that or I'll cry.

Grow up. Get real. Don't cry.

So instead.

"By the way, thanks for all the help back there," I say.

He yanks the binoculars out of my hands and uses them to search the wide-open space behind me. "I'm not some damn army ranger. I didn't train in Max Marshall's secret militia. I'm not Jinx. Or Navarro. You made the choice to run off without them. Now here we are. Alone…and we—" He breaks into a laugh.

A dry, monotonous laugh.

He releases the binoculars. The eyepieces leave red marks on his face. "Oh, I don't believe it."

He gives the binoculars to me and turns me in the direction he was looking. Jutting out from the desert sand like a painted fingernail is a large square industrial building all by itself.

With a large sign in front.

WELCOME TO DOLLAPALOOZA.

Perhaps God will show mercy to our enemies.

I know I sure as hell won't.

–GEN. HARLAN S. COPELAND to
COL. C. MAXWELL MARSHALL
Log of the Interim Committee
re: Project Cold Front
Stamped: Top Secret

JINX

In the end, I get to keep only one small streak of blue hair.

We're at the bottom of the ocean, and Amelia has brought a hairdresser to help with my image. Her name is Avery. She has perfect hair and is the nicest person I've met in a while.

It's early in the morning. A little after five, the *Perun* returns without MacKenna and Terminus. We don't ask about them, and no one says anything. If Toby is worried about his sister, he doesn't say so. I heard that Copeland is back too but we don't see him right away.

Amelia takes us to a makeshift hair salon they've set up in one of the other dorms. The beds are gone, and someone has taken the mirrors out of the bathroom and attached them to the wall with thick swashes of duct tape. There's an office chair and a small utility cart loaded with brushes and hair dye. Scientists should be down here, and instead I'm getting a haircut.

This is the hair salon of the postapocalyptic, cold fusion future.

I rock slightly on my heels, trying to shake off the mounting dread.

Avery brushes her long honey-brown hair off her shoulders and motions for me to sit in the chair. "I like the blue too," she tells me, with a wink.

Amelia enters the room, dressed in her usual uniform of expensive T-shirts and jeans. Also carrying her e-tablet as per usual. "The blue hair interferes with her likability scores." She holds up a complicated pie chart for me to see. "Look. Positive responses to the statement 'Jinx Marshall reminds me of my daughter' decrease by 8 percent among women in the thirty-five to fifty-five age demographic."

Avery has a fistful of hair swatches and is pressing them against my face. She holds up a school picture of me with my old hair and compares the swatches to that.

Amelia taps again. "Here, for males eighteen to forty-nine, we see an almost 20 percent drop in positive responses to 'I'd help Jinx Marshall escape from danger.' That's a real problem—"

I roll my eyes. "I don't need a guy to help me escape from danger."

Navarro is in a chair in the corner reading material from one of the mission binders. He looks up at me. "Really?" he says.

My face heats up.

Avery is ignoring all of this. She waves a piece of hair in front of my face. "This is the closest to your natural color, but it's awfully ashy."

"Something warmer would be better," Amelia agrees.

They settle on a shade of brown that's slightly chestnut and more red than my natural color. A jolt of shock bolts through me when I realize.

This is Mom's hair color.

I want to object, but Avery is already swiping the white,

whipped foam on my head. She isolates one lock of blue with a strip of aluminum foil. When the color is done processing, she trims my hair, turning the sloppy pixie I created myself into a sleek style with a swath of hair that falls into my face like a French girl in a cosmetics ad.

Somebody must have lugged a bunch of 3D printers and sewing machines to the bottom of the ocean, because Amelia disappears for a few minutes and returns with our new "uniforms."

I have to say, they are sort of cool. I have a fitted pair of dark blue denim pants, a T-shirt with the hawk printed on it in an interesting, distressed way and a jacket made of waterproof scuba fabric with a hawk pin on the chest. Navarro's outfit is similar except in darker tones of blue. His jacket is more of a windbreaker.

We could form our own emo synthesizer band.

From my chair, I can see the image of him shrugging into his T-shirt reflected in my mirror. I have to force myself to look away.

When we're done, Navarro smiles at me. "I like this hair better," he says. "You look more like yourself."

Which is a strange comment really. I'm always myself no matter what I look like. And isn't every version of me still me?

Well. We're all dressed up and have somewhere to go.

Toby and a couple of other soldiers arrive. My stepbrother wears the uniform of the Provisional Army of the New United States. Navarro glares at him. If there was ever something that expressed the fact that there is now Us versus Them, it's our new clothes.

We have to wait in lockdown for about an hour with all the alarms going off and announcements played over the loudspeaker while Rosenthal is escorted to the *Perun*. When that's done, the rest of us are able to board. I'm given a waterproof backpack with two e-tablets, a laptop and basic rations like water and trail mix. There's a small pocketknife. Navarro has a bag full of camera equipment slung over his shoulder.

"What about weapons?" I ask.

Amelia frowns. "You'll get a gun when you need one."

It ends up being me, Navarro, Toby and Amelia walking together to the sub. I'm sort of relieved to be saying good-bye to the white hallways, the stuffy environment, the same sandwiches for lunch. But we were safe.

We're heading back into the unknown. And there's something else. Today, we land in Washington. I'll be a couple hundred miles from my brother. I'm going to rescue Charles.

Except, what if I fail?

I fight off a shiver.

I have to get my brother back.

I can't fail.

Today, they've turned the lights on around SEALAB, revealing a sort of blue desolation in the area around the station. There's something beautiful about it though.

Amelia stops in front of the ramp to board the *Perun*. "Copeland wants me up in the control room. Remember what I told you. We're looking for engagement here." She turns to Navarro. "Send me as much footage as you can. It will help the team to have options."

We enter the *Perun*, and it's exactly the way it was before. Two soldiers guard the pathway that leads to the front of the sub. Rosenthal is probably that way.

She doesn't tell us where she's going or where *the team* will be. Amelia gives me an awkward hug. "Well, this is it."

We won't see each other again.

I try for a smile, but I'm pretty sure what I achieve is an

odd mixture of terror and tension. Amelia casts me one final look, like she's rethinking the whole arrangement. The guards press their backs against the steel support beams to make room for her to squeeze by.

Our commander, Captain Toby Novak, leads me and Navarro into the same room we arrived in. We even strap ourselves into the same seats. This time, Toby sits in our row.

"Hey, Captain America," Navarro says. "Are you going to tell us where we're going?"

This had been the stumbling block in our discussion. Copeland withheld the location of the facility that would receive the *Perun*. While we know we're headed to Washington, we don't know exactly where.

Our plan is to get away. But it would help to know where we're running away from.

Toby stays silent.

Sigh.

"MacKenna was right," I say. "You *are* one of them."

"Cape Disappointment," Toby says through clenched teeth. "The Spark has constructed a dock and receiving facility there. I think it's Rosenthal's idea of a joke, actually. With sea levels being what they are, the cape is difficult to access and almost under water. So, naturally, that's where they built the marina."

This is where we really needed MacKenna. She had all the background information.

Sigh again.

"Where in Washington is that?" I'm forced to ask.

Toby shakes his head. "On the border. A little north of Portland."

I should have paid more attention in geography class because I don't know much about the Pacific Northwest. Dad's evac plans always focused on going south.

He understood what they were building at AIRSTA.

And trained us to get away from it.

"We have to stay buckled in our seats." Toby makes a show of trying to relax. Trying to conceal the tension and seem like his old self. "They want to come to the surface quickly. The *Perun* can make it to Cape Disappointment and depressurize us in about four hours."

"What's going to happen when we get there?" I ask.

Toby shrugs. "The general says they'll have ground transport organized for us when we arrive. The operation is supposed to go down tomorrow night, so we won't have a lot of time to hang around the dock."

Navarro and I exchange a look.

When we get to the marina, we have to be ready to go.

Toby yawns and stretches his arm over his head.

Something tells me that I shouldn't ask, but I have to. "Do you have any idea where MacKenna is?"

Toby freezes. His shoulders tense. "The general told me she was trying to get to our father. Apparently, he sent her back to Fort Marshall. To wait until…"

"Why would she do that?" I ask.

"Until what?" Navarro asks sharply.

"I don't know." Toby pulls out a binder from his own bag and buries himself in reading.

I'm not even sure if it was me or Navarro he answered.

"Four hours, huh?" Navarro says, yawning himself.

"Yep," Toby says, not glancing up from his reading.

We travel on in silence.

It's a pretty boring trip. We mostly talk about how we're either too hot or too cold. I power on one of the e-tablets.

Navarro and I play hangman and tic-tac-toe. One good thing is that they gave Navarro a watch with a calendar.

Which is how I know it's Tuesday.

That our games of hangman average four minutes.

And that all hell breaks loose at 3:26 p.m. PST.

First, the yellow warning lights that are all over the place begin to flash. Then an alarm sounds. Then tons of announcements over the intercom. Specific people being called to specific locations on the sub. We must be coming up fast, because I'm freezing and my stomach is turning over and over.

Whatever else happens, I absolutely don't want to puke.

Toby is already unbuckling his harness. "I'll find out what's going on. Wait here."

"Did they warn you this would happen?" I ask.

I'm alarmed by the expression on Toby's face. "I don't think this is supposed to be happening at all," he says.

He's out the main door before I can object or ask any more questions. I have a little more sympathy for Terminus, because it's taking everything I've got not to barf all over my brand-new hero outfit.

Breathe.

We're bumped up hard, and the straps of my harness dig into my shoulders. There's a clank and scraping metal. It's the same as before. But not exactly the same.

Something hit us.

Navarro cranes his neck in every direction, as if he thinks whatever's pounding us might push through the metal walls and into our small room.

Don't stand around waiting to die.

I unsnap my buckle and grab my pack. "Come on!"

"We need to get the hell off this thing," Navarro says.

My father never made us drill for what to do when the

high-tech submarine you're riding in is under attack. I push open the door, and there's absolute mayhem in the cramped hallway. The lights flicker and the tile floor is slippery and wet.

We're taking on water.

Soldiers shout instructions to each other, a mishmash of words I barely recognize. But there's one sentence I do understand.

Deploy the lifeboats.

We squeeze along the hallway, searching for Toby and hoping that some plan will present itself. Soldiers give us odd looks as we pass, and I'm starting to think we might have been better off in the waiting room. Things must be really bad because Rosenthal is at the end of the long passageway with soldiers moving all around him.

Copeland stands behind Rosenthal. It's the first time we've gotten a look at him since MacKenna went missing. He's just as cold as ever. "Sir, we're deploying two lifeboats full of armed personnel to draw their fire," he says. "Stay down once you're in the boat. Our first priority is getting you safely to the transport."

The Opposition is in the marina.

Shooting at us.

There's another hit, and I'm barely able to brace myself. From behind me, I hear a *bong* that sounds like Navarro's head knocking against a metal beam. My heart lurches.

"You need to stop hitting your head," I say, turning around. The nasty cut he got from that rock in the river outside Fort Marshall has finally begun to heal.

"Thanks. I hadn't thought of that," Navarro says, rubbing his forehead. "Good thing you're the brains of the operation." He whirls me around so I'm facing forward.

As the *Perun* pushes on toward the marina, I see everyone has congregated at a steel ladder that leads to an escape hatch. The soldier at the top is talking into a radio, trying to time the release of the hatch door with the moment we reach the surface of the water.

Toby is making his way toward us, moving with more ease than I'd expect, through the cramped space.

He's got guns.

I'm sort of grossed out by the excitement that pulses through me at the thought of having a weapon again. But they're modern, trackable, DNA-A guns.

"Good. You're here," he says, handing me an M4-DNA-A carbine rifle. I've never fired one of these before. Toby also gives me three magazines. That's ninety shots. It must really be a mess out there. I press my thumb onto the DNA pad on the mag. A small green light appears on the plastic, meaning the ammo can be used. And any bullet I fire can be traced back to me.

"These are already programmed?" I ask.

Toby nods.

Great. I guess Copeland's people have our thumbprints and DNA.

"What's going on out there?" I ask.

"What's going on," Copeland shouts from farther up the hall, "is that we're under attack. All convo not mission critical needs to stop. Now. Even for civilians."

I guess our little fake hero squad doesn't count as an actual operation.

The noise level suddenly gets a lot louder.

The hatch is open, and a new symphony of the pops of rifles and the bangs of antiaircraft guns fills the sub, echoing off all the metal. Toby gives Navarro the other carbine.

"Sooner or later, I'm going to need a decent weapon," Navarro says.

Rosenthal catches my eye and gives me a small nod before disappearing up the hatch.

Toby has kept a silver, weird-looking, futuristic handgun for himself.

I point at it. "What is that?" I yell over the noise. Except before he can answer, I already know.

It's a plasma rail gun.

Something outside explodes, and a bright light floods the hall. More water wells up around my boots. We need to get the hell out of the *Perun* before it becomes our sinking grave. Copeland moves into the hatch, and we press close to the open door.

I'm surprised he doesn't say something to us.

While we wait for the soldiers to clear the hatch, I do the only thing I can. Focus on what's in front of me.

I point to Toby's gun again. "Gun companies were supposed to stop researching those. They're supposed to be illegal." Back when the military used to build these things, they made large guns that could fire projectiles at up to 560 miles per hour, pierce all known kinds of body armor and efficiently deliver bioweapons. The only saving grace was that they weighed a ton and you had to be superman to cart one around.

The Spark has a version that fits in the palm of your hand.

Cold dread almost overtakes me. Who knows what other weapons were out there?

Toby frowns. "Yes, it's a rail gun. The Spark was concerned that The Opposition was gearing up for war. They *had* to do something."

What else did The Spark have to do?

Navarro shakes his head in disgust. "Typical," he yells. "The Spark regulates everybody except themselves."

Toby ignores him. It's our turn to enter the hatch. He goes first.

Soldiers I vaguely recall from SEALAB form a line behind us.

Navarro inspects the rifle. "Okay. You remember Dan Hassle's lecture at PrepperCon, right? SPORTS?"

Toby's feet pound on the metal ladder. Navarro ushers me up next.

"SPORTS…yeah…of course," I say. Who could forget old man Hassle screaming, *Are you prepared to join America's army?* at the top of his lungs. I put my thumb on the authentication pad on the gun to activate the weapon.

I place my foot on the first rung of the ladder. The bottom of my boot is wet, and my leg nearly slips off. Gripping the bars tight with my arms, I pull myself up.

Rung by rung.

Breathe. Breathe. And…

SPORTS.

S = Slap the magazine.

P = Pull the charging handle.

O = Observe any round in the chamber.

R = Release the charge handle.

T = Tap Forward Assist.

S = Squeeze the trigger.

The closer I get to the hatch door, the more things get impossibly loud. There are crashes, gunfire and screams coming from all directions. A boat motor cranks on and then another.

I stick my head into the late afternoon in the Pacific Northwest. For a split second, I think I'm looking at a sunset. But my face heats up and I realize.

It's a wall of fire.

Someone must have spilled fuel into the bay, because a blaze has spread along the surface of the water. There's so much commotion that the water is rolling in small waves and carrying the fire along with it.

Waves of flames.

We're in a kidney-shaped bay with the ocean at our backs. The *Perun* is about a half mile away from the shore, which is covered in long green reeds that sway in the breeze. A wooden dock is barely able to poke out from all the vegetation, and the water threatens to swallow it up. Above the wild part of Cape Disappointment that the sea is trying to reclaim, there's a dirt road with dozens of vehicles on it and an old lighthouse. Soldiers duck behind car doors and fire at each other. It's almost impossible to tell who's for us and who's against us.

It's probably about four o'clock, but the sun is behind thick blue-gray clouds, creating a gloomy scene and making it hard to pin down the time.

The sub is barely above the surface of the water, and it seems to be sinking. Several other soldiers are crouched on top, trying to stay low as they fire weapons. Three motorboats speed toward the shore, and the soldiers draw fire away from the group. That has to be Rosenthal's entourage.

Toby's splashing around and when I make it up there, the water hits my knees. He shouts at me to join him at the side of the *Perun* closest to the dock.

"Stay down!" someone screams.

I duck as a bullet grazes my hair.

If I don't survive, they'll kill my brother.

My pants are soaked with water that is shockingly cold.

With Navarro on my heels, I slosh along and pretty much fall into an inflatable boat. Our boat doesn't have a motor, and I'm almost hit in the face with an oar as we get situated in the raft. We're all barely inside and have paddled less than five feet from the sub when the *Perun* is hit by an antiaircraft gun.

A wide piece of steel explodes from the sub and hits our raft, tossing us all into the bay.

My rifle is knocked out of my hands and lands in the water with a plop.

Salt water burns my nostrils and eyes as I plunge below the water's icy cold surface. My heavy jacket fights against me. I struggle to the surface, and when I finally emerge, I can barely force air into my tight, freezing lungs. I have no choice but to shrug out of my pack.

As I manage to doggy paddle, I scan the mayhem for Navarro. His head pops above the surface a few seconds later. Fumes from the fuel floating on the surface of the water create a toxic stench. I gasp and splash frantically, Navarro swims in my direction. Progress is slow as he avoids paths of fire and waves push him farther from the beach.

Navarro really isn't a good swimmer, and he's hung on to his weapon.

"Come on. Come on," I pant as he reaches me.

I end up tugging him along toward the shore, not to the dock, but to a spot shrouded by long, wheat-like grass that the wind is whipping into a fury. Tufts at the top of the stalks poke me in the face.

Navarro scales the grassy, rocky surface first and reaches down. I take his hand, and he helps me out of the water.

We kneel down for a second, shivering. On the opposite side of the bay, a group of soldiers flank a rock, surrounding a silhouetted figure who can only be Rosenthal. They're drawing heavy fire from several large, black SUVs in the dirt road, about fifty feet away. I don't see Toby anywhere. I hope he's okay.

I've got scrapes on my hands and arms and face. I flop back onto the muddy earth. I'm wet and filthy. My brand-new clothes are stained and ripped.

So much for my hero outfit.

More gunfire.

Dad's voice rings in my ears. *Don't stay there waiting to die.*

I sit up, trying to remain hidden in the grass.

Navarro is looking in the other direction. He picks up his rifle and leans toward me. His breath on my face is the only warmth I've got. "There's a car up there. By the lighthouse. Let's go."

I glance that way. He's right. The lighthouse looks abandoned, and there's a lone SUV parked near a squat building that's probably a maintenance shack or something.

"It seems almost too easy," I whisper.

"What? You want to go search for a car that's harder to steal?" he says.

"We should go that way!" I say as I point to the gunfight.

"Are you serious? For what?" Navarro says.

"Rosenthal!" Who else? What would MacKenna say if I let her hero get shot? Assuming Mac is even alive.

Navarro is tugging me toward the lighthouse.

"They're gonna kill him!" I try to wrestle my arm away.

"They're not going to kill Rosenthal," Navarro tells me in a tone of exasperation. Like I'm missing something of critical importance. "That would be like the Yankees killing the Red Sox. You need two teams to have the game."

"This isn't a game," I say.

"Yes, it is," he snaps back. "One with the ultimate stakes."

I don't know if that's true, but I don't want to play.

"If we're going to have any hope of getting Charles out of AIRSTA, we need to go now. Now, Susan!" Navarro says.

Charles.

He's right. I let Navarro continue to hold my hand, but I begin to run toward the truck without him dragging me.

We creep up the edge of the cliff, staying as low as we can. As we come closer to the vehicle, I can see it's a new SUV, very similar to the one Jay used to have back before all this mess. That means it has features like autodrive. I can probably override the computerized ignition. But it also has GPS. Whoever owns this thing can track us.

Also, the windows have thick, dark tint.

Someone could be in there.

"We have to risk it," Navarro says, as if sensing these thoughts.

There's really no other choice. We have to get away. That was our plan all along and, honestly, all this pandemonium is a good distraction.

We approach from the passenger side. Navarro gets ready with his rifle. As slowly and quietly as I can, I pull on the door handle.

It's unlocked.

Navarro nods.

Tension fills my body.

I throw the door open and Navarro jumps forward with his weapon.

And.

The truck is empty.

It's almost anticlimactic.

I slide in and climb over into the driver's seat. The car's fob is in a cup holder in the center of the vehicle, and the ignition has been left in ready mode. Meaning we can start the thing without even hacking the car's computer.

Navarro gets into the passenger seat. "This *is* a little too easy."

"Maybe they wanted to be ready for a hasty retreat?" I say.

My finger is hovering over the power button when the back door opens and a gorgeous blonde girl is pushed into the backseat.

My mouth falls open.

It's Annika Carver.

She's carrying a large army green duffel bag and tries to remove the tension from her face as she gives me a friendly wave.

Toby squeezes in next to her.

He played us.

Absolutely played us.

I wish Mac were here.

I wish that I could say whatever she would have said, instead of, "You...you...you..."

"You were going to leave without me," Toby says.

"Why would we leave without you, Captain?" Navarro mutters.

I stare at Toby in the rearview mirror. "Mac was right! All along you only wanted to—"

To help Annika Carver.

"That's not true!" Toby interrupts. There are more shots, and it sounds like the gunfire is getting closer. "We can discuss this later."

Navarro pulls the charging handle of his rifle and turns around in his seat, brandishing the weapon. "Or we could toss you from the car right now."

Annika clasps her hands under her chin in a perfect damsel-in-distress gesture.

I hadn't seen her since that day in the Arizona desert when she'd all but left us for dead. Her grandmother, Ramona Healy, had talked my dad into taking Annika with us when we left for Mexico. We were supposed to keep her safe. Instead, Mac and I had had to keep *us* safe from Ammon Carver's daughter. Annika had betrayed us and, if push comes to shove, she'll probably do it again. Now, she is in the backseat with Toby.

"You're really going to shoot me, Navarro?" he says with an eye roll.

There's a brief pause.

No. No, Navarro is not going to shoot Toby.

We have to move.

I press the power button. Before I can put the car in Drive, the rear door opens again. Another thin figure forces its way into the backseat.

Annika screams.

I gasp.

It's Amelia Aoki. She's pointing a camera with a light mounted to it in our direction. She turns her camera toward Annika.

"Well, well. Plot twist," she says.

It seemed like everyone knew how to start a war. But no one knew how to end one.

—MacKENNA NOVAK,
Letters from the Second Civil War

MacKENNA

"We can't just stay here forever," I say.

Terminus is the anti-Jinx. She's all instinct and nerve and prepared for anything and he's, like, the guy whoe needs a supercomputer to figure out if he has to go to the bathroom. Honestly, I can't really believe they were ever friends.

He makes us camp out about a half mile away from Dolla-palooza underneath a billboard for chewing gum. Terminus insists that we stay there overnight, using our sweatshirts as blankets and backpacks as pillows.

Reconnaissance, according to him.

We take turns watching the building for hours. All morning and into the afternoon. Until we're covered in dust. Until we've played a zillion games of tic-tac-toe in the dirt. Until we've gone through all the water and food. We don't see anything or anyone.

I think Terminus would be happy to stay out here until the world ends.

It's getting cooler and late in the afternoon. "I'm going," I say, leaving him with no choice but to stumble along behind me toward the sign that says "DOLLAPALOOZA General Hospital: Your new best friend is almost here."

The closer we get, the more it seems like no one has been here for a long time. Wherever here is.

"What is this place, anyway?" I ask.

Terminus has the binoculars. "I think it's a tourist attraction. Like a doll factory. And they give tours."

That makes sense. My mom took me to a place like this when I was little. I spent hours designing my own doll and then begging my mom to buy a doll camping set that cost more than four hundred dollars. That didn't work but, like, Mom did let us have high tea in the factory's fancy pink café.

There's only one car in the parking lot. An inexpensive red compact.

"Maybe the security guard," Terminus says.

I take the binoculars. The car looks…abandoned. "Not unless the guard lives here. We haven't seen anyone come or go. And that car is covered with dust. Like it's been out here for a while."

Terminus shrugs. "I think the place might be closed."

"Maybe it's the weekend."

This thought hits me like a lightning bolt. I'm a journalist, and I don't even know what day it is. I don't know, and I don't have a way to find out.

I force myself to breathe normally.

"Okay, let's go inside," I say.

"We're going *inside*? Why?" he asks. "Let's steal that car and get out of here."

I shake my head. "There might be supplies in there. Maybe a computer. Maybe money. We won't get very far in that car if we can't get gas."

"Okay," Terminus says.

We creep into the parking lot. This is the setup from a horror movie. Like, I'm way sure that someone in a mask is following us.

LEAD: Student journalist murdered by creepy dolls.

I bet that would get a ton of clicks.

We snake around the empty parking lot and go toward what, from a distance, looks like a gray boulder in front of a large building. As we come within a few feet of the thing, I realize it's really a metal statue, all in white, of several leaves of cabbage with a big creepy baby's face poking out. The scalloped edges of the leaves cast ghastly shadows across the infant, giving it black vacant eyes. An oversize pacifier shrouds the baby's chin.

Even though I don't want to be *that* girl.

I'm *that* girl.

I grab Terminus's hand.

It's kinda sweaty and gummy, to be honest. Plus, he was the one hiding in the car. So really.

I'm gonna have to save us.

Yay.

Slowly, we approach the front of the building. It's a basic, boring factory around three stories tall made mostly of gray concrete. But the entrance has been designed to look like an old-timey Southern mansion, with fake white columns on either side of the wide oak doors. There are signs taped all over the place. Some have been created on a printer and some are scribbled in hasty script in black marker. Most of them are in Spanish. In English, one sign says Closed until Further Notice in handwritten script. A printed one reads "Adopt your new best friend at Carl's Toys in Puerto Peñasco."

Terminus eyes the signs. "Probably not much point in keeping a tourist attraction open with no tourists around." He tries to peek in the window made of a stained glass, which is probably quite attractive when it's not so dusty. "Let's try the back."

I'm not sure why the back will be any better than the front, but there also doesn't seem to be much point in arguing.

The rear of the Dollapalooza building must have functioned as a break area for employees. There are a couple of picnic tables. A coffee can full of cigarette ashes. A small orange plastic playset for toddlers.

Also, the back is muddy.

Some kind of liquid leaks from a pipe that runs off the roof and empties near the back door. My boots make squeaky squeals as I walk through the muddy grass. I pass a couple of large buckets full of doll parts. Little dirty legs and arms, and a few heads without hair.

Gross.

Two steps lead to a narrow door. There's a sign with blue block letters. *ADVISO Solo Empleados.* Employees Only. There's a steel keypad above the doorknob, but Terminus looks around for something else.

He points at a greenish-beige rectangle on a short post to the right of the door. "Perfect," he says. "That's the main PBX box. Give me the knife."

I dig around in the pack until I find the Swiss Army knife.

He hesitates. "What if someone is inside?"

"Just do it," I tell him. What choice do we really have?

Terminus jimmies the box open and uses the knife to cut through the wires inside. "Okay. It seems like they've got a pretty basic setup here. But if their burglar alarm sends data to a monitoring company, this should cut off that access. So once the alarm goes off, nobody will show up to turn it off."

"Once the alarm goes off?" I repeat. "Like, shouldn't we stop the alarm from going off?"

He shakes his head. "There isn't a way to do that from out here. We'll have to silence the audible device once we get inside. But that should be easy. We need to find it. Fast." He stares at me.

Clearly, I'm expected to deal with the door. Wow. I'm the supersoldier in this relationship. But also...

What do I do now?

Jinx would kick in the door.

Okay. Okay. Go for it, Mac!

It's harder than it looks.

The first time I kick the door, nothing really happens other than I call out, "Ow!" as Terminus snickers.

Believe it or not, kicking in a door was one of Navarro's drills. First, I aim for the strike zone. This is the weak point right around the doorknob. I try to remember one of the ten thousand lectures on three-quarter-inch screws and structural weak points. But all I can really remember is *kick the area around the knob.*

On the fourth kick, the door bursts open.

Whoa. I. Am Too. Cool.

A siren blares as we enter the building into a break room with a refrigerator and a few wooden tables with chairs. Crock-Pots line the counter. From the looks of it, the Dollapalooza people loved nothing so much as a good potluck.

Terminus locates the alarm master control next to the employee time clock. He rips the panel off the wall and cuts through the wires that attach it to the wall. The building falls silent. Poor little dolls. They had bad security.

We make our way through the inside of the building. There are a few lights on here and there, probably for emergencies. The place is decorated like a cutesy hospital. I have no idea what Dollapalooza was like during its heyday, but now, with everyone long gone, in the nighttime half-light, the smiling dolls lean out of white cribs to whisper warnings. Floppy, dimpled arms hang from the windows of miniature school buses, like they're reaching out to grab me.

It's totally silent in the place, and I seriously doubt anyone else is inside or they would have come running at the sound of the alarm. We walk past a large, plastic version of a tree surrounded by a modeled rock surface where more doll heads pop out from openings every few feet. A plaque reads "Please don't climb on Mother Cabbage." Some of the fake cribs are decorated with red velvet bows and Christmas wreaths. I get the feeling it was always Christmas in the cabbage patch.

Past the giant tree, there's a series of child-size desks. Each one has a cheerful sign describing how to print a birth certificate for "your new special delivery."

My pulse quickens.

It's just a big, empty office building. Chill out, Mac.

We keep walking and walking and walking and we're finally in the center of the building, in front of a dramatic split staircase straight out of *Absalom, Absalom!*

"I bet the offices are upstairs," Terminus says.

It's dark up there, but he heads up anyway, taking the stairs at a fairly fast clip. They're covered with a super-gross green shag carpet.

I cast one more glance at Mother Cabbage. A row of empty baby swings beyond the bank of birth certificate computers sways and creaks. There's something odd about the way they move. Swinging out of sequence and out of time. Like someone pushed them. "You think we're alone in here, right?"

Terminus freezes. "How would I know? It was your bright idea to come in."

Even though no one can see, I roll my eyes. I have to pull it together. I mean, someone around here has to be brave.

"Hang on," I tell him. "I'm coming."

As I take my first step onto the staircase, there's a loud *bang*, and something whizzes past my right ear and makes a huge hole in the drywall ahead of me.

My heart seems to freeze as I immediately drop to my knees, just like we practiced so many times in Navarro's drills. Heavy, booted footsteps echo through the large, empty building, coming from the direction of Mother Cabbage. The instant a shadow forms in front of the staircase, I gather up all the courage I've ever had. The power of every time Mom kissed my head and told me to be brave, of every time Dad wiped away my tears, every smile from Toby. All the times I've believed in myself even when no one else did.

You got this, MacKenna.

I lunge at whoever or whatever is coming our way.

My shoulder slams hard against something cool and metal as I knock into a solid, slim figure. I grunt in pain.

That's gonna leave a mark.

A shotgun slides across the floor, and I watch as it gets wedged under a doll hand. It's the kind of gun Dr. Doomsday would love. An old shotgun. Probably some kind of Winchester. The part that I always call the butt is made of wood.

Jinx always corrects me.

It's the stock.

Someone yanks me back sharply by my hair.

The intruder releases me, and I land flat on my back with a familiar face upside down in my field of view.

Josephine Pletcher.

"Girl," she says. "You aren't quite as smart as you think you are."

Here she is. Her straight, military posture. Her neatly coiled bun at the base of her neck. Jo's standing over me in the hollowed-out area in front of Mother Cabbage where Dollapalooza workers probably greeted visitors. Of course, she was able to find us. It probably didn't take them long to figure out what happened.

For a second, I'm relieved. Dad's people found us. They'll drag us back to Fort Marshall, and it will suck. Dad will yell, and eventually Jinx will catch up with me and she'll yell. In a few hours, I'll be in that bizarro mansion getting another lecture. It's better than being killed by The Opposition.

Except that Jo Pletcher seemed to be shooting...at me.

In the low light, I can't read her expression, but she makes an impatient noise. "The colonel left for Los Alamos an hour ago. They're maintaining radio silence and as far as he knows, you're on your way to Fort Marshall." She grabs another fistful of my hair.

I grit my teeth, first to work through the sharp, burning pain in my scalp and my throbbing shoulder, and second to stop myself from screaming as Jo drags me along the tile floor. Trying to work my way free, I dig my fingernails into the hand wrapped around my hair.

Jo grunts in frustration and slams me against the fake plastic rocks. She crouches down next to me, and two smooth, capable hands grab my neck.

I choke and gasp for breath.

LEAD: Rogue soldier strangles student journalist as creepy dolls watch.

Crap. *No.* That statement totally lacked objectivity. And it contained unneeded info. Like, who cares about the dolls? I'm gonna get my ass kicked, and I can't even come up with a good headline for the story.

I gasp for breath. As I thrash from side to side, trying to pry her fingers off my throat, I manage to choke out the words, "What…the hell…are you doing?"

Jo smiles. "Solving a problem. Permanently."

It hits me.

IMPORTANT FACTS:

-They don't need us.

-My father will soon be dead.

-Jinx doesn't know where we are.

We are expendable.

Jo came in here with a shotgun.

To kill us.

The crowd is moved by symbols, by icons, by archetypes. The crowd has its own morality, its own religion. We must create a series of images that are powerful enough to motivate the resistance, and we must model what we need them to do.

–AMELIA AOKI
Report: *The Image of the Second Civil War*
Stamped: Top Secret

JINX

"What the hell are you doing here?" I call back. Who am I talking to? Amelia? Annika? Toby? The only people who are supposed to be in this car are Navarro and me.

More gunfire rings out, and the shouting is getting closer. I have no choice but to put the SUV in gear and steer the vehicle into the dirt road.

Amelia lowers the camera and climbs into the backseat. This puts her right behind Toby and Annika in the middle row. "Copeland is crazy if he thinks I'm going to let the three of you run this operation. I mean, seriously, you didn't even make it to shore with the bag of gear!"

She was right. Navarro didn't bother to take the camera with him from the sub. But then, at the time, we didn't care about making a mockumentary.

In the rearview mirror, I watch the car kick up a cloud of dust.

The Spark sending Amelia to supervise us makes a great

deal more sense than putting Toby in charge. But then…why did Copeland put Toby in charge in the first place?

I punch the gas, and as we take off, a sharp *smack* sounds on the rear window.

Annika screams again.

"Oh wow! I wish I would have got that on camera," Amelia mutters. "Ammon Carver's daughter screaming her head off would really boost our metrics."

A round crack appears, like we've been hit by a giant rock.

The Opposition knows we're up here.

And they're shooting at us.

Okay. Breathe.

"We'll try to do more dangerous stuff to accommodate you," I say.

"You're welcome, by the way," Amelia says. She doesn't seem bothered at all by the yelling or the gunfire. And unlike Toby, Navarro and me, she's not wet, which means her boat made it safely to the shore. She's dressed in a teal waterproof jacket with a hood and black fitted pants. Chic. And expensive.

"For?" Navarro says.

"She put the SUV here," I say. It's the only explanation for the convenience of the car. Why it was in a location that was so easy for us to see from the harbor. And how she knew where to find it.

I glance in the mirror to see Amelia fiddling with something, probably the camera, in her lap. "You have no idea how much paperwork I had to do to get the bullet-resistant windows," she says. "Biesecker in Special Effects wanted regular glass. You know. For the look. It took me three meetings to convince the team that your survival was more important than a money shot."

"Uh. Right," Navarro says with a grim scowl. "So this vehicle is being tracked. By The Spark."

Our plan is already a failure.

"Where are we going?" Navarro says.

We speed along, passing by the lighthouse. A couple decades ago, the structure must have towered high above the ocean, but with the sea level rise, waves roll right up to the base. Black mold eats away at the white paint, and the door has been torn off.

"What about Rosenthal?" I ask.

Amelia passes a dark bag into the middle row of seats. "What about him?"

I see Toby in the mirror, opening the bag. It's similar to the one I lost in the ocean and full of electronic gear. Toby pulls out an e-tablet and...

A phone.

We haven't been able to use a phone since January. It takes everything I've got not to reach behind me and snatch it from Toby's hand.

Focus.

Rosenthal.

"When we last left the president, he looked like he was ten seconds away from getting captured and killed by The Opposition," I say. Also. Toby is smiling at Annika and being super casual about, well, everything. He takes her hand. "Toby! Give Navarro the phone."

"Jinx. I'm still in charge and—"

"Somebody needs to be *in charge* of finding a map by the time we hit the main road!" I tell him. He doesn't even notice my reflection scowling at him.

"We've set up a bed-and-breakfast in Astoria as a safe

house," Amelia says with a yawn. "Turn on the phone. I had the techs preload the map."

Well. That solves that problem, I guess. But I really hate this. The whole point of the plan was to take charge of our own destiny. Now Amelia is calling the shots. And she cast us in her war movie.

Toby tosses Navarro the phone. A burner smartphone in a plastic bag. Navarro turns it on and activates the map. The road has become steep and muddy. We barrel up an incline and onto a two-way highway.

"Go left," Navarro tells me.

I steer left. I should be asking if it's safe to stay on the main highway.

But.

"What about Rosenthal?"

Amelia leans forward into the space between Toby and Annika's captain chairs, forcing them to stop holding hands. "I assume the president will be fine. We outnumber them in the bay three to one. But I can get a status update when we get to Astoria."

The way she says this. Like it doesn't much matter whether Rosenthal lives or dies.

Sigh.

I have to force myself to relax.

I hate to say it, but the drive is gorgeous. The ocean is on our left, a beautiful gray-blue that stretches on and on. Tall trees that lead to a thick forest flank our right. Above us, puffy swelling storm clouds roll by.

In the seat next to me, Navarro is making clicks on the map. "We need to get off the main road."

"I don't think that's necessary," Amelia says. "I doubt

anyone will follow us. The Opposition believes you're with Rosenthal."

How does she know what The Opposition believes?

My teeth are chattering again, and as the gunfire fades into the background, my hands and fingers ache. A couple of the cuts on my palms are pretty deep, and fire shoots through me as I grip the steering wheel.

Navarro reaches for the console and turns on the heater. He must be thinking the same thing as me, because he says, "So are we all thinking that Copeland sold us out?"

Speaking for the first time, Annika says, "General Harlan Copeland? He's working for The Spark now?"

Warm air hits my face.

"Copeland wouldn't sell us out," Toby declares.

Annika doesn't seem so sure.

I glance behind me. I can't understand how Annika always manages to look the way she does. The wind blew her hair into an attractive poof, and her camo leggings and green sweatshirt are somehow both distressed and neat.

Also.

"It was Amelia," I say. It had to be. "Amelia contacted The Opposition."

Amelia's face pops up and, for a minute, she stops messing with the camera. "Well, not me personally," she says. "We needed a compelling sequence to kick off our broadcast." She resumes digging in her bag and pulls out a small laptop. "We only gave The Opposition about ten minutes' notice so they wouldn't have enough time to pull a whole operation together."

The Spark gave away our location. Because it would look good on TV.

I try to focus on the road ahead. "And you were willing to sacrifice Rosenthal?"

"The general won't let anything happen to the president," she says. She bounces up and down in her seat. "Copeland isn't bad, you know. I mean, unless you think the idea that society can only be sustained by perpetual war is bad."

"I *do* think that's bad," I snap.

Amelia has her camera back up.

Navarro remains hunched over the phone. "Okay, in a quarter of a mile we should see a farmer's market on the right-hand side. There's a dirt road a few feet after that. Turn there, and I think I can keep us off the main road until…"

"Until what?" I ask.

Navarro is muttering to himself as we arrive at what was once the farmer's market. The once-cheerful red building is covered in grime and bird poop. A faded sign reading U PICK CHERRIES hangs crooked on a wooden post. Squares of the dirt where cherries once grew are empty. I turn on the road immediately after the market, which leads us into a deeply forested area. Meanwhile, Amelia is crouching down in the space between Annika and Toby, pointing the camera at my face.

"Just like I think that making a TV show when millions of people are dying in a war is bad," I say, putting my face closer to the camera lens.

What is the point of all of this? And where is MacKenna when I need her?

"But your father meticulously researched how to change popular opinion and use forms of media to influence behavior. Most political campaigns today are using his theories." Amelia puts her hand on my armrest to steady herself.

Navarro glares at her. "We're coming to a fork in the road. Take a left."

I slow down and make the turn. Without looking at the camera, I say, "Dad believed that something had gone really wrong with this world. He felt that he could create complex data models and computer programs to manipulate people into making the right choices. He thought that the ends justified the means, that you could do something wrong as long as you were trying to do something right. But that was a mistake. That road leads to corrupt leaders and a bunch of people with broken moral compasses. Dad lived to regret those theories. They got him killed."

Navarro shifts uncomfortably in his seat. I doubt he agrees with what I've said. The idea that he still sympathizes with The Opposition sticks in my throat a little. But we didn't have time to drill down on our ideologies.

As usual, Navarro sticks to Dad's advice.

Focus on what's in front of you.

"You're probably going to need the four-wheel drive," he says.

He's right. And what he's calling a road is becoming more of a trail that's littered with rocks. I have to steer sharply around tall pine trees, and it's hard to maintain our speed.

Annika moans. "I think I'm going to be sick."

Amelia pivots, flipping her camera into Annika's pretty face. "Last week, your father, Ammon Carver, made the controversial decision to drop the cold fusion bomb on California. Casualties are estimated as high as thirty-five million. What would you say to the families affected by the violence?"

"Okay, wait a second," Toby says. He taps me on the shoulder. "Maybe you should turn on autodrive."

"Naturally, my heart goes out to anyone personally affected

by the violence of this terrible war," Annika says in a voice that's pretty polished for someone clutching their stomach. "I desperately pray for a resolution before anyone else is hurt."

Amelia lowers the camera. "Okay, nice. Good job, guys. We've got some strong character development footage to use in between the action sequences."

Action sequences? I have no choice but to ignore this.

"No autodrive," I tell Toby. "I'm not letting a computer drive this car." It strikes me like lightning that *that* is something my father would say.

Navarro snorts. "The autodrive would never let us maintain this speed. And despite what you think, *Captain*, it's critical we get off the road and into a less recognizable vehicle. Fast. But…"

"But *what*?" I shout.

I take a steep decline way too fast. The bumper scrapes against the leafy, rocky forest ground, and we bob up and down.

Amelia is climbing back to her own seat. I'm almost glad when she bonks her head on the roof of the SUV.

"Okay, well," Navarro says, scooting back from me. "We can stay off the main roads for a while. But the Columbia River is up ahead. There's an old bridge that may or may not be flooded. Even if it's not, it's several miles long and only two lanes. Once we get out there, we're exposed."

"Can we go around it?" I ask.

"Not really," he says. "That would take hours. Really throw off our timeline."

"What timeline is that?" Toby asks, leaning into Navarro. "Our mission clock begins tomorrow."

Navarro jerks his chin at Annika. "I don't think we're on the same mission, pal."

In the backseat, Amelia actually yawns. "I already told you. My team has taken care of everything. Both Washington and Oregon are states controlled by The Spark. The Opposition was already unable to maintain control of federal property in these areas. We lured them to the bay. Put four squads of our best people over there. Provided a super high-profile target. Believe me. The Opposition has their hands full with the resources they've got."

"You've never seen how The Opposition operates, have you?" I ask. If Amelia had ever seen Tork in action, she'd know that we're in real trouble.

"If we could see this vehicle, so could they," Navarro says. "I guarantee you, someone saw us. And they're coming."

We take another small hill and emerge from the trees into a clearing. The area looks like it was once a small neighborhood and is now a perfect place for serial killers to retire. The houses have been abandoned for a while. Long grass grows in front of doorways. Everything is muddy and moldy. Windows have been broken out. We pass a sage green house with a huge hole punched in its roof.

"Someone?" Amelia repeats. "Someone like who?"

After we leave the neighborhood. I follow Navarro's directions and steer through another thicket of overgrown trees. I barely miss sideswiping a pine tree's spindle-like branches. I stop the SUV before we emerge from the forest, facing a wide waterway.

The Columbia.

The bridge is about a quarter mile ahead and, like Navarro suggested, it's a mess. Almost like one bridge built on top of another—like they tried to raise the bridge height once the sea levels really started to change, creating a road on stilts. But even still, waves crash over the sides, some so high that they splash the side windows of the handful of cars driving over it.

"So?" I turn to Navarro. "We could ditch the car and..." Even as I'm trying to come up with a plan, I realize there's no good option.

"It could take hours to find another car," Toby says.

"We're just going to have to hit it," Navarro says, staring straight ahead.

Okay.

Breathe.

I put my foot on the gas pedal, hard, and we skid out of the forest. We're only a few feet from the bridge ramp when another vehicle emerges from the trees at a fast clip. It's a black SUV very similar to ours and makes fast time. In a few seconds, the other car is driving alongside us, entering the bridge in the lane reserved for traffic going in the opposite direction.

"*There's* the someone we're afraid of," Navarro calls to Amelia in the back.

I glance in the rearview mirror. Amelia's mouth has dropped open, and she seems to be experiencing her first real emotions ever.

"Oh shit," Toby says.

"If you have any weapons back there, now would be a great time to hand them out," I shout at Amelia. She doesn't answer and my anger surges as I realize she's actually filming all of this.

Navarro is getting his carbine ready, but he doesn't have his pack. That means he's got thirty rounds.

The SUV rams our side. We're pushed into the side of the bridge. Sparks fly as our car drags along the metal of the railing. *Boom. Boom. Boom. Boom.* Four shots are fired in rapid succession into my window.

Annika screams one long continuous scream.

The glass is able to withstand the first three shots, with cracks the size of small rocks breaking out, but the fourth one does it.

The glass shatters.

It shoots across my face. I fight back a scream of my own as a shard scrapes my cheek. Wide chunks of glass land in my lap. I'm waiting for Navarro to fire the damn rifle, but next to me, he's breathing heavily. The SUV knocks us again. I hold the wheel with all my strength, but I steal a glance at Navaro.

Blood runs down his face and pools up around his neck. A piece of glass the size of a corn chip juts from his left eye.

Oh holy hell.

"Toby!" I yell. "Help!"

I feel around for the rifle.

The window of the SUV next to us rolls down.

I flinch and duck, expecting to face the barrel of a weapon.

I fight against the impulse to close my eyes.

Instead of a gun.

It's my mom.

Her chestnut hair is pulled up in a high, flattering ponytail that swings as her vehicle hits the potholes in the bridge. The collar of her red jacket flaps in the wind.

"Susan," she calls out. "Stop that vehicle.

"Now."

In a world where everyone was fighting for what they believed to be right, I couldn't stop thinking about this one question. Could justice ever be achieved at the end of a gun?

–MacKENNA NOVAK,
Letters from the Second Civil War

MacKENNA

I frantically wave my arms around and feel all over. The only thing I'm able to grab is a fluffy baby doll wearing a silky nightgown. I toss it at Jo as hard as I can. But she ducks, and the doll's yarn hair grazes her cheek.

Where in the hell is Terminus?

LEAD: Rogue soldier murders student journalist in abandoned doll factory while morally flexible hacker saves himself.

IMPORTANT FACTS:

-Terminus won't help me.

-Dad can't help me.

-Jinx can't help me.

-I have no weapons.

I have to remember the drills.

Do what you have to do to survive.

I'm on the verge of passing out and of using my last measure of air. But I have to survive. I rally the memory of everything that's happened since we got stuck in that burning building. The memory of all those people lost at sea on the *Booker*.

Of all the victims of Carver's weapons of destruction.

My anger is enough.

I find my footing on one of the rock sculptures and use it as leverage, kicking my leg over my head and into Jo's face. She stumbles back, crashing into the wide fake tree.

"Leave me alone!" I force the words out of my throbbing throat and roll to a standing position.

Jo jumps up too. "God. Why can't you die already?"

She walks calmly in the direction of the gun on the floor.

I need to do something. I can hear Jinx's voice in my ears. *Disable with a strike to the nose. Then immobilize with a hit to the lower body.* Maybe I can crack a kneecap.

But Jo is an experienced soldier and I am...

Me.

I let out a scream. A high, shrill scream. The kind of scream that would be really embarrassing in another time. I charge at Jo again, this time like a linebacker going after a quarterback at a football game. With minimal effort, she puts one arm out and pushes me away. I fall down.

On my butt.

Again.

A baby doll pops out of the cabbage patch and onto my lap. It has dimples and red yarn hair and smiley brown eyes. This is a pretty damn embarrassing way to go out.

I can almost read my obituary.

MacKenna Novak, killed in the cabbage patch.

Where in the actual hell is Terminus? Did he run out and manage to steal that craptastic car in the parking lot?

I'm gonna cry.

LEAD: MacKenna Novak is pathetic.

I crawl over and slump down against Mother Cabbage, the weirdo plastic tree that will be serving as my headstone, and I wait for Jo to return to shoot me.

I close my eyes.

"Stand back…and…and…" It's Terminus's voice. Scared. Uncertain.

Opening my eyes, I see Terminus over by the cribs. He has the shotgun, and Jo is about five feet in front of him. She's halfway between me and Terminus. She isn't about to take orders from him.

Jo steps forward.

A loud, low *bang* erupts in the quiet night.

The shot sails by, missing both Jo and me. A cloud of white stuffing and exploding doll faces rises from the cabbage patch. A piece of plastic doll face lands at my feet, and there's something horrifying about the half of a green eye that stares up at me. Some of the doll's forehead is attached, along with a few pieces of black yarn.

"You know you can't shoot me, Partridge."

It's Jo's voice, but I can't tell where it's coming from now.

The thing is, she may be right. Like, Terminus might not be able to aim the damn gun. I scramble around the plastic tree trunk and hug my knees in tight as a bunch more shots crack out. Four or five.

The other thing is, I didn't pay any attention whatsoever back in the bunker when Navarro made big charts of guns and talked and talked and *talked* about how much ammo each could hold.

Click. Click. Click. Click.

"You're out of ammo, idiot," Jo calls out, confirming my fears.

Then it's like everyone and everything is in motion.

In hopes of finding something to use as a weapon, I make a break for the twisting staircase, using the wrought iron railing for support. Jo darts up from under the birth certificate computers. Terminus isn't too far behind us. One of the white cribs shimmies and falls forward as Terminus makes a break for it.

I glance over my shoulder to see him skid to a stop by the cabbage patch. He tosses the dolls from the patch at Jo as she chases me up the stairs.

I take a right at the landing and make my way up to the second floor. From where I am, I can see the legs of a sofa. When I'm nearing the top of the stairs, Jo gets hit by a preemie swathed in a blue blanket with an "It's a Boy" tag attached. She grunts as it bounces off her and falls near my foot. The fake boy had a name.

Connor Dean.

He'll never be wrapped up and put under the Christmas tree.

Terminus launches more dolls into the air. They mostly hit stair railings, making weird *bong* sounds, like the ringing of a large bell, as they hit the iron railing.

I arrive at the top of the stairs at what looks like a waiting area with velvet couches and a few walnut-finished, round-back chairs. It's a loft lit by low emergency night-lights, and it has more of the fancy wrought iron railing on the side that overlooks the fake baby hospital below. A coffee table is covered in doll catalogs and magazines. Mostly in Spanish.

More footsteps stomp on the stairs.

Terminus must be on the way up.

Then. All three of us are upstairs.

Jo goes for me. She grabs the tail of my T-shirt, pulls me toward her and then pushes me back against the railing.

Hard.

A section of the wrought iron railing gives out as I crash into it. I struggle for my footing, managing to grab the remaining railing, but my balance falters and I fall back and wind up dangling over the side, hovering in the space over Mother Cabbage. The edges of the metal cut into my fingers, and the railing creaks where it was attached to the staircase bannister. I scream again as a few drops of blood trickle down my fingers.

It won't support my weight for long.

The dark tile floor is a dark void beneath me.

Jo kneels in front of me. For a second, she watches me uncertainly. Sweat beads on the skin above her upper lip. Maybe she's gonna toss me off, but even if she doesn't, my arms are aching and are about to give out.

I should have done more upper body workouts.

I could let go. It would be so easy.

Jo smiles and leans forward.

Before she can pry my bleeding fingers from the bar of the iron railing, there's a crack, a gurgling grunt, and Jo's eyes roll back in her head. I'm barely able to swing myself to the side before she falls through the hole created by the missing rail bars.

Even still, Jo almost takes me down with her.

Something wet drags along my leg.

There's a *smack*, almost like the way eggs sounded when my mother broke them on her stainless-steel mixing bowl to make fritule.

Terminus grabs my forearms in the nick of time.

He's flopped down on his stomach and has one hand around each of my arms. Since neither of us will be winning any weight lifting prizes, it takes a couple minutes to drag me up. Terminus keeps his feet dug into the green carpet and scoots back as he yanks me back onto the landing. I groan as I scrape my arms on the jagged wooden edges of the landing as he pulls. But we do it.

Terminus falls back, sitting cross-legged. The empty shotgun rests next to his legs. The part that I know as the butt is all bloody. Terminus must have whacked Jo over the head.

It takes me a minute to catch my breath. It's Jo's dark red blood. I swat at it and make a gagging sound. "Ah…oh… ugh…yuck…" I have her blood on my hands.

I've helped kill someone *and her blood is on my hands.*

I have, like, literal blood on my hands.

Terminus stays as frozen as one of the dolls.

I dig my fingernails into my own palms to stop a growing panic.

"Okay. Okay. Okay." I'm pretty sure I spend a whole minute muttering to myself. I want to scream and run and scream some more and go hide somewhere. But. "We need to get out of here." Maybe I didn't pay enough attention when Navarro talked, but I do remember that you can't run all over the place firing your gun. Sound like that carries. For miles. "We don't know who might show up to investigate."

Terminus says nothing. His blue eyes are huge marbles, wide with shock. His face has turned greenish gray. Like a Halloween mask.

"Hey!" I say grateful for the annoyance that floods through me. "Let's go."

"Go?" he repeats. "Where are we gonna go?"

Perfect.

I was the one who was dangling off the side of a balcony, swinging back and forth like a pendulum, about to crack my damn head on that checkerboard tile floor. It was me Jo tried to choke to death. It ought to be me sitting there panicking.

"And Christ. I just killed someone." His voice is stuffy. I think he's crying. Or about to cry.

Oh yeah. There's that.

I hold out my hand to help him up. He doesn't immediately take it. I actually feel kinda bad. For Terminus. And even for Jo. "You saved my life. You had to do something. You had no choice. We didn't have a choice."

He finally takes my hand. The nonbloody one.

The warmth of his palm is a relief.

Once he's up, I try to clean my other hand on my pants, but all that happens is that I smear blood on my only clean pant leg. I look like roadkill.

"I don't suppose you passed a bathroom?" I ask.

He runs his hand though his cropped hair. I don't think he's gotten used to his new cut. "Uh. Yeah. Actually. And I found the office supply room." Terminus motions for me to follow him. I notice he has a flashlight and a bag of stuff. Supplies like bottled water, candy bars, more flashlights and batteries poke out of the top of the unzipped green canvas bag.

I feel even worse. He wasn't hiding like I thought. He was searching for supplies.

I trail behind the path of Terminus's light. He opens a door a few feet from where Jo fell off the landing. The charming, Southern-style loft gives way to a generic gray office. We pass cubicles and desks loaded with cheap computers, family photos, toy boxes and dolls in various states of undress. I can't read any of the paperwork, but it looks like order forms.

"From the looks of it, people still work up here," I say.

Terminus nods. "Until recently anyway. When I was looking around, I found a memo in English. They stopped the tours at the beginning of the year. But they were shipping dolls until two weeks ago, when the border closed."

We arrive at a small room full of Post-it notes, pens, regular paper, extra staplers and spare computer parts. There's even a stack of e-tablets.

"Somebody left their gym bag in the supply room," he tells me.

Terminus picks up a black duffel bag and tosses it to me. He notices me staring at the e-tablets. "I put a few of those in the bag. But I need to inspect them before we turn them on. I don't know if they have network cards or what."

He leads me to the bathroom, gives me the flashlight, and I go in there, hoping that there's something in the bag that fits. The bathroom has three toilet stalls and a long steel sink. I open the bag. Inside, there's a green shirt with an illustration of a sleeping doll and the words DOLLAPALOOZA DREAMS in script letters, a purple headband and some black leggings. The shirt and leggings are too short and too tight, but they're better than wearing the bloody pants. I change and put my old clothes in the trash can.

I leave the bathroom, and out in the main office area, Terminus seems a bit more stable. "I checked all the desks. I found a jar of coins and an envelope that must be petty cash or something. To be honest, I'm not sure how much money it is."

Checking out the container of gold and silver coins, I can't tell either, but at least it's something.

Okay. Good.

"So, what now?" Terminus asks.

I sigh. "All we have to do is make it to that dusty car. Hope

The Opposition or Jo's friends or whoever else might hate us isn't out there. Hope we can start the car. Hope we can make it to the border and hope Antone will help us."

I've got the flashlight, so I lead us toward the stairs.

Terminus follows. "Who's Antone?"

"Dr. Doomsday's friend at the border."

After a minute, we're back in the loft. It's quiet out there. Which should be reassuring.

But somehow, Terminus hesitates near the velvet sofa.

Truth is, I don't want to go down there either.

LEAD: Journalist and hacker hide in doll factory forever.

I creep to the edge of the loft, along the part that has the railing intact. We're gonna have to go down there. But some part of me needs to know what we'll be facing. It's probably a mess. I grip the iron railing, expecting to see Jo's body contorted in the shape of a chalk outline like in one of those crime TV shows.

Oh. My. God.

I wave the flashlight all around.

"What?" Terminus asks. And then with more urgency. "What do you see?"

"Nothing," I whisper.

Josephine Pletcher is gone.

Visceral violence is an essential spectacle to motivate a crowd.

—AMELIA AOKI
Report: *The Image of the Second Civil War*
Stamped: Top Secret

JINX

There she is.

That killer.

That murderer.

That same face I see in the mirror each morning.

We're driving at full speed across the bridge. In similar vehicles.

Are we the same? Do we have the same stuff inside?

"Where is Charles?" I scream into the fading daylight, even though I know where he is. And anyway. It's not like Mom will help me get my brother back.

Mom leans out her window. A guy who's basically Tork 2.0 is in the driver's seat next to her. "Last chance. Pull over now," she yells. She adds this little carrot. "I'll let your friends go. You won't get a better offer."

The same offer Tork made the night that Mom let him push us out of the back of the truck. Mom, who made up a song to help me memorize the quadratic formula. Who brought me breakfast in bed every birthday. That same person wants me to bargain for my life.

"Should we stop?" Annika asks.

"Why do you always want to surrender?" I snap.

Toby kneels in the space between the seats. "Not helping, Jinx." He's got a small first aid kit, but it's no match for the giant piece of glass sticking out of Navarro's eye.

"Gus! Tilt your chin to minimize the blood loss," I say. Apparently, Toby's brief induction into the Provisional Army of the New United States didn't include first aid. "We have to get him to a doctor." I'm not sure who I'm even talking to. Who the *we* even is.

Navarro moans.

Annika mutters, "What are we going to do?" over and over.

"I don't suppose your team can help us out here?" Toby calls to Amelia.

She remains in the backseat, wordlessly filming.

"Give me the gun," I say to Toby. When he hesitates, "The rail gun. Now. And get ready to drive."

He activates the small silver weapon and then passes it to me. "It's only got four projectiles."

Okay.

Out of the corner of my eye, I can see the backseat window of the other SUV open. Mom is going to give the order for them to take us out. I slam on the brakes, letting Mom's car go sailing past us. We skid to a sharp stop in the middle of the bridge. Up ahead, a small green car is traveling in the opposite direction. It's still about a mile away but is flashing its lights at Mom's SUV.

Hoping to avoid getting shredded by broken glass, I take off my jacket and do my best to cover the bottom window with it. But I don't have time to be slow or careful as I hoist myself out the window and onto the car's roof. Jagged shards drag along my arms and rip my new pants.

"Susan… Susan…what are you doing?" Navarro says with another moan.

Using the handles of a luggage rack mounted to the roof, I hoist myself up. I poke my head back through the window. "Count to five and then drive," I say to Toby.

I climb into the center of the roof, take off my belt, loop it around the steel bar of the part of the rack nearest to the back bumper. After I loop the belt back around my waist, I'm barely secure when Toby hits the gas and we resume traveling toward the Oregon side of the bridge.

Rifle fire breaks out as we speed toward the other SUV. I keep myself as low as possible. Annika is screaming again. It would help us if she would just shut up. But her reactions are the only part of this situation that feel normal.

I'm doing my best to contain my terror, to hold in the part of me that would like to jump off the roof of the car and into the ocean. I have to save Charles…and now Navarro.

The rail gun feels cold in my palm.

I've never fired a gun like this before, but the design mirrors that of a more conventional weapon. It looks remarkably like a Colt 1911. And I do know how to use that.

Bracing my feet on the front bar of the roof rack, I squeeze the trigger.

Dad never told me much about rail guns. They were illegal. Supposedly giant and only for the military. But I vaguely recall him saying that they use an electromagnetic system to fire projectiles at a superfast velocity. Faster than a speeding bullet.

Literally.

The projectile explodes from the gun, creating an unusual, bright spark, almost like a firework. I'm unprepared for the recoil and I don't hold my arms nearly still enough. I miss Mom's car by at least five feet. The projectile dart hits the metal concrete and rebounds into the metal railing on the other side of the bridge. It bounces back and forth like a pinball.

If it doesn't stop, we're going to drive right into it.

A huge wave crests over the side of the bridge, covering our SUV for a minute and soaking my clothes. I'm totally wet again. Toby swerves uncertainly.

Okay. Okay. I force myself to take three quick breaths. The sharp wind pushes my hair into my face. My teeth chatter and I fight to keep my eyes open even as they burn from the salt water. I have to hit the tires of Mom's SUV. I *have* to immobilize them.

Keeping my arms as straight and as stiff as I can, I aim for the rear passenger side tire. I squeeze the trigger again, keeping my knees tense and firm and my feet stiff against the bar of the roof rail. I suck in a breath.

This time—

—it's a hit.

The speed and power of the projectile is incredible. It lifts the bumper of Mom's SUV at least three feet off the ground. The dart is so fast that it passes through both rear tires, which burst with a boom that sounds like it's just inches from my ear, despite all the noise. Shots explode from the roof of the SUV before silencing altogether. Clearly, whoever is in there with Mom lost control of their gun.

The other SUV is fishtailing and swerving across both lanes of the bridge. We'll be caught up with it in a matter of seconds.

Okay. I need to take the thing out. I need to take *Mom* out. Here.

I.

Go.

Holding my breath, I aim for the gas tank.

Boom.

Fire.

The SUV becomes a violent bomb.

The green car is getting quite close. It's slowing down, but Mom's SUV does a sharp circle and hits the green car. Both the SUV and the other car are blown across our lane and pushed over the side of the bridge.

Disappearing into the Columbia River.

Whoever was in that green car probably wasn't trained for this.

Whoever was in that green car is probably dead.

More death. More loss. More pain.

There will always be casualties.

How many more people will I kill before this is finished? Will this war ever end?

My mom is fine. That accident wouldn't have killed me, and she's better than me. Certainly, more dangerous. I grip the rail gun. It's got one shot left.

I could make Toby turn this car around. One shot is all it would take. I'd have plenty of time. They're going to have to swim to shore.

But. Could I really kill my own mother?

Plus, Navarro desperately needs a doctor. And I have to save my brother.

I bounce up as we run over some kind of car part and then a pothole full of seawater. Another massive wave splashes over us. Toby swerves but manages to keep the car from skidding.

I stare at the gray sea. "Where is my brother? Tell me where he is. Where is Charles?" No one can hear me over the wind and the waves. That's all I really want. I want Charles back.

I unbuckle my belt, wrap it around my hand and crawl along the roof of the car. I'm almost knocked off when we hit another pothole. But I'm able to swing myself back into the driver's seat, sending Toby into Navarro. Gus has passed out in the passenger seat.

I'm too cold to feel anything at all.

Toby climbs into the middle row of seats to console a crying Annika.

I glance in the rearview mirror.

We can't go back.

I push down the part of me that wants to.

We were simultaneously haunted by Dr. Doomsday's theories.

And ruled by them.

—MacKENNA NOVAK,
Letters from the Second Civil War

MacKENNA

She was *right there.*

Terminus had smacked Josephine Pletcher with the butt of a rifle, and she'd fallen off the second-floor balcony onto a hard tile floor. But in the time it had taken me to change my sweats, she'd gotten up and disappeared. Maybe the zombie apocalypse is nigh.

I've always wanted to use that word. *Nigh. Nigh. Nigh.*

Okay, MacKenna, this is not the time for witty wordplay.

"What are we gonna do?" I ask Terminus.

He keeps peering over the side of the loft and gripping the wrought iron railing and checking and rechecking the floor.

"Why am I asking you?" I mutter. "Come on."

There really isn't that much to talk about. The only option we have is to go to the parking lot and hope that Jo isn't waiting to ambush us *and* hope that we can get that old car to work. Yep. Great plan.

I grab Terminus's hand and drag him down the stairs. I hold the flashlight in my other hand and keep it pointed at the ground to make sure we don't step in any blood. We creep out the way we came in, through the employee break room and out by the door with the creepy buckets of doll parts.

I open the door only a crack, peeking out into the night with one eye.

Behind me, Terminus breathes heavily and jiggles the bag he's holding. If there is someone outside, they probably know we're back here. There isn't much point in being timid. We take off at a run, using the flashlight to guide ourselves around to the front of Dollapalooza, where the lone, dusty car is parked.

I'm in front with Terminus a few feet behind me. When we arrive at the corner that leads to the front of the building, from what I can see in the moonlight, two military-type vehicles, like Humvees or something, squeal across the Dollapalooza parking lot. The caravan is coming right toward us.

It has to be Jo. Or whomever she was with.

I need to stay calm.

Keep it together, Mac.

LEAD: Two idiots waste a ton of time fighting a super-soldier only to be gunned down in a parking lot.

No. That's too emotional. Also, not much of a story.

"She's gonna kill us," Terminus says, and then keeps repeating, "She's gonna kill us."

Real cheerful.

"We have to run! Now!" I yell. I sound like Jinx.

We run into the parking lot and my flashlight rolls over the fake Southern columns that flank the front door. The Humvees are getting closer. They'll be right by the door in about ten seconds.

The little crappy car is…gone.

We are so so so so *so* screwed.

I skid to a stop. Terminus is right behind me and almost shoves me into a small, motorized scooter that's now parked by the front door. How many people are here at the damn doll factory? What the hell is going on?

Like, maybe we could steal the scooter, but even if we can get it to work, there's no way it will hold both of us. Or be fast enough to get away from a bunch of all-terrain vehicles.

"Okay. Okay. Maybe we can…" I stammer.

Terminus sees the scooter too. "You take it. I'll see if I can buy you some time."

"Oh hell no," I tell him. Every time we've ever split up has been a complete mess. If I'd stayed with Jinx, this wouldn't be happening. The only thing to do is go back inside Dollapalooza and attempt to hold Jo's team off as best we can.

The Humvee motors grow louder, filling the quiet night.

I take Terminus's hand again and draw him back around the corner in the direction of the rear door.

We almost run into the small blue car as it barrels onto the grass yard that surrounds the building. Terminus's hands slam onto the dusty hood. We can't run back. We can't fun forward. My knees shake and are about to give out.

The passenger door opens.

MacKenna Novak, prepare to meet your maker.

I close my eyes. I wonder if death is like in those old movies and cartoons where you float around in the clouds and listen to harp music.

"Get in," a voice says. A familiar voice. My eyes fly open.

It's *Galloway.*

The car only has two doors, and I don't have time to locate the button to move the front seat forward, so I squeeze into the backseat in between the two seats in the front as Terminus gets into the passenger seat. I hit my face on the rear window as he pushes me so he can close the door.

I say *oof* and Galloway also grunts.

I must have knocked into him as I climbed in. I notice his left arm is in a sling. The skin under his eyes has turned bluish black. Galloway's got scrapes all over his arms and face. He's been beat to all hell from when we tossed him out of the Land Rover.

But he's alive.

Galloway hits the gas.

This car is a real piece of crap. It's old and not computerized. Like, a vehicle Dr. Doomsday would have preferred. But it's got an engine that sounds like a lawn mower. We'll never outrun Jo in this thing.

Galloway keeps the little car close to the Dollapalooza building. He holds a small black fob in his right hand. He goes too slow. Way. Too. Slow. Slow enough that shots ring out into the night, grazing the edge of our unmarked POS.

I grip the edge of my seat. Hard. "They're shooting at us!"

Oh, real smart, Mac. Everyone knows they're shooting at us.

I turn around to watch the brown Humvees gaining on us.

We circle around to the front door, and I'm seconds away from asking Galloway if he's planning on driving round and round in a circle like some bizarro NASCAR race through a baby doll hellscape.

He pushes a button on the fob.

A huge explosion rocks our small car. I turn around in my seat to see flames push up over the hatchback. Galloway must now have the pedal to the metal, because the engine screams as we try to outrun the fire. Right as it seems like we'll be sucked into the mess behind us, Galloway is able to put some distance between the explosion and us.

I catch my breath as we get close to the parking lot exit. Galloway's bomb took out both of the Humvees. I can see the silhouettes of soldiers climbing out and surveying the mess. A couple of them continue to fire at us, but our situation is improving by the second.

It's going to be enough. We're gonna get away.

For now.

LEAD: Student journalist and morally flexible hacker rescued from attack at doll factory by ex-marine.

That's okay, I guess. It has the *who, what* and *where*. But not the *why*.

Okay. Fake it 'til you make it. Confidence. Go.

"So. Where we headed?" I ask.

"You tell me," Galloway says, between clenched teeth.

"What are you talking about?" I ask.

"Let's stop playing games. I think we've established that if I take you to Fort Marshall or to the safe house, Copeland's people will have you executed." He glances at Terminus. "You must have suspected as much. That's why you were so hell-bent on ditching me."

Well. It helps that Galloway assumes we were smart enough to actually have some plan or motivation beyond getting back to my dad.

Terminus opens his mouth, but I speak first. "That's right," I say in a strong tone that I don't really feel. "Dr. Doomsday has a friend at the border. We were heading there."

Galloway's shoulders relax at the mention of Dr. Doomsday, and we near what I think is the same road we were on before. It's dark and there are no streetlights. I don't know what exists beyond the tiny headlights of this small car.

"Uh. Um. Sorry for kicking you…and…uh…" I stammer.

"Tossing me from a moving car?" Galloway says with a humorless laugh. "Considering Captain Pletcher tried to take you out, I won't hold it against you."

"Thanks," Terminus says. He digs around in his bag and offers bottles of water to me and Galloway.

"So where is the colonel's contact?" Galloway asks.

I reach for a bottle, twist off the top and take a long gulp. "At the San Miguel gate on the border. I think it might be—"

"I know where it is," Galloway says. "I was briefly stationed at one of the inspection stations during the Border Patrol Strike."

The Border Strike. I did a report on this. Since the New Depression started, labor strikes are common, but the strike of the border patrol agents was particularly contentious. The Spark called out the marines to staff the border, and The Opposition wanted the agents fired and blacklisted.

I check behind us again. No one appears to be following us, and the flames in front of Dollapalooza are now like a small campfire in the distance.

I tap Galloway on the shoulder. "Do you have any idea what's really happening?"

"What do you mean?" he says, sharply.

"I think Copeland has a plan. Something we haven't thought of."

"Like what?" Galloway asks.

"I don't know," I say. "But deactivating those cold fusion bombs isn't his endgame. Plus, I don't believe he gives a damn about helping Rosenthal."

Even as I say these words, I know they're true.

All these things. Peter Navarro. Dr. Doomsday. General Copeland. AIRSTA. Los Alamos. All these pieces of a puzzle. They don't seem to go together.

Galloway thinks for a minute. "All I know is what they probably told you. That Rosenthal wants the other cold fusion bombs deactivated and destroyed. But..."

"But what?" I ask. My pulse slows to a dull thud.

He sighs. "The last time I saw Colonel Marshall, he talked about Copeland. He said, 'The general won't be happy until the whole world is at war.' The way he said it chilled me to the bone."

"Is that why you're helping us?" I ask.

"Not really," Galloway says slowly. "Regardless of what happens, I consider Max Marshall my commanding officer, and he gave me a standing order."

"What was the order?" I ask.

"Follow Jinx Marshall."

Right. Only Jinx isn't here. So, what does this mean for us?

A set of headlights approaches us. I hold my breath.

The car whizzes by us without any event.

Terminus speaks in the silence. "One of the classes Dr. Marshall taught was about political systems modeling. Specifically, how leaders could use disaster situations to consolidate power."

"I remember," I say. "Dr. Doomsday talked about that the first time I met him. You create a little chaos. Blame your enemy. Get power. That's what he said."

"Right," Terminus comments, also thinking hard.

Doomsday also said, *When I realized that Carver didn't want to fix this world, that he wanted to remake it in his own image, I left. But it was too late.*

All along we assumed that Max Marshall left The Opposition because he didn't want to participate in the attacks on First Federal. But what if it was bigger than that? Whatever Dr. Doomsday learned at AIRSTA, well, he wanted no part of it.

Cause chaos. Blame your enemy. An icy chill runs through me as I realize.

Copeland is still working for The Opposition.

LEAD: General Copeland leads a mission to detonate two cold fusion bombs and blame devastation on The Spark.

"So, San Miguel?" Galloway says, cutting through my thoughts.

"Yep," I say absently.

Both sites were in states dominated by The Spark. By bombing major cities in those areas, The Opposition eliminated population centers that were important to the enemy. Blaming Rosenthal for the attacks was brilliant.

Holy crap. I *have* to get to Los Alamos.

And I have to warn Jinx.

"You're sure this guy will help us?" Galloway asks. He catches my gaze in the mirror.

Even though I'm about to lie my face off, there's something reassuring about the fact that Galloway considers himself one of us. The last time we saw Louis Antone, he'd pretty much told us to leave and not come back.

"Oh yeah," I say, leaning back, going for a casual look. "He'll help."

"That makes sense," Galloway says, relaxing even more. "Like the colonel said, *Always have a backup plan.*"

Terminus shakes his head, a small gesture only I notice. Probably because I'm the only one staring at him all the time.

Focus.

"Oh yeah. For sure."

For sure.

When I was a little girl, my father used to tell me that people can see only what they can understand. What he meant, of course, was that the population at large could be controlled by their inability to understand complex affairs. But I always wondered if the reverse was true.

If I could get the world to see me, would it understand me?

–ANNIKA CARVER
Unpublished memoir
Property of Pembroke Press; Archive; Not for release

JINX

Amelia's team is going to get us all killed.

Somehow, we finally make it into Astoria. I've never been here before, so I don't know what it's supposed to look like. But I don't think *anywhere* is supposed to be like this.

Old hotel buildings line the shore. At one time, they were probably beautiful places to stay with a view of the Columbia River. Now they're all either partially or fully underwater. We see an old man in a canoe paddling around a faded pink and turquoise building with a sign that reads ATOMIC MOTEL VACANCY. He ducks to go under what was probably once a porte cochere and continues to steer his canoe to a staircase.

Amelia's directions take us away from the shore and into a hilly area but, even there, it seems like the apocalypse has come and gone. Buildings are boarded up and riddled with bullet holes. Everywhere I look I see peeling strips of brightly colored paint and rust. It's a village that the wind is trying to knock down and the sea wants to reclaim.

A lady wheels a shopping cart full of junk up the street and visibly jumps when we pass.

"What happened here?" Annika whispers.

"The war," Amelia tells her flatly.

I pull the car into the driveway at Angeline's Bed-and-Breakfast. Years ago, people were probably writing reviews about this place that called it romantic and charming.

But now.

The blue sign has a hole punched through it. The stairs are missing a step. Several of the windows are cracked. The flower beds have been trampled.

"There's a doctor in here, right?" I say to Amelia.

"Yes," Amelia says.

I run around to the passenger side to help Navarro out. He almost falls on top of me, and I'm relieved when Toby appears behind me. Together, the two of us carry Gus inside. We enter a wide living room with water-stained hardwood floors and a grouping of furniture that faces a wall of wind-swept bookcases. There's a registration desk in front of the wall opposite the front door. From the looks of it, no one's been behind that desk in a long time.

A man in a lab coat paces around in front of a navy blue Chesterfield sofa.

"This is Dr. Knudsen," Amelia says, turning off the camera.

The doctor gives us a curt nod.

"Let's get him into the drawing room," Knudsen says. The doctor is short and squat. He has cropped black hair and is balding on top. There's something sort of familiar about him.

Navarro grunts as Toby and I drag him into a narrow hall-way and then a smaller carpeted room that has been outfitted like a makeshift hospital. A tall, young woman with blond hair is inside, attaching IV fluid bags to stainless steel stands.

Another man wearing a surgical mask is placing small medical tools on a tray with wheels.

"Get him on the cot," Knudsen says, gesturing to one of three padded beds in the room.

Toby and I rest Navarro on the cot as gently as we can.

I grab Navarro's hand, which is cold and lifeless.

The woman passes Knudsen a mask and assists him in donning a pair of vinyl gloves. The doctor jerks his chin out the door. "You can wait in the sitting room," he says.

"Don't you even want us to tell you what happened?" I ask. I feel like a complete idiot. Navarro has a giant piece of glass sticking out of his head. Anyone can see what happened.

"Wait outside," the doctor repeats.

"I should stay because—"

Knudsen's wide mouth sinks into a frown. "Because *rule number six. Trust no one.* You don't remember me, do you?"

Uh. No. I don't.

"From PrepperCon? I wrote *Your First Kit of First Aid for Surviving the Unsurvivable*," Knudsen says impatiently.

Oh yeah. I remember seeing a little bald man in a red shirt run all around the convention center. "And you were the consultant Dad hired to read the medical chapters of his book?"

"Right," Knudsen says, nodding. "I must say, your father was always far too concerned with packing light. You can't solve every problem with gauze and QuikClot." The doctor is backing Toby and me toward the door. "Gustavo here worked my booth two years in a row. If I wanted to kill him, I've had ample opportunity."

"You're contaminating this environment," the blonde woman says.

"I'll be fine, Susan," Navarro calls out weakly.

Ugh. I have to let Knudsen get that thing out of Gus's eye.

Toby and I return to the sitting room, where Annika has positioned herself on one side of the blue sofa. As always, she's neat as a pin. You'd never guess she was just in a firefight. She has the air of someone whose picnic got rained out.

Toby takes a seat next to Annika.

There's a large window on the wall to the right of the front door. I peek out at the Astoria neighborhood in twilight.

We are really, really screwed.

Suddenly, I realize I'm wet and freezing, and every part of my body absolutely aches.

I turn to Toby. "As soon as the doctor dresses Navarro's eye, we need to be ready to rock," I say. "And we need to do something about that SUV."

Toby stares into space, as if he's thinking hard.

Amelia is placing her laptop on the registration desk. "I had my crew move it into the back and cover it with a tarp. We know what we're doing."

My anger ignites. "I don't think you do. Otherwise we wouldn't be here. This is the worst type of place to set up," I tell her. "There are three or four residents on this street. If it were busier, we might blend in. If it were deserted no one would see us. You've put enough people here that we'll stand out like a sore thumb."

Amelia freezes in the middle of digging a long cable out of her tech bag. "They had to evacuate this area last week. The cold fusion bomb in California caused flooding all up and down the coast. There was no way to predict that."

This is going along with the notion that The Spark didn't know about the attack.

"Right. And how long do you think it's going to take my mother to swim out of the river and make her way to a phone?

We've got an hour, two at the absolute tops, before The Opposition shows up here," I say.

"Um...well..." Amelia stammers. "You think she survived and..."

"Yes," I say flatly.

"We need to discuss what to do next," Toby says.

Toby can't be trusted. He's here to run off with his girlfriend.

"I know what *I* have to do. Save Charles."

If the maps that Navarro spent so much time staring at are right, we're around two hundred miles north of my brother's position. This knowledge lights a fire in me. I don't care what Amelia said, or what Toby thinks is best. I'm going.

I must have said that last part out loud, because Toby stands up.

"You're going?" He comes to stand inches from my face, his eyes dark and stormy. "You're not going anywhere without me. We have an agreement. We said we'd stay together."

An agreement? Is he really referencing what we said that night in the desert?

"We *had* an agreement. First, you tried to run off. Then, you joined Copeland's team of supersoldier wannabes," I tell him. "Finally, you're shacked up here with your girlfriend and, let's face it, that's all you really care about."

"I didn't get to choose Ammon Carver for my father any more than you got to select Stephanie Maxwell as your mother," Annika says in a bitter voice.

I want to smack her.

"I'm not running off with my girlfriend," Toby says. He sits down again next to Annika and motions for me to take a seat in the armchair next to him. "We're trying to come up with a solution to a difficult set of problems."

Since I feel so tired that I might fall down if I don't sit, I take the chair.

Amelia is fully situated behind the registration desk. She's got two laptops, a video editing monitor and a large modern modem that probably communicates with a satellite.

Whatever else happens, I'm taking that stuff with me when I go.

Toby leans forward. "Listen. I *was* going to take off that day in Mexico. That was wrong. I felt so defeated all the time and... I messed up." He puts his hand on my arm, the way he used to when MacKenna and I would be fighting about some stupid thing and he wanted me to calm down. "But everything I've done since then has been to help get Charles back. I joined Copeland's team so I could get on this mission and so that I could find out whatever I could. We needed an inside man."

This makes some amount of sense. And I desperately want to trust Toby.

But.

I make a dramatic show of tilting my head in Annika's direction.

"She's here to help," he says.

"She's here because you're in love with her!"

Toby's face turns red, and he steals a glance at Annika. "I don't know what's going to happen in the future, Jinx. But that's not why she's here. She hates Ammon Carver as much as we do. As much as you hate your mother. She risked everything to come help us." He gives Annika a gentle prod. "Tell her what you did."

For the first time, Annika actually looks a bit flustered. "Oh. Well. I overheard my father on the phone, talking to someone about..." She gives Toby a perfect damsel-in-distress look.

He takes over for her. "She overheard Carver discussing arrangements to add additional security to AIRSTA."

"And something about a prisoner they're keeping there," Annika adds.

Toby smiles at her. "Right. I made contact with her when we were at Fort Marshall."

"How?" I ask. They wouldn't let me near a terminal, and Toby is no hacker.

"I had access to the computers," he says impatiently. "They gave me basic credentials when Dad and I were commissioned. I told you. The whole point of joining was so that I could put a real plan together."

"Um. Excuse me. What?" Amelia says, glancing up from a monitor where she's reviewing footage of the car chase. "There's already a *real* plan."

"Right," Toby says with an eye roll. "That we're going to roll through Portland in a giant SUV and try to bust into AIRSTA with like forty marines. Sure. Never mind that all major US cities are under curfew, that there are checkpoints all over the place and—"

"We have all the necessary documents," Amelia says, hotly.

"We'll get caught," Toby says, shrugging out of his camo jacket. "Or in firefights with any number of violent mobs that are running around raising hell. Three days ago, fourteen people died during a raid on a food distribution center in the Pearl District."

"Violent mobs? Portland is out of food?" I ask.

"Almost everywhere is out of food," Amelia says quietly.

Toby glances at her. "Anyway. We have a better idea. As you know, to cover up Project Cold Front, The Opposition closed the Tillamook State Forest and the Siuslaw National Forest and cut off access to that part of the coast. But Annika got us a vehicle and forestry credentials. All we have to do is make it to a monitoring station about five miles from here. We can go on foot."

"On *foot?*" Amelia repeats.

This is a good plan. It will let us stick to the woods. We probably won't get stopped in a government vehicle.

I point at Annika. "What makes you think she can be trusted?"

Toby makes an impatient noise. "She risked her life coming here. *She's* got the uniforms and badges. Show her, Annika."

Annika opens the large bag she's been carrying, which is resting by her feet, to reveal green National Park Service uniforms, name tags, fobs and plastic badges. "I've even made sure that these credentials won't trigger any alarms. They're from employees on sabbatical."

Amelia stands up and starts to pace in front of the bookcases. "Wait. Wait."

When I continue to glare at Annika, Toby prompts her again. "Annika, show her the note," he says.

Annika puts her dainty hand in her bag again. She hands me a folded piece of cream stationery. I open it. At the top, I find the words Beverly Wilshire, Beverly Hills in fancy red script.

And then my brother's handwriting.

Oh God.

I jump up.

My dear sister…

Of course, Charles would write like this. Like he's eight going on eighty.

Things are fine here, although I do miss you terribly.

"Annika saw Charles. Last month. Probably when Stephanie was moving him to Oregon," Toby says.

"How was he?" I demand, coming to kneel beside her.

*My good friend Miss Carver tells me she might be seeing you
soon. I asked her to give you my regards.*

"Physically, he was fine," Annika says, slowly. "But emo-
tionally…"

I nod. He's doing about as well as can be expected when
your mother murders your father, kidnaps you and then leaves
you alone on a military base.

"Charles trusts Annika," Toby says.

Charles is a small child.

I'm waiting for you to come back.

And he never really understood the rules anyway. He never
understood the most basic rule. *Trust no one.*

But I'd made the decision that I didn't want to live like my
father. Look where his rules got him.

The letter is signed:

All my love, Charles

Like it or not, I'm going to have to trust Annika Carver.

Toby rises again, coming to stand near Amelia, towering
over her. "From now on, I am in charge of this mission."

Amelia casts a glance toward the registration desk. Toby
blocks her so she can't move in that direction. "Jinx, check
that equipment. Give me a report on what it's doing. Ms.

Aoki, please have a seat." He gestures to the sofa, urging Amelia to sit alongside Annika.

I move to the desk. From here I can hear the chatter in the drawing room. The low rumble of Dr. Knudsen's voice. The clink of instruments. I force myself to concentrate on the laptop. "Uh. It's a ruggedized UNIX system with a proprietary video editing suite. Something fast. Sophisticated. There's a satellite modem currently uploading an eight-minute video clip to a peer-to-peer file sharing site" It's a good setup. The IP address has been cloaked, and the upload is lightning fast.

Toby nods. "Okay. Let it finish and then get everything packed up. No more transmissions without authorization from me."

As he says this, the progress bar fills, and an alert tells me that the upload is done. I power off the laptop and begin winding up cables. If I'm going to trust Toby again, I have to ask.

"Do you have news about MacKenna?" I ask.

Toby hesitates for a second. "She and that hacker friend of yours made it to Mexico at the staging location for the Los Alamos mission. Dad sent her back to Fort Marshall." He pauses again. "You really don't know why she went there?"

"No. But…" I say. If we're really going to be a team again, I have to tell him. "Right before she left, Terminus and I stole some data off a research computer at SEALAB. I think she must have seen something important."

Toby sighs. "She didn't stick around to tell anyone about it."

MacKenna is impulsive. Reckless. That's what Navarro kept saying.

"All right," Toby says. "So we'll get on the move and try to come up with the best way to infiltrate AIRSTA."

Amelia's face scrunches up in anger. "I already told you. My team—"

Toby cuts her off. "We don't trust your team." He faces me. "The communication that Annika intercepted said the prisoner was being kept in a bunker adjacent to the cold fusion bomb silo. Clearly, that's where The Opposition is trying to lure us. Maybe we can get Charles out of that bunker without going into the silo at all."

"Without going into the silo? Are you serious?" Amelia says, shaking her head. "Millions of people could be killed by leaving that bomb potentially operable. I mean, let's imagine you rescue Charles Marshall. If The Opposition finds a way to detonate that cold fusion bomb before you get out of the blast radius, little Charles will be killed anyway."

"What are we going to do if Gus can't travel?" Annika asks, biting her lower lip. "That thing in his eye…it looked serious."

I don't want to think about what will happen if Navarro isn't okay.

He has to be okay.

I grab the bag of computer equipment and join everyone at the sofa. "Toby's right though. There's something about this that is just off. Some part of it we don't understand. The Opposition has done everything but dare us to go there. And The Spark knew about that bomb that was headed for California before The Opposition deployed it."

Amelia frowns at me.

"I'm not sure that's true," Toby says.

I make a face. "You saw Jo on the *Booker*. She knew that bomb was going to blow."

"Rosenthal didn't know. But I think Copeland did," Toby says.

"Harlan Copeland is deranged," Annika comments.

Toby nods. "One of my assignments was guarding Rosenthal's quarters. SEALAB really wasn't made for top secret conversations. Rosenthal and Copeland were really going at it. Basically, Rosenthal was saying that after spending all that time with The Opposition, the general's intel sources ought to be better. I can't see why they would have put on that display for my benefit. I really think Rosenthal didn't know."

"So, all we really know is that both sides need me to log in to the AIRSTA mainframe, and neither side is being honest as to why," I say, thinking hard.

"Rosenthal is honest," Amelia says.

I have to hand it to her. She's sticking with her story.

"You really think your father would program the mainframe to allow you to log in?" Annika asks. She hands me a pair of green pants, a beige short-sleeved shirt, a green jacket, a black belt and a green tie.

"It sounds like something he would do," I say, taking the stuff from her.

"Because you used to do a lot of work together?" she asks.

"Because if my credentials are needed, it means The Opposition can't kill me and my brother," I say.

It's silent for a second.

A chill runs through me. I don't want to think about what it means that Dad had to build so many safeguards to keep people from executing us.

Amelia glares at Annika. "You got a uniform for me?"

"Oh, you're not coming," I say.

We need to travel light, and the last thing we need is some stranger with questionable motives tagging along.

Annika is already giving Amelia a uniform.

"She has to come with us," Annika says, in a hard, firm voice.

"Why?" I ask, squinting at Carver's daughter.

"Because she's right. Public opinion is the ultimate weapon. Like it or not, we need her," Annika says.

Toby nods in agreement as Amelia looks on.

"The doctor and nurses both work for me, and there are five soldiers in the backyard. A word from me, and you three will spend the rest of your lives in Guantanamo Bay," Amelia says. "Plus, I'm on a video upload schedule. If I don't make my deliverables schedule, there will be even more people out trying to kick your asses."

"You're producing a TV show," Annika says flatly. "You want excitement. We're going to give it to you."

Amelia appears to think this over. She points to the bag in my hand. "Fine. But if I go along with this, I want control of my equipment. And if you guys don't deliver something good, all bets are off."

Toby nods again, and I release the bag into Amelia's grip.

It's Annika who answers. "I've been making personal appearances since I was four years old. Audiences love the unpredictable. You've got four kids battling the collapse of an empire. Your mission is already a success."

Amelia gives Annika an appraising look. It's as if she's finally met her match.

I find out that there are showers upstairs and hustle up there to change because I want to be ready when the doctor is done with Navarro. The water in the shower is hot, but I can't get warm enough.

No one knows for sure where MacKenna is. And we have two new members in our party.

A hacker. The son of a bomb builder. A sociology student turned soldier. An American princess. And now a television producer.

This is us.

I feel ridiculous getting dressed up like a forest ranger. I've never tied a tie before. And I can't shake this sinking feeling. Like my father always said.

You can never tell what some people are capable of.

Dr. Doomsday said, "Trust no one." What he should have said was "Trust yourself." Trust the little hairs that stand up on the back of your neck. Trust that punch-in-the-gut feeling that makes you think something is about to go wrong. That voice in your ear that makes you leery of someone claiming to be a friend.

When you override your sixth sense, that's when things go really wrong.

—MacKENNA NOVAK,
Letters from the Second Civil War

MacKENNA

It takes a little over an hour to make it to the gate at San Miguel.

It's around seven when we get there. The plan is to ditch the car a couple miles from the border and walk to the gate that Antone took us through back in January.

Of course, we're picked up by The Opposition before we can implement this plan.

I want to kick myself because I seriously should have seen this coming. Like seriously, we'd seen the news footage at Fort Marshall. We knew that Ammon Carver and The Opposition were guarding the border and working with the Federales to catch Americans sneaking around. Plus, how many times did Dr. Doomsday warn us that the various gates would become inaccessible? Like one million?

LEAD: Inept student journalist pays no attention to the news; gets self killed.

Yay.

The Opposition has set up a series of portable trailers on the American side of the San Miguel gate to deal with Americans trying to illegally cross the border. The site is lit up by a bunch of tall stand lights powered by loud generators. We're taken inside one of the portables, where we find ourselves in a bland interior with basic metal desks, elementary school–blue carpet, folding chairs and stainless-steel racks.

There are signs all over the place. Some are written in both English and Spanish.

Like.

REFUGEE PROCESSING CENTER

And.

"Notice: One candy bar and bottle of water per person."

Great. The Opposition is rounding up political dissidents and giving them a bottle of water and a candy bar before sending them to some kind of death camp.

IMPORTANT FACTS:

-We have no identification.

-They took the phones we stole from the baby doll factory.

-Oh yeah. We broke into and pretty much demolished a factory.

-I don't even remember Galloway's first name.

Galloway scowls at me. "Well. This is quite a plan," he says.

Terminus glares right back. "*You've* been living in Mexico for months. *You* chose the route we used to get here."

The officers haven't bothered to separate us, which doesn't seem like normal police procedure. But maybe when you round up three fools and plan to lock them up and throw away the key, you really don't need to follow some mega-official checklist.

They're holding all three of us together on the far side of the portable trailer. We're sitting on a metal bench in an area that's been fashioned into a makeshift cell with pieces of chain-link fence that have been hastily welded to the floor. Outside our cage, a man sits at a desk, typing rapidly. He's got a name tag. Jamie Evans.

"Sir? Excuse me. Sir? Mr. Evans?"

I pace and keep that up for a useless ten minutes. All attempts at conversation fail.

Finally, I fall down on the bench. "What are we doing here?" I ask. I'm mostly talking to myself at this point but it's the first thing that gets any reaction.

"Waiting," Jamie Evans tells me flatly. No expression on his face.

"For what?"

He looks up for a second. "For who."

"For who?" I repeat.

Jamie nods. "Yeah. For who? That's the question you should be asking."

Ugh. My face gets hot. "Fine. *For who?*"

He smirks. "You'll see."

Okay, then.

We're waiting.

So Jamie Evans types really, *really* fast. Prints out a paper. Places it in a short filing cabinet next to his desk. Wash. Rinse. Repeat. Over and over. Whatever is going on generates a lot of paperwork.

So…we're waiting and waiting and waiting and waiting.

We're waiting for…gunfire.

At first the shots are faint and in the distance. But they get closer and louder and closer and louder, until it's like someone is popping a bag of popcorn three inches from my face.

"What's happening?" Galloway asks.

"You're the adult! Aren't you supposed to know?" I shout.

"Ow!" Terminus says.

At first, I think he's been shot or something. But, no, I'm digging my fingernails into his arm. Unlike Galloway, Terminus doesn't look like he's on the verge of having a heart attack.

There's a bunch of yelling, and Jamie glances at the three of us in confusion. He opens his desk drawer, grabs a handgun and leaves the trailer.

"Okay," Galloway says. "Up you go."

Before I can ask important questions like, *Up where?* or *What the eff are you talking about?*, Gallow has grabbed my lower legs and hoisted me up. My head crashes through one of the fiberglass tiles of the portable building's suspended ceiling.

My reporter's brain is busy indexing facts for articles I'll never write.

BACKGROUND INFORMATION:

Suspended ceilings use square, removable tiles placed in a metal grid. Schools prefer this construction technique. The tiles conceal plumbing and electrical features and muffle sound while allowing easy access for repairs.

My forehead brushes a metal pipe.

Okay, MacKenna. Pay attention!

I hear Terminus stammering. "Uh. Do you really think that's a good idea?" he asks. He sounds nervous. For the first time since the cops picked us up.

"Jump in here if you have a better idea, Partridge," Galloway says. To me he calls, "Crawl forward a little bit past the cage, then come down and see if you can get us out of here."

I grab on to the thick steel pipe. Galloway continues to push on my legs and after a minute I'm up there, scrambling around like an overgrown spider.

"Keep your weight on the steel grid," Galloway shouts. "Or you'll fall through."

Right. Right. Keep my weight on the grid.

I balance myself on the thin metal of the grid. As I crawl along, I knock and hit and jostle the other tiles. One falls down and lands on Jamie's desk.

Okay. The guy's desk is as good a place as any to bring myself down.

I'm about to lower myself down. When.

The portable door opens with a sharp knock.

My. Heart. Stops. Beating.

Through the hole created by the missing ceiling tile, I'm staring at the top of Josephine Pletcher's head as she passes by me and comes to a stop directly in front of the cage. She's got another shotgun slung over her shoulder.

"Galloway?" She's trying to sound snotty. Like she usually does. But there's an edge to her voice. Something is going wrong. "You are becoming a real pain in my ass. And where the hell is Novak?"

Outside, the gunfire continues.

For some reason I can't quite explain, I don't want to give anyone the opportunity to answer that question. Without giving myself even one single second to think things over, I crawl forward a couple feet, lift up the panel directly over Jo's head. I let out a yell and let myself fall through the hole in the ceiling.

I fall down like a kid doing a belly flop into a pool. I sort of land on Jo. At least I kinda hit her and knock her down. She's already got her leg in, like, a medical boot or something and her head is all bandaged up. Which honestly is pretty weird. The Opposition has more soldiers. Why not send someone who wasn't beat all to hell to pick us up?

But whatever. Their planning problems are their problems. The rifle flies out of her hand and land's on Jamie's desk.

As I go for the gun, Galloway shouts, "The keys! They're on a hook by the door."

I run to the door, grab the ring of keys and thrust them at the guys. Terminus takes them, hands shaking, and fumbles with the lock but makes fairly quick work of it. The instant he's outside the cage, his fist hits my nose.

Hard.

I see stars as I fall back into Jamie's desk chair. I'm wheeled back into a rack full of boxes of candy bars. Jo snorts with laughter as a box of Snickers falls from a shelf, knocks me in the head and lands in my lap.

At first, I think it must have been an accident.

Okay. It's gonna be okay. Blood runs onto my lips, but my nose isn't broken. I'll be okay.

Galloway rushes forward, probably to get the gun and cover Jo.

Oh. And. Then.

Galloway skids to a stop as Terminus recovers the shotgun.

"Hold it right there," Terminus says with the rifle up.

"I'm docking your pay for every second I spend in here, Partridge," Jo says with a smirk on her face.

Oh. Holy. Hell.

Jo didn't need reinforcements.

Because.

She already *had* a man on the inside.

Terminus gives me one of his looks. One of his attempts to appear charming. "Come on, now. Don't look so betrayed. In another version of reality, I'd love to take you out for a veg-gie burger and a movie. But this is not that world. And I did tell you I'm in it for the money."

Yes. He's said as much all along.

"Good luck spending it when you're dead," I say. My teeth grind.

"I'm the one holding the gun," he says with a laugh.

LEAD: Harold Partridge cannot be trusted.
LEAD: Harold Partridge is gonna kill me.
LEAD: Harold Partridge is a villain.

Galloway stays frozen with his arms in the air.

I remember one thing that Jinx told me.

Terminus is a coward.

"You really think you can shoot me?" I ask.

Jo is limping in his direction.

"No," he says as he hands her the gun. "But she can."

Dear Lord.

I am such a fool. I always wondered how my dad had gotten involved with Stephanie. But here it is. This is how. You take a little bit of a chemical reaction, add a person who's agreeable, who seems to go along with your plans, and…boom. Dad and I are the same. Getting our strings pulled like little puppets.

Outside the trailer I hear more yelling and shooting and…

A helicopter?

A distracted expression crosses Jo's face and for a second her gun falls a bit slack. Whatever that sound is…it's some-thing…unexpected.

The trailer door slams open again. There's an audible gasp from everyone in the room. The only way I know I'm not hallucinating is that Jo is wearing this mask of shock and chokes out these words.

"Mrs....Carver?"

Well, yeah. It's Ramona Carver. Or Mrs. Healy or whatever she calls herself. It's Ammon Carver's mother. Right there, in her faded blue jeans and a cowboy hat and ranch boots. Toting a rifle. Like a character from one of those Larry McMurtry novels she's so fond of. If there was one person I never ever thought I'd ever see again in my whole entire life, it was her.

"Good evening, Miss Pletcher," Ramona says with a pleasant smile. "Please give my regards to your father." She then fires twice into Jo's midsection.

Jo stumbles back into the chain-link fence.

I cover my mouth to stop a scream.

Josephine Pletcher falls face forward onto the cheap carpet. This time, she won't be getting up and crawling away.

I'm expecting it to be like when Jinx had to shoot a guy next to me when we were first escaping America for Mexico, and I couldn't hear anything for like two days. Instead, the sound is like someone playing drums. A few loud noises that leave my ear drums intact. I notice there's a long black cylinder attached to the end of Ramona's rifle.

Once more, I know I should have paid more attention to Navarro's lectures. Especially the one entitled "How and Why to Use a Silencer or Suppressor."

A deep, dark crimson stain spreads under Jamie's desk and creeps in my direction. I pick up my feet and look away.

Terminus shifts his weight from foot to foot and his eyes travel all over the room. "Wow. I'm relieved that's over."

He's gonna try to spin this.

"Are you?" Ramona says coldly, before I can say anything.

He nods and opens his mouth to speak.

Boom. Boom. Ramona shoots him too.

I make a squeaking noise as I choke. Harold Partridge is dead. His body right there next to Josephine Pletcher.

Forever.

Shock and horror ripple through me and then a bit of revulsion as I realize something else. I am a bit relieved.

Galloway raises his hands higher in the air and whispers, "Whoa. Whoa!"

"He's with me." I force these words out of my dry throat with as much energy as I can muster.

Ramona lowers her rifle. Slightly.

It occurs to me for the first time that she might be here to kill all of us. I remember when Jinx ran around acting like she was terrified of Ramona Carver, and I had laughed and wondered why someone who carried, like, ten thousand guns was frightened of a dingbat old lady.

Don't you understand? That dingbat old lady *raised Ammon Carver,* Jinx had told me, all panicked and freaked out. She even used damn air quotes.

Yep. Shoulda paid more attention to that too.

Ramona nods. "All right. Let's go."

She turns. Her long gray braid swings and hits her back as she heads for the door. Galloway and I have no choice really but to run outside after her.

Outside, a blue helicopter with a white swath on the side waits with its engine churning. Gunfire and shouts continue. The Opposition fire at a trio of vehicles kicking up dust as they speed away from the portable buildings.

No one pays any attention to Ramona Healy.

Part of me wonders if this is what Jamie meant—if Ramona Carver Healy is who we were waiting for.

"That's our ride," Ramona yells over the noise, pointing at the helicopter.

"What are we doing?" I shout back.

"I'm going to end this thing," she says. "And you're going to help me."

Max used to tell me we train to survive at any cost, but that in reality we all have a price that we're ultimately unwilling to pay. Things we won't risk. Lines we won't cross. If you push someone to that point, they become especially dangerous. Volatile. Unpredictable.

A man who knows he won't survive is capable of anything.

–SPECIAL AGENT STEPHANIE MAXWELL to
GENERAL HARLAN COPELAND
Meeting memo; Operation name redacted;
Date redacted.

JINX

"It's out of the question," Dr. Knudsen says.

The doctor and his nurses are sitting on the sofa, all shaking their heads in unison. Navarro can't travel.

It's been an hour since the surgery. Dr. Knudsen believes it was successful. *Optimistic outcome* is the term he uses. He thinks Gus will have some sight loss in his left eye but mostly he'll be okay. Navarro is still in the other room on the cot, barely waking up from the anesthesia.

The clock is ticking.

Despite the fact that all of Amelia's people want to act like we have all the time in the world, my mother is coming. It's scary how scary that thought is.

"We can't stay here," I say.

"Even if it's not medically safe, we *have* to risk moving him," Toby agrees.

The two of us stand in front of the bookcase facing the sofa. Annika is still getting ready. I'm sure she'll manage to look gorgeous in one of these awful uniforms.

"Amelia tells us you destroyed the vehicle that was following you," Dr. Knudsen says.

"That won't be enough to stop my mother," I say.

"How do you know?" Amelia asks, pointing the camera at me.

"Because it wouldn't stop me," I say in a tone of frustration. The stiff fabric of my forestry service uniform itches, and the shirt's pointy collar pokes into my neck. "You don't know these people. You don't know what they're capable of."

Knudsen frowns. "You sound like your father."

Amelia stands in the corner swiveling the camera from face to face.

"I'm in charge here," Toby says, drawing himself up to his full height so that he towers impressively over the short doctor, who is also seated.

The doctor snorts. "How old are you, son? Eighteen? Nineteen? I've been a doctor for twenty years, and I don't care what uniform you put on. I won't allow you to override my judgment on my patient's care."

I exchange a look with Toby. "You're really not getting this. None of us can stay here. We'll all be—"

Before I can add "killed by The Opposition," a phone in Amelia's pocket rings. She's forced to turn off her camera.

She turns her back on us as she pulls out her small phone and says, "Hello?" then speaks in hushed tones, but even Knudsen starts to look nervous.

"We need to go. Now," I say to the doctor. "All of us."

Amelia returns her phone to her pocket. "The Opposition has landed at the Port of Astoria. They'll be here—"

Outside, a vehicle screeches to a stop.

Now.

"What do we do?" Toby asks me.

He's supposed to be in charge. But this isn't the time to take issue with the chain of command.

"We need weapons. Ideally explosives. A bag of medical supplies. A vehicle…"

Even as I'm saying these words, I'm concerned that they're futile. That by the time we even get our jackets on, we'll be surrounded.

"We've got everything in a bedroom at the end of the hall." Amelia gestures to the hallway that leads to the drawing room where Navarro is resting.

I'm about to break for the hallway when…

There's a knock on the door.

A light, casual knock.

I force myself to go in that direction. Step by step. Breath by breath. My heartbeat thudding along. Would Mom send someone to kill me? Or would she do it herself? The brass door handle is cool in my palm. I tug the door open. Slowly.

Mom.

Mom is alone on the porch. She has a trim, leather satchel with her. Underneath her jacket, I can see the outline of a handgun, but her weapon isn't ready.

Clearly, she doesn't regard me as much of a threat.

There she is. Impossibly cool and collected for someone who was tossed in a freezing river a couple hours ago. She's wearing a variation of The Opposition soldier's uniform. All in beige. A fitted beige skirt. A crisp beige jacket. Red tie and beret perched at an appealing angle on her head. Her long brown hair in a neat braid.

"They'll be here soon," she says.

They? I don't know what I was expecting, but that wasn't it.

Left with nothing else to say, I go for, "Hi, Mom."

Mom. I almost choke on the word.

I glance around her. Outside, it's finally getting dark. I'm surprised she's alone. There's a small green hatchback that's covered with rust parked in front of the bed-and-breakfast. It's not a military vehicle. It's probably been stolen off the street.

I nod at her crappy car. "You came here alone? In that?"

From a house across the street, someone peeks out of closed shutters. People know we're here. We're being watched.

Mom rolls her deep brown eyes. She's still about an inch taller than I am, which is trivial but somehow reinforces the fact that I can never seem to get the upper hand. "Susan, let's not waste time. I need to speak with you. It's important." She pushes past me and into the Angeline. I close the door behind her. Everyone in the sitting room has remained frozen, Toby and Amelia by the bookcases, the doctor and the nurses on the sofa.

"I don't know what you believe is happening," she says, coming into the foyer. "But whatever it is, it's not what you think."

I follow Mom into the sitting room. Her boots squeak on the wood floor.

Mom gives Amelia a grim nod of recognition. "Ms. Aoki. Of course, Harlan would get you. You *are* the best."

Amelia remains by the bookcase with her mouth open, her camera dangling from her limp hand. Which strikes me as strange.

My mom is the head of The Opposition secret police. The ex-wife of Maxwell Marshall. A woman with the ear of Ammon Carver. She was personally responsible for the operation that triggered the New Civil War. If you want to film something shocking, it isn't going to get much better than this.

Amelia's camera stays off.

Mom smiles. "And what Amelia is *the best at* is manipulating the perception of reality. Until you're no longer sure what, or who, is real." She continues to stare at me. "Lyle. I'm going to need the room."

For a minute, I wonder who Lyle is. Like, is she calling me Lyle? But when Dr. Knudsen stands up, it clarifies things. "Stephanie, you shouldn't be here."

"I appreciate your loyalty to Max. But if you're still here in thirty seconds, we'll have a problem, Lyle." Mom steps into the center of the sitting room, positioning herself between Toby and the doctor. "And by *we*, I mean you," she says.

Toby regards my mother like he's seeing a ghost.

She smiles at him, "Hello, son."

I think for a second that Toby might charge Mom, but Amelia crowds up behind him, ushering him into the hall. The nurses follow. Dr. Knudsen casts one uncomfortable glance at Mom before being the last one out of the room.

"Well, well," Mom says, eyeing my uniform. "Joining the National Park Service, are we?" It's the type of cheerful voice she might have once used to ask me if I'd done my homework. Or folded all my laundry.

"You murdered my father, and this is what you want to talk about? My choice of clothes?" I ask.

"You know that was an accident." Mom takes a seat on the sofa where Knudsen was a moment before. "You must have seen what I've done to honor his memory. To ensure that he'll live on in the pantheon of the greatest Americans."

"He didn't want to be a hero for The Opposition!" I tell her.

Mom frowns. "He was my hero. You may not want to believe that. But he was."

I can't seem to find the words to say how much I hate her and what she's done to our family. And to the world.

"I want my brother," I say.

"Susan," Mom says, leaning forward. "I know you hate me. And I probably deserve it. But you must understand, everything that's happened, everything I've done, I did it all for our family. Your father and I used to stay up late and watch the stars and talk about what we hoped for in life. What a perfect world would look like. I thought we could make that world a reality."

Mom's eyes are a little misty, and she's talking to me in that same soothing voice that she'd use when I had a cold and she'd bring me chicken soup. In this moment, I can totally understand what my dad was up against. I want to forgive Mom. To hug her. For things to be what they once were.

Why didn't I make more of a point of getting a gun?

Always be prepared.

Rule number one.

Mom takes me in with her warm eyes. "Things have changed. I always assumed that I'd be able to bring you in. That we would be a family again...somehow. But I discovered...well... Copeland plans to have you killed. You and Charles. He thinks killing Max Marshall's children will make great live TV." That last part drips with a cold bitterness. Like it never occurred to her that the general would have his own agenda.

It's like Mom has forgotten the rules. *Trust no one.*

We already thought Copeland couldn't be trusted, but why did he care what happened to me and Charles specifically?

She sighs. "Of course, Copeland wants a war. But I think this really has to do with your father. Copeland doesn't want there to be anything left of Max Marshall in this world."

"You're the one who trusted him," I shoot back.

She glances out the window. "I trusted your father. Your father trusted Copeland. Clearly, we were both mistaken. About many things." Mom goes on. "I don't know how exactly he intends to kill you both. But they've set a trap at AIRSTA."

I frown in confusion. "You're saying Copeland is with The Opposition?"

Mom nods. "As much as he's for anyone but himself."

"But..." I stammer. I have so many questions. Why would Copeland pretend to help Rosenthal? Why not just kill Carver's nemesis when the opportunity presented itself? "What about your buddy Ammon Carver?"

"With Max gone, I'm of limited use to him." She rises from the sofa and walks in the direction of the front door. "We're out of time. There are still men loyal to your father. One of them helped me smuggle Charles off the base. He's being kept in Coquille, a small town south of here, in a place called the Paulson House."

Why is she telling me this? And is it the truth?

But Mom *is* alone. In a stolen car.

"The Opposition. They don't know you're here?" I ask.

Mom hesitates. "They've sent a team," she says, trying to sound unconcerned. But there's a nervous edge to her voice. "It hit the port about five minutes ago. It won't be long until this place is teeming with National Police who will make Marcus Tork seem like a cuddly teddy bear. You better not be here when they arrive."

"What are you talking about? Why should I believe you?" I stutter.

"Do you know me to be a liar?" she says with a frustrated grunt, smoothing the small wrinkles in her beige skirt.

My heart drops. "Are you serious? You pretended to be for The Spark. You lied about Jay. Do you have *any* idea how many times I heard you say that you loved him?"

Mom sighs. "I was doing my job." She holds up her elegant hand to stop me from speaking. "Listen to me. Get your brother. Get as far south as you can, far away from the mess we've made."

I frown. I don't know who *we* even is, and this sounds like a trap. I'm not sure what to say. "What are you going to do?"

She answers in a sad, small voice. "What I think your father would have wanted. I'm going to make it as hard as possible for the National Police to have you executed. I'll buy you as much time as I can. Follow the drills. You know what to do."

When I stand there, unsure, uncertain, part of me wanting to believe Mom and the other part wanting to go for her gun, she rolls her eyes at me.

Outside, heavy booted footsteps sound out.

The Opposition is coming.

"I don't believe you," I say. "I don't think you'll really try to help me. Or help me get Charles back. So, if you're going to kill me, let's get on with it." With no weapon and in a uniform that has a patch with a brown grizzly bear, I feel ridiculously nonthreatening.

Mom takes a step in my direction.

I could go for her gun.

"Susan, for God's sake," she says, pressing her lips together. "I'm not going to kill you. You're so stubborn. Exactly like your father. You think I would stand around here chatting with you if I wanted you dead? And why would I send you to Coquille if Charles wasn't there? I could simply let you go on to AIRSTA and walk into whatever trap Copeland designed for you."

"But...but..." I stammer. Suddenly, our mission has become so uncertain. This morning, we had a plan. Get to Charles. Destroy the cold fusion bomb. But now...

"Listen to me," Mom says through her teeth. "This might be our last two minutes together. Ever. You have to listen. Whatever happens, don't go to AIRSTA. I had Charles moved to Coquille specifically so you wouldn't have to go there. When Ammon finds out... I don't know what he'll..." She shakes this thought off. "You have to believe me. What I did... I thought I was building a better world for you and your brother and even for Max. I never meant for..." She trails off and sniffles.

How much of any of this is real?

And.

How much of Mom's perspective is the result of Dad's theories? I wonder if that's why he couldn't bring himself to stop her.

Even from the sitting room, we can hear the front door creak open, and the growing noise from outside spill into the house. Tires squeal. Yells fill the streets.

Someone else is in the house with us.

Whoever it is must have closed the front door because it's quiet again in the hall.

Jerking my head in every direction, I will myself to remember the drill. *Strike to incapacitate. Go for a weapon.* I move closer to the large, heavy, metal lamp resting on a scuffed-up end table. I could throw it.

Do it.

Do it right now.

Don't stand around waiting to die.

Mom stays calm, like she was expecting this new arrival. She runs her fingers over the outline of the handgun bulging in the pocket of her jacket.

Rows of National Police officers in black riot gear file past the window. In ten seconds, the whole house will be sur-rounded.

The footsteps continue, and a tall, muscular man with steel gray hair walks into the sitting room.

General Copeland.

He's changed out of his provisional military uniform and is outfitted in the camos and badges of a conventional marine. Clearly, he's fully back on The Opposition's team.

"Well, well," he says cheerfully. "Can't decide which side you're on, eh, Stephanie?" He gives Mom a humorless smile.

Her hand inches inside her jacket pocket. "I might ask you the same question. How is your pal David Rosenthal these days?"

Copeland shrugs. "He was alive and well as of an hour ago when I left him on the beach back at Cape Disappointment."

Mom's about to pull her gun. "I don't suppose you ever considered taking him out."

The general shakes his head. "You can't have a war with-out an opponent."

Navarro said much the same.

Mom has her gun drawn now. It's one of Dad's old guns. "So, that's what you think you're doing? All-purpose war-mongering. As usual."

"I know what I'm doing," Copeland says. "What are you doing?"

"Saving my children," Mom says, in a sharp voice.

Copeland's eyes widen in mock credulity. "And who, may I ask, will save them from you? From this mess you and Max created?" He gestures at Mom's gun. "Let's not insult each other here, Stephanie. There are dozens of troops out in the street waiting for my signal."

I muster up all the bravado I can. "Why don't you give your stupid signal, then?"

The general glances at me, giving me the same annoyed look that he did so often at Fort Marshall. "Ah, youth truly is wasted on the young. Always so eager to fight and die. At the wrong time. For the wrong reason." His attention returns to Mom. "You could shoot me, of course. But it would accomplish nothing."

The fake smile falls away from the general's face. "I'm doing what we agreed we'd do. What we all *said* we'd do from the very beginning. This fight. This war. It's about whose ideas will prevail. Which society will survive. It's a battle for the *soul of the world*. Maxwell Marshall knew that this world teeters on the edge of a dangerous collapse and that it needs a strong leader to push the reset button. All his work led up to this moment."

Mom frowns and lowers her gun. She continues to clutch the leather case, even though it would be better to have her hand free for her weapon. "This isn't what Max wanted. He thought Ammon could lead us. With real leadership, the type of destruction you're planning wouldn't be necessary."

Copeland smiles again. "That's not my interpretation of his work. We could ask him for clarification. Except, of course, you killed him."

A terrible grimace contorts Mom's beautiful features. It seems like she might really feel something. For Dad. Or for me and Charles. She's staring at me the way you look when you're visiting a sick relative in the hospital. "Susan's not going anywhere with you."

Copeland leans against the wood-paneled wall behind him. "I'm not here to hurt her, and I certainly don't want her anywhere near me."

Mom pauses, and she's clearly thinking hard. Probably about which drill to run. "Well, then, what—"

Navarro comes into the sitting room, flanked by Toby. Both are carrying rifles. Not DNA-A guns, but old-fashioned ones. Remington Model 700s.

Dad would be thrilled.

"He's here for his little television show," Navarro says.

Amelia is a few paces behind them with her face flushed.

"Those soldiers outside are here to make sure we die on camera," Toby adds, his angry stare boring into the general's forehead. Annika stands behind him, looking like an impossibly elegant forest ranger in her stolen uniform.

Copeland shrugs. "Not necessarily. Carver wants his little three-ring circus. Because, as Max was fond of saying, chaos creates opportunity. You can get out. If you're good enough." He stares right at me when he says this.

More boots echo on the porch.

"That sounds like my father," Annika mumbles, wringing her elegant hands.

But. There's something wrong with this. "Why give us a chance to escape when you're just going to kill us at AIRSTA anyway?" I ask.

Amelia's shoulders slump. "It's a show. A story. It needs a finale."

Right. They not only want us to die on camera. They want us to die on cue.

Jerking her chin at Amelia, Mom says, "She's with The Opposition. She needs dramatic confrontation to attract viewers to your little show."

Amelia's face turns red as we all glare at her. "Well, um, technically, I work for an independent production company that has been—"

I go over to the window and peek out the blinds.

At least thirty National Police stand in the back and I can guess there are even more in the front. Even if we have a hundred Remingtons, they're gonna take us out.

As if sensing these thoughts, Copeland goes on, "The only way out is through the roof." He gestures to the hall behind Navarro. "There's a service staircase at the end of the hallway that leads to the master bedroom. You can access old cabling that connects the houses, left over from the days when telephone and utility cables were aboveground." He moves toward the hallway.

Navarro clutches his weapon with white knuckles as the general passes.

Mom is already following Copeland, breezing past Navarro, who stares at her like he's seeing a jackalope. Amelia follows uncertainly.

"Get your gear and follow me," Mom says.

I don't know what to do other than go along with this plan. At least there's some chance of survival. At least I might see my brother again. We hit the supply room. It's a small bedroom with ornate dark wood furniture that's all scratched up. Amelia must have had her people leave us supplies. There are a bunch of brightly colored backpacks tossed into the center of a four-poster bed. The packs are pink and yellow and every other color that can probably be seen from outer space.

Perfect. Basically, Amelia doesn't want us to survive.

I unzip one of the packs. It's decent. A handgun. A few magazines. Basic supplies like a canteen and waterproof matches. More than that, there is a stack of what must be zip-lining gear. Dr. Doomsday would give it a C+.

This is a violation of the rules.

Don't put your fate in the hands of your enemy.

But.

There's no choice. There's no time.

We each take a pack. I go for the neon green one.

It might blend in with the trees. If you squint really hard.

Mom goes in and grabs a rifle. A Colt AR-15 and several magazines.

Copeland remains in the hall, watching all this happen with an amused expression.

Mom marches us to the end of the hallway that narrows into darkness. On the way, we pass Dr. Knudsen and the nurses. They join our odd procession.

Wood splinters. Glass breaks.

The National Police pound down the door.

They're coming in. Okay. Okay. *We can survive.*

I'm so close to getting Charles. I have to survive.

Dr. Knudsen is breathing hard. One of his nurses, the blond lady, is crying. The male nurse has the hiccups.

Mom points to a heavy, retro, canary yellow chair. "Grab that," she says.

We all file into the stairwell. Toby's the last in. He grunts as he maneuvers the chair into the narrow doorway. It gets stuck halfway through, and Toby has to climb over. It's a good idea. It will create a bit of a delay.

Mom is better than I am. Copeland gives her a sanctimonious little nod of approval.

We take the stairs at a fast clip and enter another bedroom full of old, abused, dainty furniture. A twin bed has a fluffy blue down comforter with a long stain along the edge. The door to a tiny bathroom creaks open.

Amelia raises her camera, but a stern look from Mom makes her lower it again.

I shut the bedroom door, lock it and push a chest of drawers in front of it.

Light streams in through an open window opposite the door. Flimsy indigo curtains flap open in a light breeze. There's a gorgeous secretary's desk in the corner near the window. Old copies of Nancy Drew books are arranged in artful stacks in a case over the writing surface.

I approach the window and peer out. The room overlooks the rust-and-mold-covered side of the Angeline. A row of National Police crouch in the space between trash cans. Their helmets bob back and forth. A female officer shoos a stray cat away. The cat releases a high-pitched screech before taking off toward the front of the house.

Thick silver steel cables extend from the corner of the roof right above our window and run from house to house, and occasionally to rotting wooden poles. Remnants from the days before The Spark converted most of the country to a combination of natural gas and wind power.

"You're sure these aren't still electrified?" I ask, pointing upward.

I'm expecting Amelia to answer, but it's Copeland who says, "I'm sure. The Spark shut down Pacific Power ages ago. These lines haven't been used in years."

Being as quiet as possible so as not to attract attention from below, Toby climbs out onto the windowsill and pokes one of the cables. Nothing happens.

"Why didn't they remove them?" Annika asks.

Mom sets her leather case down gingerly on the desk. "In large cities, they did," she says with a shrug. "But maintaining these less urban areas was never a priority for The Spark. And this area was hit especially hard by the sea level changes."

Her inference is clear. The Spark allowed this terrible mess in Astoria to develop and never bothered to clean it up.

Toby attaches the progression carabiners to the cable. He never did this drill with Dad, so it had to be Copeland's people.

From downstairs, a man's voice shouts, "We're in."

More scuffling of boots and echoes as the downstairs doors are kicked open.

Shouts of *Clear!*

The National Police are methodically checking the building.

Toby draws Annika to the window. There's a set of handlebars attached to a metal pulley. It's basically like a trapeze. We'll have to hang on for dear life. Hope we don't fall before we make it to the next house.

Perfect.

Mom removes her gun from her coat pocket. For a split second, I think she's going to shoot me, and I brace myself.

Until she says.

"Earplugs."

Then I understand her plan. Navarro and I open our packs and pull out several pairs of military grade earplugs. I toss packages to Knudsen and the nurses.

"What the hell are you doing?" the blonde nurse whispers, her brown eyes wide, traveling from me to Mom's gun.

"Distracting the soldiers below so they don't shoot at us while we go out the window." This is a classic play from Dad's book.

Copeland sits casually on the bed and watches us, almost like he wishes he had a bowl of buttered popcorn. "It really is a shame we're gonna have to execute you when all this is over, Stephanie," he says.

I put the plugs in my ears. As Toby sends Annika swinging out the window, Mom moves toward the tiny bathroom and fires a single shot through a rectangular window over the shower.

Annika remains graceful as she glides through the air. Her blond hair billows and her jacket puffs out heroically behind her. If there ever was a money shot, that was it. I can almost feel the frustration radiating from Amelia's skin.

Down below, the National Police scatter in all directions searching for the origin of the shots. The stomping down below increases. People seem to be running all over. Another shot rings from outside.

Toby sets up another pulley and motions to the doctor and nurses. The doctor reluctantly climbs out the window, tightly clutching the handles of his pulley. Mom fires another shot. I stare at Knudsen as he zips away from the Angeline. He loses his grip just as he reaches the roof of the next building. He lands too soon, falling several feet onto the sloped roof of a beige house around two hundred feet downhill.

Toby waves for the nurses to go next.

"I can't go out there," the woman says.

Mom points her handgun in the nurse's direction. "Go now. Or I will shoot you."

The first nurse reluctantly takes the pulley apparatus from Toby. The male nurse goes next. Mom has to fire several shots to cover his screaming. Toby and I exchange a look. I give him a small shake of my head.

I'm not leaving before him.

He reluctantly climbs out the window. Navarro helps Toby with the pulley. That leaves the two of us alone with Mom.

A speck of blood appears on the white gauze covering Navarro's eye. Knudsen was right. Navarro shouldn't be traveling.

Mom goes to the desk and places her handgun down. She gets ready with the rifle. The top drawer from the chest falls to the floor in a crash I can't hear. I've never seen my mom in action before and...

It's terrifying.

She marches to the door as the National Police break through using a Halligan bar. The first man through the door is shoving the chest of drawers aside when Mom takes him out.

With a single shot to the head.

She doesn't allow his body to drop. Instead, she grabs him underneath one arm and uses his body as a human shield, no doubt capitalizing on the confusion of those who recognize her uniform. She continues to fire, eliminating the whole team in the hall with cold precision. When she's finished, she shoves the first man's body into the stairwell with as much force as she can muster. To maximize the number of obstacles in the hall.

I shiver.

Sticking my head out the window, I can see that the National Police are in chaos. They're dragging high-tech bullet shields from their vans and running toward the doors of the Angeline, preparing to storm the building en masse.

"Susan! Come on!" Navarro says.

He takes my hand and tries to drag me to the window.

But right then I can see it all. Mom is drawing all the National Police into the building because...

Mom rests her rifle on the desk. With her back to Copeland and blocking his view, she opens her leather case, pulls out a padded envelope and very carefully unpacks its contents on the writing surface.

Explosives.

Strips of yellow plastic explosives.

I pull out my earplugs.

It's Semtex. It has to be.

Dad kept some of this in his workshop, but he'd never let any of us touch it.

"Mom..." I say uncertainly.

Behind her, Copeland remains relaxed, waiting for the next round of action.

If it is Semtex, it's enough to take out the house and even part of the street.

"Susan! We have to go!" Navarro yells.

With my earplugs out, I can hear the sounds of the National Police carry from the porch.

Mom has a small metal hammer and a candlelighter. A really simple detonation scheme. Light the explosives. Then combust them with a hammer. It'll work great. If you don't give a damn about killing yourself in the process.

Mom leans close to me. "Susan," she whispers. "Get your brother and run. Don't go to AIRSTA. Do you understand? Do *not* go there."

My blood runs freezing cold. She's going to blow up the Angeline.

With herself inside.

All this time, I thought I would kill her. To find out that I can't, and even worse...

"No! Not for me!" I say. "Mom..."

I don't want you to die for me.

"Susan!" Navarro screams.

Mom's eyes tear up. "Susan. Jinx. You have to go."

I'm still muttering, "No," when Navarro yanks my arm. Hard. He presses the pulley handle into my palm.

As I'm climbing through the window, I glance back at Mom. She's lighting the Semtex.

"Go," Mom says. "Go as fast as you can."

Copeland has noticed the flames, and he's getting off the bed as I grab the handles and sail out the window. I think I hear Mom say *I love you* as I push away. But I'm not sure. My upper arms burn, and my dangling legs feel like they weigh a million pounds.

Hold on.

I pass over the lone National Police soldier left in the alley. Over the tops of metal trash cans. An abandoned, rusted-out fishing boat. Old, worn-out tires. Stacks of wet firewood.

Hold on.

I'm barely able to keep my sweaty fingers wrapped around the plastic-coated metal bars.

The instant my feet hit the asphalt tiles of the gable roof, I drop onto my knees. I put my hand down on a spot missing a tile, and it punches through into the insulation. Tiny scratches sear my palm as I pull my hand back. I can't catch my breath.

"Be careful." Toby's alone on the roof. He's already sent everyone else farther down the hill. "This roof is in awful shape."

Navarro's right behind me, and he's barely got his feet on the roof when the Angeline explodes into flames that creep out nearly to our feet. A few screams break out near the back door but are silenced almost immediately. A series of secondary explosions, probably from the gas appliances in the house, send black flames higher and higher into the air.

Mom is gone.

And she's taken Copeland and most of the National Police out with her. Only a couple people remain down on the ground. One is bent over, probably throwing up. The other crouches behind a flaming Suburban, yelling into a phone.

From the roof, I can see the sun finally beginning to set. Toby helps me to my feet.

"We have to keep moving," he says.

"They'll be back."

Dr. Doomsday told the world that it was possible to outrun the past. He and Ramona Healy were the same in that respect. In a strange way, it made perfect sense that they were friends. They both wanted a world where what's done didn't need to be reckoned with.

But the past will always catch up.

It will always outrun you.

In the end, time moves faster than you do.

—MᴀᴄKENNA NOVAK,
Letters from the Second Civil War

MacKENNA

Ramona tells me and Galloway to climb into the rear of the helicopter.

There are three orange leather-covered seats back there, but Ramona takes the front seat next to the pilot. I can't see what the guy looks like. He's wearing a helmet, and his eyes are covered by a pair of reflective goggles.

That leaves me and Galloway in back with an empty seat between us.

Galloway was a marine. He's been in the war. Maybe he's used to what we just saw.

But me.

My stomach will not settle. My heart will not slow. The lump in my throat will not go away.

The instant we're inside, the pilot lifts off smoothly. Galloway points at his seat belt, and I take heed and fasten mine as well. I want to ask Ramona what in the hell is going on and how she knew where to find us and where we're going, but it's insanely loud in the cockpit. The engine whirs the way a giant might moan, and the continuous clicking sound of the propeller is almost like sitting on the wing of an airplane.

We drift up and away from the brightly lit portable trailer and the speeding vehicles. Away from where Harold Partridge took his last breath.

Galloway reaches into a pocket mounted on the seat in front of me and hands me a pair of headphones with a headset microphone attached. He's already wearing a pair. I put them on, and they muffle most of the noise.

Ramona and the pilot are in conversation.

The pilot is yammering on in a bland professional voice. Like he picks up fugitives every day. "—has been confirmed. We'll reach our cruising speed of 158 miles per hour in about five minutes. I'm still recommending that we stop to refuel in—"

"No." Ramona's voice fills my ears. "We'll continue on."

"We'll be outside the recommended flying distance of—"

"Duly noted," Ramona says. Real cold-like. "If needed, there are any number of places we can land. I can have my team come to us."

Her team?

LEAD: Ramona Carver is running a covert operation.

"Excuse me…uh… Mrs. Healy. Where are we going?" I ask.

"There will be plenty of time to discuss that, young lady."

The pilot ignores me. "Very well, Mrs. Healy. I estimate flying time at three hours and four minutes following your desired route. This gives us an expected time of arrival of 1:14 a.m. local time."

Of course, he doesn't say what locality he's talking about. The pilot's microphone clicks off.

"Okay but, Mrs. Healy—"

"You can call me Ramona, girl," she says brusquely.

"Okay but, Ramona..." I'm too overwhelmed to form a question.

Why are you helping us? Can you help me contact my father? I need to find Jinx. She's walking into a trap. Where are we going? What are we doing?

"Get some sleep. When we land, we'll talk." Her microphone clicks off, and I get the idea that if I keep talking, I'll be talking to myself. Ramona appears to be taking her own advice. In front of me, her long braid falls behind her seat as she rests her head against the leather.

Galloway turns away from me and stares out the window.

I feel around on my headset and notice there's a button below the earmuff that turns off the microphone. I press it so that no one who might be listening can hear me sniffle. I don't wat to cry. Not for Terminus of all people.

Certainly not for Josephine Pletcher.

Yet.

The tears come.

Terminus betrayed me, but did he really deserve to be executed like that? It was simultaneously not enough and also way too much. In the end, will any of us get what we deserve?

We fly north across the border.

I press my nose to the cold glass of the helicopter's window. My father took Toby and me on a helicopter ride once, over Colorado. It was beautiful.

This is...dark.

Like, totally dark.

I mean, I don't know where we are, but we're probably traveling over Southern Arizona. We should be passing over the occasional town or truck stop. There should be some sign of life.

Instead.

We fly over a two-lane highway packed with cars that don't appear to be moving. Their headlights pulse and flicker. Every few minutes, there's a red–yellow pop. No cities. No towns.

Just.

Campfires.

I close my eyes and hope to unsee everything.

Galloway shakes me. His mouth moves, but I can't hear anything.

I realize I fell asleep with my headphones on. *Cool.* I lift them away from my ears.

"We're here," is the first thing I hear as the helicopter engine quiets down.

Where is that, exactly?

Wherever it is, it looks a lot like the same desert we started in.

We all get out of the helicopter. As soon as the engine stops, it's as silent as the grave.

"Wait here," Ramona tells us. She takes off toward the silhouette of what in the dull light of the early morning half-moon looks like an abandoned shack. It's about two hundred or so feet from where we landed in the helicopter.

From what I can see in the beam of the flashlight Ramona Healy is waving around, we're in a dry, brownish landscape. Blue-black blobs, probably trees, dart the landscape. Ramona's light flashes over a large turquoise-and-pink sign that's shaped like a bird and says STOP! YOU'RE IN PIE TOWN.

"Oh, come on! There's actually a place called Pie Town?" I say. "Pie Town, what? Arizona? Nevada?"

Galloway waves his hand. "Keep going."

Um. "New Mexico?"

Galloway gives me the thumbs-up.

I can't help but feel relieved.

We're going to Los Alamos.

We have to be.

A second later, Ramona returns, flanked by a group of people pushing a huge cart of supplies. The cart's wheels squeak and rumble on the rough, dirt terrain.

"Don't get too excited. They ain't got no pie," Ramona tells me.

Why is it that, no matter where we go, there is never ever any pie?

An older man is with her. "We haven't had any pie since February. Do you know how hard it is to get butter? Even that damn vegan stuff? And fruit? Forget it. Last time we had a can of fruit was on February 18. A dented can of pumpkin filling."

"Yeah, yeah," Ramona said. "Like I said. There ain't no pie."

Oh. My. God.

The old man. It's Bob Healy. Ramona's second husband.

We left him for dead in Wilcox, Arizona. He'd been shot at least once and was facing God only knows how many soldiers from The Opposition.

"You're alive? In… Pie Town?" I stutter.

Healy grunts. "Everybody's got to be somewhere, girl."

"Yeah. Only I thought you'd be…like, six feet under or something," I say.

To my surprise, Healy laughs. "Only the good die young," he says.

Behind us, two men work on refueling the helicopter.

Ramona taps my arm. "We have to get moving." She turns and walks back toward the building, her braid bouncing up and down. Healy follows at a fast pace. Galloway and I run along behind them.

Healy names pies as we walk. "The Pie-O-Neer used to be right proper famous in my day. They had a pie bar. All you could eat. Let's see, there was blueberry. Cherry. Chocolate…ah…coconut…oh yeah and…apple and Hatch green chile. Delicious."

The guy is busy naming every kind of pie on earth when we get to the building.

This is the Pie-O-Neer, all right. But unlike whatever Healy is going on about, this place is covered in dust. The windows are boarded up. He pushes the door open. I'm expecting an old restaurant. Maybe like Maybelline's diner back at the crap motel in Gila Bend.

Galloway crashes into me as I make a hard stop.

The interior is lit by a bunch of green camping lanterns. There are portable desks arranged neatly, each with a soldier in fatigues at a laptop. Some are typing. Some are talking into headsets. Some are using small cell phones. Everything is operating on battery power.

LEAD: There is no electricity.

IMPORTANT FACTS:

-All we saw from the air were fires.

-No streetlights glow anywhere on the highway outside.

-No lights shine outside the building.

-Cases of batteries are stacked along the walls of the Pie-O-Neer.

Healy nods at me like he can hear my thoughts. "Power is rationed. If you're lucky, you get four hours a day. If you're

in Pie Town, you get nothin'." He turns. "You're called Galloway?" Healy asks, nodding at Galloway. "Come with me.
I'll get you some fresh gear."

They take a right and go to what was once the kitchen. The
EMPLOYEES MUST WASH HANDS sign has been covered
by a handwritten piece of paper with *Supplies* scrawled on it.

"Okay, girl. There isn't much time," Ramona says.

"Are you gonna help me save my father?" I ask. "He's walking into a trap."

"That's what you think," Ramona says. "But it's The Opposition who's gonna be surprised this go-round."

LEAD: Ramona Carver is working with my dad.

BACKGROUND INFORMATION:
-What the actual hell?

She leads me to a wall covered with maps and aerial photos.
"Let's get down to brass tacks." Ramona has a long wooden
pointing stick, and she taps a red dot placed on a huge aerial
photograph of a square building. "Since you were hell-bent
on getting yourself to New Mexico, I'm gonna assume that
you know that Copeland is still working for The Opposition. His plan is to use the cold fusion bomb to take out two
states that are loyal to The Spark, while making it look like
the whole thing is a Rosenthal operation gone wrong."

"It both hurts The Spark and interferes with its ability to
get future support," I say.

It's a good plan.

Except The Opposition set a trap that my father and Jinx
are walking into.

"But my father—"

Ramona interrupts me. "You must think your daddy is

dumb as a doornail, girl? Jay Novak fought with Copeland in Operation Cedar Hawk. Anyone who's ever spent ten minutes with Harlan Copeland knows that the general would sooner don a turkey costume and strut around in the Thanksgiving Day Parade than go along with a plan designed to *prevent* a war. He made contact with me right after you made contact with Copeland in Mexico."

"Wait. What? How did he—"

The woman takes off her hat, tosses it on one of the desks and pushes her long heavy gray braid over her shoulder. "He got a message to someone loyal to Marshall, who got it to me. How? I don't know. You'll have to ask him when you see 'im. The long and the short of it is that Jay Novak is gonna try and destroy the cold fusion bomb while the fusion material is inert. Unfortunately for my dear son, Ammon, I've got enough contacts and money left to help Jay pull it off."

I remember from before that Jinx could barely get a word in edgewise when the old woman was talking.

"Okay, but..." And again, I can't get my words out fast enough.

What are we going to do? What about Jinx?

Ramona leans on the empty metal desk nearest the photo we're both staring at. At the next desk behind her, a male soldier reads a long list of coordinates into a cell phone. "So, I'm gonna get Jay Novak enough troops to blow that facility back to God."

Okay. Sure. This deluded old lady is gonna march on Los Alamos and destroy The Opposition's ability to build the weapon of the future.

"With who?" I ask. "The thirty or so people in this room?"

Ramona snorts. "Don't make the mistake of underestimating me like my son does, Miss Novak. You do so at your own peril."

Um.

"But what about Jinx—"

She doesn't know about any of this.

I ran away before I could tell her.

LEAD: MacKenna Novak is the worst.

"I've got somebody on that team. Susan Marshall will be told what's what when the time is right," Ramona says.

"*Somebody?* Who?"

She ignores this too. "You got ten minutes to get yourself in new gear and grab something to eat. Then we head out."

Precisely ten minutes later my belly is full of pink lemonade and a can of baked beans and I'm wearing a new set of green fatigues. My green T-shirt almost fits correctly. I shove a few granola bars into the pocket of my camo jacket.

Ramona waits for me near the rear door of the Pie-O-Neer.

We walk outside. The sun is beginning to rise over the flat, dry desert. The golden light rising might be beautiful.

Except.

As far as the eye can see, green jeeps and cargo trucks are lined up in neat rows behind the Pie-O-Neer. Soldiers in various types of fatigues call out orders to each other. Old gas engines turn on. People climb in and out of the vehicles.

Oh hell.

Ramona Healy has her own army.

It's about to take to Los Alamos.

BACKGROUND INFORMATION:

Ramona Carver Healy, now well into her seventies, served as trustee of the Carver Company for fifteen years after the

death of her husband Cornelius. When her son, Ammon, grad-
uated from college, he gradually took over operations. Dur-
ing her time as trustee, Carver Healy successfully negotiated
massively profitable land transfer deals with the governments
of Russia, China and Iran. She became the world's third rich-
est woman. She successfully faked her own death and avoided
contact with her powerful son for over a decade.

Back when Dr. Doomsday was still alive, Ramona had sur-
rendered to The Opposition to save our lives. Back in Arizona, she had helped us escape.

But here she is. I touch her soft hand lightly. "How did you
get away from Ammon Carver?" I ask.

She leads me through the back of the restaurant, past an
employee break room and a small office. "Well. Let's just say
that my boy ain't quite as smart as he thinks he is." The old
woman turns to me. She's wearing a uniform that matches
mine except she's got her cowboy hat back on. Her hard face
is etched with long lines of worry. "And now. I'm gonna teach
my son a lesson he ain't never gonna forget."

My heart slows almost to a stop. "What lesson is that?"

"I brought Ammon Carver into this world, and I can take
him out of it too."

The Spark believes this is the best of all worlds.

The Opposition fears that might be true.

—PRESIDENT AMMON C. CARVER on the issue of Executive
Order 17996,
Declaration of the State of Rebellion

JINX

Navarro's eye is bleeding.

Again.

"I still think we should have brought the doctor," Annika says for the millionth time.

We left Knudsen and the nurses in Astoria with all the supplies we could spare. Knudsen rebandaged Navarro's eye one last time before we left. The three of them were hiding in a vacant house when we took off on foot.

They're not wanted by The Opposition. They could stay on the coast. Forever.

"Knudsen was too slow," Toby says.

"And he panics," Navarro comments. "He once almost lost it during a drill in Ajo."

Those who panic don't survive.

I shiver.

It's well past dark when we arrive at the vehicle Annika stashed outside an abandoned inspection station alongside the overflowing Youngs River. So far, she's come through like

Toby promised. The place is deserted. The vehicle looks exactly right, a light green SUV with a wide backseat and a large cargo area in the back. It's old enough to not have autodrive or built-in computer monitoring but well-kept enough for it to make sense for it to be on the road. There's an official Forestry Department seal on the door, but a couple of digits of the brown unit number have been casually scratched off.

Smart.

Now, we drive.

I remain on edge as long as we're on the highway and relax a bit only once we're able to cut into the Siuslaw Forest. Going off road is theoretically better.

But.

"It's like the land that time forgot out here," Navarro says, peering out the window with his good eye.

Since The Spark had this area closed off, no one has been maintaining it. It's almost a marshland, everything wet and muddy. The headlights of our car pass over rotted tree trunks and a blackish moss that seems to cover everything. Once in a while, we pass old cabins and campsites. Overturned ice chests. Smashed canoes and kayaks. Paths of plastic trash. Thanks to all the water and mold and rust, it's impossible to tell how long it's been since anyone has been out here. Maybe a day. Maybe ten years.

We drive all through the night.

Toby's driving and we give Navarro the front seat so he'll be comfortable.

So. I'm stuck in the back with Amelia and Annika.

Annika Carver has elbows like sharpened pencils.

Amelia is trying to get what she describes as "establishing shots," and she makes very little effort to stop from crashing into Annika as she stares at her camera screen. "It would be really helpful if someone would explain where we're going," she says.

It takes a lot of discipline not to push her from the moving car.

"You want your little show, you go where we go," Toby says.

"I still think we should shoot her," Navarro mutters.

We'd already had this conversation too. The truth is, we need her. She's in charge of gathering video footage that The Opposition wants. Having her with us increases our odds of survival. But it runs counter to the drills.

Dad said, *Keep your friends close. Keep your enemies in the morgue.*

I wish Dad were here to help me deal with all this stuff.

I wish Dad were here. Period.

"You should get some sleep," Toby tells the three of us.

I try but end up staring at the dark forest beyond our headlights.

When we're about three miles from Coquille, Navarro says, "We need to hide the car and stay out of sight until sunrise."

He's right. There's the curfew. And even though the sun will be up in an hour or so, our vehicle becomes compromised if anyone sees us in it. Also, we don't know what we'll find in town. We need the element of surprise.

We hide the car behind a dumpster of a Walmart with boarded up windows and a parking lot full of overturned shopping carts, coffee cans full of water and even a smashed-up couch. One of the pieces of wood has the words NO LOOTING spray-painted on it in loopy orange letters.

Toby takes a flashlight out of his pack. We're able to creep along through unfenced backyards of houses ruined by bullet holes and broken windows. We pass a stray dog who gives

us a low, single bark before settling back down next to the
trunk of a wide, bushy tree. Everything we see is broken. A
picnic table with benches that have fallen to the ground. An
outdoor playset with the swings torn off. A row of boat motors in various states of breakdown.

Our light coats aren't much of a match for the cold morning, and I catch myself shivering. Blades of long, icy, overgrown grass brush my ankles the farther we get into town.
As the sun rises, gray smoke rises from the rooftops of a few
houses.

The air is full of the citrusy, smoky scent of smoldering
pine, which is odd. Wood burning fires have been illegal for
a long time.

Right around sunrise, we crouch behind a row of bushes
that have grown as large as a school bus and stare across the
street at the house where Charles is supposedly being kept.
During its heyday, it must have been a mansion.

Annika confirms this when she whispers, "This place was
once owned by a timber executive. It's old. Probably built
in the late nineteenth century." She points. "See the Queen
Anne architecture. The Dutch gable roof. It must have been
quite beautiful."

Queen Anne architecture. *Right.* Sometimes I really miss
MacKenna.

Navarro rolls his one eye.

Amelia is panning her camera all around. "Yeah. Now it's
quite a mess though."

She's right. It's like the wind has blown off half the shin-
gles of the roof and the rain took care of the rest. A bunch
of broken, gray tiles are strewn in the mud in front of the
house. The porch railing has been busted through in several
spots, and the concrete steps that lead to the door have large

holes gouged out. Not much is left of the building's white paint. A citrus tree has grown so large that it almost covers the front door.

The place has all its windows though, which makes it an improvement over the other houses in town.

"Okay, we'll go around to the back," I say.

We take turns creeping across the street and snaking around the side of the house until we flank the sides of the rear door. Navarro, Toby and I all have our handguns drawn. Annika wears her usual panicked expression and stays a foot or so behind.

Amelia's arms stay tense as she points her camera at the door.

"On my count," Navarro says.

"1, 2, 3."

Toby kicks open the door with an impressively powerful strike to the area next to the old brass knob. I'm the first in the room.

Breathe. Okay. I'm ready.

Do whatever you have to do to survive...

Breakfast?

We crash into a cheerful kitchen, where Charles is sitting at a pinewood table with a steaming bowl of oatmeal and a pile of fresh fruit in front of him, his spoon frozen midway to his mouth. And sitting across from him...

Ammon Carver.

Did my mom set one last trap?

My father's old army pal. The man who ruined my family. Ruined the world. Here he is. At the breakfast table in a chair across from my brother. Reading a paperback book and eating oatmeal. He's wearing a long-sleeve red cotton shirt and a pair of neatly ironed khaki slacks. His silver-gray hair and beard are perfectly trimmed, and a pair of gold metal-rimmed glasses are perched on the end of his nose. He looks like the guy in line behind you at the grocery store. Or the dad that tells you to stop playing loud music at a slumber party.

He could be in a paper towel commercial.

There's a square, cast-iron wood-burning stove a few feet behind the table, creating a comfortable warmth. From elsewhere in the house, a radio softly plays polka music.

I feel equal parts terrified and ridiculous.

"Jiiiiiiinxxxxx," Charles says with his mouth full, his gaze traveling to the broken door. "You could have jussssst knocked. We would...have let you innnnnn."

My brother is calmly eating breakfast with a mass murderer.

Charles casts a pointed stare at my gun, which I hastily return to the holster. Everyone else files into the kitchen as I rush to Charles and scoop him out of his chair. His spoon falls to the ground as I hug him tight.

"Wow!" I hear Amelia say. "We're lucky we're not doing this live. That was pretty embarrassing." She mumbles something about making some edits.

I lean back from Charles, keeping my hands on his shoulders. He's grown since I last saw him. He's heavier, and a tiny bit taller than I remember. But he's clean and well-fed and smells like lavender soap.

He's even had his hair cut.

Charles is all I have left.

What am I going to tell him about Mom?

I squeeze him again, hard, and sob into his shoulder.

"Jinx, you're getting my shirt all wet," he says. But he hugs me back, tight.

Apart from Amelia fussing around, the room has fallen silent. I glance up to see Annika standing there like she's in a trance. She finally says, "Dad?"

"Hello, dear," he says in that gravelly voice that's become way too familiar. Carver pushes the cereal bowl and book into the center of the table.

The man who rules the world eats his oatmeal with thin banana slices.

The instant I let Charles go my brother runs over to hug Navarro and Toby. "See," he says to Carver. "I told you my sister would come."

Carver smiles. Fatherly. Benevolently. "So you did, son. So you did." He glances at Amelia, who lowers her camera and turns it off. Then he tugs at the sleeve of his red, plaid shirt, revealing an oversize gold watch. "A bit later than expected though."

Annika taps her booted foot on the wood floor. I know exactly what she's feeling inside. Carver is a lot like my own dad was, always involved in some big master plan, when what I needed was a hug.

Charles grins. "Miss Annika! You made it. I was hoping that you would."

That's an oddly cryptic comment.

Before I can think much about that, I notice a bowl of brown sugar and a jug of maple syrup on the table. "Charles are you eating that? What's your number?" I demand.

He can't answer right away. He's wrapped in Annika's arms, and she's smooshing his face into her shoulder. "I don't need to worry about that anymore." He lifts up his shirt to reveal a small surgical scar on his pale abdomen.

"You got a SNAP?" I say in disbelief.

Charles has type 1 diabetes and, for as long as I can remember, he's been on the waiting list for an artificial pancreas.

But since The Spark nationalized the medical industry, wait times went on indefinitely.

He nods. "Mom got it for me."

Mom.

I'm relieved when he doesn't ask about her.

Instead.

Carver clears his throat. "No doubt you're eager to get on the road," he says to no one in particular. He strokes his silver beard in a way that reminds me again of my father. He stares directly at me when he says, "Charles, why don't you get your bags ready, son? I have a few things I'd like to discuss with your sister."

Carver gestures for me to take the seat across from him at the round table, where my brother was just a moment before.

Navarro shakes his head. He's still got his weapon out, which is smart. I probably shouldn't have put my gun away. Navarro is always running the drill. He opens his mouth to speak, but Carver raises a hand to silence him.

"Young man, if I wanted you dead, you'd be dead," Carver says in a cold, firm tone. "I need to speak to Miss Marshall. She has a weapon. I don't. Whatever else happens, you'll leave here alive. You have my word. And I always keep my word."

I wrap my arms around myself to keep from shivering.

It's Annika who sighs and takes Navarro by the elbow and then leads both him and Charles out of the small kitchen. I remember that morning when we were on the run. When I still hoped that everything was a big mistake. Dad came to our makeshift camp in the desert to tell us our old lives were over. It had felt so useless to argue with him. All those same emotions live in the slump of Annika's shoulders. Toby follows behind her with a shocked expression on his face.

Carver gestures again at the empty chair, and I take it.

"What happened to your eye?" Charles asks Navarro as they leave.

"It's a long, thrilling tale," Navarro says with a weak smile. "As always, it involves your sister and a high-speed car chase..." The conversation trails off as everyone disappears into the house.

Here I am.

Alone.

With Ammon Carver.

Carver and my gun.

I should do it now.

I've got the Beretta M9. It's probably from some military surplus that The Spark was supposed to destroy but didn't. The metal of the gun almost burns a hole in the pocket of my silly fake forestry jacket. When I tuck my hand into the pocket, the edges of my fingertips graze the synthetic grip. If Ammon Carver carries the world on his shoulders, can I knock it off? Can I force him to shrug and make everything right again?

I could.

One shot and it will all be over.

Back when I was trying to save MacKenna from that mercenary in the casino, I killed a man. Even though he was trying to kill us, I still thought I'd never be myself again. Never be good or decent again.

I *can't* do it again. I can't kill someone unless I absolutely have to. And more than that, I know I can't kill Carver specifically. There is something about him that won't die. Like my father. His memory would live on and become a force that would be impossible to ever fully reckon with.

Carver gets up and moves around the small kitchen, then returns to the table with a pot of coffee. He drops a cheerful yellow mug with a happy face on the table in front of me. "Care for a cup?" he asks.

No.

No, I do not want to drink coffee with the man who destroyed half of California.

When I don't answer, he shrugs good-naturedly. "Suit yourself," he says and returns to his seat, refilling his own mug. "So, as a matter of housekeeping, can I assume that Harlan Copeland is dead?"

"Yes," I say flatly.

"Right," Carver says as he stirs a lump of sugar into his coffee. "Probably for the best. There was never going to be an expedient way to explain the general's complicated relationship with Marshall. Or the need for him to infiltrate Rosenthal's inner circle." He gives me another benign, almost charming smile. "Saves me the disagreeable task of having the poor fellow publicly executed."

There will always be casualties.

The dread inside me continues to build. "So did my mom—"

Carver taps his metal spoon against his mug. "Tell me about bringing your brother here? Oh heavens no. I believe she thought she was stashing little Charles in the last place I might look. Of course, I've been monitoring this situation *very* carefully." He pauses and gazes thoughtfully into his mug. "She was a true believer, you know. You can take heart in that. She and Max truly believed they could save the world from itself."

He sighs. "But I don't think they ever really understood that we would need to destroy the house before rebuilding. The foundation was rotten. It had to be replaced."

"By killing everybody?" I ask through gritted teeth.

"If necessary," Carver says.

He takes a long, slow sip of his coffee. "More than two thousand years ago, Julius Caesar got dressed and left his house, heading for the Roman Senate, where he was assassinated by an odd coalition of men who had only one thing in common. They all wanted Caesar's power. The previous night, his wife, Calpurnia, had a nightmare that her husband was killed. Of course, Caesar must have known that his adversaries wanted to move against him, and yet he dismissed his bodyguard and went alone. Why did he do that?"

I shrug. Why, indeed? And why did it matter?

"I read once in a book that Caesar was a risk taker. Or that he needed to prove he hadn't lost his edge. But that isn't why," Carver says.

"Um. Okay. But—"

Carver shakes his head. "He went because he had to. Because the confrontation was inevitable. The question of whether Rome was a republic or an empire had to be answered. Susan, we can't escape our destinies. We can't outrun them."

A chilly breeze travels through the kitchen. "Maybe I'm faster than you are."

Carver actually has the gall to laugh. "I believe, my dear, the fact that I was sitting here eating breakfast with your brother when you arrived means you are not."

I hate him more than anything right now. "So, what now? You're going to just let us walk out of here with the expectation that we'll voluntarily go to AIRSTA? Where you plan to have us killed?"

He holds his hands on the table in front of him, creating an arch with his fingers. "Neither of us knows what the outcome of this struggle will be. We haven't been informed of our own fates. If there's one thing I learned from your father, it is that people with resources can always find a way to survive." Carver leans forward and, for a moment, seems to be lost in his own thoughts. "Max and I started this together. He tried to run. To forget about the past. It didn't work. Because we have to finish it. Together."

Carver smiles again. "Susan, if you run, the next thing your brother will need to be saved from is you."

I dig my fingers into the palms of my hands. I have to get Charles and get out of here. But part of me understands what Carver is saying. Dad helped to set something terrible in motion. We won't be able to hide from it forever. If I try, I'll be forced into making the same desperate decisions that Dad did. The ones that led to his death. And put us here.

"I have to go," I say, getting up from the table.

For some reason, I push in my chair. Like it's somehow important to keep that tiny kitchen in order.

"Yes, you do," Carver says. He returns his attention to his book as I leave the kitchen.

Even though it's a chilly day, beads of sweat form on my forehead, and my hands are sticky and clammy. I push myself farther into the house. The inside is in much better shape than the outside. The hardwood floors have been freshly waxed and polished. I move through a spacious entryway, taking in its staircase with an ornate carved-wood railing opposite a tall front door, and come into a plush furnished sitting area with cozy, cream-colored armchairs.

Navarro is sitting in an oversize armchair staring into space while Charles is busy giving Annika a rundown of the state of plant life in Oregon. "One interesting thing about the rising sea level has been its effect on the various types of grasses on the coast," my brother says. "I don't know if you noticed, but the grass along the beach is much taller and denser than what one would have expected in…"

Annika doesn't appear to really be listening to him. She looks up when I enter the room. "Did he ask for me?"

I shake my head, unsure what to say.

Toby sits next to her on the sofa and pats her hand. "It's probably for the best. We need to go."

Annika's stricken expression fades away. "It is for the best," she says. "When I leave here today, I won't be Ammon Carver's daughter. I'll be Annika. I'll be whoever I decide to be."

Amelia sits on a stool in the corner farthest from the door with a computer in her lap. She regards Annika with a thoughtful look.

I finally get a good look at my brother. It seems like Mom was honest. Charles has been warm and comfortable. He's gotten good medical care. He had more food than most people.

He's even wearing a cardigan and a bow tie.

Navarro stands up.

I suck in a deep breath. "*We* should rebandage your eye," I tell him, even though I know he won't let me do it.

"What did Carver tell you?" he asks.

Annika's deep blue eyes point in my direction as well. She clutches a little pillow with cats and the saying Meow or Never cross-stitched on it.

"We should take the car," Toby says, almost to himself. "Go as far south as we can."

"Carver said we have to go to AIRSTA," I say, rubbing my sweaty palms on my forest ranger pants.

"That's what I keep telling you," Amelia mutters.

The small spot of blood on Navarro's eye bandage has grown larger. He gives me an electric look. "*We* don't have to do anything. We got what we came for."

Navarro gestures at where my brother was on the sofa. But Charles is now moving around the living room while Amelia follows him with her camera. He approaches a window seat near the door to the sitting room. Bags of gear and supplies are stacked on top of it. There are boxes of protein bars, self-heating meals and a case of bottled water.

"Mr. Carver is right," Charles says.

Navarro joins him at the window and opens a black waterproof bag. It contains a laptop and a selection of networking cables.

"What is all that?" I ask, waving my arm at the pile of stuff. "Where did it come from?"

"We have to leave," Charles says. He's starting to look so much like our father. "I promised we'd be in place by eleven."

"He's right," Amelia says again.

Navarro scowls at Amelia and says through clenched teeth, "Can someone please remind me why she's still here?"

I ignore this and remain focused on my brother.

"In place? You promised Ammon Carver that we'd go to AIRSTA?" I ask Charles. What else did the two of them talk about?

"No, no," Charles says, shaking his head. "I promised Mrs. Healy, when she called here."

My heart turns icy. "You've been talking to *Ramona Carver*?"

Charles smiles sweetly. "Yes. And we have to go. Now."

We waste more time than we should arguing.

And in the end, Charles is right.

We have to go.

As much as I want to run as far as I can, as fast as I can, get my brother out of here, go somewhere—anywhere—else, doing whatever we can to stop The Opposition from detonating one of those bombs is the only thing left we can do. To fight.

To help.

Even if it probably isn't going to work.

Still. There's something pretty terrifying about following directions from Ammon Carver's mother. Charles explains that Ramona will send additional people to help us take AIRSTA. She's hooked us up with maps and a ton of gear.

And she's planned a route for us across what was once a state conservation area for salmon and great blue herons. Like everything else around here, it's been hit hard by climate change, and The Spark had it declared a wasteland. Everything looks wrong. There's too much water in all the wrong places, and trees that grow out of other trees. The water is a strange reflective green. I can't imagine that the salmon are happy in there.

"I thought Ramona Carver was like, dead, or something," Amelia comments.

With all our people and gear, it's pretty cramped in the forestry vehicle. Like before, Toby drives with Navarro in the passenger seat, leaving me again packed in the backseat with the girls. Charles is in the cargo area, and he sticks his head into the backseat to answer Amelia. "She was in seclusion on a ranch in Arizona."

I resist the temptation to laugh at an eight-year-old using the expression *in seclusion*.

In spite of the fact that the whole world is probably doomed, I feel a little lighter. I've got Charles back. Finally. I grab his hand and squeeze it.

Even Annika looks less *in distress* than usual.

But. Also. Mom.

I want to ask if Mom knew Charles was in touch with Ramona. But I don't want him asking about Mom.

Instead I say, "You haven't mentioned MacKenna. Do you want to know where she is?"

He shrugs. "I saw her this morning. She's in New Mexico. With Mrs. Healy."

"Mac is with Ramona Carver?" Toby asks. He glances at Charles in the rearview mirror.

"Charles," I say, frowning in confusion. "What do you mean you *saw* her?"

Charles nods. "We had a video call this morning. Mrs. Healy called early. She didn't want to have to talk to her son. MacKenna says hi and also sorry."

MacKenna says sorry. Great.

"Oh, and Ramona prefers to go by Mrs. Healy."

Amelia snorts and murmurs, "If I'd given birth to Ammon Carver, I'd prefer to go by Mrs. Healy too."

"Where are they?" Navarro asks.

"In New Mexico," Charles says. "When Jinx has fixed the computers, MacKenna and Mrs. Healy are going to deactivate the bomb at Los Alamos."

Sure, that sounds like it will work.

We're following some bonkers old lady into battle.

We are doomed.

But at least we have a plan for how we're going to die.

Amelia's head stays buried in her laptop. Toby let her upload her latest movie on the way to Coquille, and she's checking the stats. "Our number of views on that house thing are through the roof," she says.

That house thing was the death of our mother.

Toby stops the vehicle in front of a clearing in the forest. There's a mishmash of different types of grass and patches of wildflowers here and there. He pulls out the map that was in one of the bags that Charles had. "Okay. According to this, there's another forested area and then we'll come to the main base. We're supposed to keep to the trees and meet someone called Volcheck near the rear gate."

"That sounds right," Amelia says. "Our intel indicates that there's a communications building on the east side of the base. We think—"

"No," I say. I'm using the binoculars from my pack to check around. "My dad wouldn't put the system that interfaces with these bombs in a communications building. That introduces too many security vulnerabilities. He'd want the systems to be directly connected to the missile without any way in or out."

"She's right," Navarro says. "But we have another problem. Do you see any planes around here? Or even any landing strips on that map?" He's looking at the electronic map on his phone, scanning the area with his finger.

"No. But so what?" Toby asks.

"*So* if this cold fusion bomb is an air-launched ballistic missile, where's the airplane supposed to come from?" Navarro responds from the passenger seat.

There's nothing but trees as far as we can see.

Charles pulls his own pair of binoculars out of his pack. He points to a patch of purple flowers. "We have to go there," he says. "That's where Dad wants us to go."

I squint in that direction. "Why?"

"It's checker mallow," he says, in a way that makes me think I'm in for a long lecture on perennial plants. "Dad took me to see some once at the botanical garden. They plant it because it attracts butterflies, and—"

"Okay, Charles," I interrupt. "But why should we go over there?"

"*Sidalcea cusickii* is almost extinct," he says in his know-it-all professor voice. "You'd never find big patches of it like that anymore except in a garden. Dad planted it. So we would know where to go."

Navarro ruffles my brother's hair. "Good to have you back, buddy."

Toby steers the car close to the chain-link fence that surrounds the clearing containing the pinkish-purple flowers. We all pile out of the vehicle and begin to search the area for some sign that my brother is right. That Dad wanted us to find this place. Navarro digs weapons out of his bag and puts a handgun in a side holster, then steps out into midmorning Oregon air. He opens the cargo area. After we climb out, Navarro unpacks some of the larger rifles.

Outside, thick gray clouds roll by. The air is wet, like it might rain.

Charles takes delicate steps through the rows of wildflowers that come up to his knees until he steps onto a wide piece of metal that covers an area about twenty feet wide. Some effort has been made to blend the door into the short grass.

The six of us crowd around the metal slab.

The wind blows my hair into a massive troll-like poof. As usual, the atmosphere gives Annika a glamorous edge. Amelia takes her camera out of her pack.

"That's a silo closure door," Navarro says. He points at an area a few feet away from the metal. "I think that's a handle. Probably for an entrance hatch. But if this missile is underground, then…"

Amelia points her camera first at him and then at the metal door.

Then we have a massive problem.

"We have to check it out," I say.

"Uhhhhh…" Toby says, his face turning red.

There's a small steel box next to the hatch door. I open it and find an electronic access pad with a red light above a label that reads LOCKED.

"Okay, Susan," Navarro says.

So now we'll find out if this plan has any hope of success.

I hesitate for a split second.

Then.

I press my thumb onto the pad.

The light turns green, and we all exhale in unison.

Navarro yanks the hatch door open and jumps back. We're all expecting something to happen. Normally, whenever we show up someplace, people are waiting in line to kill us.

Nothing stirs.

We creep up to the open hatch door. There's a long steel tunnel with a ladder that descends as far as I can see. It's lit by green emergency lights.

"That's really deep," Navarro says.

Annika's jacket blows in the wind, creating an action-hero silhouette. She wrings her hands. "You're saying a bomb like the one that destroyed half of California is right beneath us?"

No one has much of a reply to that.

"I'll wait here and cover you," Navarro says, as he gestures for me and Toby to open the hatch. "We have radios in our packs."

"We have to go together," Charles says flatly.

I shake my head. If we're going in, it will be better to have some hope of being able to get out. "He's right. Someone should serve as a lookout and you'll be safer here with Gus."

My brother frowns. "Mrs. Healy said we *have* to go in together."

We've been reunited all of two hours, and we're already

having an argument. "I don't care what Mrs. Healy said, Charles. We have to follow the drill. We're going into an unfamiliar area that's under enemy control, and—"

Charles sounds exactly like our father when he says, "Susan, I *have* to go."

I glance at the gray clouds rolling by.

My brother stares at Navarro with his wide green eyes. "And Gus has to come. Because…"

"Because what?" Navarro says as he loads his rifle.

Charles sighs. "Because Dr. Navarro is down there."

Navarro almost drops his gun.

I don't know how we'll all be remembered.

I only want to make sure we're never forgotten.

—MacKENNA NOVAK,
Letters from the Second Civil War

MacKENNA

When we show up, Dad spits out his coffee.

He's set up a command center about a mile from Los Alamos. It's around eleven when Ramona takes me and Galloway alone in a single jeep, keeping the rest of her force out of sight and several miles away.

Dad paces around his jeep and mutters about me being grounded...like that's even a thing in the middle of an apocalyptic war. Ramona gets him calmed down when she explains that Copeland planned to have me killed before I could ever make it to the safe house.

But he frowns at me. "You really believed that I'd march into certain death?"

The way he's looking at me.

MacKenna Novak is the absolute worst.

"You could have told me that you were in contact with Ramona. That you had a plan," I say. I try to keep the guilt out of my voice.

"I was trying to keep you safe," Dad says. "For the plan to

work, Copeland had to believe that you were following his instructions." He puts a hand on each of my shoulders. "*You* could listen to me every once in a while." He wraps me in a hug.

After that, he gets to work.

I gotta say… I'm kinda…impressed. Dad makes quick work of organizing teams using a combination of his original soldiers and Ramona's people. By noon, there are jeeps heading out in every direction, circling the base.

Lead: The battle for Los Alamos has begun.

BACKGROUND INFORMATION:

The Los Alamos National Laboratory used to be a huge research compound. In the twentieth century, the atomic bomb was developed here and for a while they did other kinds of energy research. It was mostly closed when The Spark developed the national solar power grid.

He has a few soldiers set up a tent with a card table, some folding chairs and a giant orange jug of water.

It's around twelve thirty when Dad leaves our position. "I'll be back as soon as we take the silo," he tells me.

"I'm coming too!" I say. I scramble toward his Jeep.

He actually picks me up and carries me to the tent. He's shaved, and his hair has been cut into a clean military crop. He's in khaki fatigues with a NOVAK name tag sewn on.

"You're staying here," he says, flatly. "That's an order."

I'm about to put up one hell of a fight when I notice that Ramona's remaining in the tent too. I definitely know she's not planning on waiting out the battle from here in the middle of the desert. She's got her own jeep and, no doubt, she plans to head out the minute Dad is gone.

I make a big show of letting my shoulders slump in disappointment. "Promise me you'll be back," I say.

"I promise," he says.

Ramona sits in one of the five folding chairs.

About five minutes after Dad leaves, Ramona dons her cowboy hat. "All right, Miss Novak. Here is where I must take my leave."

I scramble up off my chair. "Okay. I'm ready. I need a gun."

"Like your daddy said. You're staying here." She pulls the tent flap open a couple of inches to reveal two soldiers.

"Wait. Wait. What?"

No answer.

"You're not gonna let me fight?" I demand. "Why did you even bring me here if you're not gonna let me help stop Ammon Carver?"

Ramona's wrinkle-lined mouth presses into a frown. "I done told you, girl. *I* am gonna stop him." She reaches in her bag and gives me an e-tablet. The kind that can publish stories online. The kind that real journalists use. "There are other ways to fight besides picking up a weapon, girl." She holds the flap of the tent open so I can see the chaos outside. "Some of these people are gonna die doing what's right. You're here to make sure the whole world knows it."

An alarm begins to wail.

With the e-tablet in my hand, I peek out of the tent in time to see a small building in the distance burst into red flames.

The Second Civil War will have a story…and I will tell it.

In this world, we will not fear death.

We will be afraid of life without purpose.

–PRESIDENT AMMON C. CARVER on the issue of Executive
Order 17996,
Declaration of the State of Rebellion

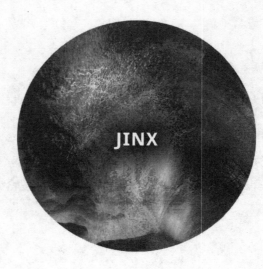

JINX

"We're going live," Amelia announces. She points a camera with a green light mounted to it right next to my face.

There's no time to argue.

"And we're live...now," Amelia says, clicking a button on an antenna attached to her camera.

The light flashes as Navarro says, "What? What are you saying?"

Charles is already climbing down the hatch as I try to talk to him. "Peter Navarro? You're saying Gus's father is down there? Charles, why would you say that?"

Annika pulls at the loose strands of her hair. "You're saying that the prisoner I overheard my father's people talking about is Peter Navarro? He's still alive?"

There's no answer besides the clank of my brother's boots on the metal ladder.

I hustle into the hatch and make my own way down. I just got Charles back, and now he wants to disappear again into a deep, dark void.

"Charles, Charles," I whisper.

A *tap, tap, tap* noise rises from the base of the silo.

Navarro is next, and he almost slips on the ladder a couple of times. There's still the issue with his eye, and clearly Charles's pronouncement has freaked him out. He's not doing as well as he's trying to appear.

We come to a landing at the base of the ladder. It's darker down here, and I get my flashlight out. As Toby and Annika come down, I wave my light all over. It lands on a stainless-steel box. Like an elevator, but it's been disconnected from the pulley system.

The closer and louder we get, the more frantic and erratic the tapping becomes.

Where the elevator doors would normally open, someone has welded a pair of industrial hinges and installed a strong black titanium lock.

There's somebody in there.

Charles stops in front of the doors, clearly not at all surprised by this development.

"Did Mrs. Healy tell you that Peter Navarro is down here?" I demand, waving my flashlight across his face.

"Yes," he says simply.

Navarro runs his fingers over the door's hinges. "Susan, can you get this door open?"

The tapping continues in a steady beat. Tension radiates off Navarro's body.

This is wrong. All wrong.

"Yes," I say, slowly. "But…this silo is at least a hundred feet deep."

"What's the significance of that?" Annika asks as she arrives at the landing.

"It means it's an ICBM. These dangerous, fanatical assholes built a cold fusion intercontinental ballistic missile," I say, kneeling down and getting my laptop out of my backpack. I connect a cable to the lock.

Toby is coming down the ladder.

"I still don't see—" Annika begins.

Navarro continues to face the locked door. "An ICBM is essentially a bomb that's strapped to a rocket. The bigger the rocket, the farther it goes. A missile that needs a silo this deep…"

He should know. His father is a rocket scientist.

"I'm not so sure this is a good idea," I whisper. I can't even really bear to say it loud enough for Navarro to hear.

"Open the door, Jinx," Charles says.

Okay. Okay.

I can code a simple electronic lock hack in my sleep.

```
rbddat
        ORG $4000
r_dat       FCB 1              reboot pointer addr
            FCB 2              address $4000
            FCB 3
            FCB 4,5,6
Crc         RMB                1reserve a byte for check bits

            ORG $4100          start of our code
            CLRA
Again       SETA 1,$r_dat      set reboot pointer
            INX                X points to next number
            ADDA 0,X           add next number to acc A
            INX                increment pointer
            CPX #crc           see if X points to sum location
            BNE again          keep trying if response
            STAA crc           store acc A in crcsum
            RTS
            END
```

The pace of Navarro's little speech gets faster. "...like we're talking about going back to the nuclear area...like Titan II and..."

The lock clicks, and I remove it and toss it onto the metal floor.

I get ready with my rifle. "Stand back, Charles."

Rule one: Always be prepared.

Slowly, slowly, I pry the elevator doors open with my fingers. I can't stop myself from gasping.

Looking back at me is an older, more gaunt version of a face I spend half my time staring at.

Navarro's mouth drops open. "Papa?"

And right then it is so clear.

Why The Spark and Ramona Carver and everyone else was so damn desperate to destroy this thing. Whoever has control of this missile is truly an angel of death.

The Opposition wanted to fire it.

And they all needed me to do it.

"You shouldn't be here," Peter Navarro says. And he's looking right at me.

"Papa, you're alive?" Navarro asks.

"Son," Peter Navarro says. We all wait for him to go on. But he doesn't. After a few seconds, he says, "You need to..."

Peter Navarro is incredibly thin and his skin has an odd, gauzy texture. Like he hasn't been outside in quite a while. He's wearing a pair of baggy green sweatpants and a T-shirt with long oily stains all over the front. He eyes my gun. "The safest thing is to shoot me."

"We're not going to shoot you," Gus says in a horrified voice. "Does Mama know you're still alive?"

"No. That information would put her in great danger," Peter says. "No time but...what happened to your eye?"

I touch his arm lightly. "We need to destroy that missile."

"We can't go into the control room together," Peter says. His eyes widen in terror. Like I scare the absolute hell out of him.

An alarm blares, and the green lights begin to pulse.

"What is he talking about?" Toby yells, above the sound of the alarm. "And how is he still…" He trails off before adding *alive.*

I sigh but force myself to be equally as loud. "The Opposition wants to *fire* the missile. My father and Dr. Navarro must have programmed the system to require both of them to launch it. They probably figured that Rosenthal would have one or both of them killed, making a launch impossible or extremely difficult."

"That's right," Peter says. "You obviously know that Dr. Marshall gave you system access in the hopes of giving The Opposition one less reason to have you killed."

Peter gives my brother a sad look. Beyond the silo, an echo sounds as a heavy door opens. "The crew is coming."

"Launch the missile? At what?" Annika asks.

Peter Navarro looks very startled to see Ammon Carver's daughter. But he answers her. "Both of the missiles have primary targets inside Russia."

A wave of shock washes over Toby. "Carver wants to start a war with *Russia?*"

Peter Navarro nods. "Indeed. And he wants to blame Rosenthal for it."

In spite of herself, Amelia murmurs, "This is good stuff."

"No it isn't," Navarro snaps. "Papa. You're scaring me."

I step in front of Peter Navarro. "Dr. Navarro, we have to go to the control room. I think I can take the software off-line."

His head jerks in my direction. "Once we get up there, they could torture us or trick us or manipulate us into firing the missile. Your father and I came up with this system, precisely so that would not be possible."

"Given enough time, The Opposition will probably figure out a way to fire the missile. What do you think will happen to us then?" I ask.

The hatch door creaks open. Something silver drops from the opening.

A tear gas canister.

Thank God Ramona Carver considered this possibility. I dig in my bag for our masks. I'm shoving one on Charles's face when I yell, "Toby! You have to hold that door. As soon as I get to the control room, I should be able to lock it down. Until then, shoot anyone who isn't us."

"That sounds a little violent," Charles says before I cover his mouth.

"Annika! Go!" Toby tells her.

"I'm staying with you," she says, tugging her own mask on. She gets her gun out of her pack.

Dr. Navarro motions for us to follow him through a huge steel door opposite the elevator that served as his prison cell. I tug Charles's arm and drag him along behind me. Gus and Amelia follow.

Peter slams the door behind us.

We enter a tall, wide tunnel made of thick, green metal that ends in another heavy steel door. It's well lit in here and our flashlights aren't needed.

Navarro tries to say something that sounds like *Flash mores* through his mask. After a second, I realize he probably said, "Blast doors." The silo needed a system of fireproof doors to keep the crew and equipment safe when they launched the missile.

The alarm continues to sound, but it's slightly more quiet in the tunnel. I flinch as gunfire explodes in the silo behind us. Ahead of us, the door opens slowly.

I push Charles behind my back.

Navarro doesn't hesitate. He fires his rifle repeatedly at the door.

The bullets dent the door but accomplish little else.

Peter Navarro rips off his mask. "Harker? Is that you?"

"Dr. N.?" a male voice asks.

"We're coming into the control room. We'll allow you to surrender," Peter says.

There's a pause. "Who is *we*?"

"A team from The Spark is on the base. I'm here with Max Marshall's daughter."

Another pause.

More gunfire from behind us. Toby doesn't have unlimited ammo. We have to hurry.

"Jinx Marshall is out there?" the voice asks.

Peter nods at me.

"I'm here," I say.

The steel door opens, and a short, stocky man in sweats like Peter Navarro's joins us in the hall. "Jinx Marshall!" he says. "We've been watching your show."

He says this like it's something fun we've been doing together and not me fighting for my life. But I keep my temper in check.

I guess this is Harker. "I was a big fan of your father's," he says, as I pass.

Beyond the door, we find the control room.

It's...

What the hell is this?

The walls and floors are about what I would expect. The same green, ruggedized metal and rubber, no static flooring. But then. There are computers made of materials I don't recognize, and thin glass displays everywhere. Technology that isn't supposed to exist.

We remove our masks.

Two other soldiers are in the room with their hands in the air. Everyone watches me expectantly. Amelia points the camera at me. Everyone expects me to know what to do.

Except.

I glance around. This stuff is light-years ahead of anything I've ever used.

But I have to *do* something.

There's a desk in the center of the room that seems like it's intended to be an opps center of sorts. It's surrounded by more of the glass monitors. One shows an outline of the underground base. It's actually more like three silos connected by a network of tunnels. In the center is the entryway we came in. The actual missile itself is on one side, and the control center, where we are now, is on the other. Red dots that must represent people pulse on the screen.

Sliding behind the desk, I press my palm onto one of the glass monitors. Dad had a real love affair with touch screens, so this seems like tech he'd implement.

Luckily the screen turns blue. A pleasant chime sounds, and a computerized voice says, "Good. Afternoon. Susan. Marshall."

And then.

"How can I assist you?"

A menu appears, and I press the security button. It's pretty easy to figure out how to lock the doors. A few seconds later, Annika and Toby burst into the room. They're out of breath.

"We managed to chase the first patrol from the silo but I'm pretty sure they went for reinforcements," Toby says. "Whatever you're going to do, you have to do it fast."

I turn off the wail of the alarm. Normal yellow-white lights pop on.

When Annika removes her mask, there's an audible gasp from the soldiers, who all freeze and stare at her. Toby glares at all three of them.

"Whoa!" Annika says. "I thought they had to stop working on tech like this because of the New Depression."

I thought so too.

"Are we gonna be on the show?" one of the other soldiers asks Amelia.

I doubt she intends to answer him, and luckily our attention is diverted by Harker.

"Hey! That's new," he says, pointing at the Doomsday logo now on the screen.

I let my finger hover over the glowing illustration that reminds me of the cover of Dad's book. It's almost fitting that we should follow *Dr. Doomsday's Guide to Ultimate Survival* until the very end.

Amelia hovers in front of me, breathing hard.

I press the button.

Dad's face fills every one of the glass monitors.

Charles steps close to where I'm sitting at the desk. I reach out for his hand and squeeze.

The warmth is real.

On-screen, Dad begins to speak. *"My dear Susan, if you are*

here, it can only be because my worst fears have been realized. I be-
lieved that I was helping the world by developing theories that ex-
plained how it worked. I believed it was wise to assist in the creation
of dangerous weapons. For me, these were swords that would inevita-
bly be forged, and all I could do was control who would wield them.
Now I have left it to you, not to finish my work, but to destroy it. If
the world is to have a future, you must create it. I love you, Susan.
You and your brother."

Charles chokes out a little sob.

A timer replaces Dad's face on all the screens. It's counting down from 03:00.

"Auto destruct in three minutes," the computer voice says.

As usual, there's no time to mourn.

An odd, greenish smoke fills the glass computer towers.
It's a type of acid and creates streaks of melting plastic on the
glass. Harker and his men are already running for a blast door
opposite the one we came in.

"We have to go," Toby says.

I get up from the desk, keeping Charles close to me.

Twenty seconds have already ticked by.

"Will we be able to see Dad again?" Charles asks, staring
at the monitors.

Peter Navarro coughs and points to the door Harker went
through. "Follow that tunnel. It leads to an escape ladder.
Hurry. You can be topside in two minutes."

You?

Navarro catches that too. "Come on, Papa," he says, taking a squeaky step on the rubber floor.

Peter Navarro puts a hand on his son's shoulders. "Son, I
am so proud of you. Of the man you have become."

Gus looks absolutely terrified. "No. No."

"I have to do it," Peter says.

"Do what?" Gus yells. "Susan turned on the auto destruct!"

Peter walks with his son toward the door. "Marshall's auto-destruct sequence will destroy the computer systems. That's only half the problem. I have to take out the fusion apparatus, or it will be too tempting for someone to attempt to rebuild this thing."

"Auto destruct in two minutes," the computer voice says.

"Tell your mother I love her," Peter Navarro says.

"Come on!" Toby shouts before drawing Annika through the door.

Amelia follows behind him walking backward, keeping her camera on us.

I have to get Charles out of here.

"Gus!"

Navarro stares at his father with an expression I recognize. The way that you see someone in their last seconds on this earth. The way you look at someone who is already a ghost.

I push Charles in front of me and down another green tunnel like the one we used to get here. The lights flicker, and the alarm is going again. We come to a narrow tunnel with a ladder going upward. My first thought is that I hope I'll fit.

The metal rungs of the ladder are cool beneath my sweaty fingers.

Toby is nearing the top. As Charles enters, Toby must be opening the hatch, because daylight streams down. We climb as fast as we can. I'm out of breath when we get to the grassy surface. A few dragonflies flutter about, blissfully unaware of our problems. Shouts echo from the forest beyond the clearing. The reinforcements Toby told us about will probably be in the clearing any second.

Even though I'm exhausted, I know we need to get as far away from here as possible. Navarro is almost dragging both Charles and me toward the forestry vehicles.

Run. Go. Run.

We're nearing the car. Annika has the backseat door open.

A pillar of red flames shoots out of the silo and into the sky like an oversize cheap firework. It's followed by a loud *boom*. The ground beneath our feet quivers, and an explosion bursts up.

I'm barely able to pull Charles out of the way to avoid getting hit by the silo closure door.

A flaming metal ring lands on the top of the vehicle with a smack.

Toby gets behind the driver's seat.

I shove myself into the backseat headfirst and put Charles on my lap. Amelia crowds in. Toby's got his foot on the gas before she can even close the door.

Fire creeps along the grass and flaming pieces of equipment from the silo drop into the clearing. Annika screams as Toby barely misses part of a bunk bed that lands right in front of us.

"What the hell is going on?" she asks.

"My father destroyed the missile," Navarro says in a cold, dull tone as he gets situated in the passenger seat.

Amelia's eyes are wide with fright. "I thought the whole idea was to *not* destroy the missile." She's still recording us with that stupid camera.

"The whole idea was to avoid detonating the bomb. We destroyed the cold fusion computer system. But Dr. Navarro wanted to destroy the hardware too. And it's a long-range missile…all that rocket fuel is…" I glance at Navarro. I can't bear to add *highly explosive.*

"Look out!" Charles shouts.

The car screeches to a stop.

Through a break in the drifting smoke, I see the thin, sweatpants-clad legs of...

Peter Navarro.

"Oh my God," Annika whispers.

Navarro jumps out of the passenger seat and pushes his father into the vehicle. He then squeezes into the backseat with us. I end up almost sitting on his lap. Two seconds later, part of a metal bookcase lands where the scientist was standing.

Toby hits the gas, taking us back into the forest. He very nearly hits a flaming tree.

"Where are we going?" Navarro asks. Even though we're driving through a fiery hellscape, he can't keep the smile out of his voice.

From the direction of the main base, we hear a series of small explosions. More black smoke rises above the tops of the trees.

Charles leans forward. "We need to find Ramona's man. Volchek."

"He's a good guy," Peter Navarro says.

I press my ear to the glass of my window. It vibrates with the sound of rifle fire.

AIRSTA is at war.

Amelia points the camera all over the car before landing back on me.

"So, you've saved the world?" she says with the camera about three inches from my face. I grab it from her and hold it, pointing it at my face. And then... I speak.

"This war began as a quest to decide whether we are a nation of individuals fighting to each keep our own personal rights or a collective that must work together to ensure each individual person is respected. My father believed that this world could survive only if a strong leader stepped forward to correct the excesses of democracy. To Maxwell Marshall, the world was a broken machine in need of a strongman operator. But he was wrong. Because no single person should be allowed to completely override the will of the group. Just as no group should be able to take away our right to exist as individuals. Each side in this struggle seems to expect more of their enemy than they do of themselves.

We have been on the run. Almost lost our lives. Almost lost each other. I've seen bad people doing the right things for the wrong reasons. And good people doing the wrong things in the hope of achieving something right. Basic values like love, altruism and compassion are not forms of surrender that make us weak.

This world can survive only when each person loves their friends more than they hate their enemies. When hope for the future equals nostalgia for the past.

When we all understand that we must survive together because no one person can survive alone. We can't save the world. People need to save themselves.

If you believe in fairness and freedom…if you love truth and justice…

No one can take that kind of stuff from you.

The feeling that doing what's right is too hard…or costs too much…

In the end that's what breaks you down.

What breaks the world down.

Because it turns out that the small ways in which we

mistreat each other become a big deal. It turns out that compassion and honesty and basic human decency are what make life worth living.

What I want is a life worth living."

I roll down my window and toss the camera out. The show is over.

LETTER #2: ENDINGS AND BEGINNINGS

Los Alamos, New Mexico

Ramona Eleanor Carver Healy spent her last five minutes on this earth reading from a paperback copy of an old Western called Horseman, Pass By. *She told my dad that a wiser person might turn to the Bible. "But I'm minutes from meeting my maker, and I want to have something to make conversation about," she said. She was able to destroy the missile created by her son. She almost made it out too. In one of life's little ironies, she collapsed as we fled the base. Dad thinks it was a heart attack.*

Against all odds, Dad survived. We all did.

Except Ramona.

She was seventy-five years old.

I watched the remnants of Los Alamos burn as the soldiers regrouped around Dad and our small camp. The black smoke rose, meeting Ramona Carver Healy in the heavens. The stench of burnt plastic and sizzling fuel filled the desert for hours. We'd won this battle, but could we win the war? Or could we dismantle the war machine?

Ramona made arrangements for Jinx to meet us in Pie Town. It's a strange place for a reunion. But at least we're all together again. Navarro's father is alive. He's still trying to find a safe way to call his wife back at home. We're happy. Even if we're stuck with Annika Carver. Even though there's still no pie.

After the destruction of Project Cold Front, sixteen more states joined California in seceding from the union. Rosenthal's strategy of driving states aligned with The Opposition to economic devastation appears to be working. Nearly all of the coastal states are for The Spark. Rosenthal has taken Washing-

ton, D.C. The Spark has disconnected The Opposition from the power grid. Dad says that the war will be over within a year.

It will have to be.

That's as long as The Opposition can last without replenishing food and clean water.

Sometimes I think about that little girl clutching her doll back on the Booker. Her careless smile. The thin, light strands of blond baby hair that blew behind her. About her last moments waiting for death at sea. That girl has a story, and it has to be told.

There's always a last moment. A last kiss. A last breath.

When will I draw mine?

AND THEN...

I used to dream about saving the world.

But like Dad said, you can't save people from themselves.

That feels like another lifetime ago.

Amelia and Galloway set off for the capital. Rosenthal is there.

We leave the desert at night with all the supplies we can manage.

On foot.

Leaving everything behind.

We're going into the heartland.

I want safety. Toby wants peace. MacKenna wants the truth.

I don't know if we'll ever find what we're looking for.

Is there a world free of this war?

Gus thinks there isn't.

But there is a dream of such a world.

And I believe we can find it. Or create it.

Until then, we keep going.

Until then, we survive.

★ ★ ★ ★ ★

ACKNOWLEDGMENTS

Thank you for reading this book. I am especially grateful if you started with *Day Zero* and stayed with me, Jinx and Charles as we finished this journey.

I am so appreciative of the entire team at Inkyard Press, most especially my incredible editor, Natashya Wilson. I will always be proud of the three books we worked on together.

Thanks as well to Bess Braswell, Brittany Mitchell, Laura Gianino, Justine Sha and Connolly Bottum, who work tirelessly to bring engaging books to teen readers and readers of all ages. Special thanks to Kathleen Oudit for art direction and Elita Sidiropoulou for design for the covers of both *Day Zero* and *Day One*. Linette Kim, Heather Foy, Andrea Pappenheimer and the Harper Children's sales team brought my work to bookstores and library shelves, and I will be forever grateful for their efforts.

Thank you to my friends and family, especially my mom, May Porter, Cassidy Pavelich, Amie Allor, Shanna Weissman and Debbie Pirone. As always, thank you to my BFF, Riki Cleveland, for friendship and always being willing to read my horrible first drafts, and to my trusted critique partner, Amy Trueblood, for your wit, wisdom and on-point notes.

To the AZ YA/MG writer community. Thank you all, especially Dusti Bowling, Stephanie Elliot, Kristen Hunt and Lorri Phillips, for all your wit and wisdom.

Thanks to my early readers, including Laurie Forest and Nancy Richardson Fischer. Any mistakes are my own.

To my wonderful husband, Jim, and amazing daughter, Evelyn, thank you for putting up with my coffee runs, late nights and strange Google searches. I am so lucky to have your love and unconditional support.